He cursed himself for a fool, swung wide, came around in a steep descent and as they leveled off, the corridor a black maw before them, he snapped on his landing lights and went to full power. If they were hit with any unexpected downdrafts he'd need every ounce of power and speed he could get from this thing. And the brilliant lights would reflect from spray and keep him from getting too close to the titanic plunge of water to their left.

It was magic all over again, spray reflecting with dazzling dancing brilliance from the landing lights. They were almost through the corridor, winds pummeling and hammering at them, when the pilot called out, *"Enough!"* and hauled back on the yoke. The Cessna burst upward in a powerful climb.

Instantly they were struck blind.

This is what it's like to be inside the fireball of an atomic bomb when it explodes. The thought speared the mind of Angel. It was green, the world went green, as the ▓▓▓▓▓▓▓▓▓▓▓ strangely green, as ▓▓▓▓▓▓▓▓▓▓▓▓▓▓▓▓ and there exi▓▓▓▓▓▓▓▓▓▓▓▓▓ ultimate blinding ▓▓▓▓▓▓▓▓▓▓▓ than blinding light, more than paralyzing glare. It was the End and the Beginning of Everything.

Novels by MARTIN CAIDIN

MARTIN CAIDIN

This book is for a lady.

SUSAN SIMMS

BEAMRIDERS

Copyright © 1989 by Martin Caidin

A Baen Books Original

Baen Publishing Enterprises
260 Fifth Avenue
New York, N.Y. 10001

First printing, June 1989

ISBN: 0-671-69823-0

Cover art by David Mattingly

Printed in the United States of America

Distributed by
SIMON & SCHUSTER
1230 Avenue of the Americas
New York, N.Y. 10020

Chapter I

My God, what a body. What breasts! And those legs! Ah, that tiny waist. Oh, what I could do with this woman! This time I'm going to tell her right out what I'd like to—

"Good morning, Miss Angela!"

The security guard turned off the switch on his deepest thoughts and beamed his greetings in a huge smile to Angela Tirado, storming the entrance to Venezuela Monitor Nacional Television Studios. Angela Tirado knew what Carlos Tinoco was thinking. They'd gone through this routine for years. One look at her across the sidewalk and before she covered twenty feet to the studio doors his pants bulged with signals racing back and forth between brain and groin. Carlos Tinoco kept the wide smile on his face as Miss Tirado swept by him, the barest touch of her perfume sending renewed frenzy through his system. He wet his lips with a suddenly thick tongue as she swept through the doorway he held open, her slender athletic body festooned with a minicam camera, power packs, tape recorders, and microphones.

Ah, the shame, mused Carlos Tinoco. *She could be making babies, but she is in love with all her electronics.* Another wave of painful desire stabbed his loins. He forced the smile to stay wide and handsome.

Angela Tirado stopped directly before him, and Carlos Tinoco kept in mind her temper was as close to that of a jaguar as her body was to perfect; he stood at a very strict and respectful attention.

Miss Angela smiled. *God, she is dazzling. If only I—*

1

"Knock it off, you sidewalk lothario," she snarled. "If you were any more obvious you'd be drooling down your chin." He opened his mouth in surprise and before he could move, a strong hand with fingers arched into a long-nailed claw stabbed toward his crotch. Instinctively he gasped, bending forward to protect the jewels so honored in his own bed at home. *Damn, she's done it again!*

Angela Tirado smiled as her hand curved smoothly from dead aim at crotch level to Carlos' face, patting his cheek gently. "There, there," she crooned. "Dear, sweet Carlos, so horny and with a great fat wife and six daughters at home."

"Uh, yes, I, uh—"

"Get your fat arm out of the way!"

He jumped back, her words scalding, and she swept by with equipment clanking and leather heels cracking hard against the marble floor of the studio lobby. Carlos signaled frantically to the elevator operator in a time-honored gesture and received a brief nod in response. The moment Angela Tirado moved into the elevator car the operator's arm shot out to block waiting riders. He ignored their protests, slid the door closed and started up.

"And how are you this morning, Miss Tirado?"

"You running a medical service, Juan? Ambulance chasing for any lawyer friends?"

"Why, no, I was just—"

"Sixth floor. *In silence, Juan.*" Little shards of ice seemed to fall gently to the floor of the elevator.

"Yes, ma'am," he said dutifully.

She entered the sixth-floor corridor with a silent crash, her presence an impact mental more than physical. Angela Tirado was the hottest property in news broadcasting throughout all of South America, Central America, *and* the huge Hispanic belt through much of the United States as well. Her broadcasts reached Puerto Rico and Cuba and through the Antilles islands, and she was the *only* newscaster who delivered her special reports in both Spanish and English language editions. Sponsors clamored to pay enormous sums for commercials on her broadcasts, and in television news that's the name of the game.

Whatever is *it* before the unkind and often unfriendly television news camera, Angela Tirado had *it*. The dazzling smile, the windswept hair that seemed to be blowing even within a studio, the perfect grooming, the clothing that spoke volumes of her on the edge of rushing off on a trek to the Amazon, or broadcasting dazzling space launches from French Guiana, flying patrol missions to hunt down Russian subs prowling off the Venezuelan oilfields—her viewers expected her reports from deep within the jungle camps of guerrilla fighters, and gave equal attention to political or fashion reporting.

To the Latin world, Angela Tirado was the long-awaited Madonna of the television airwaves. Daughter of a stunning Venezuelan mother and an American father who'd become a millionaire developing oil fields in half a dozen countries, Angela had compressed a dozen years of special education, training and experience into six frenetic years of intense work. She had inherent brilliance, a stunning face and body, an almost maniacal courage and acceptance of danger, and a zest for living that reached out and embraced her audience. Women adored her and men lusted for her, and she overwhelmed them all with explosive news reports.

Angela Tirado spelled power.

Angela Tirado at this moment was spitting mad. She burst into the newsroom, drawing and ignoring sudden long and quiet stares, and stopped before the desk of Nelson Sanchez. She glared at the big and burly Venezuelan draped loosely across his chair, cigarette dangling from his lips, his feet propped on his desk. Tirado slowly and carefully separated her equipment from her body to place it on Sanchez's desk. He smiled at her and she smiled back and with a sudden swift motion knocked his feet from the desk. The unexpected move half-tumbled the big man to the floor. Balanced on one hand he looked up with surprise at his partner.

"What the hell's the matter with you?"

"Where's that Greek ape?" she demanded.

"Pappas?"

"How many Greek apes do we have for a pilot!" she shouted.

"Hey, lady, I'm not his keeper, remember? He works for *you*."

"*Where* is he?"

Sanchez smirked. "In bed." The smirk became a leer. "Of course," he added.

Tirado showed her disbelief. "He's asleep in the middle of the afternoon? I'll kill him. We've got a story to—" She took a deep breath and Sanchez moved quickly in the respite.

"Now, Angela, I *didn't* say he was *sleeping*."

"Wipe that smirk off your face," she spat. "*What* bed's he in? His? Carmen's? Grace? Lorena?"

Sanchez was genuinely surprised. "How do you know all his women?"

"Tell me *where*. I'll get the bastard on his feet."

"But why?" Sanchez asked, his question as honest as he could manage. "We don't have any flights scheduled."

"To hell with the schedules," Tirado retorted. She leaned forward and turned Sanchez's chair. "There." Her finger jabbed at several studio monitors. "Don't you even listen to what's going on? Down at Devil's Plateau and also by Jungle Rudy's camp. There are hundreds of reports of UFO's coming in and—"

Sanchez held up both hands in defense. "Hold it, *hold it*, lady," he said quickly. "Angela, we've been getting UFO reports from that area now for weeks. You know that yourself. Everybody's seeing idiot things in the sky. Which means the jungle down there is full of idiots."

"Or frightened people," she added.

Sanchez shrugged. "Superstitious, frightened, bugged out of their minds on jungle juice. What's the difference?"

Tirado placed both hands on Sanchez's desk and leaned forward to an almost threatening closeness. "This time, you big lummox, it's different."

"It's *always* different!" he said impatiently. "You couldn't put together a story on UFO's even if—" He broke off, impatient with himself. "Angela," he said earnestly, *"it's not news.* It's hysteria, hallucinations, airplane lights, satellites, whatever, *but it's not news.* Not even *you* can make it news that will get on the air."

"Are you through?" Angela now stood straight, arms crossed over her heaving bosom, generating all the warmth of a drill instructor. Sanchez shrugged and held up both hands in mock surrender.

"Now, *listen* to me," she said, all nonsense gone from her voice. Nelson Sanchez recognized the Angela Tirado he'd worked with for years: the sharpest newshound in the business, hot on the trail of *something.* So now he did what he'd have done if she hadn't asked. He listened, and carefully.

"Last night the weather down in the area of Devil's Plateau—by Angel Falls—"

"I know the area," he said quietly.

"All right. Then you know that at night all airliners fly *high* through there. At least twenty-eight thousand feet and as high as forty-two. I've checked with national air traffic control. Last night the weather was lousy. Thunderstorm buildups to as high as fifty and sixty thousand. So everybody was extra careful. As much as they could they were diverting the airliners around the worst storms. Everybody was on their toes, clicking right along."

She took a deep breath, reviewing her notes in her mind. "At least a dozen airliners, commercial airliners, saw them last night. Venezuelan, American, Brazilian and Mexican. Got that? Pilots from four different countries." Her face flashed a quick smile of triumph. "We also intercepted a coded report from one of the Americans' Blackbird reconnaissance planes. It was at seventy-four thousand feet when the crew reported a glowing sphere snapped past them no more than a hundred yards away."

"*Snapped?*" Sanchez asked. "That's a strange description."

"Their word, not mine." She accepted his hint of criticism. "It could mean almost anything," she admitted. "A light flashing by them. Or a glowing object passing them in the opposite direction. That airplane flies at two thousand miles an hour. If they even went past something standing still that was close by it'd be almost gone before you saw it. It would *snap* by. Whatever. We don't know yet. But it *is* significant that their crew would break radio silence to send such a message."

"All right," he yielded. "They saw *something*. But I can't accept even a glowing sphere as reliable. Not in the middle of the night at high altitude in storms and at that kind of speed."

"Done," she agreed. "So we consider only the importance of the crew making the report."

"What else?" Sanchez asked.

Tirado sat on the edge of his desk. With deliberately slow movement she opened a gold case for a cigarette and lit up with a flourish. Her Dunhill lighter clicked closed with an audible sound. He knew this woman. That was almost an announcement.

"Angela, my sweet, you have your own cloud around you. Canary feathers."

She smiled. "I haven't told you the really *big* news."

He sat back, silent. He wasn't going to ask a damn thing when she played cat-and-canary.

"It's the Russians," she said and went silent.

He knew when he was beaten. "What about the Russians?" he asked, as much playing the part as genuinely querying her.

"The cosmonauts in the Mir station orbiting the earth," she began.

"I know about Mir," he broke in gruffly.

His mood didn't touch her. "The Russians are claiming that the Americans set off an atomic bomb, or some such similar device, down at Devil's Plateau."

"That's crazy and you know it," he snapped, his irritation genuine. "There isn't anything *like* an atomic bomb. It is or it isn't."

"Oh, I agree," she said smoothly. "I'm not arguing for or against a *bomb*. I emphasize what several cosmonauts a couple of hundred miles out in space reported to Moscow. Whatever they saw, it *was* a flash visible for over a hundred miles. And that's along the surface of the earth, not just looking down from a space station passing almost overhead."

"That's also a lot of bullshit. Light or no light, there aren't any Americans setting off *anything* down at Devil's Plateau. Come on, Angela! That's along the edge of the Amazon basin, for Christ's sake!"

"I know where it is," she said coldly. "Try to keep things in perspective, try to see the whole picture, instead of arguing the details."

"I'll argue details all day and all night when they're ridiculous," he growled.

"There's more," she went on quickly. "For a remote area that's an international preserve, there's an extraordinary amount of sudden flight activity down there. All kinds of aircraft and helicopters—"

She stopped as she noted the quickening interest in his expression. Sanchez knew the *Auyan-Tepuy*—Devil's Plateau—as well as any man she knew. He was one of the few newsmen who'd been atop the Plateau, who had flown down through Corridor Diablo, the terrifying stretch of black-walled ravine filled with enormous boulders at the smash area where Angel Falls impacted after a watery plunge of more than three thousand feet. Nelson Sanchez looked at her carefully.

"You've accounted for the local aircraft?"

"Yes," she told him. "Three Cessna Two Oh Sixes, two Caravans, three Augusta helicopters. But only *one* of those ships has been airborne during the past week."

"What about the Seven Twenty Seven? It goes into that new strip once a day. You know where, about two miles from the jungle camp."

Angela Tiraco had a look of quiet triumph. "The Boeing hasn't been in there for the past five days. The weather's rotten, Nels, and I mean way below minimums. So we've got *one* local airplane confirmed as active, but," she added for emphasis, "the locals *and* the natives are talking about hundreds of flights! And they're *not* all aircraft."

"I know, I know," he said with a groan of resignation. "Glowing green spheres. Bright lights. The Russians saying the Americans are setting off atomic bombs. I said before that's all bullshit and you know it as well as I do."

"The bombs, yes. The green sphere?" She shook her head and he marveled at the sight of her, as he had marveled for so long at her beauty. No wonder she paralyzed her television viewers. He shook his head mentally to clear his thoughts as she went on. "But I won't give an inch on that Blackbird crew report. That's *too* hot. Breaking radio silence over Venezuela only confirms that the Americans have been violating Venezuelan airspace in— "

"I know, I know. Sovereign rights and all that."

"You speak very lightly of it," she said with a sour note in her voice.

"My love, my good friend Angela, my partner in crime, do not climb on your white horse with patriotic indignation." He sighed. "I'm as defensive of our borders as you. But when you're flying at night above seventy thousand feet, in storms, at two thousand miles an hour, and you're over jungle on the edge of the whole Amazon Basin, the word *border* simply has no meaning." Sanchez rose to his feet, fishing in a shirt pocket for a cigarette, then patting his pockets for a match. Tirado tossed him her lighter; he lit up and returned the Dunhill.

"Okay, I've been as unpleasant as I could, considering all the circumstances and your voodoo stories," he said finally. "I know what you want. There's a story down there— "

"Right," she said with growing enthusiasm.

"And you want us to go there."

"Right again."

"And it's late afternoon and it's also more than seven hundred miles from here to Devil's country."

"I know!" she half-shouted. She quieted suddenly, tired of the new path the conversation had taken. "Sanchez, old buddy, let me change something you said. It's not that I *want* us to go there, it's that we *are* going there. Got it?"

"Uh huh." Nothing else in the way of confirmation was needed. Once Angela Tirado made up her mind that was *it*.

"Now, in just what bed and between whose sheets can I expect to find Tony?" she demanded.

"He said something about soft lights and champagne and that he—"

"Never mind," she broke in quietly. "I know the drill. Hard as it may be to believe, he's actually using his *own* bed." She began gathering her gear and shoving it at Sanchez. "Let's *do* it, my friend. You take all my equipment and your own gear as well and move your big fat Swedish butt down to La Carlota Airport. You call Margarita before you leave so that she'll have a fast ship ready and waiting for us. I want at least a hot turboprop that'll get us to Auyan-Tepuy in three hours or less. Have it fueled and ready to start."

She spun away from his desk. "I'll get our Greek lothario." She started down the corridor, looked back. "And don't be late!" was her parting shot as she rounded the far corner.

A flamingo-pink Corvette hit the parking curb at La Cruz Apartments and screeched to a halt, tires smoking, the heavy sportscar rocking on its shocks. Angela Tirado exited the driver's seat with that special appeal of indifference to people who had stopped and stared at car and driver, many of them recognizing a vehicle that had become well known through its owner's broadcasting fame. In a country where an American sportscar's garish coloration and even appearance was hardly the most popular choice to people whose average income was distressingly far below that of the average citizen of the great Yankee colossus to the north, *this* eye-abusing Flamingo-'Vette was the exception to the rule. Angela Tirado was as well known to the Venezuelan public as the most popular stars of film and television's ghastly soap operas that five days a week ground out their hamburger tales for the ever-faithful. *This* was a lady of and for the people, the woman reporter who told the truth and defied the authorities and told the public the way it really was, and the devil take the hindmost.

Angela strode briskly to the La Cruz entrance where the doorman held open the glass doors for her. She paused briefly to drop a handful of coins into the outstretched reach of two street youths who would, until her return, guard her car with all the ferocity of dobermans. One of the best street-urchin games in town was to anticipate where Miss Tirado, the angel of television, would park the Flamingo thing. She was *always* good for a fist of money.

Angela waited impatiently through the elevator ascent to the eighteenth floor, one toe rapping a keyed-up tatoo until the car stopped and the door opened. She stormed down the hallway to stand before the apartment numbered 1812, took a deep breath, bent down to remove one shoe and then beat a hammering barrage against the door. The number 2 fell unnoticed to the floor.

"Open up, you Greek baboon!"

Angela stopped pounding, stared at the door, replaced her shoe and stabbed the doorbell with her right hand and began pounding with her left. Her voice rose in volume as the seconds passed.

"Pappas, you hairy son of a mountain goat, *open this damn door!*"

She heard a metal chain tinkling. Angela went silent, watching the door open barely an inch. One eye beneath long lashes peered at her. Angela shoved against the door. It opened a few more inches. A naked girl stared at her. Wide eyes failed to hide her sleepy state.

"Who are you? What do you want? Never mind. I don't care who you are or what you want. Go away."

The door closed; Angela caught it an instant before the lock clicked and shoved with all her might. The door flew open and the girl stumbled aside, full breasts bouncing. Angela swept past her, made a mental admission that Tony Pappas if nothing else had consummate taste in his women, and stormed her way to the bedroom. Naked feet pursued her. Angela stopped at the door and snapped on bright overhead lights, giving her a brief view of a buckass-naked Tony Pappas *and* two more beautiful and equally naked girls diving beneath satin sheets.

"For Christ's sake, Angie! You can't—!" Pappas got no further in his protests as Angela swept onward to bedside, grasped sheets in both hands and whipped them from the bed. The girls ran screaming from the room and a large, hairy, and red-faced Tony Pappas covered his crotch desperately. Angela grabbed a handful of thick curly hair atop Pappas' head and yanked him upright.

"Ow!" Pappas still clung to modesty with this woman and kept his hands buried against his groin. "Have you gone crazy? What the hell do you think you're—"

"Get up. *Now.*" Angela released her grip and moved back to a comfortable chair. She fell smoothly onto the cushiony mass and smiled. "We're on a story and you're flying. Remember? *I'm* the reporter and *you're* the pilot?"

"You're crazy, you know that?" Pappas wrapped himself in a sheet. "*What* story? Where? When?"

She spoke with cool, deliberate recitation, entirely the professional. "We're going after those UFO reports. They're coming out of the southwest like mad and I want to be airborne tonight when they start again."

Pappas' face was a blank. "UFOs?" he echoed.

"The area about Auyan-Tepuy."

"Angel Falls?"

"You've got it. *Churun-Merun.*"

"And what do you expect us to do? Fly down along the bottom of the falls?"

"If there's a UFO there we go there," she said firmly.

"Woman, you've slipped a cog between your ears. That's the Devil's Corridor. The route of the devil himself. When they named it *Diablo* they knew what they were talking about. It's crazy in daylight. It's suicide at night."

"Oh, piss off, Tony. You've got lights and we can kick out some flares—"

"You're out of your mind. *No.* I'm not going."

She was already out of her seat and rummaging through his closet. She grabbed clothing, turned and threw everything onto the bed. Flight suit, jacket, boots, even his flying cap. "Get dressed, Tony. Now, immediately. *Pronto.*"

"You crazy broad, I said I'm not going!" he shouted.

She stopped at the door leading into his living room, turned, and smiled sweetly. "Tony, my friend, in five minutes I walk out of this place. If you're not with me, you're fired." She waved her hand and closed the door behind her. She had no doubt he was already slipping into his flight gear.

She saw Nelson Sanchez and the night line crew waiting by the Cessna 425 turboprop. She urged the cab driver through the gates directly to the airplane and she piled out with Tony. Sanchez greeted them with a nod. "The bird's ready. Full fuel, the ground crew ran up the engines and topped off the tanks again. All my gear is aboard. Yours, too, Angela."

"Very good," she said crisply. "Let's do it, friends."

Sanchez climbed the steps into the cabin. Tirado turned to Pappas, who seemed lost in thought. "What are you waiting for?"

"Something, something," he murmured. He looked at the horizon. "Sun's going down," he said absently.

"Good for you!" Tirado exclaimed. "It does that every night, remember? *Get aboard*, Tony!"

"There's something I forgot."

"Well?"

"I can't remember what it is, dammit," Pappas growled.

"It can't be that important, then." She went into the airplane and forward to the copilot seat in the right of the cockpit. Moments later she heard Pappas coming forward, grunting as he slid his bulk into the left seat. She smiled to herself. This big hunk was like a fish out of water when he was on the ground, but once he moved into a flying machine he became part of the metal bird. She'd never admit it to Tony Pappas, but he was the best she'd ever flown with and she would go anywhere with him at the controls.

Even now he had shed the cocoon of clumsiness that afflicted him. His hands flowed among the myriad controls and levers and instruments of the powerful turboprop. Motors whined as pressures rose, lights glowed in a fantasy of colors; he checked the bird through its innards and moments later he signalled the line crew and received a signal in return that his propellers were clear to start. Less than three minutes later they were rolling from the line onto the taxiway. She sat back, watched and listened.

"La Carlota Tower, Monitor Tango Quebec Victor ready to taxi to the active for immediate takeoff. Over."

"Monitor Tango Quebec Victor, cleared to taxi south to runway three six. No other traffic. Hold short of the active."

"Roger, La Carlota."

He busied himself with his ground checks and runups as they taxied, made a ninety-degree turn at the end of the taxiway and eased to a stop. "Monitor's ready to roll, tower."

"Monitor Tango Quebec Victor, you are cleared for immediate takeoff. What is your direction of flight, please?"

Pappas released the brakes and started a right swing onto the runway. "Ah, La Carlota, we'll take a heading of two one zero and report en route."

"It's all yours, Monitor."

He eased the power levers full forward to their stops
and the Cessna went forward like silk, shoving them
back into their seats. Pappas never seemed to make a
deliberate move. Everything *flowed* through him to the
machine. The slight rumble of the runway faded as the
earth fell away, the gear came up with dull thumping
sounds and with the nose pointed high into the sunset,
just off to their right, they soared toward darkening
skies.

For ten minutes they flew in silence. Angela Tirado's
whiplash comments had been left behind on the earth's
surface. This was a different world, a different time and
space, and she would not intrude on Pappas' feeling out
the aircraft, blending his senses with the energy flow
and vibrations and murmurs of their machine. At over
two hundred miles an hour they soared magically into a
sky streaked with deepening reds and dark blues left by
the vanishing sun. Pappas yielded his control to the
automatic pilot as once again he checked the lifesigns of
the machine. Finally he settled back, staring straight
ahead. For the first time since takeoff he spoke.

"*Goddammit.*"

Her glance was sharp but her voice gentle enough.
"What is it?" She felt Sanchez moving behind her. That
one word could signify anything, including a problem
with their aircraft. But Pappas' hands remained calm
and he moved one hand only to rub a stubbled cheek.

"I forgot to file a flight plan," he said finally.

"So? When we get back someone will slap your wrist.
You know we can take care of such things," she told
him.

"You don't understand."

"Spell it out, Tony," she said.

He sighed. "It's against some very strict regulations
to fly at night in this country, *especially* where we're
going, without filing a flight plan and getting permission to do what we're doing."

She tried not to show irritation at his remarks. This
wasn't like Tony. "You sound like an old woman," she
said, more tartly than she intended.

He turned with a knowing smile. "Oh, really? This isn't a matter of breaking a regulation, Angela. If they catch us up here, and apparently there's some sort of prohibited area where we're going—you never gave me the time to check it out—they'll send up fighters to intercept us. Since we're *not* supposed to be here, and there's no good reason for us to be here, or down at Devil's Plateau, those fighters are just as likely to shoot first and worry about questions later."

"You're not serious."

"The hell I'm not." He wasn't smiling.

"We're *not* going back," she said, her face grim with purpose.

"Well, who the hell wants to live forever," Pappas said, surprising her. He glanced at her again. "You might as well catch a nap, then. We're going up to thirty-two thousand and it's like flying inside an inkwell, especially when we bust through that front."

"*What* front?" She was angry with herself. She'd never considered the weather. As quickly as the thought came to her a sharp blow struck the aircraft and the hiss of rain smashing against the windshield filled the cabin.

"*That* front," he said, smiling. He was enjoying her sudden discomfiture.

"A little weather doesn't frighten me, Tony."

"Hooray for you, lady. It frightens *me*."

They lapsed into silence. She was determined to stay awake, but the steady drone of the turboprops, the softly glowing lights and rocking of the airplane was soporific and she was sound asleep in minutes. She could hardly believe more than two hours had passed when Tony roughly shook her awake.

She looked outside. They were soaring over another planet of great silvery clouds beneath them, a full moon low on the horizon. It was stunning, magical. Tony Pappas didn't seem to be impressed by the magic. He was pointing and she followed his lead.

For a moment she saw only the silvery mantle beneath them and the distant cold orb of the moon. Then it happened. An incredible flash of green. Nothing sharp: a huge green pulse of light, a silent explosion of green flashing through the clouds. The green was not there and then it *was* there, in an instant transforming the clouds, lifting upward and out away from the world. It was just that, a pulsation, and it was gone, leaving only a memory.

The voice came from behind them. "What the hell was *that*?" Sanchez, fully awake, a television camera in his hands but nothing to shoot.

"I don't know, but if we *all* saw it then it's real."

"I saw it," Pappas said immediately. "I also saw it twice before, but it happened so fast I thought I was seeing something that wasn't there." He rubbed his eyes. "It happens when you're flying at night. Color pulses in the eyes."

"*I* saw it, Tony," Angela persisted.

"Oh, I know, I know," Pappas told her. "We're not the only ones to have seen something."

"What do you mean?" *This is maddening*, Angela Tirado told herself. *Something is happening out there and—*

"The radio's full of pilots reporting strange lights," Pappas explained.

"Anything about those UFO's?" Angela said quickly.

"Uh huh," Pappas nodded. "You name it and they're calling it. A lot of confusion. Nothing official. Just airline pilots up real high. You can see for hundreds of miles. Green flashes and a couple of pilots reporting glowing green balls, or spheres, or *something*, going past them so fast they're not sure what they saw."

Triumph raced through Angela. "How far are we from Devil's Plateau?"

"Thirty miles or so." Pappas pointed ahead and down. "The cloud front ends just ahead of us. It's clear the rest of the way."

Angela Tirado made an instant decision. "Take us down, Tony."

"You mean, down to—"

"Down to Devil's Plateau. Take us down *now!*"

"You're the boss, you got the elevator ride downstairs." His hand moved smoothly, the throb of power eased, and the nose fell earthward. "You're crazy, Angela, and I'm crazier for going along with your crazy ideas."

She ignored him, turning to Sanchez. "Nels, you have every camera you've got ready to work."

"I'm all set, Angie."

They fell silent, searching the skies, straining to see anything. The full moon gave them an astonishing amount of light. A soft horizon showed mountains and mesas coming into view against the lighter background. Moonlight reflected like quicksilver from streams and rivers and swampland. That was not hospitable country down there. Pappas tracked their exact position with his electronic navigation systems. They didn't really need them. A wide river flowed toward Devil's Plateau. Enormous mesas stood up like ancient flat-topped pyramids and temples.

"See that area? Just left of the nose," Pappas described Devil's Plateau to them. "The top of that mesa is filled with dozens of streams. When I bring the nose more to the left you'll see everything down there reflect moonlight. And you'll see the falls breaking off the edge of the plateau."

Quicksilver and moonglow with lights flash-reflecting. They swung beyond and Pappas brought the airplane around in a wide circling bank. Angel Falls shone brightly in the moonlight, a luminescent ghost stretching downward from the plateau for more than three thousand feet. At its bottom the water spread out in a huge bowl of shifting spray.

"It's incredible," Angela said softly. She hesitated a moment and then gestured. "Can you see the corridor, Tony?"

"Diablo?"

"Yes."

"Yeah, I see it. Why?"

"Make a pass right through the corridor. About two hundred feet off the deck."

"You're out of your mind! The winds are wild down

there, Angie! We make one mistake and we'll be splattered against rock like— "

"Do it! *Please!*"

He stared at her. She *never* said please. He had never heard the word directed to him by Angela Tirado. He cursed himself for a fool, swung wide, came around in a steep descent and as they leveled off, the corridor a black maw before them, he snapped on his landing lights and went to full power. If they were hit with any unexpected downdrafts he'd need every ounce of power and speed he could get from this thing. And the brilliant lights would reflect from spray and keep him from getting too close to the titanic plunge of water to their left.

It was magic all over again, spray reflecting with dazzling dancing brilliance from the landing lights. They were almost through the corridor, winds pummeling and hammering at them, when Tony Pappas called out *"Enough!"* and hauled back on the yoke. The Cessna burst upward in a powerful climb.

Instantly they were struck blind.

This is what it's like to be inside the fireball of an atomic bomb when it explodes. The thought speared the mind of Angela Tirado as her eyes went green, as the world went wildly, savagely green, as Everything became green and there existed nothing else but the ultimate blinding green glare. It was more than blinding light, more than paralyzing glare. It was the End and the Beginning of Everything.

She thought she heard Nelson Sanchez scream or cry out in pain in the seat behind her. Even as the verbalization punched into her mind and she realized the pain ripping through her optic system, vision was returning. Sparkling lights, dazzling reflections within her eyeballs, a madhouse of green optical energy racing between eyes and brain. Mouth gaping open, gasping for air from the shock, she half-turned and saw Tony Pappas transformed into a green statue, his body frozen, hands locked, one on the yoke, his right hand on the throttles.

She couldn't believe his control. "I'm all right." He

spoke the three words like an automaton. He was busy
with saving his life. Saving their lives. He was flying
brilliantly. Just before they were struck by, by—*whatever*
it was that hurled them into green blindness, he had
pulled back on the yoke and booted the turboprop into
a steep climb. The direction in which he was flying
would take them up and away from between those
crushing vertical rock walls that formed Corridor Diablo. If he continued on this same path, unerringly, they
would burst free of the rock that could turn them into a
momentary splash of gruesome flame, to fall in gushes
of burning wreckage to the floor of the devil's canyon.
Tony still could not see. You do not have vision when
you are green-blinded and flying into a sky as dark as
the inside of a cat. But he needed only a few more
moments; he knew if he held on to their angle and rate
of climb and their speed they would be in free air. But
they wouldn't be safe. Not yet. He was still blind and a
pilot doesn't fly well at all when he's blind. He can't *see*
what his airplane is doing. You're as good as dead, but
you're seconds away from the final act.

Tony Pappas knew his airplane. He knew every switch
and control and dial and knob and button. He spoke
again calmly, looking straight ahead and seeing nothing,
and using his fingers for his eyes.

"I'm going to autopilot," he said in that same monotone, only a part of him communicating with Angela
and Nelson, and most of Tony Pappas' awareness and
skills devoted to keeping control of their machine. His
fingers brushed the quadrant, slid along familiar territory, found the ON switch for the autopilot and depressed the switch. In that instant the electrical system
activated the automatic pilot and the Cessna was locked
into its zoom climb and heading of flight. They weren't
yet out of the woods. The airplane couldn't sustain the
dangerously steep angle he had used for their zoom
burst upward from the lethal canyon now far below
them. His fingers moved again and brushed the electric
trim, and he slid the ridged surface forward, hesitated,
slid it forward again, *feeling* the nose lowering just a

bit. He listened. His fingers had been his eyes. His ears also became his vision. He listened to the cry of wind changing, shifting. The roar of great speed had subsided; now they labored upward. He went forward again on the trim switch. Wind speed sounds increased. They climbed now at a flatter angle. They were *safe* in the great emptiness of the sky. For the moment, anyway.

They sat quietly in their pain that receded slowly. Lines and shapes became visible as vision crawled and fought its way back to the three of them. Angela turned; she was able to *see* Nelson behind her. She remembered now; he had cried out in pain. Had it been the light?

No; the side of his face was a darker mass. "I'll be all right," he said in a subdued voice. "The light. When the light came my head jerked back. I cut it on the camera." He was grateful for the deep gash that poured blood from the side of his head. That was their only injury, and he pressed a handkerchief into the gash to stem the flow of blood. "I'm okay," he reassured them.

"Can you see?" she asked Tony. She made out his face now. Tony nodded, slow but careful. He was holding a flashlight on the gauges. He couldn't see in the normal dim light of cockpit night illumination. She didn't bother him for the moment. "We're going to be fine," he said finally. "We're at eight thousand and we're still climbing. Everything is okay with the plane."

Her hands shook as she lit a cigarette. She took a long, deep drag, felt a shudder sweep through her.

"God, what in the name of hell *was* that?" she asked finally, knowing they knew no more than she.

Tony laughed, a short and humorless sound. "It sure wasn't no hallucination." He glanced at Angela. "I take it all back, Angie. Everything I said about how crazy you were to come here. I don't know what it was. Just that I've never known anything like it. And that it nearly killed us." He rubbed his eyes. "Well, there's good news with the bad. My vision is almost normal now."

"Me, too," came Sanchez's voice from behind them.

Angela nodded. "Just in time."

"In time for what?" Sanchez asked.

"Get your camera, Nels," she said with a sense of urgency in her voice. "I don't believe this party is over yet." She pointed. Behind her she heard the sound of the television camera as Sanchez went to video recording.

"Good God," Tony said, as much to himself as to them.

Two dazzling bright lights raced swiftly through the sky, rushing toward them, expanding swiftly with their approach. "I don't see anything else," Angela said. "Those lights . . . Tony, what is it?"

Pappas peered ahead, squinting to see better. The two lights now were brighter, sharper, rushing toward them in a great curving sweep. "Holy Mother," Angela murmured as she stared. "Nels! you getting this?"

"Yeah, yeah," he mumbled, concentrating on locking the lights in his viewfinder.

The lights became great glaring eyes, starting to blind them as they came rushing in with tremendous speed. Tony snapped off the autopilot, got ready to kick the Cessna into a steep curving drive, and then he was through thinking. Hard forward and to the left with the yoke, he stamped left rudder and chopped power to drop beneath the lights almost on top of them now. Angela and Nelson fought for balance as they were thrown against the side of the airplane, their stomachs giddy with the sudden violent maneuver.

"They've got to be UFO's!" Angela shouted, all reporter again. "Oh, what a story! Nels, keep shooting, keep shooting!"

An incredible sight unfolded before them. The lights vanished, then reappeared out of darkness behind them, and split swiftly, spreading away from each other horizontally, racing ahead and taking up position on each side of the diving Cessna.

"Oh, shit," Tony said to himself, the words unbidden to his lips. He brought the airplane out of its curving dive and eased again into level flight. "I can't believe this," Angela said to them. "Right through everything you did, I mean, those lights, they held perfect formation. That's incredible."

Tony Pappas didn't share her wonder. "Get ready for some *more* lights," he said, almost sullenly. She stared at him, caught by surprise. Her surprise was even greater as bright light beams stabbed at them from either side of their plane. She saw Tony's hand reach out to turn on the cabin speakers from the pilot's radio. A voice was already speaking to them in clearly annunciated, *very* official Spanish.

". . . are in violation of federal security regulations. Consider yourselves under arrest. Take up a heading of three four zero degrees and initiate your descent now. Hold that descent rate at four hundred feet per minute. An airport is sixty miles directly ahead of your line of flight. You will make a straight-in landing. Radio permission will not be required. Any attempt to change your course or to escape will result in our shooting you down without further warning. If you read this message either flash your lights or respond on frequency one two one five. Over."

"What the hell kind of UFO is that!" Sanchez shouted from the back seat.

"They're better known as F-16's," Tony Pappas said sullenly. "Air force fighters, and they are *very* serious." He reached for his radio frequency controls.

"Are they serious? Would they really shoot us down?" Angela Tirado's voice made her disbelief unmistakable. "They wouldn't do that, would they, Tony? Shoot us down? *Kill* us, I mean?"

"Little lady, you can bet your sweet ass they would." He thumbed his microphone. "Ah, fighter escort from the Cessna," he said slowly, unable to avoid a sudden grimace. "I read you five by five. We will comply, and we will keep this frequency open. Over."

"Very good, Cessna. Do not initiate any further radio communications. Confirm, please."

"Ah, roger, sure, you've got it," Tony said. He stared ahead, monitoring his descent at exactly four hundred feet a minute. The lights on either side of them snapped out. Darkness rushed in like a blanket.

"Hey, they're gone," Sanchez called out.

"The hell they are," Tony Pappas growled. "One mistake by me and they'll blow us right out of the air. They're out there. We can't see them but *they* can see *us*."

For several moments they were all silent. Angela reached out to gently touch Pappas' arm.

"I'm very sorry, Tony," she said softly.

He didn't turn. "Shut up," he told her.

Chapter II

Earlier that same evening there began a sequence of events, totally unknown to Angela Tirado, that would soon snare her and her news team in a web of inescapable consequences. Had Angela remained in Caracas, or flown to virtually any other part of her country in pursuit of strange lights and reported UFO's flashing through Venezuelan skies, she would have avoided the hair-trigger escape from death down the Devil's Corridor and the equally lethal missiles and cannon of Venezuelan Air Force F-16 jet fighters. To say nothing of the less lethal but no less aggravating events of being forced from the skies, landing unexpectedly at a remote military airfield and, in unsportsmanlike manner, placed under arrest and tossed into an inhospitable and most uncomfortable military prison, there to contemplate the official charges being arrayed against her, Nelson Sanchez and Tony Pappas. The more she dwelled on the matter the more foolish became her insistence on the flight she'd demanded from her news crew. They and their lives had been jeopardized, their equipment *and* their aircraft seized, and Monitor Nacional Television now faced a crushing fine from their government, to which might be added severe restrictions on other reporters to prevent the very actions committed by Angela Tirado and her team.

The saving balm of the whole crazy parade of events was that all along *she'd been right*. In the ruckus storming about her and her crew violating federal air regulations, and the other assorted charges she considered (to paraphrase a close American woman reporter) so much "cockamamie bullshit," there remained the one point: the Venezuelan military refused even the most distant comment.

That savage green light, the explosion in silence of a light so fantastic it transcended anything she had ever known. No wonder the cosmonauts orbiting overhead in their Mir space station were reporting to Moscow that nuclear devices were being exploded along the rim of the Amazon Basin! The location had been pinpointed, according to the "outraged" Russians, as within Venezuelan borders, and therefore an insidious criminal pact must exist between Venezuela and the United States for the testing of strange new atomic weapons. None of it made a shred of sense, at least where *weapons* were concerned. No fallout, no fireball, no radiation, no mushroom cloud— *Bah!* she punctuated her own thoughts, because there still was no explanation for that damning light. The *only* light with which she could compare the devastating glare were the reports she'd read of atomic explosions. *The light of a thousand suns,* many observers had said, shaken and stunned. *The light that was seen when God created the world.* . . . Superlatives piled one atop the other. When people had seen the light to excess, even through *black* eyeshields, it had taken from thirty seconds to an hour to regain their sight.

She thought about that. She and the others began to regain limited vision within five minutes or so. In ten minutes they were seeing reasonably well. Fifteen minutes left them with a headache but normal vision. It couldn't have been an atomic bomb, she insisted to herself. *Yes, it could,* her own critical alter ego snapped at her. *Stupid girl.* You're trying to rationalize final answers with nothing more than a glare, no matter how bright. What if it were a bomb that went off directly behind you and more than twenty or fifty miles away? It would still have been just as bright!

She paced her cell, impatience and frustration competing for attention. That, and discomfort. Tony had only had time to tell her he didn't even know the name of this field. It wasn't on their charts, no signs appeared anywhere; in fact, there wasn't any identification of *any* kind on any vehicle or building, and the uniforms of the guards carried no patches or nameplates. *Why all this mystery?* her inner voice shouted at her. Impatience, frustration and helplessness. She couldn't make any telephone calls to her home office. Pappas and Sanchez were in the same position. Individual cell lockups, everything on their persons other than their clothing confiscated, and for answers to their questions only stony silence.

She stared moodily through the single small window of her cell. Nothing so prosaic as thick metal bars. The transparent pane providing her a minuscule glance at the outside world, made of armor glass, was far more effective than old-fashioned bars. It prevented the passage of anything save filtered light. It blocked off almost all sound, except for the building shaking from the roar of jet fighters slamming into afterburners for takeoff. There was still plenty of *that* going on.

Then, perhaps twenty minutes after the last sound trickled to her of jet blast, she heard the thin wail of sirens. Not *a* siren. *Many* sirens howling their massed chorus. Klaxon warning horns also could be heard, and then the lights in the cell flicked off and back on three times and then stayed off. She went to the window to look out, to find some explanation of what might be happening. It was a mistake.

The savaging green flashed, daggers of teal brilliance ripped into her eyes, and she staggered back from the brain-wrenching punch of the light.

Not until twenty minutes later, seated on the floor, tears streaming from her eyes with returning vision, did she use her brain for something other than emotional outrage. It could *not* be a nuclear device exploding. She'd gone through almost everything before—radiation, a mushroom cloud; all of it. This time she was on the surface, in a building, from within which she could hear the roar of jet fighters. *No sound accompanied that terrible light.* Ergo; no sourcepoint of millions of de-

grees of an atomic explosion. *No explosion.* Heat and
sound went together, inseparable. So it was something
else. *What?* No answers came from anywhere and she
lapsed into a deep emotional funk, head resting against
her knees, feeling crushingly isolated.

One hundred miles away, the experiment that had
brought her and her associates to the prison block of
the ultrasecret military airfield continued. Had Angela
Tirado made her flight just a few hours earlier, and had
she known where and how to look, the mystery drowning her now in emotional bonds would have been
revealed.

Sunset along the southern rim of Venezuela is never
calm. Here great stretches of river and grasslands rising
to rounded hills that warn of not-too-distant Andean
ramparts mix with massive buttes and mesas. They are
unlike the stone ramparts of the American West, the
glories of Monument Valley spread through Utah and
Arizona. There the world is sand and rock and the
multihued presence of the Painted Desert, the latter
visible only when the sun angle best reflects its colors.
If one could transform Monument Valley into a new
world of thick, rich vegetation, rivers and streams, lush
foliage and the marching giants of thunderstorms that
wander the countryside like homeless colossi, the picture would be more complete. Here is *Auyan-Tepuy*,
the Devil's Plateau. Water races along its tabletop-flat
surface with a major stream, like a huge artery, surrounded on all sides by hundreds of smaller streams
and gushing founts. Much of the water pauses an instant on the sharp rim of the plateau and then slides,
slips, tumbles and cascades downward. But the main
stream, well before it reaches the edge of this immediate world, broadens suddenly, widens to a powerful
stream, and with swiftly increasing bottom depth accel-
erates its water to a powerful thrumming roar and furiously boiling liquid. It is flung by speed and pressure
outward from the edge of the plateau and then begins
the greatest drop of water in all the world. This is Angel

Falls, and the water will plunge straight down for more
than three thousand two hundred feet, a height so
stupendous it makes the drop of better-known Niagara
seem a localized event. The water crashes down with
increasing fury until it smashes into the ravine known
as the Devil's Corridor, a black and murderous passage-
way dangerous even for large birds, which fall prey to
sudden violent winds that without warning can hurl
them against unyielding rock.

Angel Falls owes its name to no indigenous saint or a
gathering altar for corporeal folk. Nor does it honor any
local hero. Long before her time, Tirado knew, an
American pilot, a wild and tempestuous adventurer,
had flown over Devil's Plateau in a machine that for its
day was one of the best but by modern standards was a
dangerous and unpredictable craft. Sure enough, his
machine failed, and Jimmy Angel crashed atop the infa-
mous Devil's Plateau and was given up for dead. Even
had he lived he was in deep jungle, high atop a mesa,
and far removed from even a vestige of civilization. In
fact, Jimmy Angel survived his crash. He also fought,
walked, scraped and crawled his way out of the jungle to
a river and a dugout canoe with jungle natives who
stared in disbelief at the tattered human wreck before
them, Jimmy Angel made it back, alive, and a stunned
and marveling Venezuelan government honored his incredible feat by naming the world's tallest waterfall
after him.

In the years that followed, Angel Falls and the surrounding countryside became recognized as an environmental pearl in the rough. It was declared a national
preserve by the Venezuelan government and, in years
subsequent to that initial protection, and through the
United Nations, was further declared a planetary treasure. No new roads could be built, no old roads could
be repaired, and all movement into and out of the area
was placed under the strictest government supervision.
In short, the Venezuelan authorities gave you permission to enter the area; if found there *sans* that permis-

sion you faced some heavy and bad legal medicine. Fines and jail sentences went hand in hand.

So for every reason that might come to her mind, Angela Tirado *knew* that there could be nothing of the modern world either existing in or taking place in this pristine treasure trove of natural and powerful beauty.

She was also dead wrong. Had she been within this area, either on *or within* the massive butte that formed the base of Devil's Plateau, she would have been witness to another world as strange and forbidden as that created by nature. A world of men and machines and staggering energies they sought to control and put to their own use.

And that by comparison paled the UFO story she sought so diligently to confirm.

The events that led to their brush with disaster and her confinement in the lone prison cell were already under way at the same moment she was scattering naked women from the bedroom of Tony Pappas.

But unfortunately for Angela Tirado she was unable to see *within* the mountain that wore Devil's Plateau as its crown. Nor could she hear the voices borne along secret government frequencies that had been sounding the signals and events of the most stupendous scientific program in the history of Venezuela. A program that, if successful, would shake all the world.

This day's test neared its initial blazing culmination as the sun fell beneath the horizon along the edge of the great Amazon Basin, when the huge mesas seemed to march in silhouetted formation along the final deep orange hues of last daylight.

"All stations from Control, I repeat, all stations from Control, Test Five Two Nine is now at ten minutes and counting. On my mark, we are at ten minutes and counting. *Mark!*"

The technician sat within a room jammed with electronic control and communications equipment. All about him were walls of solid rock, yet he felt a touch of nervousness that all was not as secure as it might have been. It was strictly a psychological reaction, and to the test crews of PROJECT BEMAC the prickling of hairs along the back of the neck had become standard fare. High overhead the river rushed white and boiling to the rim of the plateau and hurled itself outward. That rushing water, tumbling rocks along its river bed, scraping and gouging, created the trembling transmitted through the rock itself. The water fell more than three thousand feet to crash against huge black boulders as large as houses, and the grinding shifting of those enormous hulks also brought a quivering to the earth and up through the seeming solidity of the mesa mountain.

Far below the technician in his man-gouged cave there roared still more violent energy: enormous hydro-electric systems powered by the force of Angel Falls rushing downward to its final doom of crashing spray. The power of the water was not enough for the BEMAC tests; an enormous river of electricity was also needed, and here in this isolation of *Auyan-Tepuy* the scientists and their teams could carry out their secretive work.

The technician who had called out the countdown mark saw his receiving equipment glow red; simultaneously he recognized a woman's voice as it fed into his earset. "Control, this is Jaguar. We're all in the green here and ready to go. Standing by for any further instructions."

Control moved a dial. "Very good, Jaguar." He paused a moment before speaking again. "Condor, your status, please."

"Ah, roger that, Control. This is the big bird calling back. Condor is ready to flap. Standing by."

Control frowned. He glanced up to a scientist listening to the exchange. The scientist shook his head slightly. "Control to Condor. We'll do without the flippancy, please, and that is official. Do you read?"

The voice tone changed immediately. "That's affirmative, Control. Sorry."

Another twitch on the frequency dial. Later, Control would gangswitch all transmissions so all stations would receive him simultaneously. But for the moment, they wanted singular responses. "Piranha, your status, please?"

"Okay, Control, Piranha here. We're in great shape, all systems green, but we, ah, I've been told to ask you if we're going to get a plasma shot to do a recheck of our gear before the main transmission."

Far upriver from the plateau, along the banks of the Canaima River, Jungle Rudy stared at the sky of early evening, his gaze in the direction of Devil's Plateau. No one even remembered his full name. He had been Jungle Rudy for nearly forty years in this isolated and primitively beautiful jungle camp just upstream from Thunder Falls. He had raised his children here; his eldest daughter, Hilda, was at this moment by his side. About them were another dozen men and women, technicians and observers. Excitement built among them. The skies above the Canaima had for the past several weeks exceeded anything nature ever provided with the aurora of the polar regions, and they knew another silent crash of light was about to instantly transform all the visible world to dazzling green. Here at the edge of the rushing waters they also listened to the voices ghosting among the scientific and engineering camps of the secret project. A radio receiver in the back of a helicopter carried its sounds by small loudspeaker to the group.

Within the mountain, Control went to gangswitch transmission. "All stations, counting down for pulse test. I repeat, this will be a pulse test at only five percent power transmission. Check your monitoring and intensity systems. Ten seconds and counting."

Throughout the now-darkened jungle and plains of the deep Venezuelan interior the scientists and technicians waited. The seconds vanished and a barely perceptible green haze ghosted through jungle and sky. Control listened to the reports coming in. He nodded to the lead man in Control. "Everything's right on the money."

"Very good. Do a final stations check and continue the count."

"Yes, sir." Control confirmed again he was on gangswitch transceive. "Skyhook?" he called tersely.

He recognized the voice of Captain Ali Bolivar, still thought it amazing that the voice came down from a speeding aircraft at thirty thousand feet. In that plane Bolivar checked his gauges, glanced at two technicians behind him in the cabin. They nodded and one held up his thumb. Bolivar spoke into his lip mike. "Control, Skyhook's with you and ready to monitor. We've got the count."

"Very good, Skyhook." Control paused a moment. "Chopper One, you read?"

A flashing red light sped down the Canaima River, swung toward shore and began flaring to set down on a broad grass area. The pilot thumbed his mike. "Control, Chopper One's about to put down in the nest. We'll be set in a minute."

The helicopter settled smoothly, rocked on its gear, and a moment later its cabin door swung open to reveal two scientists carrying instruments fixed atop tripods. They walked thirty feet from the helicopter, snapped out the tripods, leveled them on the ground. A woman followed them with a glittering electronic display panel she placed on the ground. Carlos Alberto Silva, chief of the science team, shouted to Judy Morillo over the slowing helicopter sounds.

"We're ready here, Judy. You?"

She smiled, showed her rising excitement. "Ready! I can hardly wait!"

"Any moment now," Silva told her, glancing at his watch.

"Thirty seconds and counting." At all the monitoring stations, aboard the aircraft high overhead, in Jungle Rudy's camp, in stations deep within huge caves, men and women either studied their gauges and control panels or, if they were fortunate enough to be in the open, looked out to the sky.

"Five, four, three—"

Ali Bolivar held his breath and looked down on the earth six miles below. Pale afterglow of sunset reflected from the water rushing across the flats of Devil's Plateau. He saw three tiny but intense marker lights against darkness. He didn't need them. He knew the Devil's Corridor better than any man. He'd flown through it more than a hundred times. In his mind he counted seconds. His body tensed and he ground his teeth together.

One instant, blackness. The next, an explosive bolt leaped into existence down the length of Devil's Corridor. It didn't race down that hellish ravine, it didn't flash—*it appeared*. One instant it was not there and the next a river of green fire snapped into existence. Its flash whipped outward and with the speed of light, so fast that were it measured it would have raced seven times around the earth's equator in but a single second, it transformed the world to green. As quickly as it appeared it was gone. But not to the visual observers. Retinal afterimage clung to the green, kept the world green, sent sparkling and flashing green through and around blinking, quivering eyeballs.

What people saw depended upon where they were. To Ali Bolivar and the observers high above the world the green light was a single needle, impossibly miles long, snapping into and out of existence, gaining thickness only through the inability of the eye to retain afterimage tight focus.

Indians in dugout canoes and within their riverside villages, depending upon their angle of sight, suffered the inability of eye or mind to comprehend. Since a single flash of light could not instantly appear over a distance of many miles, their eyes gave them a false picture of a huge spearpoint of light racing over the jungle, above the hills, across the rivers, with tremendous speed, faster than any bullet, making the fastest airplane reduced to the speed of their own dugouts. Since they accepted what they saw and it never occurred to them they might be plagued with visual inadequacy they never doubted that an *object* ripped through the jungle night, covering many miles in barely a second.

Even within the jungles the natives knew of great

machines that sped high above them. Machines carrying men that moved about the earth *at five miles every second*. But how could a man survive racing through the air at three hundred miles a minute? To a man paddling a dugout canoe there is no distinction between atmosphere and absence of atmosphere; the latter is too ridiculous to contemplate. They did not even need to know such names as Vostok, Voshkod, Mercury, Gemini, Skylab, Apollo, Soyuz, Salyut, Mir or the many names of the great winged beast other men called Columbia and Challenger and Discovery. Even here in the jungles they had seen the flame paint the clouded heavens as enormous French boosters ripped skyward within shouting distance of Devil's Island off the South American coastline. If men could run through the dark skies at five miles a second, what could be so strange about a glowing ball of green light doing the same through their jungle?

They had seen it before but still they were awed and amazed. Jungle Rudy and Hilda, Carlos Alberto Silva and Judy Morillo; all of them who saw with their own eyes the silent crash of green that took over the world and then vanished. Scientists checked their instruments and gauges, looked at one another and shook hands or embraced in jubilation. The airwaves fairly crackled with the good news between the many monitoring stations, the aircraft and the helicopters, and the leaders of science and government waiting many hundreds of miles distant in Caracas and on a broad mountain outside of the capital of Venezuela.

Deep within Devil's Plateau, on a platform above and looking down on the electric transformers, banks of mirrors, thick cabling and an orderly nightmare of equipment, all arranged about what appeared to be a monstrous cannon barrel of superscientific design, a young man took a deep breath. His name was Benito Armadas and he wore a jumpsuit with strange insignia and the lettering of BEMAC. Dark wavy hair, powerful muscles bunched beneath the suit, a touch of perspiration along his upper lip, all swept away by his look of determination. He stood on a circular platform as if claiming ownership and stared hard at Doctor Vasco de Gama. De Gama stood with a slight stoop, clear sign of the tremendous responsibility he shouldered at this moment. He wished he could avoid the clear and unblinking gaze of this young man. He wished he were not here within this mountain, blazing incredible new avenues into the future, for it was one thing to titillate nature, and quite another to know that if he nodded affirmation, this young man might well be dead minutes later.

"They're all ready, sir," Armadas said. His eagerness betrayed him as he leaned forward. "*I'm* ready, Doctor de Gama. Let us do it, sir!"

De Gama nodded slowly, more with his own inner turmoil than recognition of Armadas' entreaties. He raised his eyes. "You are so sure that you do not fear for your life?"

"I'm *sure*."

"It is really the unknown, Benito." The scientist spoke with genuine warmth for the younger man. "It frightens me. It could be worse than merely your death."

Armadas grinned. "No one lives forever." He shrugged. "I know the risk." He laughed. "It can't be any worse than our flight down here through that thunderstorm. Half our people were convinced they were going to die, and the rest of them were so sick they were afraid they would *not* die." He stopped, knowing now that anything he said would be brushed aside. Vasco de Gama must answer to himself. Again he nodded.

"All right," he said, his sigh tremulous and weary. "Take your position." De Gama motioned to technicians. "Attend him. A final check. *Everything* again." He offered a flicker of a smile to Armadas, then walked slowly to an observation booth where he donned a headset and lip mike.

"This is Doctor de Gama," he spoke slowly into the mike, knowing his voice carried to all BEMAC personnel. "Doctor Hernandez, confirm your contact."

Doctor Edith Hernandez, Chief Biologist and Medical Doctor for the BEMAC team, squeezed the transmit pad in her left hand; simultaneously she continued to monitor the panels reporting on every critical biological function of Benito Armadas. He was wired up like one of the early astronauts. The simile was so close the doctor smiled. In both instances they were breaching a new frontier. Unaware of the movement, her right hand lifted to stroke a rosary as she scanned her panels and answered de Gama's call.

"This is Hernandez, Doctor." She didn't wait for a response. "The subject is in excellent condition. In fact, considering what he's about to do, he is calm beyond all expectations. A perfect example of the Cooper Syndrome."

Everyone listening in smiled; they understood her words perfectly. The astronaut from the American Project Mercury, that country's first manned space flight program. Crammed into his tiny Mercury capsule, atop a great Atlas booster vibrating and thrumming with unstable and tremendous explosive energy, listening to the countdown that would end with a hellish roar and a Niagara of fire, Gordon Cooper fell fast asleep. Mission Control knew a moment of panic when strange, completely unexpected sounds carried through all control positions and down through the tracking ranges. *It was the sound of Gordon Cooper snoring*.

Vasco de Gama appreciated the comparison but no smile creased his face, and his frown remained. Cooper at least was following in the footsteps of others. Americans and Russians had leaped the barriers of gravity and slipped into free-fall orbit. Their unknowns had been whittled down to very acceptable odds. Not so the case, he mused, for this bright-eyed and eager Armadas. He would stand upright on a circular platform. All about him in a sphere of energy made visible by pulsating currents there would be created an electromagnetic field of a very precise frequency. At a specific moment, an enormous storehouse of energy would smash into a cold-electron laser generator, a beam eight feet in diameter would snap into existence at the electromagnetic field. At that instant Benito Armadas would snap *out* of existence as a molecular and cellular body of familiar physical substances such as flesh, blood, bone, sinew and the multiple trillions of parts, small and large, from viral and bacterial elements to sparkling connections within his brain. Everything about Benito Armadas would be disassociated from the physical reality of his entire lifetime. He would *become* a part of the supercharged blast of coherent light.

If all went well—de Gama offered himself a wry grimace for the phrase that had attended so many dangers in space flight—Armadas, in the form of an electromagnetic pulse embedded within the laser beam, would leap the distance from his transmission point to a receiving station several miles distant. The trip would take the barest fraction of a second. Armadas would be traveling, after all, with a speed of 186,271 miles per *second.* For his vehicle would be light itself.

The word to describe his transmission—laser—seemed woefully inadequate for this incredible gamble they were taking. A laser beam was, after all, light, albeit a truly fantastic manipulation of light. Laser—*Light Amplification by Stimulated Emission of Radiation*—was a super gun. And guns, even scientific devices, kill.

Yet, as de Gama knew so well, they had made over a thousand such tests with live animals. In the first six hundred such tests more than half the creatures died in sickening fashion. Then the failure rate plummeted and success became theirs as they learned to manipulate these incredible forces of man-altered nature. And the last one hundred and eighty-two tests with live animals had been perfect.

Time for a man to fly by light. That was the motto of these eager, shining faces all about him, de Gama noted sourly. Well, there comes that time when one must release the sword from its scabbard—

"*Sixty seconds and counting,*" intoned the speakers. The very air seemed to become brittle with rising tension.

"Open the doors," de Gama spoke into his lip microphone. At the far end of the chamber within the mountain large metal doors opened swiftly. *"Doors open and secured,"* came the confirming voice response from an unseen technician.

Vasco de Gama kept his hand poised over the large red button that would stop the test in a split second. But his hand remained in strike position, rigid, while the rest of him eased through the count in concert with dozens of skilled engineers and scientists.

"Confirm receiving station," de Gama called out, as he had so many times in the animal tests. Another voice came back in response, this one originating from miles away through the darkness.

"Station Two ready," the voice said crisply.

"Thirty seconds and counting . . ."

De Gama thought of Beatriz Armadas. Young, beautiful, intelligent, deeply in love with her husband. He could be—

"Fifteen seconds . . ."

He felt the power building up from the generators, ready to hurl raw electrical current into the giant laser generator, the cannon, as they called it. The signal of scientific and human triumph, or the sound of death—

"Five, four, three, two—"

Vasco de Gama held his breath. Every man and woman in the generating station did the same. The world poised on this last second, hung suspended, the count slipped through its crack of time to zero and the countdown timer released its dragons. It came in a viciously swift sequence of events, too fast for the human mind to know in any detail. De Gama knew the succession by heart. First that tremendous crack of pure energy, current blast, then the ripping blast of light from the laser cannon. A bolt of dazzling, incredible green, a shaft of light seemingly as solid as steel, a rod eight feet in diameter. It tore from the laser cannon to a huge multifaceted mirror and rebounded *instantly* through the transmission lab, snapping from one mirror to another. The teams hadn't even time to flinch from the savage fury of light, let alone the crawling scrape of sound, as the single beam split and resplit and converged in a huge bowl of light centered about, on, into and within Benito Armadas.

The light flashed through the open space of the cave lab between the opened doors. Beyond those doors tumbled a massive river of water, the roaring bulk of Angel Falls. To this laser strike the water had no more substance than a few electrons floating in empty space. In effect it didn't exist in the universe of the laser.

The green bolt one instant was within the mountain; in the next tiniest slice of time from a single second it leaped the darkness from beneath Devil's Plateau to the receiving platform thirty miles away.

The firing crew stared at the platform. Not even a wisp of smoke, not a single tendril, marked where Benito Armadas had stood. He was gone, transformed and hurled away.

Doctor Edith Hernandez clutched her rosary. "My God," she whispered.

Chapter III

Condor Station stood atop a soaring butte in the southern jungles of Venezuela, one of a group of giants rearing upward from jungle lands. The mesa rose in perfect position to receive straight-line transmissions from BEMAC ONE where Benito Armadas was a moment of eternity away from flash dematerialization. Atop the mesa, Condor Station rose as a prefabricated geodesic structure concealed from the world by an upper surface cover of soil, brush and trees, and even a false brook kept flowing by concealed pumps. This removed its visibility from cameras using either regular or infrared film; Condor blended into its terrain features because it *was* part of that terrain.

Except for the now yawning-wide doors that faced directly the distant open space behind the cascading fury of Angel Falls. From that not-visible but assuredly open space of BEMAC ONE would emerge, faster than any eye could follow, the powerful green laser beam with the electromagnetic imprint of Benito Armadas. *They all hoped . . .*

The men and women of Team Condor had nearly been "frozen" to their assigned control panels and work stations for the past several minutes, grinding their way emotionally through the countdown for their friend. Either Benito Armadas would go down in history for the first flight unlike any other, or he would be committed to their painful memories. They kept glancing from control panels and gauges to the receiver platform where there should appear, simultaneously, the eye-stabbing glare of the green laser and the unharmed body *and mind* of Armadas. That *should* be the instant result of the test but they all shared the same thought. The word *should* belongs in that distasteful word category that includes maybe, perhaps, could be, possibly, and other abused copouts of reality.

Doctor Rogelio "Roger" Delgado, Chief Scientist for BEMAC's Laser Division and de Gama's opposite number in this test, ran nervous fingers through his thick wavy hair. He hated moments that seemed to stop time, when every second dragged laboriously across the face of the clock and he felt a hundred heartbeats between every jerky movement of the second hand. Delgado was a man of *active* science. To him lasers had always been the magic wand of science and medicine. He had a genius's flare for lasers as other men do with metals or quantum mechanics or the violin. Almost buried in the hierarchy of Venezuelan science—for the world's leading nations judged anyone not in their immediate camp as distant and as good as buried—he was nonetheless recognized by a key group of American scientists as the world's leading genius in laser development. Delgado wanted to blast tunnels through mountains of rock with his own designs for huge laser cannon. He had designed enormous rolling lasers to surgically carve out canals and irrigation ditches with geometric precision. He could nick a wisp of tumor from a human eye or explode an armored car into blazing slag, all of it performed with equal ease. He was the Merlin of the laser world, recognized as such by his own peers and his government—and by those few Americans who very secretly funneled huge amounts of financial aid into the Venezuelan laser programs. The Venezuelans, for their part, accepted the funds with gratitude and an unbreakable condition: *no interference*. The Americans complied with such requests. They understood only too well the implications of laser genius on the near future and, like their Venezuelan compatriots, they didn't give a diddily fig for any massive Star Wars programs.

What they were about to attempt here made all military programs pale to measly insignificance. But at this moment Delgado, unparalleled genius that he was, tottered on the brink of being a nervous wreck. He glanced across the open space of the receiving platform to the central viewing stand. His glance caught and held the eyes of two men vital to this secret, magnificent adventure. Jorge "George" Wagner, rotund and jolly, concealed behind his beaming visage and brown skin his own genius for energy control and management, especially in the gravitic and electromagnetic fields. By his side stood Claude McDavid, a bear of a man with huge bulk of body and a bushy beard, from within which shone chromed teeth as a platform for a great pocked nose and eyes that appeared as penetrating as steel pins. McDavid was a crazy combination of Scot, American and Venezuelan and his chosen field was critical to PROJECT BEMAC. He was a shaper of metals and ceramics. He could form any kind of alloy or bring to life any ceramic for structures, generators, power transformers or electromagnets of staggering power.

The three men looked at one another and whatever message they might have remained within their eye contact. Delgado was the man in the saddle at this moment, not Wagner or McDavid. They could only watch. Watch and wait, even if their own professional fortunes and future were locked into what would happen any moment now. Only a few people knew that Wagner and McDavid were of yet another unusual breed. To bypass or circumvent the often-gnarly rules of procedure and security of both the Venezuelan and American governments, they had been granted dual citizenship in *both* countries. They carried the passports of each government, and virtually all doors of scientific research programs thus opened and remained open to them.

But now they were observers, not even as involved as the technicians and aides who stood nervous or frozen at their posts. As if from a distance, in headsets and through the dome speakers, the final count intoned. A gush of cold air blew through the opened doors. In the far distance were the lights of BEMAC center, unseen, dimmed automatically when the firing doors opened.

"Three, two, one, z—"

Green brilliance flashed simultaneously from the multi faceted Receiver Mirror, through the grouped reflectors in the receiving area, concentrating in the center of the platform. If all went as planned and hoped for Benito Armadas would literally snap into existence, having gone through the miracle of travel at the speed of light, dematerialized and rematerialized in that onionskin-thin slice of a long second.

Magic. One instant only the empty platform; then the flashing glare of light *and then Armadas materialized instantly before their eyes.*

Exultation, tears, shouts all began welling up in throats and from eyes. It was incredible. *They'd done it!* There he was, right before them; a moment before he'd been miles away.

A shout of joy choked off, shock whipped through the observers, his friends, his coworkers. *Benito Armadas wasn't in the center of the receiver platform where he belonged. His body stood on the edge. It should not have been that way. They had a faulty "catch" at the end of the transmission.*

They could barely comprehend the sudden flickering of light that spelled a problem, then a flash ripping outward and a godawful moan of tortured energy that seemed to well upward from the bowels of the mountain.

A moment, only that, not a shred of instant more, of horror on the face of Benito Armadas. An invisible force whipped him about violently, a twist so tremendous they saw one arm being pulled from its socket. Too fast for the watching eyes to discern details, his body leaped from the platform edge to smash into the sharp edges of a computer console. The terrifying explosion of mirrors, glass, metal and sundered electrical cables tore Armadas to shredding pulp.

The explosion rebounded from the wall in a huge grisly shower of a body exploding from within, mixed with steel and glass and spattering flame.

For long minutes the only sounds in the station high atop the mountaintop were of shocked friends vomiting and crying, and the distant radio voices of BEMAC CONTROL calling desperately to learn what had gone wrong.

"Everyone have their belts on?" The pilot of the large Sikorsky helicopter glanced behind him. Passengers in their seats nodded slowly or gestured. No one felt the need to speak. Delgado, Hernandez, de Gama, Wagner and McDavid sat wrapped in the complexity of personal grief mixed with hammering questions of *why?* The answers lay beyond the remote jungles and plateaus of southern Venezuela. The pilot advanced power and the helicopter trembled as its great rotors bit into moist air. Theirs would be a short flight to just beyond the camp of Jungle Rudy where a private jetliner awaited them. They made the flight in silence, then walked stoically from the helicopter to the F-28 standing by. They filed aboard the jetliner, listless, self-occupied.

The captain came back, stopped next to Claude McDavid. "Anyone else, sir?"

McDavid shook his head. He tried to smile but only a grimace showed. "No. That's all, captain. Straight back to Caracas. You'll have instructions there when to come back for some more people tomorrow."

"Yes, sir." The pilot disappeared into the cockpit. Moments later the engines started.

McDavid had to get these people out of their deep funk. Bad enough that Benny Armadas was dead. Far worse psychologically was that they'd all been spattered with chunks of intestine and a lot of blood. That's enough to stomp anyone's id deep into the ground. McDavid leaned over to Edith Hernandez and Vasco de Gama. He knew Roger Delgado was listening.

"I need to talk about tomorrow," McDavid began.

De Gama shook his head. "No, no. Not now. Tomorrow, maybe."

"Yes, *now*, goddammit," McDavid said angrily. "Grief can wait but not what we have to do. Listen to me, all of you. We're all through working down here with experimental programs. From now on we use these facilities only for tracking and monitoring. We do everything at IVIC. The Caracas station has everything we need and above all else it can avoid the problem that killed Benny."

They stared at him. They weren't aware he'd chosen his words very carefully.

"You _know_ what killed Benito?" Hernandez asked, her eyes wide.

"Yes."

De Gama almost came out of his seat. "Then for God's sake, tell us!"

McDavid shook his head. "No. Not yet. _Tomorrow._ I could be wrong. I don't believe I am, but—" He shrugged. "You think about the technical and engineering parts of all this. Tomorrow we'll meet with Felipe at IVIC and we'll lay it all out. That's all for now." He leaned back in his seat. "I'm tired. I'm going to sleep."

Seconds later they heard him snoring. "The son of a bitch," George Wagner muttered. "That's how he always gets out of these things."

"What? How?" Delgado asked.

"He's in a post-hypnotic trance, dead to the world," Wagner said, gesturing at McDavid. "He's sound asleep. He's tuned us out completely. Can't hear a bloody thing we say." Wagner sighed. "I envy him at times like these."

Vasco de Gama shook his head at Wagner. "Do not be so quick with your envy," the elderly scientist said. "Tomorrow, at the first light of day, when we occupy ourselves with our silly little technical problems, when the birds greet the new sun with singing, when the schools fill with laughing children . . ." His voice broke off; they waited. "It is then," de Gama continued finally, "that Claude will do what none of us have the courage to do." He leaned back in his seat and stared into space. "I would not wish to be the one who tells Beatriz Armadas, that young woman with a child growing in her belly, that she is a widow."

* * *

Tony Pappas stretched out on the bare cot in his cell, his open eyes unseeing. He felt no concern about his arrest, the charges being gathered against himself and Tirado and Sanchez. He gave no thought to the many violations he had himself committed. He cared for none of these. He had a *feeling*. Not the kind one describes or can even describe to another. Not so long ago . . . he had stood by the single window of his cell, staring into the night sky. Too many clouds for the stars to shine through, no single gleam of a bright planet and the moon only a ghostly shadow through the low scudding clouds. Then he saw it, barely visible against the confusion of muddied night: the green flash from an enormous distance. A light seen from *over the distant horizon*, around the bend of the curving earth's surface. A flash more of a glow than the searing light he had known earlier.

At first he smiled. He knew that light. A secret he kept to himself. A moment later the glow was gone and the muddied sky darkened fearsomely. A stab of ice raced through his body and Tony Pappas shuddered. Something was very, very *wrong*. Something was out of time and out of place. He struggled to locate the source of disturbance. He was a child of two worlds. His boyhood Mediterranean, the hills of Greece, ancient columns and monuments and ghosts drifting along hillsides in the soft moonlight. Then the long journey to a distant continent, the feeling of emptiness he shared with his father. They had both lost their most deeply beloved: his father's wife. *His mother*. Wrapped in something they called death. A stranger, invisible, just as his mother was now. Invisible and gone and whispering to him only in shadows and his dreams.

Then the new world, strange tongues and people and customs, and a brown-skinned woman, kind and with deer eyes, began to fill the space of his life. He watched the woman and his father become closer, spend more time together, recognized the small, warm-smelling familiar touches and they told him he had a new mother.

And a new country *and* a new language. Strangely, from the emptiness of the past grew the fullness of this new future, and the Greek youth became a strapping Venezuelan man. Icarus flew in his traditional past but now Tony Pappas had his own wings and he was not afraid to fly too close to the sun.

Now, in this cell, beneath the troubled sky, he felt terrible, remorseful. A great loss. Somehow he knew, though he did not know how or why, a close friend had died. *Badly.*

The Fokker F-28 slid downward on a long invisible beam of microwave energy toward the large military airfield twelve miles to the southwest of Caracas. With the cloud deck barely a thousand feet above the ground the machine remained invisible until it slipped beneath the clouds on its final straight-in approach to de Miranda Aerodrome. In the very late hours of the night, only a few hours from dawn, the twin-jet machine attracted little attention, for it was but one of many military aircraft that took off and landed all night long. Besides, the entire area of Caracas filled with the flashing beacons and the red and white strobes and glowing red and green position lights of hundreds of aircraft. Aerodromo de Miranda was but one source of this constant activity. La Carlota stayed busy day and night, and the sprawling commercial airline hub hosted dozens of airlines large and small.

The F-28 eased earthward, touched lightly on its main gear and rolled to the far end of the runway, unnoticed by any save the military airfield personnel.

So they believed.

Cheyenne Mountain was a hollow mockery of its name. The great mass rising from the flanks of the Rockies, adjacent to the plush resort area of Colorado Springs, was but a shell of its former self when the local citizens wore thick animal furs and handsewn moccasins. Those days were irretrievably in the past. The new local inhabitants were more likely to be found wearing Reeboks and Playboy casuals and driving Corvettes rather than riding horses bareback. All this fluffery was incidental to the *interior* of Cheyenne Mountain, which many years before had been removed from civilian access and spectacularly gouged, tunneled, modified, cabled and equipped as a massive electronics command and control center for key personnel of the United States Air Force, either in peacetime or under the painful ministrations of a Soviet nuclear strike.

The long-expected warheads with Made-in-Russia plutonium never arrived, yet Cheyenne Mountain continued to expand its goals and purposes by growing with the times. Its initial command facilities tracked incoming Russian aircraft and prepared intercept by fighter planes and missiles against such grim interlopers. The winged raiders began to yield the position of dominance to giant missiles that were kept poised to leap from ground silos and lunge upward from submarines, aimed at the heartlands of America with as many as a dozen hydrogen bombs in each flowering warhead. Again the calendar pages fell away and times changed, and men and machines journeyed on spears of flame to beyond the planet's atmosphere, there to place in invisible tug-of-war webs between gravity and centrifugal force thousands of strange objects, a few with men, many crammed with exotic instruments and power sources intended to look down and ferret out the secrets of what lay beneath the deliberate cover of nations friendly and unfriendly.

The inevitable invariably follows the formerly inevitable, and the exigencies of the times, spurred on by the absence of nuclear war, had transformed the purpose of Cheyenne Mountain. No more the simple tracking and planned intercept of unfriendly objects, either whistling through atmosphere or creating ionized trails beyond the wispiest tendrils of planetary air. Cheyenne Mountain had become a critical intelligence center for all the military, covert and intelligence agencies of the government. From the depths of the great mountain, its intelligence functions connected by tunnels and tubes, stairways and cables as if the mountain itself were a huge brain and its connecting links a mixture of cybernetic axons, synapses, neurons, and electrical pulses, the government maintained a round-the-clock surveillance not simply of enemies or potential enemies, but of *everyone* in the world capable of forming a group of meaningful size.

Or of developing a new system, machine, device or function that would impact the future.

Which is why Colonel Jack Westphal, A-2 Command, United States Air Force, had Venezuela on his mind as he strode purposefully down a gleaming corridor with buffed floor and shining rock walls in the nether depths of Cheyenne Mountain. Westphal was scanned, covered, examined, tested and scrutinized by an astonishing variety of security systems during his passage deeper and deeper into the mountain, until finally he made an abrupt right turn down a final corridor, stopped to permit hermetically sealed doors to open in response to his beamed security code, and then moved with a gliding granite motion into Tracking and Data Center Number Nineteen. Jack Westphal, slim of build, neatly bristling of moustache, and impressed with self as he pushed his career toward wearing stars instead of eagles on his shoulders, impacted his heels against the floor with just enough additional force to turn heads to notice him and his majestic passage to the desk of Major Harry Vaughan. It was quite the show. Westphal was greatly impressed with his performance and absolutely convinced no one knew how carefully he had planned his driving walk past desks, consoles, computer arrays, data banks, tape recorders, glowing maps, three-dimensional terrain holograms of various parts of the world including the ocean floor, satellite tracks, realtime films of critical Soviet activities and other esoteric elements of man's glorious new age of the atom and the long-range missile.

Colonel Jack Wesphal came up abruptly before the sign reading VELA HOTEL FLASH WARNING, beneath and behind which was arrayed a series of readout panels and consoles that made a mockery of the wildest video game arcade ever assembled to collect the massed coinage of wide-eyed teenagers. Westphal ignored the equipment that had been cost-accounted at better than one hundred and thirty-eight million dollars. Instead, he rapped his left palm with a sheaf of papers neatly coiled in his right hand and locked eyes with the major.

"Harry, what the hell is going on?"

Major Vaughan laughed aloud; he couldn't help it in the face of the verbal incongruity. He leaned back in his chair and held out both arms in a gesture of supplication. "Hell, Jack, look for yourself. This is the best place in the world to find out what's going on."

"Ditch the snotty crap," Westphal retorted. "You know what I'm talking about. Your Vela Hotels."

The dumb son of a bitch talks like it's a Monopoly board, mused the major, but he kept his thoughts to himself and his face properly curious and impressed.

Harry Vaughan slipped a slim Jamaican cigar from a neatly zipped breast pocket of his uniform shirt and lit up in a slow and deliberate series of small physical actions. He could almost hear teeth grinding in the jaw of the martinet before him. Vaughan had the faint but still persistent sensation that Westphal was what the Russians had in mind when they ground out propaganda against the United States, and he was also the very one-and-the-same representative figure of government who scared the hell out of Americans afraid the good old U.S.A. was on a plunging sleighride straight to nuclear hell. He pushed the sudden forbidding thoughts from his mind. *You're a major and he's a colonel and you're in a sensitive job and the son of a bitch can stick it to you. Now act subordinate, you dumb bastard.* He grinned at his own self-image and tried to act subordinate.

"Sir," and he sat up straight as he spoke, "I want to be absolutely certain I understand just what the colonel wants answered. And I mean that seriously." He removed the cigar from his teeth and held it lightly between thumb and forefinger and locked his baby blues on the martinet before him. "Sir," he appended.

"Harry, you've got the Pentagon *and* the White House in an uproar," Westphal said with grave overtones.

Vaughan blinked. "Me?"

"Jesus Christ, Harry, is it every day you report nuclear detonations from down in fucking South America!" Westphal leaned against a twenty-million-dollar computer. "You know you're not supposed to smoke that kind of shit in here," he said testily.

"Yes, sir, we're not supposed to smoke *any* kind of shit in here," Vaughan said immediately. "But not to worry, Colonel. I've cleared it with the computer. It's all been worked out." He held up the cigar and studied it for a moment. "Something to do with golden tobacco leaf. I don't know. But the computer *did* say it was okay." He didn't pause a single beat between changing subjects. "You said they were in a flap at the White House, meaning no disrespect, Colonel, *and* at the Pentagon?"

"The urinals are overflowing, Harry."

"That *is* some kind of flap, sir," Harry Vaughan, Major, said respectfully.

"You didn't make any mistakes, did you, Harry?" Westphal jerked a thumb at the huge computer array whose functioning and operation escaped him, although he would have denied such heresy to his mother *and* God.

Vaughan went wide-eyed. His hand fell over his heart and he looked pained. "Sir, just *look* at these reports!" He grabbed a computer plastisheet readout and gestured wildly with it. "*I* don't make up these reports, Colonel Westphal, all I do is monitor Baby, here," he tapped the computer console, "and I take the reports Baby spits out and I send them on to the coded distribution master list." Vaughan spread computer data sheets, covered from one end to the other with technical data and geometric figures whipped up by the computer. The colonel made a face he believed he kept to himself. He *hated* children. The only thing he hated more than children were *infants*. Vomit slingers. Linoleum lizards. Now he had to listen to Vaughan talking about *Baby* and *spitting up*. Holy shit. He leaned forward to study the printouts. Vaughan tapped the plastisheets. Any vestige of levity was gone. This was serious goddamn business and now he was suddenly all business himself.

"Here," Vaughan said. His finger swept about the data sheet. "Two, sir, I repeat, *two* Vela Hotel monitors *and* a Keyhole all flashed their reports at the same time. Let me emphasize that. At the same *instant*, and—"

Westphal broke in, his irritation now an honest emotional and professional reaction. A sort of unspoken truce had snapped into being between them. No more personal in-the-head jostling. "Dammit, Harry, they've *got* to be *wrong!*" His own hand came down with a crash on the printouts. "Those Vela Hotel satellites are at, what, fifty thousand miles?"

"Sixty one thousand two hundred thirty-one miles, sir," Vaughan said crisply.

"All right, all right. So the Velas are at better than sixty grand, and they reported a light flash that could come *only* from a nuclear detonation, fission or fusion doesn't matter. Harry, we're talking about something on the level of a fucking *hydrogen bomb*."

Vaughan relit his cigar. He had felt as perplexed as did Westphal and he let his own confusion leak through. It would bond them a bit better and it sure as hell was an honest reaction. "I know, I *know*, Colonel," Vaughan said drily. "I didn't send in this stuff half-cocked. Sir, I've already checked all direct radiation systems. You know, the works. Gamma, neutron, x-ray; we swept the whole spectrum. *Nothing*. Besides, Colonel, did you really expect the Venezuelans to be testing a thermonuke?"

Westphal shook his head. "Those people are still in the stone age," he admitted. "I mean, they're still flying hand-me-down War Two equipment—"

"They're flying F-16 fighters, sir," Vaughan broke in quietly.

"They *are?*" Westphal looked incredulous. "I had no idea." He took a long breath and studied the papers

Vaughan had placed before them. "All right, can we make any sense out of this? That's why General Freeman sent me here directly. Got my ass out of bed and gave me a direct order to be here with you. So let's get to the rest of it. First, you're confirming the flash report of one Keyhole and two Vela Hotel satellites as you transmitted?"

"Yes, sir."

"No change in any of the details?"

"No, sir."

Westphal sighed. "What about all these whackos sounding off? You know, all the UFO sightings. Did those come in to you also?"

"Not from the Velas or the Keyhole, Colonel. Another system, in fact, several of them, brought in those reports. Computer Central does an immediate breakdown and distribution. The fact that the flash and the UFO reports are time-coincidental brought them together here."

"What's your opinion on the UFO reports?"

Vaughan laughed. "Man, here we go again. That's old hat stuff around here. And today, just about sunset, that's EST, we started getting a whole rash of UFO's. Sightings, I mean. All over Venezuela. But some from Brazil, as well. But then," he reflected, "we've been getting UFO reports from Brazil for years."

Vaughan frowned. "No, that's not enough, Colonel." Vaughan leaned over to his panel and tapped in instructions through his keyboard. A large screen came alive with a map of the northern half of South America. Another tap and the area covered by the map expanded. Bright lights began to glow at different points. "Those lights, sir, represent hard sightings for tonight *only*."

"What constitutes a hard sighting?" Westphal obviously held little stock in alien things from space.

"The report comes from a reliable source," Vaughan replied. "We've got them tonight from Venezuela, Colombia, Panama, Brazil and—I want to emphasize this point—we've got reports from the crews of at least a dozen airliners, *and* another coded report from one of our Blackbirds on an overflight to Cuba. *That* crew, sir, one of our best, gets to be on the same footing as all your whackos."

Westphal grimaced and shook his head in frustration. "You know, Harry, I'd feel better if the Russians also had this headache to go with—"

Vaughan grinned and broke in. "Excuse me, sir, but you go right ahead and enjoy yourself."

"What the hell does that mean?"

"Colonel, the crew aboard the Mir station saw not only the UFO's but also that crazy light, what we're calling the bomb flash, or *whatever* it was, from their orbit. They had detector alarms go off and one of the Russians happened to be eyeballing the local scenery when the whatever-it-is kicked into gear. He was still complaining about green an hour later." Vaughan studied the colonel. "You, ah, wouldn't know anything about the Russians kicking over any cans at the White House, sir?"

Westphal said, "No, I don't," but he nodded his head vigorously. Vaughan took the signals quietly. So the Russians *were* mystified and raising hell and Washington wanted *that* kept quiet.

Westphal suddenly pounded a fist into his other hand. Frustration hovered about him like an electrical spark. "Dammit, Harry, it doesn't add up! No sense at all!"

Vaughan looked up and offered the colonel a crooked smile. "No, sir, it sure don't." With those words he also offered his unspoken message. *Better you in the barrel than me, Colonel* . . .

Both men turned as a sergeant approached them. From the look on her face she was all business. From the look on Major Vaughan's face he had looked at this sergeant many times before and was still as impressed with what her breasts did to a uniform. The colonel started to appreciate buxom beauty but had his reverie cut short as she extended the message to him.

"Sir, top priority. Orders to deliver this to you in person. You're to bring all reports on the anomaly to the Pentagon immediately." She handed him a clip-board. "Please sign here, sir."

Westphal scribbled his signature, returned the clip-board and held the message in one hand as he watched the beautiful female form departing.

"War is hell, Colonel," Vaughan offered.

"What does *that* mean, Major?" Westphal snarled.

"Hell, sir, you're going to talk to some lean machines in the crazy house on the Potomac, and I get to watch that glorious ass walking back and forth here."

"You're not funny, Major."

"Have a great trip, sir."

Chapter IV

Black.

No; *almost* black. Darkness sieved by faint glows the eyes demand time to confirm as real. Glowing reds so faint they're easily mistaken for the red glow a man gets from squeezing his eyes tightly.

Then other dim colors. Amber, green, blue; tendrils and whorls and blocks and patterns coming into focus. Gauges, dials, instruments. An advanced machine of some kind. A gloved hand comes into view, turns a dial and the lights glow brighter. No question. A cockpit. Through a sharply angled slab windshield a round goblin light hangs in nothingness. It's the moon seen through the armored glass windshield of a Lockheed SR-71 Blackbird, cruising at eighteen hundred miles an hour through air so thin an unprotected man would die of stricken lungs within seconds of exposure.

A single brighter light at the very bottom edge of the armor glass. The world tilts to give two men and their camera a better view. One instant the single light, green and fuzzy, is unknown miles away and before the eye can blink the light *is here* and just as quickly, faster than a man's thought, *it is gone*.

Darkness again, time for the eyes to adjust, and before they can define the now-remembered glowing tendrils and whorls a greenish mass fills all the world before the shark nose of the machine, appears, disappears, all faster than the thought of remembering it all.

Green light, instruments, armored windscreen, gloved hands vanish in sudden bright white lights as the screen goes dark and the conference room fluorescents ripple into eye-banging brightness. As eyes adjust to the light the motion picture screen slides upward magically to vanish within its ceiling recess.

"Holy shit," a man's voice is heard

"Take your seats, please," asks another voice, ignoring the mild epithet, understanding it as well.

It's strange. Looking at that film taken a hundred thousand feet above the world while we're inside a room that's six stories below the ground. How silly! Kim Seavers smiled with her thoughts, and as she looked about the round conference room and studied the other six people here with her. Few people had ever heard of this particular room, which was a great spheroid imbedded in steel-reinforced concrete and surrounded with a living web of electromagnetic patterns always shifting under computer random ministrations to assure the room's security from outside attempts to learn what went on within. Kim Seavers sighed. She felt that all this was so grossly unnecessary. *We're like elves and gnomes meeting in some technological forest, doom and gloom all about us, and what we're trying to do is bring a marvelous new light into the world. . . .*

She rubbed a pulled muscle in her left shoulder, a reminder of the intense physical training she and Morgan Scott, to her right, went through every day, seven days a week, unremitting and intense, to sustain their superb physical conditioning. Morgan Scott she could understand. His middle name could have been dedication. Rugged from head to toes, craggy and scarred, as tough as nails and as quiet as a deacon studying in the privacy of a church bell tower. A mixture of man and mood she didn't *always* understand but a man on whom she could always rely. Morgan had long before earned her respect; physically the man was a superbly functioning machine, yet he was detached from his skills and abilities. He could not be insulted. She felt Morgan went through life communicating on some lofty plane, letting his physical body carry through the motions demanded of it. He seemed to have no driving force

that impelled him through his brutal physical conditioning, yet he might as well be driven by a fervent religious fever. She had quit trying to understand; more
important to *trust*.

Their relationship, shared with a dozen other young
men and women, was as much a mystery to themselves
as to outsiders. They had been recruited through a
government front working through the Olympics. Once
their competitions were behind them they were offered
a most extraordinary arrangement. A woman cracked
the subject in a gym; not until their conversation had
ended did they discover that the gym was mysteriously empty of anyone save their own group.

"This is an offer from your government. Two governments, actually. Both friendly. Both working together.
We are not military or paramilitary. You won't be trained
for lethal purposes nor will you be asked to train for
such work. You *will* be required to remain in nothing
less than terrific physical conditioning and you will
work day and night to develop certain physical and
mental skills, and technical skills, that are presently absent
from your own abilities. You will be sworn to both
secrecy and loyalty and the penalties for breaking either
will be severe. But if you fit within this envelope of
what we're asking, we can promise you the best physical training in the world, additional training that will
prepare you for a dozen different disciplines, a great
deal of challenge, travel and excitement. We'll attend
to all your bills and your needs and each of you will
have twenty thousand dollars, tax free, deposited in
individual accounts of your own choosing every year."
The young blond woman seemed to gain in strength
and power as she talked.

Kim Seavers was the first to break in. "Is what you're
asking us to do dangerous?"

"There are three answers to that question," came the
immediate reply. "First, *everything* is dangerous, even
if you can't see the danger. Second, not necessarily.
Third, I guarantee the danger. There'll be danger, risks,

rewards, challenge. Let's say your horizons of the future
will be tremendously expanded."

"What if we're killed?" one of their group queried.

"Then you'll be dead and I assure you that you won't
complain."

They did it. Signed up. They'd been training for
more than a year. Mountain climbing, skydiving, underwater work; they became skilled in demolitions, communications, electronics, computer operations; they drove
huge trucks and large and small airplanes, boats and
ships and submarines. They became mechanics and
paramedics and learned at least four languages each.
They learned to live off deserts and jungles and the
worst cities in the world.

And they still didn't know why.

Kim Seavers shrugged to herself. She caught the
glance of Morgan Scott and offered a smile. She would
have been surprised at Morgan's evaluation of her. She
knew he respected her professional abilities. She was a
linguistics genius, a master in world cultures and all the
other areas demanded of them. Seavers had a strange
attractiveness about her from a Venezuelan mother and
an American father. There must have been some Andean Indian; Morgan looked at this woman and saw an
extraordinary high-cheekboned beauty.

They both turned their attention back to the room.
The Egg, as it was known. Full global situation maps
along curving walls. Digital computer displays with staggering quantities of information about which neither
one of them really cared much. Everything was very
expensive, horribly complicated, and smacked of grave
overtones of covert government operations. They judged
with some accuracy that all this was tied in to the
National Security Agency and perhaps even to the Central Intelligence Agency, but the latter organization
most likely had been or was being shoved aside, its
buttery sheen of America's best interests having turned
sour with Irangate and the explosive uncovering of vast
personal fortunes secured by allegedly fervent patriots.

"Remember how we were convinced this was all

NSC and a few other outfits like it?" Morgan Scott
whispered to Kim Seavers. "There's another side to
this. I don't know who is who and what ball teams are
playing here, but I *do* know quite a bit about that cat
over there."

She looked at a physically huge man with broad
shoulders and intense blue eyes beneath a wild shock of
pure white hair, and instantly she liked whoever-it-was.
"What's his name?"

"That's Senator Patrick Xavier Elias, the hound from
Hell as far as most government operations are concerned." Scott chuckled. "Officially he's the Chairman
of the Joint Committee on Government Operations. A
hound dog with a cocked shotgun and a very big whistle
he can blow on anyone. He runs what they call the
Watchdog Nine. See the man to his right? That's Craig
Mancini. He and Elias are like two pit bulls in a deep
well. Mancini hates Elias and I mean hates."

Well, she didn't much like Craig Mancini after no
more than a studied look of the man. Tall, dark, intense, he had the brooding look of the lead vulture
from an immoral flock of the filthy creatures. "What's
he do?" she whispered to Morgan Scott. "He looks like
an undertaker who's had all his cadavers stolen."

Scott grinned. "You're going to find this tough to
believe, but that dude, and I can tell already how fond
you are of him, is the big mocker of the science division
of the NSC. More to the point, he's a direct advisor to
the President."

"*Him?*"

"Don't let the buzzard beak fool you. He's a genius in
his own right in a dozen scientific disciplines."

"Then what's his problem?"

Scott laughed to himself. "Some people were born
with a shitty attitude. He's one of them, that's all."

Seated near Senator Elias was a face she'd seen on
television many times, and even more often found in
the pages of *Newsweek* and *Time*. Caleb Massey, the
renegade of the scientific world, Peck's Bad Boy of
physics, the crazy man who mixed the metaphysical

with quantum mechanics and made it all work, to the devastating consternation of his conservative associates. He was revered and hated with equal passion, and he'd brought his career onto the jagged edge when he told the President of the United States where he could get off, and to stick his SDI program as far up the presidential blowhole as it could go. What blew so many minds in government and industry was, first, that what Massey objected to with the Star Wars program wasn't the program or the concept but the muddling screwups by so many captains of industry and science who were all working overtime to gain fiscal weight as fat cats of that dollar-dazzling endeavor. "Throw out the whole lot of them," he'd told the President. "Bring in fresh minds. Bring in the strongest opponents of SDI and make them work seven days a week to prove it can't work. That way they'll probably get the job done faster than anyone else."

And second, as far as mind-blowing was concerned, was that the President hadn't taken any umbrage at the brutally frank mannerisms and colorful expressions of speech referring to the aft presidential anatomy as a repository of a national program. He and Massey had been friends for many years and they remained friends. That bound them together as if by steel wire, and it was behind the intense dislike Massey and Mancini had for one another. "Goddamn Wop immigrant bootlicker," is what Massey called Mancini. "Smartest son of a bitch to come out of Italy since Michelangelo and he hasn't got the common sense to pour piss out of a boot without a roadmap. If he'd stop sucking the big presidential toe he might speak some common sense, but he's so busy trying to wield the presidential whip for a president who's too occupied to do it himself that we've got a skinny Mussolini with a fat lip on our hands."

"I thought Massey was all through with government work," Kim Seavers whispered to Morgan Scott.

"He was. Quit cold."

"Then—"

"He and the senator are old warhorses from way

back. Been in the same harness pulling together many times. Elias leaned on that friendship and talked him into coming here."

"But *why?*"

"You ask a hell of a lot of questions."

"And you've just stopped answering them!" Seavers hissed back.

Morgan Scott gave her a rueful grin. "Because I just ran out of answers." He nodded to take in another figure across the conference table. "You know him?"

"Uh uh. I'm a fish out of water in here," she replied.

The man who was a stranger to them was a chameleon. They *should* have known Jack Kilgore because Jack Kilgore knew them and their parents and friends and in fact had reams of data on Morgan Scott and Kim Seavers. That was his job. He worked for the Latin Division of the State Department and he was terrific at his job. No one who met Jack Kilgore could remember, within two hours, what he looked like. First introductions indicated a man in a pale grey suit with pale sandy hair and pale brown glasses and a limp-nothing handshake and a voice that sounded like a couch cushion wheezing softly.

"You're looking at a chameleon."

"You're not making sense."

"Try to remember this conversation. Above all, try to remember what that man Kilgore looks like," Morgan Scott urged. "I guarantee that two hours from now you will not be able to describe him to me."

"That's ridiculous!"

"That's the whole point." Scott pushed a slip of paper and a pen before Seavers. "Go ahead," he urged. "Write yourself a reminder to tell me, later tonight, about Jack Kilgore." He watched her write the note and slip it into a shirt pocket.

"I feel silly," she said.

"You'll feel like an idiot later," he promised. He nodded at Colonel Jack Westphal, wearing a comfortable tan jacket with leather elbow patches. "That one is military," he told Seavers.

"He sure hides it well," she said with a shade of sarcasm.

"He hides it lousy," Scott contradicted. "I know what to look for, you don't."

"All right—"

"That jacket has been selected for its casual look, but if he were a civilian he would absolutely have left it home. The leather patches cry out for attention. Also, it's been packed too long. Hasn't had time to have the packing creases pressed out. He's not wearing a necktie, right? That's a bola tie. Zuñi Indian most likely; maybe Navaho. Thunderbird figurine, silver tips on the leather. Rare in the east. Oh, specialty shop might have it, and you can order it from a catalog, but the leather shows he's had it a while. One gets you ten, little love, he's at least a light colonel and he's stationed out west."

Before Kim Seavers could reply, the angry voice of Craig Mancini cracked across the room with dead aim at Westphal. "Colonel Westphal, you brought me here to look at some stupid lights flying through the air?"

Scott nudged Kim Seavers and grinned, but they kept silent and listened as Mancini turned to Senator Elias. His voice went from acid to hot-peppered scathing.

"A goddamned UFO, Senator." Mancini's hands went into the air and he fairly threw himself backward in his chair. "A UFO, for Christ's sake! What's next?" He jerked a thumb at Westphal. "This idiot's impression of Santa Claus? Ollie North in a false beard and a red suit sailing through the sky?"

Elias barely contained his pleasure at the bubbling anger in Mancini. "Well, hell, Craig," he said with a jolly lilt to his voice, "I do believe you'll admit you never saw anything like it before."

"There's a hell of a lot I haven't seen before! There's a hell of a lot I have no reason *ever* to see!" Mancini shouted. "And all I saw just now was *a light!* A stupid light about which you can't tell me a damned thing!"

Westphal swallowed hard, jumping in as if he were naked. "Sir, Mr. Mancini, that light is something pretty special."

"It could have been another plane! There's no way to tell from that asshole film you just showed us!"

"If it was another plane then it would have to be something that can fly at better than a hundred thousand feet with our Blackbird, sir."

Mancini calmed himself, looked at Westphal as if he'd just discovered something slimy emerging through a hole in the carpet. "You cannot possibly be that much of an idiot, Colonel. No, no, I take that back. You most assuredly can. I begin to wonder if you didn't obtain your commission from the Sears catalog."

"Dammit, sir," Westphal said with growing desperation, "that light went past our aircraft at one hundred and six thousand feet, and sir, I'll tell you that there's nothing in South America that flies at a hundred and six thousand feet. Sir."

Mancini offered a rueful grin to Senator Elias. "Is he one of the chimps left over from the Mercury program?" Before Elias could answer Mancini was on Westphal like a starved leopard.

"*Colonel* Westphal, you said nothing in South America flies at over a hundred thousand feet, did you not?"

"Uh, yes, sir, I did," Westphal offered with a touch of salvation.

"Where was that Blackbird when these films were taken?"

"Uh, over the southern plateaus of Venezuela, sir?"

Mancini smiled, teeth bright under the fluorescents. "My, my, what a clever little boy we have here. I'll bet you even know that Venezuela is *in* South America, don't you?"

Westphal wanted to die but Mancini wasn't about to retrieve the hook yet. "Colonel, what is the altitude record for an aircraft with an air-breathing engine?"

"I, uh, I'm not sure, sir—"

"You *are* assigned to A-2? What is loosely called our Intelligence Section? Or, in your case, what is *laughingly* called our Intelligence Section? You are allegedly a colonel of our air force in Intelligence and you are unaware that the record we discuss is one hundred forty seven thousand eight hundred sixteen feet and that this record is held by an Ilyushin E One Eight Two? Does this awaken any of those slumbering cells you call a memory between your unwashed ears, Colonel or whatever you are?"

Elias went to the rescue. "That's very impressive, Craig. The point is that light was *not* an airplane, and it *was* well over one hundred thousand feet, over Venezuela."

"The *point* is, my dear Senator, is that balloons for weather research, cosmic ray research, manned flight research and no less than another thirty-one major scientific investigations drift about this planet of ours, including all of South America, at altitudes of up to a hundred and sixty thousand feet, and they do carry lights, and they do drift in jetstreams at four hundred knots and—" He stopped for a long breath and a wicked smile. "My point, sir, speaks for itself."

"Wasn't a balloon, either," Elias said softly. He turned to the crestfallen Westphal. "Colonel, give him the rest." He pointed to Mancini. "Keep quiet until he finishes."

"Patrick Xavier, don't you tell me—"

"Shut up, Craig. Dammit, Colonel, get with it!"

Westphal turned gratefully from the senator to face the poised wrath of Craig Mancini. "Sir, the SR Seventy-One aircraft that took that film is also equipped with Mark Forty Tracking Radar." His own words seemed to give Westphal strength and he hurried on. "The radar officer followed that light, or whatever was behind that light to give a very solid radar bounce, to an altitude of two hundred twenty thousand feet. At that point tracking capability was lost."

Before Mancini could say a word, the senator moved in. "What speed, Colonel?"

"Sir, it went right off scale."

"And what is maximum scale?" Elias added quickly.

"Four thousand miles per hour, sir."

Mancini leaned forward, his eyes narrowed. Elias hadn't been misled a fraction of an inch by Mancini's performance in skinning the colonel alive. Son of a bitch he might be, Craig Mancini was also wearing a skull bulging with brainpower. He gestured for attention. "Hold it; *hold it.* Just a damn moment." He looked sharply from Elias to Westphal. "To hell with that light. I want to be absolutely certain of the accuracy of your statement. You said the light or the object was tracked over South America? Specifically, the point of contact was over the southern plateau region of Venezuela?"

"Yes, sir," Westphal said crisply.

"Confirm the aircraft type again," Mancini demanded.

"Lockheed SR-71 Blackbird, sir. Submodel D6."

Mancini used his words as if they were a spear, addressing himself to both Elias and Westphal. "What the hell was that machine doing over Venezuela? We don't have any reciprocal agreement for reconnaissance overflights with those people."

"I'll answer for him," Senator Elias replied. "This is out of his bailiwick, Craig. That flight was standard response to an unexplained light flash of extreme but unknown intensity. The aircraft was on an assigned run for Nicaragua and was diverted by code signal during flight. *I'll* confirm all of it for you."

Mancini looked to Jack Kilgore. "What does State have to say about this?"

Kilgore shrugged. "No objections are on record."

"Don't pussyfoot with me, goddammit!"

Kilgore remained an unperturbed near-phantom. "We informed the Venezuelan government of our flight. They chose not to consider the Blackbird overflight as an intrusion. Therefore there is no violation of standard operational procedure." Kilgore might have been speaking to an unruly child rather than the science advisor to the President.

Heads turned to the sound of a chuckle from Caleb Massey. He hadn't said a word. He looked like a grizzly bear contented with a huge meal. The chuckle subsided but a smile began; tolerant silent mirth for the verbal clatter about him. Whoever and whatever Caleb Massey was, he had a damping effect on Mancini. His voice lost its knifelike slash.

Mancini turned from the chuckling grizzly back to Elias. "The President has been all over my case," he said with sudden candor. "Something crazy. Reports of a nuclear detonation in the middle of the damn jungle." He held up a hand to forestall interruption. "I've seen all the contradictory material. A light flash in the visible spectrum so intense our military monitoring satellites triggered their alarms. But nothing on radiation, penetrating or subsidence. No heat, or non-sufficient to deteriorate foliage in the area in question. And so forth. It's a huge contradiction. Crazy."

For the first time Caleb Massey stirred to life and spoke. "Nothing crazy about it. We did a pattern grid on the higher intensities of the flash. Eight thousand square miles is a healthy area." He shifted position in his chair. "But to help make your day, Mancini, we now have *nine* such suspect detonations all with the same characteristics. A lot of flash but no bash."

Massey didn't rattle Mancini's cage. Mancini wanted information and he had no ego problems when it came to getting what he wanted. "Anything specific? Latitude, longitude, altitude?"

Elias motioned to Westphal. "Put it on the graphics."

Westphal nodded and tapped buttons before him. The room lights dimmed and a holographic three-dimensional map of Venezuela materialized against a far wall. Names of geographical areas appeared along with data readouts of map coordinates. The holographic map expanded, giving the viewers the impression of plunging earthward with heady speed. Motion froze abruptly.

"The greatest intensity reported is in the area known as *Auyan-Tepuy*—" Westphal began.

"English, dammit," Mancini growled.

"Angel Falls, sir. The world's highest—"

"You idiot, spare me your National Geographic specials and *get to the numbers!*"

"Hell, man, read them for yourself," Massey said with his own touch of contempt for Mancini's behavior. Massey gestured to Westphal. "Lights," he said curtly.

Massey looked at Elias and the senator nodded. They didn't need words for Caleb Massey to take on Mancini.

"Spare me the speeches and the sophomoric debating, Craig," he said, as warm as an angry warthog. "Let's have your questions."

Mancini came back immediately. "What I do *not* like about this meeting is how you people try to mix apparently actual anomalies with gibberish. The light flash—singular or plural—merits immediate and full investigation. It may be a natural phenomena about which we know nothing or it may have a more mundane artificial explanation. I grant all this to you. I have judged the autoresponse of the Vela Hotels and Keyhole satellites. But to use all this to lend credence to these idiotic UFO claims, and do *not* again base your conclusions on some cheaply made radar systems in an airplane, the accuracy of which depends upon everything from electrical glitches to an incompetent observer who cannot read his own instruments, well, I am disappointed and somewhat ashamed of what I've found here—"

"Oh, shut up, Craig," Massey broke in. "If you'd just stick to specifics instead of political stumping, we'd have been out of here long ago. Get to the damn point!"

Mancini flushed and then turned icy cold. "Just what are *you* doing here, Caleb?" A poisonous smile flashed and went. "As I recall, you abandoned our ship of state, let down our President—"

"He's here at my specific request," Senator Elias snapped.

"Well, then, as an official member of this little party," Mancini sneered at Massey, "most of whom are uptighter than a constipated cat, do *you* also have a UFO to offer up as a scientific sacrificial lamb?"

Massey toyed with a cigar, looked directly at Mancini. "Nope."

If nothing else, Craig Mancini respected Caleb Massey. "Do you have something for me to take back to the White House about the possibility of a nuclear device detonating in the area we specified?"

"Nope." Massey lit his cigar. "No ionizing radiation, no residual radiation, no thermal pulse, no fireball and subsequent mushroom cloud, no seismological disturbances, no reports of permanent blindness to anyone, so on and so forth. Ergo, tell the President to sleep easy. No bomb."

"But we can't ignore it," Westphal broke in, almost plaintive in his unspoken request for further investigation.

"We can damned well ignore it until we get more than a super flashlight!" Mancini snapped.

"No, we can't," Elias pushed between them. "Even a false reading or something that our computer systems misinterpret can put us on the edge of a war. Don't look so surprised, Craig. There's a hell of a lot of difference between scientific detachment and the realities of life." The senator met the eyes of everyone in the room before he went on. "We once went to a war footing because our warning satellites picked up a mass missile launch in Russia. It could *only* have been missiles. We went to full red alert. Pull the handles and we'd have kicked a few billion tons of hell on the way to the Russians. We also would have started something that could have destroyed the earth—because of a petroleum line fire scattered by fog and haze."

Mancini tapped the table with nervous fingers. He hated to ask *anything* of Caleb Massey. "Do you have a reliable judgement of the source or content of that light flash?" he asked carefully.

"Got a pretty good idea."

Morgan Scott nudged Kim Seavers. "That's the best imitation of a Kentucky good ol' boy I've ever seen," he whispered.

She leaned closer to Scott. "Maybe it's not an act."

Scott's brows went up and he nodded, smiling.

"Dammit, Caleb," Mancini pressed, "if you know what it is— "

"I didn't say I *knew*," Massey allowed. "Said I had a pretty good idea, which is a country mile from saying the same thing."

"I need facts to tell the President!" Mancini shouted.

"Tell the man anything you like," Massey said pleasantly. "Hell, Craig, I'm not his advisor. *You* are." Massey smiled. "You're such a smart son of a bitch, act like one."

Craig Mancini could think with lightening speed. He knew he couldn't relate the details of this meeting as they'd transpired. The President would boot him down the nearest flight of stairs. So Mancini used some of his smarts. "All right, Craig, then I'm asking you for your opinion. I want to take it with me to the White House."

Massey nodded agreeably, hitched himself a bit higher in his chair. "I'm warning you, first, you sure as hell aren't going to believe me."

"I am on the record," Mancini said quietly and with unaccustomed patience, "as asking for your opinion *and* your help."

"Well, I can't turn that down," Massey said without any touch of sarcasm. "Okay, short speech, predicated with the note that I'm not asking anyone to believe me. Them's the rules." He didn't wait for verbal response.

"I spent four years working on SDI. Star Wars. To me it's a pretty dumb program. Won't work. Hell of a waste of money. I could be wrong. Been wrong before. Even Einstein's been wrong, so if I've goofed in my opinion I'm in good company."

He paused for a moment of reflection. "But I've been in the middle of the most advanced laser research known. That light flash we've been talking about. You've been talking and I've been thinking. Gentlemen, and you, miss," he nodded to Kim Seavers, "taught me two things tonight. First, the flash in Venezuela was laser-generated. Absolutely no question about it."

He went silent again. Kim Seavers, fascinated by everything about Caleb Massey, leaned forward. "Sir, you said you learned two things tonight. What's the second?"

Massey offered a thin smile. "The second thing I've learned, young woman, is that whoever is generating that kind of laser power is years beyond anything the best scientists of this country, or the Russians, have ever done."

That was it. Massey eased back into his comfortable slouch and sucked deeply on his cigar. Senator Elias shifted his position in his chair and Massey smiled. He knew when the white-haired old bastard was getting into fighting posture. The big question was whether or not Mancini had the smarts to recognize just what was coming down. As a senate bulldozer Elias had the muscle to roll over and flatten even Craig Mancini. And they were at the point when someone had to do *something*.

To his credit, Mancini took the bit firmly in his jaws. To his everlasting discredit he did so with all the finesse of a great white tiger shark in a feeding frenzy. Mancini glared and stabbed a finger at Westphal. "Colonel, as of this moment this is a full-fledged investigation. You get a team of our best people down to Venezuela and you get them there *immediately*. You have my full authority, and I'll give it to you in writing, to take whatever you need to get to the bottom of this affair. Understand? Get our people down there, find out what kind of cockamamie bullshit is going on, and you report back to me. No in-betweens, understand?" He glanced coldly at Caleb Massey and Senator Elias. "You report to me, in person, at the White House, got it?"

"Yes, sir," Westphal said immediately.

"For Christ's sake, Craig," Elias broke in, "aren't you going to at least *ask* the Venezuelans about stomping roughshod through their country?"

Mancini laughed. No humor there: a cold laugh and a contemptuous look on his lean face. "Why? What good would that do? They're a fourth-rate country. A backward people. Most of them still live in straw huts with their goats and pigs. Damn country is swamp and mountains and natives with one foot still in the stone age."

Kim Seavers didn't know her mouth was open, that she had gasped audibly with sudden temper that began to explode outward. She felt pressure on her arm from Morgan Scott, who motioned her attention to the senator. Elias gestured for her to remain quiet. Kim pressed her lips so tightly they turned white.

"Craig Mancini," Elias spoke with deliberate spacing of his words, "you are unquestionably one of the dumbest and most insensitive human beings I have ever had the misfortune to meet."

Mancini smiled, a man who knows what power he holds. "Senator, I don't give a rat's ass for your opinions about either my intelligence or what you call my insensitivity. You remind me of that idiot British government official who refused to let his intelligence officers read intercepted Nazi messages before the second world war. Gentlemen don't read other gentlemen's mail, he said, and they got the second world war for their sensitivity. I am here with people I absolutely would rather not have for company because something strange and, in my opinion, idiotic, is going on down in Venezuela. It doesn't fit any patterns. It's crazy enough to trigger satellite warnings and everything else we've had before us tonight. You'll notice, Senator," Mancini stressed with a sneer, "the Venezuelans haven't come forward with any explanations either. So I'm doing my job. And that's to find out what's behind all this bushwah. Caleb Massey, there, acts like the damn pope at a Shriner's convention and rattles on about all this being caused by a laser, but by a laser that's too powerful to exist and that's far beyond the capability of either us or the Russians. That's some pretty far-out concluding on his part. A laser made with adobe clay and hauled around by an ox cart. Massey can't identify what's going on but he's content to act like the smug, waddling college professor, and—"

Mancini drew himself up short. "For the record. Massey, I don't want it said I didn't give you every chance to get on the record. Do you want to add anything to the report I'll be preparing?"

Massey blew out a cloud of smoke, flicked ashes to the floor, and smiled. "Nope," he said casually.

Mancini held out both palms of his hands to Elias. "See? *Nothing.* Not from him, anyway. Only supposition and maybes and that sort of noncommittal verbiage. Which leaves us no choice but to get down there to find out what is really going on. Patrick," Mancini spoke with sudden unexpected honesty, "let's say Massey is right. In his better days Caleb was one of the best—"

He paused to glance at Caleb Massey, who offered a toothy grin in response, a facial gesture of *no-one's-interested-in-your-birdshit, fella.* "Let's say," Mancini continued quickly, "that we're really dealing with a laser. *How do you know it's not a Russian laser?*"

Massey broke his silence. "You're a fool or an idiot, Mancini. I confess to not knowing which."

Anger clouded Mancini's face. "We'll damned well see," he said ominously. "For everyone in this room, *everyone*, this matter is now top secret. I'm invoking the war securities act of this country. You say one word in public about this meeting or the contents of what we were discussing—"

"What?" Massey looked up in mock horror. "You're not telling the world about our UFO's?"

"—and you'll be behind bars so fast you won't know what happened," Mancini finished with a snarl.

Senator Elias brought his hand down with a sharp cracking sound on the table, sending papers fluttering to the floor. He let out a long suppressed sigh of distaste for the man from the White House. "You're a dinosaur, Mancini. It's that simple. You're still mentally in the age of the dinosaurs. Big dumb beasts with a lot of authority and no brains."

"Shut up, Senator."

Elias smiled coldly. "You get to make that mistake only once, mister," he said smoothly. "You ever talk in that tone to me again and I'll take you out before the public, in front of the entire nation, and I'll bust you up into little pieces of dinosaur feces." He tagged on a wan smile. "Besides, you're all bluster. *You* do not have the authority to invoke any governmental acts of any kind beyond adding to everyone's distaste for you."

The senator rose ponderously to his feet, a grimace of pain in his face reflecting ancient wounds and injuries pursuing him always. "We're finished here. But with all the respect due your office with the President," he

pointed a gnarly finger at Mancini, "let me give you my
warning in a more official manner. You pull any of that
Ollie North crap by interfering in the internal affairs of
Venezuela, which is one of the best nation friends we
have on this planet, and I will bring you officially up
before the entire Senate, and I will break you personally. Not even the President will be able to help you
through *that*."

He pushed back his chair, looked neither left nor
right, and walked stonily from the room. Seavers, Scott
and Massey followed, Seavers and Scott slowing their
pace with a concealed gesture from Massey. Not a word
was spoken during the long walks down corridors, in
the elevator, or on the high landing of the building
they'd just left. They moved through a winding garden
path to the parking lot. With a clear view before and
behind them, between a high hedge to each side, Senator Elias stopped to face the three people following
him. Kim Seavers was amazed. The angry man she'd
seen in the conference room was gone; in his place was
a grandfatherly, kind gentleman of silken yet visible
power kept deep beneath the surface. She felt instantly
she could trust this man without reservation.

"It's very important that I meet with you three tomorrow," Elias said. As he saw their expressions and
they nodded assent he hurried on. "*Not* in my office. I
don't trust anyone there not to bug the place and what I
wish to discuss with you must be and remain absolutely
confidential."

Kim was startled and didn't hide it. "Senator, they
would bug *your* office?"

"My dear, my office, the men's room, the ladies'
room, the cafeteria, the rail system between the upper
and lower houses, taxicabs," he gestured with a sweep
of his arm, "even these *bushes*." He patted her arm
reassuringly. "Not to worry, young lady. My own team
is sweeping this area with both pickup alerts and sonic
brushes to mess up any attempt at recording whatever
we say here."

Kim looked from the senator to Massey and Scott. "I don't understand—"

"You will soon enough," Massey filled in. "Do you trust us?"

"You? And the senator?" She offered a short laugh of relief. "My God, *yes*. Of course!"

Massey nodded and returned his attention to the senator. "Any ideas on a place, Patrick?"

The white-maned head shook slowly. "I'm more politician than spy, Caleb."

Kim Seavers moved forward. "I have a perfect place for what you need, sir," she said to Elias. He nodded for her to continue. "I'm still not sure what this is all about, but if you want to talk in the middle of bedlam, we," she nodded at Scott, "have just the ticket."

"Go on, go on," Massey urged.

"Our training camp across the river," she said quickly. "The indoor handball courts. With the playing, sneakers on the floor squeaking, the ball, and the shouting and the echoes you can hardly hear yourself think in there." She smiled. "Senator, that's *our* turf."

Elias nodded in agreement and motioned for them to walk with him the rest of the way to his car. "Tomorrow at noon," he said as he stood by the car door. A finger waggled at Kim. "But I warn you, miss, I play a very rough game." He chuckled and moments later he was gone.

Morgan Scott turned to Massey. "We going to talk any more about tonight, sir? There are sure a lot of holes I'd like to fill."

Massey put his arm about Scott's shoulders. "I have a wonderful idea. Let's go to my club. Very private, very posh. I need a drink. I think we can *all* use a drink." He gestured and led them along the walk. "My car's this way. Besides," he went on, "I need to know a great deal more about this young lady and her, ah, associates." He smiled at Kim. "We're going to become *very* close friends."

"Fine by me," Kim said, walking by his side. "It's all

a big mystery to me. Even why we were here, you know, in that meeting."

"You were there because I wanted you there," Massey said quietly.

"You? Wanted *me* there?" She shook her head. "Now I understand even less than I did before."

"Well, let's start off by saying that nothing I said in that meeting tonight was a guess. That will do for right now," he cautioned. "Even the trees have ears, young lady."

Kim kept her silence. Finally Massey offered her another tidbit as they entered his car. "What kind of training, Kim, are you going through?"

She started to answer, held back what might have been a foolish answer, then studied the big man. "It's an everything curriculum."

"Well said," Massey told her. "What organization do you work for?"

"The Olympic Committee," she said after a moment's hesitation.

"Very good," Massey responded. "Your answer is precisely the one you were told to use whenever asked that question."

Her eyes widened. "How did *you* know that!"

Morgan Scott laughed. "Kim Seavers," he said with a sweeping gesture, "allow me to introduce you to the Olympic Committee."

Chapter V

General Luis Espinoza sat in the gunner's seat of the Sioux combat jet helicopter, as relaxed as if he'd been at home in his living room in his favorite easy chair. But he was a long way from home or even a comfortable seat. Multiple straps bound his body gently but firmly to the gunner's seat and all about him curved clear lexan so that he sat within a transparent bubble that flung itself at a hundred and forty miles an hour down a jungle plains river, twisting and turning with every bend and curve of the water, foliage to each side tearing by in an eye-watering blur. Thirty miles ahead of the howling Sioux reared the buttes and mesas that marked the area of Angel Falls. General Espinoza looked up, then to his left and right. Beneath the low clouds—he liked the weather as if it had been made to order for their mission—he saw the flashing strobes of heavy-lift Sikorsky helicopters, ungainly Skycranes that resembled nothing so much as praying mantises made of aluminum I-beams and giant rotors. Some thundered toward Angel Falls' rooftop, the Devil's Plateau. Others ground their way to sites where BEMAC facilities had worked around the clock for nearly a year. Still more droned and rumbled in the opposite direction, carrying odd shapes and cargo loads on long slings beneath their rugged bodies.

Behind the Sioux helicopter with the phlegmatic general, wide-bodied jet cargo transports moved in a steady succession from the remote airstrip. As fast as they descended steeply from the sky and rolled in clouds of boiling dust to a halt, aft cargo ramps lowered and dozens of men pushed and bullied equipment and dismantled structures into the planes, grappled them down with chains and cables, and signaled the pilots to take off immediately. General Espinoza was pleased with the pace of events. The heavy cloud cover concealed their activity from prying reconnaissance planes and satellites, and "massive defense maneuvers" conducted by the Venezuelan military, with swarms of armed helicopters, ground attack planes and swift F-16 fighters, along with dire warnings of unauthorized penetration by any kind of vehicle.

Venezuela's scientists from the BEMAC team were clearing out. They had little idea of how to do the task in less than six months. Unburdened by extensive scientific knowledge, and an unquestioned master of military logistics, Espinoza was doing the impossible. "I will have everything out of the *Auyan-Tepuy* in three days," he told Doctor Felipe Mercedes, BEMAC Director.

"That is really quite impossible, you know," Mercedes replied. He didn't doubt Espinoza. The two men were old friends, but—three days? "Impossible," he repeated.

Luis Espinoza fixed the scientist with eyes resembling steel ball bearings. They glittered unlike anything Mercedes had ever known. "Felipe, I don't waste my time saying things I cannot do. You know better."

Mercedes studied the general. Had he really known and worked with this man for more than twenty years? He marveled at Luis Espinoza, ramrod spit-and-polish military with a face and body carved from granite. Mercedes knew his record. No galloping Latino Patton here; Espinoza had earned no less than four degrees to go along with his military training: in chemistry, ballistics, geopolitics and environmental sciences. He had also earned his combat infantryman's badge, ground his way through underwater demolition schools, and wore the paratrooper wings of the United States, Israel and Venezuela. But he wore no medals or ribbons or battle stars, despite combat service in Thailand, Nicaragua, Grenada, the Golan Heights—and on certain "special missions" no one spoke about aloud. There was something else. None of his insignia, brass or silver or gold, was to be found on his uniform. "The glitter comes from within the man. Pearl-handled guns guarantee nothing." Everything on his uniform was flat, nonreflective, as enigmatic as the man. Only his closest friends knew he had graduated—under a different name—with honors from the U.S. Naval Academy at Annapolis.

Now he was doing the impossible. His pilot knew his orders. The Sioux whipped around a massive vertical wall of stone and slowed its flight through Corridor Diablo, close enough for the roar of Angel Falls to demand shouted conversation. For the next hour Espinoza studied and surveyed the many installations. He was satisfied. There was more work to do at other places. He depressed the armrest comm button. "The airfield," he told the pilot. The flight crew looked at each other. They'd be *very* glad to offload *this* passenger. Those were the only two words he'd spoken in more than an hour. He gave them the creeps.

Approximately seven hundred miles to the northeast, the aerial deliveries ended at three airfields beyond the sprawling city limits of greater Caracas. All visitors were barred from the fields and their immediate environs. Truck convoys rolled steadily from the airports, the contents of the vehicles covered with canvas and guarded by armed soldiers. From some unloading areas the cargo loads were pushed to an open area where a helicopter descended, lowered a cargo sling, and departed minutes later with the cargo swinging gently in the downwash hurricane of rotor blades. They all had the same destination: upward along the mountain slopes beyond Caracas. Helicopters landed on hastily flat-pounded pads on the ridges of high slopes. Trucks rolled in and parked in neat military formation, and hundreds of men and women in construction hardhats assembled, pounded together and otherwise recreated what only the day before had been concealed in the distant vast jungles of southern Venezuela.

That night the work continued unabated. Dazzling floodlights turned night into day, reflecting garishly from the clouds that finally dipped down and shrouded the world in fog. Felipe "Phil" Mercedes and his immediate staff smiled with the onset of cold mist. There could be no better way to conceal the details of the frenetic activity centering mainly about the sprawling grounds, buildings and other facilities of IVIC—the world-famed *Scientific Investigación Venezuelan Institute.* Several of the scientists and technicians with Mercedes were the same researchers and workers who had lived down in the marchings of the faraway mesas and buttes surrounding Devil's Plateau.

In their midst moved armed guards and civilian security teams. No one moved without an individual identification security badge carrying photo, fingerprints and laser codes, and most wore work coveralls and hardhats. As many were covered with dust, mud and grime, among them Captain Ali Bolivar, who only the night before had cruised six miles above Devil's Plateau as part of the team monitoring the eye-searing laser beams of Project BEMAC. Bolivar skidded to a halt in a jeep and climbed out wearily, waving to a group including among its number Carlos Silva, Field Operations Chief; Judith Morillo, recently returned from downcountry with Silva; Vasco de Gama, who had returned by jet from downcountry; and the BEMAC Director, Doctor Felipe Mercedes.

Mercedes was rarely recognized as a native of Venezuela. He was short and stocky, prematurely grey and sported a broad white moustache, and was given to wearing hand-me-down jumpsuits from the Venezuelan Air Force, preferring the dozen zippered pockets of the jumpsuit for his pens, pencils, computers and assorted other paraphernalia for which he was famous. "One never knows when the moment will come when it's necessary to be a genius," he often told his staff. "I prefer to be prepared for what might be my one great moment in life." He was also considered the single greatest scientist his country had ever produced, and had studied at the leading technical universities of the United States, England, and Germany.

He wore two hats, really. He had been IVIC's director for years until BEMAC came into being, the latter now taking virtually all his available time. His associates considered him still to be at the helm of IVIC, easy enough when this one-man scientific force held court in a sprawling home on the mountainside within shouting distance of the powerful IVIC nuclear reactor. Mercedes needed a constant communication with certain scientists in the United States, and for this purpose he had the two men perfect for such a task—Jorge Wagner and Claude McDavid. They were a startling combination of physical oddity, Wagner rolling about on his short and pudgy frame and McDavid moving like a furry bulldozer smiling at the world with his chromed teeth gleaming through his grizzly-like beard. Together they had mastered energy control in gravitics and electromagnetism, and what Wagner established in theory McDavid brought to life with his own genius in forming ceramics and exotic alloys.

Equally important to the long-term goals of BEMAC was the well-concealed fact that Wagner and McDavid held dual passports for Venezuela and the United States. Even more hidden to any public eye was the role played in this twisting of national laws by none other than Senator Patrick Xavier Elias, as much a mystery figure to the Venezuelans as he was to the Americans.

As the head man in BEMAC, Phil Mercedes was as practiced in human psychology as he was in administration and science. He understood the extraordinary relationship stringing together genius, emotion, competition and the fanaticism of radicals bruising their way through the scientific world. Few descriptions could better fit McDavid.

Problem: Something terribly wrong with the laser transmission system had killed Benitos Armadas. *Problem*: The BEMAC team had no hard answers as to the transmission bias that hurled Armadas with body-shredding force from the receiver platform. *Solution?*

Word had come to Felipe Mercedes that Claude McDavid stated without any ambiguity that he knew why Armadas was killed or, more specifically, what caused the anomaly resulting in his death.

The problem wasn't solved, or perhaps even within reach, because McDavid hadn't said a solitary word on the matter to Mercedes. And Mercedes, notwithstanding his burning desire to hear what the grizzled scientist had to say, knew from painful past experience that McDavid would talk to Mercedes only when he felt the moment was right. Prior to that moment he'd be tighter than a clam that used superglue for mouthwash. Flaming tongs couldn't drag the words from him. It wasn't a matter of being a prima donna; McDavid believed implicitly that timing was the essence of all life, and that a vital statement made at the wrong time was a wasted statement.

As shocked and saddened as he was with the death of the young man, Armadas, whose family Mercedes had come to know only too well, and as anxiously as he wished to hear what McDavid had to say, Mercedes yielded to the inevitable and forced patience, at least outwardly, upon his actions and words. Besides, events were proving McDavid all too right.

Ali Bolivar's voice, carried by a battery-powered megaphone, rose above the clattering roar and din of trucks, bulldozers and helicopters. "Professor! There comes the last helicopter load!" he called out to Mercedes.

A storm of dust exploded outward as the huge machine lowered itself on diminishing lift and eased its cargo onto the sloping ground. The whirlwind ripped into the group of scientists and technicians, blasting their hair and clothes, covering them from head to foot with grit. Judith Morillo huddled close to Doctor Silva as she marked her cargo manifests on a clipboard. "Thank God for small favors!" she shouted to the scientist. "I'll need to shower for a week to get this dirt off me!"

Silva glanced at the manifest and waved Bolivar to join them. For several moments Bolivar turned away, crouching, as the helicopter howled to full power and lifted away. The sound of trucks and construction equipment was almost a muted hum in comparison. "Ali!" Silva called. "How much more equipment at the airport?"

Bolivar wiped his mouth with his sleeve and spat out dust. He pointed to a long line of trucks winding their way up a distant and lower hill. "That's the last of the shipments from the devil's playground."

"Excellent! Everything is going directly to the assigned positions?"

"Everything," Bolivar confirmed. "And none too soon, if you ask me. I feel like I'm in Africa again."

Morillo shook her head. "Ali, something's not right here." She extended her clipboard. "The electrical generators. They're not shown anywhere on the delivery sheets."

Bolivar nodded. "And they won't be. You can thank McDavid for that. He told our director they weren't worth the trouble to move. Much too heavy. They would have to be dismantled and, well, he's right. It would take weeks or months."

"But what happens to them?" Morillo asked.

Bolivar grinned. "Think of *Auyan-Tepuy* as the first pyramid tomb of Venezuela, my lady. The caverns beneath the plateau and behind the falls are sealed off. The great doors are welded shut. Everything has disappeared behind rock falls. Those are orders from the government. Everything left behind is entombed. It is never to be opened. Angel Falls is now officially what it was before. A treasure for the entire planet."

Silva nodded his agreement. He took Morillo's arm gently, turned her to face the mountain sloping upward. "From now on, Judith, this is where we work, where we live, where our future lies. From now on—"

He cut short this own words as Felipe Mercedes and Vasco de Gama approached. "Bolivar, what's the schedule for the last truck?" Mercedes called out.

"Two hours to arrive, sir. Eight hours to unload," Bolivar said quickly.

"We're running behind schedule," Mercedes said, glancing at his watch. "Everybody who is on assignment to the tunnel, have them report immediately to their stations."

"Yes, sir. I'll call out on the van radio."

Mercedes peered beyond Bolivar. "The IVIC van?"

"Yes, sir."

"Have it brought here. Ali, attend to the assignment call, and then tell the vehicle chief I'll need that van for a while."

Ten minutes later they were all inside the van mounted on a four-wheel-drive truck bed, rocking and bouncing wildly as the driver pushed the vehicle upward along a steep and crudely bulldozed road. They hung on to keep from being thrown about. In the front right seat, Mercedes grinned at his scientists bouncing about like potato sacks.

"Ali, you made a personal inspection before you left from downcountry?"

Bolivar nodded. "Sir, I personally flew about the entire area. Helicopter. You can't tell anyone ever did any work there. All that's left by the high mesas are the helicopter pads, and they have been there for years. We thought it wiser to leave them."

"Very good. And Jungle Rudy? How is his camp? And Hilda?"

Bolivar laughed. "They prefer what they call their old quiet returned to them. Besides, Professor, Rudy enjoys his new role as a mystery man of the jungle. Some American news reporter has described him as 'a refugee from a Hemingway novel.' " Bolivar shrugged. "And who knows? He has many stories to tell about UFO's and native superstitions."

Mercedes nodded. For several moments only the labored sounds of the van grinding upward could be heard. Mercedes closed his eyes, reviewing, seeing in his mind's eye a vast myriad of details. When he opened his eyes again they knew he had brought himself up to the moment. Again he directed his attention to the pilot.

"Ali, you have talked with General Espinoza?"

"Yes. Personally."

The name *Espinoza* brought everyone else to instant alertness. That man was a military officer, a general. BEMAC had nothing to do with the military. Why would Professor Mercedes, their very own director, be concerned about the military man? Mercedes observed their reaction and ignored it, concentrating on Bolivar.

"We, ah, had company?"

The others in the van exchanged questioning glances, but no answers came forth. They turned back to the exchange between Mercedes and Bolivar. The pilot was now unexpectedly serious.

"Yes, sir. At least twelve overflights confirmed. We believe there were more. The electronic countermeasures people were swamped."

"As we expected," Mercedes said mysteriously. He smiled. "Both sides, I expect?"

"No question. We tracked them between eighty and one hundred twenty thousand feet. We know the American machines. The Blackbirds, of course. The Russians?" Bolivar shrugged. "Likely either the new MiG Forty-One operating out of Cuba, or perhaps their Ilyushin stealth aircraft. We can't be sure of that." Bolivar leaned back in his seat and smiled. "I admire the ingenuity of the Americans, Professor. They dropped one of their, what they in their strange humor call the Inquisition satellite, on a pass at only fifty-six miles, then powered the satellite back up to orbital altitude. Their cameras must have been very busy."

"And our neighbors?"

"Two night passes, low. French, as you expected." Bolivar hesitated. "How could you know they—"

"Ah, the French also are inquisitive, Ali. And their launching site is not far from here. It is so easy to make a mistake in navigation. Of course, it is several hundred miles, but we all know the French. Too much wine for their pilots, perhaps." Mercedes laughed, then grew serious again. "What trick did you finally use, my young friend?"

The others in the van were baffled. For a moment Ali did not answer, as he studied a line of trucks crawling like beetles up a distant road, heading for astronomical observatory domes perched like balloon birds along the ridgebacks of the lesser Andes that overlooked Caracas. "Ali?" Mercedes prompted gently.

"Excuse me, sir," Bolivar apologized, turning back. "The trick. Yes, yes. There was a very bad crash, sir. A large transport carrying magnesium ore. It burned most fiercely. An incredible light. From the air you could see it clearly even from several hundred miles away."

Vasco de Gama and Carlos Silva had struggled to remain silent, but the latter description was too much even for them. Silva threw his arms upward in exasperation. "*What* crash is this? I have been downcountry all this time! There has been no crash, no great fire!"

Bolivar looked at the scientist, his face expressionless. "It was very bad, Doctor Silva. The load of magnesium from the mine. It was already in a highly volatile state since it was to be used for the manufacture of incendiary warheads."

Vasco de Gama had listened to the exchange with a look of growing disbelief on his face. He moved forward, nose to nose with Bolivar, their foreheads almost banging together from the lurching motion of the van. Bolivar saw scientific teeth grinding. "Captain Ali Bolivar," de Gama spoke in angry but carefully measured tones, "it would seem you have gone crazy or you are taking some strange drug. Everything you have said is mad. *We don't have any magnesium mines in the area of Devil's Plateau.*" He took a deep breath. "And if we did there is certainly no mining of any kind going on!"

Felipe Mercedes, looking back on the growing tension, smiled. "Of course," he said to de Gama.

"Not only that," Silva sputtered, "but *I* certainly would have been informed of any such crash!"

"That is true," Mercedes allowed.

Vasco de Gama shared his bewildered expression with the others in the van. "Then what is all this about?" he protested. "Is it a game? A very *strange* game? You both talk as if you've gone mad."

Mercedes broke out in a wide smile. "My friend, *we*

know there are gold mines and diamond mines in downcountry, and we both know there are no magnesium mines to be found. But who else," he shrugged, "really *knows* of such things. And who besides our own little group, here," he gestured at them all, "and a very few people elsewhere, is not so certain about the crash of a very large aircraft with incendiary magnesium?"

He studied Bolivar. "A point occurs to me," Mercedes said slowly, "that escaped me before. There has been the fire we planned?"

"Yes, sir."

"There will be spectroscopic studies, my young friend."

"Assuredly," Bolivar said brightly. "And such studies will clearly show magnesium."

Comprehension grew among the group. The "disastrous" magnesium fire had been planned carefully and apparently executed exactly as planned. "Where did you get the magnesium?" Judith Morillo burst out. "We don't have—"

"Ah, but we did," Bolivar broke in as he anticipated the query. "Old military stock. The Americans stored them here many years ago. Incendiary bombs. Their fuzes were removed long ago and they were perfectly safe to move." He turned back to Mercedes. "One more thing, Doctor." He watched Mercedes signal for him to go ahead. "The general said they would be releasing the names of the casualties."

"If Espinoza said so," Mercedes smiled, "you may, as the Americans say in their detective stories on television, bank on it."

Carlos Silva had an expression of admiration on his face. "All this chicanery, then, our cover story? To lead all those spying on us away from the laser flash?"

Mercedes pointed a finger at Silva. "You are a scientist and we had even *you* unsure, confused."

Morillo leaned forward, desperate for another answer. "I heard of a strange report. Not merely a flash—I mean, a green light in the sky, yes, but this was a bright green *sphere*. There was a news story, I caught it on radio, about a green UFO? Is this part of everything we have heard?"

Bolivar looked immensely pleased with himself. "There *was* a green sphere. A UFO. The Americans, in fact, have photographs of the sphere at, oh, I believe over a hundred thousand feet."

"Photographs?" Morillo was almost refusing to believe what she heard.

De Gama clapped Bolivar on the shoulder. "And how did you arrange that little trick?"

"This was a most cooperative mission by the gringos." He laughed with the use of the expression. "A rocket was fired ahead of the plane. At its altitude air resistance meant almost nothing. When the rocket burned out a capsule released a large metallic balloon, inflated automatically with helium. It carried batteries, reflectors and flashing lights. The Americans, of course, knew precisely where to aim their cameras. They flew by the target at perhaps two thousand miles an hour. They took some marvelous pictures. And as we expected they have been classified and the Pentagon refuses to release them to the press. We also—"

The van bumped and rattled to a stop. Mercedes glanced about them. "Enough," he announced in a tone that left no room for argument. "Everybody out." Moments later they stood together on a steep slope and Mercedes waved off the van.

He gestured at the slope before them. At the high end of wide, steep steps loomed a large research building, spreading left and right, and in its center, behind a marbled entrance, rose the unmistakable lines and curves of a nuclear reactor.

"We're now just before the tunnel entrance to BEMAC," Mercedes told the group. "Let us proceed." He began the long climb.

Halfway up Vasco de Gama waved for the group to stop. He leaned on Bolivar, gasping for breath. "This . . . this is too much." He pointed in exasperation. "Why are we climbing steps like donkeys? We had the van," he complained to Mercedes. "We could have driven."

"Ah, but a sound body provides the best basis for a sound mind," Mercedes chided.

"There's nothing wrong with my mind," de Gama grunted.

"True," Mercedes admitted. "But listen to yourself. You sound like the pet pig I had as a child." He laughed and pointed. "We are almost there."

Vasco de Gama stared. "Where?"

"The tunnel."

"But that's our nuclear reactor," de Gama sputtered. "*Where* is this tunnel of yours!"

Two figures appeared at the top of the stairs. Jorge Wagner and Claude McDavid greeted them expansively. "Gentlemen! Miss Morillo! Welcome to Laserland!"

"What is he talking about?" de Gama said with a touch of anger. "That is our *reactor*." He shouted up to McDavid. "I see the reactor, you idiot. *There is no tunnel*."

The scientist, his chest heaving with exertion, stalked past Wagner and McDavid to disappear within the security entrance to the IVIC reactor building. Behind him Mercedes laughed. "Quickly, now. Let us watch. I don't want to miss this."

They caught up with de Gama, his anger little dissipated, waiting with a short fuze of impatience as three security guards checked his ID badge, calling in to another security checkpoint the badge details. "You are clear, sir," they told him.

"I'll wait for the others," de Gama told the guards. He sat heavily on a bench, grateful for the delay to catch his breath. Several minutes later, clearances approved for the group, they followed Mercedes into a high-ceilinged room. They paid little attention to the safety doors and systems through which they had walked hundreds of times. A huge, thick door rolled ponderously to the right, setting off a loud, penetrating horn blast. Red lights flashed, another horn boomed, and a mechanical voice sounded from speakers high on the walls.

"Stand clear. Please stand clear." Instinctively they moved back. Lights flashed above and to the sides of a massive steel door. A pneumatic hiss made them wince and the second door slid with a painfully heavy movement to the side. They went through the open space, facing yet another thick door, heard the warning again to stand clear, and the door behind them boomed closed. Now they were within a sealed chamber that filled with the sharp sound of compressed air rushing into the chamber.

As many times as they had gone through this same procedure they couldn't avoid the instinctive glances about them. On all four walls and the door interiors bright red signs warned of danger from nuclear radiation. Radiation-level monitors at eye level looked at them from each wall, then red lights flashed out and bright green lights came on. The mechanical voice came alive.

"Clear to enter. Clear to enter. Please stand clear of the door. Warning! Please stand clear of the door. It will open after a five count. Five, four, three, two, one—"

A bell rang loudly, air pressure dropped and the final safety door rolled aside. For a moment, safety instincts overcame long familiarity. There's something sinister, forbidding, ominous and plain damn dangerous about the huge curving bulk of a nuclear reactor looming before and high over you. Everyone starting into the reactor room stopped for a moment, their eyes sweeping left and right to take in the masses of plumbing, glowing monitors, gauges, control panels, computers, thick electrical cabling stretching like endless multicolored snakes in all directions. They all shared that same subtle shudder that ran through their bodies. Then, as if shaking off a cold and frightening mist surrounding mind and body, they started forward. Two technicians awaited them. Before they took more than their first few steps the white-smocked men came forward. "Doc-

tor Mercedes," the first said by way of greeting, reached
out and affixed a clip-on dosimeter to Mercedes's jacket.
Soon they all wore the cumulative-radiation instruments
that would track all radiation pouring from the reactor—
hopefully in harmless spray.

The technicians left and as Mercedes and his group
went forward they were greeted warmly by Doctor
Josefa Betancourt, the director of the scientific research
center. In stark contrast to the scruffy-appearing group
with Mercedes, Betancourt loomed tall and dignified,
dark-haired, dressed impeccably, as neat in appearance
as if his attire had been carved from cloth. His demeanor concealed a warm, dignified and brilliant scientist
with whom Mercedes and the others had worked for
years. He held out his hand to introduce his companion.

"Felipe, lady, gentlemen, my pleasure," Betancourt
said with a voice of warm honey. "Please, this is Doctor
Rosa Rivero, who has joined our little group here at
IVIC. She has been in France for the last three years
working within their most advanced nuclear programs,
and she is now in charge of our own reactor and research programs." A dazzling smile showed from a brown-
skinned, very handsome woman who looked to be forty
years old, but could have been mistaken ten years to
either side of that number. "I warn you, Felipe, be
very careful of this charming lady. She mixes a most
dangerous radioactive cocktail."

The introductions broke the ice; the groups, normally
highly competitive in their work, relaxed. Betancourt
took Mercedes' arm as they walked. "You will forgive
me, Felipe? I planned to review your new program
with you but," he shrugged, "I am overruled. I am to
meet with the president within the hour. Doctor Rivero
has been briefed fully by me, and she will attend to
your every need."

"The scenery," Mercedes said with open appreciation, "is vastly improved by her presence." He pushed
away Betancourt's arm. "I am not that much a fool not
to choose superior company. Goodbye, Josefa." He took

Doctor Rivero's arm. "I am yours to command, lovely lady."

Rivero laughed and gestured for the others to follow.

"I hope," growled de Gama from behind them, "that perhaps we shall see this invisible tunnel now!"

"Be patient, Vasco!" Mercedes called out. "There are more changes yet to be seen, and—" He interrupted his own words as two large young men, spit-and-polish through every inch of their army uniforms and gold berets, fell in neatly behind their group. De Gama stopped, studied the two men, and hurried to join Mercedes and Rivero.

"You're right. I *am* surprised, Felipe. Guards with machine guns in their hands? Do they watch over us also when we go to the bathroom?"

Rivero exchanged a glance with Mercedes, who smiled and nodded for her to respond. She turned to face the scientist who was so clearly upset with the presence of machine guns at his back. She spoke with a crisp tone, what one expected of a nurse in starched whites in a hospital, talking to a child. "You misunderstand, Doctor de Gama. Those guns are not for us but *because* of us. You see, sir, they are for your protection."

Mercedes moved to de Gama and took his arm gently; he gestured with his free hand. "Do you see that door, Vasco? Just on the other side of the reactor?" They started walking together. "The guns are because of what we have created on the other side of that door. It is a secret the entire world would want desperately, *at any cost*, to have. So, sad as it is to us all who have no need or want of guns, they are now a fact of life. For some time to come, my friend, how long I can't know, they will be a part of your life. And mine," he added, as if to ease the blow.

They stood before a huge door with massive steel plates and bolts. All about them were warning signs that the door was electrified, that entry without the highest clearance was forbidden, that attempted forced entry would be met with immediate gunfire. As if to emphasize what was increasingly that fact of life, Vasco de Gama glanced up and to his left and stared into the muzzle of a machine gun in a remotely controlled turret. He turned to his right to see a similar weapon. "A matched pair, I see," he said drily. He looked at Mercedes.

"Enough games. The tunnel, Felipe."

Mercedes nodded. He moved forward and stood on a metal platform. A voice seemed to come out of nowhere. "State your name for voiceprint and EM identification, please." Mercedes looked straight ahead. "Doctor Felipe Mercedes, Director, BEMAC. Fourteen, File Nine." Blue light ghosted down from a concealed aperture above, and Mercedes seemed to flicker where he stood.

"You will all be doing that soon," Doctor Rivero explained to the others. "He is being scanned for his body electromagnetic pattern, his voiceprint is being checked against prior recordings, and a complete holographic double of Doctor Mercedes is being computer-studied behind that door."

The light faded abruptly. Mercedes glanced up and spoke to a concealed sensor. "Fourteen, File Nine, open, please."

A deep, barely-heard thudding boom sounded beneath them, and the massive door slid to one side. Mercedes gestured to his group. "There, my friends, beyond that door, is your tunnel. It leads to your future lives and, should all go as we hope, it is a quantum leap into the future.

"Come."

Chapter VI

"Open the door!"

At the sound of the wall loudspeakers and the flashing of bright red lights, two guards moved their autorifles to the ready. They stood back to back to cover the long corridor from one end to the other. Television scanners against the ceiling moved slowly, a whining sound lost in the echoing of loudspeaker cries, the shouts of men, booted feet smacking against the gleaming floors of the military prison within *Fuerte Tiuna*, nestled conveniently within the city limits of Caracas. More bright lights came on. At each end of the corridor appeared two more men, each with a huge timber-shepherd guard dog.

The door with thick steel bars rolled back, squeaking in protest, and clanged against its stops. Dazzling light splashed into a large cell. Angela Tirado, Tony Pappas and Nelson Sanchez held their hands before the blinding glare. "Out! Come with me!" shouted a guard barely visible against the stabbing lights. They moved awkwardly. Angela stumbled and only the grip of Pappas' arm kept her from falling.

"Where are we going?" Angela asked, still half-blind.

"I don't even know where the hell we *are*," Pappas said through dry lips. "How long have we been here? This is our third prison. I don't know where we—"

He drew up short as his eyes focused on two heavily armed men holding two very large dogs on short leashes. They nodded to the guard who'd led them from their cell. The lead man with a dog started down a side corridor. "Follow me, please," he told them. They fell in step behind him, the second guard and dog taking up position behind them. "I don't think they're going to shoot us," Angela said with dry humor. "No one says please if they're taking you out to be shot."

"You watch too many cheap detective movies," Sanchez grumbled.

"Spy movies," she corrected him. "You know, James Bond, Telly Savalas—"

She fell silent as Pappas caught the attention of the guard leading their way. "Where are we going, friend?" he sang out.

"The general will see you now."

"General? *General?*" Sanchez said quickly. "His name, soldier; what's his name?"

"You don't need to ask him," Pappas answered before the guard spoke. "I recognize this whole modus operandi. It's almost his personal signature. Everything perfect."

"*Who?*" Angela shouted.

"The big man himself," Pappas replied. "General Luis Espinoza."

Angela's lips pursed in a startled O. She didn't answer. This *was* a big deal, then. You didn't go any higher than Espinoza, the mystery man of Venezuelan government. Angela smiled. If they lived through all this . . .

She *smelled* a great story in the making. Immediately her step became livelier.

The door closed behind them. Angela looked about the room. "No guards?" she murmured aloud. "I don't understand. I—"

"What is there to understand?" She spun about at the sound of the voice that seemed to emerge through a steel larynx. General Luis Espinoza, for it couldn't be any other, had slipped into the room like a phantom, then stood with awesome reality. *It's as if he's carved from granite*, Tirado decided. *His eyes . . . steel marbles . . . and yet, and yet . . .*

Espinoza seemed amused. "You are staring, Miss Tirado," he said. Now she understood the descriptions.

A voice of stone, yet clothed in velvet if he so wished. Right now he so wished, she decided. Or it pleased him. Or whatever the hell was going on.

"Yes, I am," she said finally. "You're not at all what I expected."

"You touch my curiosity," he said silkily. "Did you expect fangs? Claws? A fiend slavering in a hungry crouch?"

Unexpectedly, completely without any intention, she burst into laughter. "Yes, yes!" she sang out, relief flooding through her. "As God is my witness I do believe that's *exactly* what I expected!"

"Ah, you are disappointed?"

Her laughter cut off as if by thrown switch. "No. No, not that. Surprised. Tremendously surprised. I mean —oh, I don't know. I didn't know *what* to expect. But the last person I expected to meet with tonight was *you*."

"Then let me warn you, Miss Tirado. An effective weapon need not smile." The timbre of his voice had changed again. With those words the steel was back. *No; it's never been gone. Only controlled,* she told herself. *He's given us a warning. Careful, Angie girl, be very careful in here.*

Espinoza seemed to blur as he moved; suddenly he was behind a large desk. A gloved hand gestured easily. "Sit, please." He waited as they moved gingerly to the three other seats in the room. "First, you are not under arrest."

They stared at one another with almost explosive relief.

"*Yet.*"

Angela Tirado rose to her feet. "I didn't care much for that last word," she said, as careful as she seemed haughty. "If we're not under arrest, why have we been imprisoned for three days?"

"Venezuela is a democratic country, Miss Tirado—"

"Spare me, General, I know my—"

"And even democratic institutions require vigilance and protection," he went on, as if his own words poured syrup over and drowned hers. "You three have been detained. There is a difference. The detention was necessary and brought on by yourself." His finger gestured to her chair. "I said you weren't under arrest. I also asked that you be seated."

"I'll *stand*."

"As you wish. You are under arrest and—"

"Goddammit, sit down!" Sanchez shouted, grasping her arm.

She shook him off and took her seat slowly. He was absolutely fascinating. She couldn't believe this was a common military man, a—she shut off the yammering to herself and paid close attention to this extraordinary person, realizing at the same moment, with another mild shock of surprise, that she hadn't been frightened for her safety since she came into this room.

Espinoza reminded her with a verbal crash that she *should* bring concern to her thinking. "Are you aware," the general began slowly, again with a subtle yet unquestionable change of tone, "of the violations you have committed, singly and individually, of the laws of our country?"

Angela glanced from Sanchez to Pappas and received silent agreement for her to speak. "General, chasing down a UFO, with eyewitness reports from the ground and the air, is a *news* story. In no way did we ever intend to violate any laws and certainly *never* to endanger Venezuela. Or do you forget this is also *our* country?"

Oh, shit, it didn't take, she said to herself with sight of his humorless smile.

"I will humor you, then. Did you find your UFO's?"

Sanchez failed to remain silent. He leaned forward, almost falling from his chair. "We damned well found *something*, General!"

"Ah, I am delighted. Then describe it to me, this . . . *something*."

"Well, it was, uh," Sanchez leaned back in his seat, "it's hard to say, what I mean is, uh—"

Tirado moved in quickly. "We saw some bright lights."

Espinoza shook his head slightly, disappointment clear

on his face. "I talk with children," he said softly. "You saw bright lights. Extraordinary. What were they?"

"Well, they were, uh," she faltered suddenly. "Dammit, General, *you know* what they were! Jet fighters, for one, that—"

"Jet fighters. That is a clear identification, to be sure. Whose? Of what nationality?"

She felt herself fumbling and hated herself. "Why, *ours*, of course. I mean, they landed with us. We saw them and they intercepted us and ordered us to . . ." Her voice trailed away.

Tony Pappas felt tired before he spoke. "Sir, F-16 jets."

"Should I assume, Mr. Pappas, from what I have just heard, that the lights were F-16's, that you are pursuing a news story on the efficiency of our military aircraft in tracking, intercepting and forcing down a civilian aircraft flying in violation of federal regulations?"

"I *said* they forced us down!" Tirado said angrily. "If we didn't land as ordered, they said they would *shoot* us down!"

Espinoza didn't move a muscle but it seemed he had struck like a viper. "*Why?*"

"Uh, why?" She looked frantically to Pappas, saw a blank face, turned back to the general. "Because we, uh, well, I mean—" She sat bolt upright. "Dammit, we flew down Corridor Diablo—"

"Another violation."

"To the devil with the violations! That green light we saw! That wasn't *ordinary*, General Espinoza! And it sure as hell wasn't any jet fighter from *any* country!"

"First a white light," Espinoza said, shaking his head slightly, "and now a green light that is a greater mystery."

"It *blinded* us! *We nearly crashed!* Doesn't *that* mean anything to you?"

Espinoza made a steeple of his fingers. "Captain Pappas, explain life to these two, please."

Tirado and Sanchez stared. Angela felt her mouth open, had to force it closed before she could speak.

"*Captain* Pappas?" Her voice was a hoarse whisper. "*You?*"

"Yes, Angie. Captain. That's right, but I'm in the air force reserve. The *reserve*, dammit. I'm not on active duty and—"

Espinoza's voice cracked whiplike. "Captain, I said to *explain.*"

Pappas nodded to Espinoza. "Yes, sir." He turned back to his two friends. "We took off for a cross-country flight into the interior. I failed to file a flight plan; I've already told you that meant trouble. Then we flew through the interior without a flight plan. That's a second violation. We flew into a military restricted area. That's *three*. We—"

"*That's enough!*" Angela wasn't acting any more and she made no attempt to speak with fancy phrases or continue this double-dealing dialogue. She jumped to her feet, face contorted, locking eyes with Espinoza. "I don't *care* about all these stupid regulations he's quoting! They're all minor against what's been going on out there," she gestured wildly, "and we all know it! You *know* what we were looking for! There have been all kinds of reports about incredible explosions of light around Devil's Plateau. You can't hide behind your damn regulations when those lights were seen by airline pilots and Russian cosmonauts from space! The Americans and the Russians are talking about an atomic explosion. *An atom bomb*, for God's sake! We don't have atom bombs in our country. But there are UFO reports *also* coming in from all sides. *Whatever* was happening down there by Devil's Plateau is what we went to find out!" She gulped down air. "And that, General, your honor, *sir*, whatever the hell you are, is the right of the Venezuelan free press! If it bothers you so much and we've become a national danger, *then shoot us*! Or let us the hell out of here so I can do my job!"

She half-collapsed in her seat, bosom heaving, fists clenched so tightly her nails dug painfully into her palms. She waited for the explosion from Espinoza.

Silence. *Oh, my God, nothing I said made any impression on him. I—*

"Bravo, bravo," Espinoza said unexpectedly. The honeyed voice again. Was that sarcasm or humor? "Shall I tell you, Miss Tirado, what you want to find?"

She gaped. *"Yes!"* she shouted.

The man before her changed from general to technician, or specialist, or scientist, or—

"You chased the visible light manifestation of a vital maser test, carried out by certain research groups of our air force but mainly by a special research organization unknown to either our own people or to the world. The maser—"

"Do you mean laser?" she broke in.

"Maser," he emphasized as to a child. "In the microwave band. It was mixed with certain laser experiments as well. It's brighter than any other kind of light, especially at particular angles of sight reference. Bright enough, young woman, to trigger satellite sensors, alarm airline crews, terrify natives, confuse cosmonauts, *and* create all manner of reports of UFO's whizzing about in grand numbers."

Sanchez looked to Pappas. "What the devil's a maser? What's all this microwave stuff?"

"You may not write of that test, of what you have seen, or what you've learned in this room," Espinoza said solumnly.

"The hell I—" Tirado didn't get any further.

"The free press, Angela Tirado, also has the obligation to protect its own nation. The testing we've had under way, both laser and maser, carries the highest security classifications. You may think it is a grand exclusive, a wonderment for your news show, I am certain, but you will *have* to tell your story along with these fairy tales of unidentified objects skittering about the skies. Then what do we have for all your pains? Thirty seconds on your newscast? Page sixteen, fourth-column, bottom of page, in a paper?"

Espinoza wheeled his chair about slowly and leaned back. For a moment he stared at the ceiling, his thoughts free of this room and its occupants. He returned as he brought his steely gaze again to Tirado. "Any official confirmation of what you already know, of what has happened to you *and what I have told you freely*, interferes with our research and development program. *That*, and do not take this lightly, *is* a most severe violation of our security laws, especially," he paused and seemed almost for a moment to snort with disdain, "by people who have already broken many laws, and who *by law* I could incarcerate right now."

The general moved to his feet. The others did the same. Sanchez had a thin smile on his face. "You would do all this . . . without a trial? Without any bail? Legal representation?"

"I *could*," Espinoza said with a sudden chill to his words. "I could do all that within the embrace of our security statutes. And I inform you now these are *not* military. They are government, all-embracing, applicable both to military and civilian. Where our national safety is concerned we do not inspect apparel."

He looked down at the desk, his fingers splayed out on the polished wood, looked up again. "I'll bring this to a close." Steely eyes moved from one to the other before Espinoza again spoke. "If you will give me your word there will be no news stories, no comment, private or public, on this matter, we will be through with it. I believe you intended no harm, that eagerness overcame caution and logic. With your word to me, the government will simply forget whatever violations have occurred. The slate will be wiped clean."

A finger stabbed rigidly at Pappas. "Except for this one. He knew better and he has much to answer for."

Angela walked to the desk and faced Espinoza. "All right, General, I'll buy your little deal. But only on one condition."

Espinoza's only response was a raised eyebrow.

Angela pointed to Pappas. "You include the ape in the deal. Forget us, forget him. Otherwise," she shrugged, "it's back to square one and you toss us in the clink again." For the first time she offered Espinoza a sweet smile. "Somehow, General, I don't believe we're *that* easy to dispose of."

She didn't get the retort she expected. Or a threat. Espinoza offered what might pass for a fleeting smile. "As you say so colorfully, Miss Tirado, I'll buy your deal." He extended his hand. "I have your word?"

She clasped his hand. *Firm, even strong, but gentle. Amazing.* "My word, sir."

Sanchez came forward to shake hands with Espinoza. "My word of honor. And thank you, General Espinoza."

Espinoza shook with Sanchez and nodded. Sanchez stepped aside for Pappas to come forward. "My word as an officer, sir," he told the general. "Your word is accepted, Captain." The barest of signals, no more than eye movement, passed between them.

"Miss Tirado, I will have a taxi for you within the minute," Espinoza said to Angela.

"A taxi?" she echoed. "But where—"

Pappas broke in. "We're in Caracas. This is Fuerte Tiuna."

"You knew all the time?" she asked him.

He shook his head. "No, no. But here, in this room, it was easy to figure out. La Carlota Airport is to our south. I've been listening to all the turboprops, the executive and company planes, letting down for a final approach to the field. I know the timing and the sound." He grinned. "Just a short cab ride home."

"La Carlota Airport," Pappas told the driver as they climbed into the cab waiting for them at the Fort's entrance. They settled in, still taken aback at how they'd been shifted in the dead of night from a backcountry military airfield to the Fort so familiar to them that they looked upon its superbly manicured expanse every day. Sanchez studied the lights of the city. When they drove onto the superhighway cutting south through the city he finally turned his attention to the team.

"Angela, for the life of me," he said with exasperation, "I don't understand you. Have you gone crazy?"

She looked with surprise from Sanchez to Pappas,

who shrugged, then back to Sanchez. "How? What crazy?"

"The general. With the general!" he exclaimed. "How could you agree to a deal like that?"

"*Shut up.*"

They turned to stare at Pappas. He nodded his head in the direction of the driver. Sanchez opened his mouth, clamped it shut. Tirado nodded to Pappas and turned back to Sanchez. "It's simple enough," she said with a swift shift in her subject. "The general lets me review the film from the Grenada invasion. Especially the film the Americans captured from the Cubans. You know what I mean. The missile sites?"

"She's talking about the tactical missiles the Cubans had set to fire on our Maracaibo oil fields," Pappas contributed to their nonsense.

"So what's wrong with my deal?" Tirado snapped to Sanchez. "It's a fair exchange. I see the film, I give him the right to censor whatever he thinks will irritate the Americans."

"And what about irritating the *Russians?*" Sanchez asked.

"That's easy," Pappas offered. "Screw the Russians."

They fell silent for the rest of the ride. The cab let them off at the main office of Aerotuy by the flight line. They stood by the steps, returning the wave of a security guard who knew Pappas well.

"Why'd you shut me up in the taxi?" Sanchez asked Pappas.

"You're a baby in a forest filled with wolves, my friend," Pappas told him, grinning at his own description. He rested a hand on his friend's shoulder. "You're a great newsman. Reliable, strong, trustworthy. But when it comes to intrigue you're a newborn. You were going to talk about everything we'd said in Espinoza's office, right?"

"Why, yes, but so what? We were alone in the—" His eyes widened. "You're right. Damn me for a fool."

"Well, people forget," Pappas said, more generously than he intended. "You completely forgot about the taxi driver. He was a government agent, Nels, and that cab was wired for sound and pictures. Three minutes away from your promise to keep your mouth shut and you were going to broadcast everything. Nels, Nels," Pappas said with great patience, "there is only one way to keep your word to Espinoza. *Keep your mouth shut.*"

"Well, and happy bullcock to *you*, my fine feathered *Captain* Antonio Icarus Pappas," Angela threw at their pilot. "A captain, no less! Are you assigned to the secret police, Tony? Or do you spy only on your friends?"

"If you weren't a woman," Pappas said calmly but very deliberately, "I would break your face for those words. And if I felt for one moment you *believed* what you just said, I would walk away from you now and never say another word to you."

"I know, I know," she chided. "I also know you're in the air force reserve. It's hardly a secret, Tony. It's in your bio file at the station."

"Then why'd you squeal like a stuck pig in the general's office?" Sanchez wondered.

"Because it was appropriate, Nels. Because it looked good and sounded good for us to be surprised, shocked, and highly pissed off at our Mediterranean lothario, here." She took each man by the arm. "Walk with me down the flight line. If as you say, Tony, we may have microphones aimed at us, we can stop by one of the airplanes running up and no one will hear us over the engines."

Several minutes later they stood off the wingtip of a big Grumman Gulfstream, turboprops screaming ear-hammering defiance to the night air. Angela turned to her crew. "Do you understand, I mean *really under-stand*, the meaning of our little exchange in Espinoza's office?"

"Well, we went up a blind alley with UFO's, that's for sure," Sanchez replied.

"To hell with the UFO's!" Angela spat.

"But . . . but you were so all-fired hot to get that story, and I thought, I mean—" Sanchez stammered, honestly confused.

"The UFO story is a blind alley, a decoy, a setup, a ruse, whatever you want to call it," Angela broke in. She was as much amazed with Sanchez's myopia as he was confused with her words. "Nels, you idiot, do you know what a maser is? I mean, *really?*"

"Espinoza *told* us," he said stubbornly. "It's just a different kind of laser, that's all. Higher up in the frequency so that instead of visible light, you know, the coherent light of the laser, it's in the microwave, like radar. FM and video, also, I guess."

"Listen to me, dammit," she said angrily, grasping his arm as if that would make her words clearer. She glanced at Pappas and he only nodded for her to continue. "Nels," she said to Sanchez, "you produce a laser beam by boosting—by stimulating, that's the word the technical boys love to use—certain types of radiation. Let's just accept visible light. Normal light is chaotic, random, disorganized. Like a mob of people in a riot. But if you can get all those people—or particles of light—to line up and march in formation, you jump from chaotic to coherent. Following me?"

He nodded. "Yes, yes."

"Okay. That means you're amplifying normal light by a factor of thousands." She looked with triumph at Pappas and again turned back to Sanchez. "But to get a maser, you don't boost or amplify light. You boost a very high-energy microwave. Like a very tight, very intense radar beam. You ever see those big radar domes on the military airfields? Of course you have. Ever read the signs on the road that say don't stay here, don't linger, get the hell out? Do you know *why?* Because if you stand in front of those things for just a few minutes when they're putting out power you might as well be standing inside a microwave oven. It'll burn out your guts and fry your brain. *That's* microwave."

She took a deep breath. "Now, when you stimulate something like radar, you get a maser. It's incredibly powerful—"

Sanchez was annoyed at being lectured and didn't bother to hide it. "So? So what's the big deal, Angie?"

Angela swung about in a circle, arms high and wide, a sudden swirl of triumph. "Damn you, Nels, *a maser beam is invisible*. You can't *see* a maser! Don't you understand? Any kind of microwave, is *absolutely — invisible — to — the — human — eye!*" She grinned with her own conclusions. "Hah! General Espinoza tried to snow us tonight! Don't you get it? *He lied to us!*"

She laughed, a delightful sound brushed into the air by the thundering engines of the Gulfstream. "And when General Luis Espinoza has to lie to a mere slip of a girl—*me!*—then there is one *hell* of a big story out there!"

She calmed suddenly and grasped their arms. "And you two big cats are *my* news team, and *we're* going to *get* that story!"

Chapter VII

The bright light revolved slowly, sending out splin-
ters and gleams as it twisted, revealing an interior of
liquid curlicues. Two more lights approached, the three
sourcepoints joined, and three whiskey glasses clinked
solidly as Caleb Massey, Kim Seavers and Morgan Scott
joined in a toast to their first drink of the evening.

Massey smiled at the young man and woman, sitting
forward on the edge of their chairs. "*Prosit*," he sang
out quietly. They sipped their drinks, Massey downed
his in a long smooth swallow. Kim and Morgan eased
back in their seats, taking the moment to look about
them and study the extraordinary clubroom in which
they were Massey's guests. The big man smiled at their
expressions. "Interesting, isn't it?" he asked.

"Interesting isn't the word," Kim answered quickly.
"I mean, I've been in some luxurious digs before, but
nothing," she shook her head in admiration, "anywhere
like this." About them was an enclosed world, a packag-
ing of dark paneling in rich unknown woods, thick
carpeting, enormously high ceilings, dazzling chande-
liers, armchairs that seemed to mold to their bodies.
High overhead mahogany-bladed fans turned slowly.
Waiters seemed to glide across the floor without effort.
Kim studied the drapes: a strange material, all closed,
no windows visible. The very air was subdued, especially from their recessed alcove along a far wall of the
clubroom. Voices from other small groups scattered
through the room reached them in hushed whispers,
although from animated gesturing and facial expressions

Kim was certain no one bothered to speak in lowered tones. It was all very confusing to her.

"Mr. Massey, what—" she paused, looking about her again and gesturing, "I simply can't *not* ask the question. What is all this? What is this *place*? Don't misunderstand me," she added hastily. "It's *gorgeous*."

Massey gestured with his drink, slouching back in the huge armchair holding him like a friendly grizzly. "Once upon a time," he began, pausing as they laughed, "well, there was a call that went far and wide for a very special place for a special group of people. They weren't your ordinary run-of-the-mill crowd. Actually," he smiled, "they were the best spies, secret agents and intelligence operatives of the many arms and agencies of the United States government. They all agreed they needed a totally secure place to meet, plot, scheme, tell lies, plan, get away from the kids, have a lazy drink; whatever. That place *had* to be secure. It would be the province of them all; no one would have priority over anyone else. A secret subcommittee of the senate took over the task and assigned the people to build and run that special place. They took their orders *only* from the subcommittee. Since no one knew who they were, they were free from interference." Massey looked about the room and held up an empty glass. "You're in that room now."

Morgan Scott toyed with his drink. "The intelligence services don't run this place, sir?"

"Oh, they run it by *funding* it. All the military intelligence services, CIA, NSA, NSC, FBI and a dozen other groups you never heard of. They pay *cash*. I suppose you could say we *all* run it. By that I mean it's open-ended security. Everybody does their best to break the security of this place. No one has yet succeeded in breaching the walls, so to speak. This whole facility is tighter than the deepest sub-basement of the Pentagon." Massey smiled. "That's why we're here. The drink is social. Our reason for coming here is *not*."

"You'd never know it," Morgan Scott said. "Oops,"

he added with a laugh. "Not what you said, sir, but that all those outfits could cooperate that well."

"Either one of you have a recorder on you?" Massey asked. Before they could answer he smiled at Kim. "Well, you certainly do, young lady. Micro package, force field electronics, no sound, very sensitive."

Kim stared with genuine surprise at Massey, looked to Scott and then back to Massey. "How could you possibly know that?"

"Well, let me adopt my best Wallace Beery stance." Massey screwed up his face and his voice became gravelly. "It's my job. A lifetime of being a spy or whatever you wish to call it. I've also dealt with every kind of device you could imagine and then some. Put your recorder on that table, Kim," he said, gesturing. "It's eight feet from us. Turn your little doodad on and leave it in the record mode."

Several seconds later, the recorder removed from within her belt and left on the table, she slid back into her seat. "Done."

"Recording?" Massey asked her to confirm.

"Yes, sir."

Massey looked to Scott. "Say something, son."

Morgan Scott sat stiffly, straight-faced. "Once upon a time there was a wicked warlock who lived in Washington, D.C., and he had a terrible habit of pulling the legs of pretty young women, or, stroking their legs, and—okay, sir?"

"Well, you're original, anyway. Kim, the recorder. Bring it here, please, and play the tape."

She returned the recorder, held it in one hand, ran the tape back through rewind and punched PLAY. She was openly astonished at the warbling squeal bursting through the speaker. She grasped the recorder, studied it, shook it. Massey smiled and motioned for her to shut off the machine.

"Would, ah, Warlock Massey have an explanation for all that?" Morgan Scott asked.

Massey tossed off the rest of his drink, burped as delicately as one might expect from a water buffalo, and cocked his head to one side, a sign they would come to recognize as indicating nonjovial words would follow. "You can't record *anything* in this place," he said in no-nonsense tones. "There's complete electronic disruption of voice patterns. If you could see the pressure waves from your throat, generated by muscle action and body heat, the usual outflow of sonic harmonics is gone. Throw a pebble into a smooth water surface and you get neatly identifiable rings. Set off a hand grenade just below the surface and you get sonic frenzy. In this kind of aural environment only the human ear works. It has the sensitivity, electrical circuitry and that incredible computer between our ears to sift out sense from nonsense."

Massey pressed a button to the side of his chair and leaned down slightly to talk to his armrest. "One nine six for another round, please."

"Right away, sir," the chair said.

"That chair have brains?" Kim asked with a smile.

"No. It does have specific circuitry to recognize my voiceprint. If *you* ordered the drink from this chair there'd be a full security alert under way." He smiled again. "This place is full of surprises like that and even *I* don't know what they all are." He shifted position to rest an elbow on the armrest and prop up his chin in the palm of his hand, and his head once again cocked barely to the side. "Do you two have any idea of what went on at the meeting tonight?"

"Sir, the whole thing was weird." Morgan Scott looked about him, uneasy. "It really is okay to talk openly?"

"Fire away, son. Your mother wouldn't recognize your voice on a telephone from here."

"Yes, sir. Back to the meeting. Weird, like I said. This business about UFO's." He shook his head. "That's pretty crazy. Then the *real* mystery. The lights. The *green* lights. Just as crazy is where they're coming from. I'm equating all this with the geographical area, of course."

"*And* the numbers," Kim added quickly. "For the

Russians to get a clear definition of that green light from the altitude of the Mir—"

"Why did you use the word 'definition'?" Massey asked.

"No one used the word *flash* or anything similar. Had there been a question of light intensity we'd have heard that comment. Then, the Vela Hotel and Keyhole satellites responding the way they did?" She shook her head. "No way. Big light, very intense, doesn't make any sense about where it came from, and absolutely *not* a nuclear device such as a bomb."

"Why?" The question stabbed at her.

"By now there would have been either fallout or high-altitude radiation picked up by balloons, aircraft; all those things always on the alert for such phenomena."

Massey had a look of pure joy on his face. He leaned over to nudge Scott. "Pretty damned good for a beautiful girl whose main event in life is competition athletics," he said proudly.

"We haven't talked laser," Scott tossed into their conversation.

"Talk laser," Massey said quickly.

"Over my head," Scott said. "Not lasers, *per se*. But what I heard is of a magnitude beyond anything I know about. And then all that conversation about green spheres doing thousands of miles an hour and the films we saw and the way Mr. Mancini did everything but throw a shit fit—damn, sorry, sir."

Massey waved off the expletive and looked to Kim. "Sir, I'm no expert but I believe I have a pretty good method of seeing the *large* picture."

"The whole elephant and not just the trunk, eh?"

"That says it pretty well," Kim went on. "When you put it all together, two elements emerge."

"Fascinating." Massey was doing his best not to smile. "Please do go on."

"Well, almost nothing of what we heard *should* be taking place where the events were described. I know the area around Angel Falls. Nothing I've heard gives a satisfactory explanation for such phenomena in so isolated an area. It simply doesn't serve any purpose. If the Venezuelans, *if* they're involved, wanted isolation, they've got everything from vast swamp and river country to desolate deserts completely isolated from the outside world except for aircraft or satellites. Or," she added quickly, "in the case of the Mir, or even our own shuttles, manned observations from space. But nothing *fits*."

"Conclusions?" Massey asked with disarming calm.

"Either everything we heard is really telling us nothing, which makes everything I've said an exercise in futile conversation," Kim said slowly, "or—and this is the most likely conclusion—we're victims of an elaborate smokescreen."

"Hoax?" Massey asked.

"No, sir," Kim said immediately. "A ruse to cover something of extraordinary power or advanced scientific nature that can't be hidden because it *does* produce enormous illumination effects, so they need all this circus hoopla to cover their tracks. And the perfect vehicle is the UFO."

"Why?" Massey almost demanded the answer.

Morgan Scott picked up the response. "Because Brazil, all the way north to Venezuela, has been a hotbed of UFO sightings for over twenty years. Not only sightings, but photographs, films and even reports of landings. Thousands of them. After a while the response to such reports is to ridicule what's going on, to treat the whole thing with what I call gentle sympathy."

Massey leaned back to regard the two young people with open admiration. "Bravo," he said quietly. "In more ways than you realize you've been dead on target."

Kim smiled. "I have the feeling you're not going to tell us where we've been right *or* wrong."

"You're right," Massey told her. "I won't. Not yet, anyway. You'll learn soon enough. Now it's time to get down to business. Do you two consider yourselves volunteers for missions that may be dangerous?"

"Yes, sir." They spoke in chorus.

"I'm talking about situations that can kill you."

"We've been through this before," Scott said. "Our only restriction is that we won't get into any of this undercover stuff where we're expected to kill. Assassinations, that sort of thing. We'll risk *our* lives but we won't take a life from someone else."

"That's a position on which you're firm?"

"Absolutely," Kim said.

"Very good. Now let me review quickly." A different Caleb Massey seemed to appear before them, a subtle shifting in mood and personality and attitude.

"Morgan, you're a former test pilot, skydiver, Olympic athlete and also a chemical engineer. You speak seven languages. For personal reasons that were rather intense you quit the military. You've lived and worked in South America as a chemical and geological engineer. You're also a black belt in at least four martial arts. Unmarried, unattached and, to some extent, bored and seeking challenge to make your life more meaningful."

"I'm almost afraid to hear what comes next," Kim Seavers said, rolling her eyes.

Massey didn't hesitate. "Your mother is Venezuelan, still a citizen. You're fluent in Spanish, Portuguese, French, Italian, Russian and fairly adept in several Slavic languages. You're an amateur archeologist and well respected for your graduate work. You're obviously an outstanding athlete, a champion swimmer, you're an expert in underwater work, you've done skydiving and you've got your ticket as a pilot. More recently you did postgraduate studies in nuclear systems and electronics, and specialized in laser technology. Oh, yes, the both of you are also paramedics. Those are just the highlights. You have one phase of your life as a teenager you wish had never happened. You were married at sixteen and your father had the marriage annulled. You never told anyone why you made such a drastic move." He paused a moment as he brought a cigar from an inner jacket pocket. "Care to tell me now?"

Kim's face was stony. "I don't believe you don't already know."

"We have a third party with us, Kim. I never discuss

personal issues of this nature with *anyone* else. Yes, I do know."

Kim held his gaze, preferring not to look at Morgan Scott. "I married a nineteen-year-old boy. He had bone cancer and less than six months to live. We moved to Nevada and lived out in the desert. You're right; the marriage was annulled. It didn't matter. I stayed with Mitch until the day he died. In my arms. The doctors were wrong. He lived only two months."

Massey swept on, to Kim's gratitude. "The mission you'll go on calls for a third partner. You'll become a team, tighter than two whiskers on a dwarf gnat. Do either of you know Stanley Blake?"

"You have the unsettling habit, sir," Scott said, "of asking questions to which you already know the answers. Sure we know Stan Blake. He's the toughest competition in sports I've ever had."

"Kim?"

"I did diving with him. Believe it or not, sir, we were looking for ancient ruins in the South Atlantic. It could have been Atlantis. Whatever it was we definitely found the remains of a civilization that predated the best of Europe by several thousand years."

"Excellent. I'll do the routine condensed biog on Blake." Massey paused long enough to finish a second drink and offer up a crooked smile. "Blake's a diver and so are you, Kim. We start with you."

"I thought *you* were going to tell *us*!"

"I am in my own way. Go ahead."

She sought the memories and the right words. "Well, the impression that stands out the most is that Stan Blake is an incredible physical specimen. Not the fancy muscle type. That doesn't count for beans," she emphasized. "He's, well, I think of words like whipcord, or pure banded steel. He has athletic muscles. Long and flowing rather than the knotted bunchy type."

"Is that important?" Massey queried.

"Absolutely. He doesn't cramp up under severe exertion and that's critical when you're under pressure for a long time. He's an outstanding long-distance runner, for example, but he also has tremendous power for short, hard work. I know about his Olympics work. He was—*is*—a top wrestler, a heavyweight boxer, he's into just about all the martial arts and has a whole bundle of black belts. He flies, both fixed-wing and choppers. He's a jumper. Not *just* a jumper; he's qualified as a paratrooper, a smoke jumper with the forestry people. You already know he's a diver, everything from scuba to deep sea, and that's where the *long* muscle counts. I think he did a stint with the navy—"

"He was UDT," Scott said. "Underwater demolition team. They don't come any better."

"There's something else," Kim said, digging into memory. She snapped her fingers. "Of course. We'd talked about it. He did a special job with oil drilling rigs off the Venezuelan coast. Something about our government loaning him out for that."

"Very good," Massey said, then waited.

"Well, he's a geologist. I think he went into that because he likes to climb mountains. Loves the risk. He nearly got killed climbing down into Mt. Shasta when it was active. I know he got scalded pretty bad. He thought it was great fun. He's a maniac when it comes to that."

"You'd never expect it but he's also a gun nut," Scott interjected. "No, I take that back. Not a nut. He's a *pro*. Of course. He's won Olympic competitions in shooting. Has a hell of a collection. He's an expert in just about everything, *including* longbows and crossbows, blowguns; all kinds of weapons."

"And he hates the military," Kim said. "There's more than one dichotomy in that man. He *was* military, one of the best, and he's so against capital punishment and war and killing he's almost paranoid on the subject."

"You find that a fault? Or a problem?" Massey asked.

"I would," Kim said slowly, "except for the fact that he explained it to me once. He also has a collection of small predatory creatures. Wasps, killer bees, scorpions, beetles, centipedes, those kind of killers. He told me that nature equips all creatures for survival in the best possible way, but right alongside the venomous spiders and snakes he has a collection of the most beautiful butterflies I've ever seen. He likes to blow people's minds with that. He points out that they can't kill *anything* and they've outlasted, as a species, most of the predatory and killing creatures that nature has wiped out."

"Sounds like he *thinks*," Massey observed.

"Yeah, but don't be fooled by that," Scott threw in. "If he *has* to, he can be damned dangerous." He looked at Kim. "Did you know he was once mugged? In Detroit. He was alone, God knows doing what, in one of the worst parts of town at night, and a whole bunch of animals came down on him."

"W-what happened?"

"There were about ten of them. When it was all over the police reported a gang fight, there were so many bodies scattered on the streets. They came after Blake with knives and clubs, and *he* had a steel—I don't know what you call it, but think of a steel whip, like a car radio antenna, but much stronger than that. He went straight *for them*. It sounded like the singing sword right out of King Arthur. He cut them to ribbons. Didn't kill anyone but they ended up looking like hamburger. A few of them got to Stan, you know, hands on. He broke a bunch of arms and legs."

"Was he hurt?" Massey asked.

"I don't see how he couldn't be, but there wasn't any record of medical treatment," Scott said.

"All right. I'll add the finishing touches. Blake is a team player. If he was a lone wolf he wouldn't be any good to us. He's paramedic, speaks Oriental languages, including Japanese, Chinese, Arab, Russian, perhaps some more. Totally loyal. He's also in the same category as you two. Part of a team on special assignment but without knowing exactly what. You three will make up your own team." He held up a hand. "Later, later. The details come later. I'm surprised that neither of you mentioned one other thing about Blake."

Kim blinked. "I thought we had it all."

"Almost all." Massey's face was deadpan. "You're both white. Good old Caucasian. Even the Venezuelan in Kim, which is part Indian, only makes her lovelier. Neither one of you has said a word about Stan Blake being, well, maybe the best word is mongrel. His grandfather is as black as they come and his grandmother was Chinese. His father is a big ugly brute, and, like these things often go, his mother is Cherokee Indian."

"So?" Scott said.

"That's all? Just . . . *so*?"

"What's the difference what he is? Racially, I mean," Kim added. "I'd never have known any of these things if you didn't tell us. He has Caucasian features, but his skin color is, well, I think of Hawaiian or Polynesian. If anything he's got a permanent light tan."

"Except for his eyes," Scott added. "Black as black can be. When the light catches them just right, they gleam."

Massey smiled. "Time to get down to cases. I'm on the record now. Are you willing to take the job I've told you almost nothing about except that you may get killed? Or even worse?"

"You know our terms, sir," Scott said. "We're not in the covert operations business, this CIA crap."

"Understood and accepted. *On my part*," Massey said immediately. "One more thing. The job is for the United States *and* for the Venezuelans."

"A group? Individuals? For the country?" Kim shot back.

"You mean Venezuela? For the country. Equal loyalty. No divided feelings. No dichotomy of commitment."

"Does it have something to do with what we saw and heard tonight?" Scott asked.

"I didn't hear that question," Massey said. A smile flickered and vanished. "Yet," he appended. "Now, if you go for this little adventure you report to me. Got that? *To me*. No one else and I'll want your sworn oath on that."

"Whoa, sir," Scott said, holding up his hands, palms out. "You know we're on that Watchdog program for

Senator Elias. *He's* got our word. *He* decides what we do."

"And if the old warhorse okays my terms and tells you to shift to the side and work directly for me?"

Kim Seavers and Morgan Scott exchanged a long glance. Kim shrugged and nodded. "If the senator gives the green light," he said finally, "we're yours."

Massey looked up, ignoring the response. "Aha! A final round of drinks on their way." He rose to his feet. "Stay here. Will you excuse me? Nature calls an old body. I'll be just a moment."

"Yes, sir," Scott said. "Should I, ah, sign for the drinks?"

Massey chuckled as he walked away. "No one *ever* signs *anything* in here, son."

In the men's room Caleb Massey stood before a locked toilet stall, a door that went from floor to seven feet above the floor. It had a number 8 in brass at eye level. Massey slid the brass plate aside to reveal a lens and a telephone-style combination dial face. He tapped in a code and stared with his right eye into the lens. A dim blue light glowed, he heard compressed air hiss, and the door opened. He entered the toilet stall, closed the door behind him, sealed it with compressed air and a steel bolt. A bright light came on through the walls.

Massey sat on a comfortable padded seat and placed his palm against the wall. He barely heard the tinkling tones of a computer system, then the section of wall to his right glowed with faint lettering: SECURE. Another panel in the wall opened. Massey reached within the space to remove a featherweight oxygen mask linked by wire to two featherweight earmuffs. He donned the equipment, withdrew a credit-card-sized computer from an ankle wallet, tapped in a coded number and then the word READY appeared in place of SECURE.

Massey spoke easily into the "oxygen mask" that not only muffled his voice but scrambled all acoustical patterns within the stall.

"Well, Caleb, how did it go?" he heard.

"You free?"

"Hell no, you old bastard, I still charge," Senator Patrick Xavier Elias growled into Massey's micro headsets. "Hold your water."

"Got it," Massey said. In his mind's eye he saw the senator seated in a comfortable lounge chair in robe and slippers, his huge Rottweiler, Ajax, by his side. City lights would be showing through polarized steel-tempered glass. Massey knew the routine Elias was following, tapping in codes on his chair armrest, initiating an acoustic scrambler that brought a deep growl from the dog due to the sonics. Finally the chair itself, a marvel of microminiaturization with contacts in a dozen other cities, would sound a chime and a woman's voice would say softly, "Cleared and secure, Senator."

Massey heard the next words from Elias. "We're clean, Caleb. Let's have it."

"I have Seavers and Scott with me."

"I figured you wouldn't waste any time."

"They're ready. But they won't move an inch until you transfer them to me."

"Tomorrow."

"Good," Massey said. "There isn't any time to waste. They've had a bad setback down in Venezuela, but that McDavid fellow has a tight grip on their problem."

"He's working with us?"

"He's working with us for the good of Venezuela."

"Even better."

"I want our own team in BEMAC. Scott, Seavers and Blake for starters. Mercedes already has some opposite numbers in the pipeline and in full testing."

He could almost feel Elias stiffening. "Live transmission?"

"Yes."

"God *damn!*"

"Incomplete, Pat. Foulup on the receiving end. At least one dead, maybe more."

"You said McDavid had a handle on it?"

"Yes. He knows we're the answer to their problem."

"You keep beating around the bush, goddamn you.

Do you tell me how far they are? What results I can expect?"

"You know more than you should already."

"The devil you say! If I don't know, I can't handle the appropriations and—"

"Jesus, cut me some slack, Pat," Massey broke in. "I sure as hell don't want Mancini tumbling to what's going on. You having reservations about trusting my end?"

"*No*. I don't question your judgement or you. But the whole thing seems so incredible, beyond all possibility—"

"*That's enough, Patrick.*"

He heard Elias take a deep breath. "All right, Caleb. Back to reality. From what I have been told, and with accuracy, we can expect the Russians to do their best to get into this thing as soon as they can."

"Oh, they'll try. I'd be sorely disappointed if they didn't."

"Caleb, watch what toes you step on."

"Toes, hell, I'm going to bust their kneecaps."

"Those days are gone, Caleb."

"The hell they are, Senator."

"Caleb, you can't just—"

"*No*. Don't even try to stop me, old friend." Massey's voice was that of a stranger from a dim past when Pat Elias and Caleb Massey had been the finest killers in a Green Beret team. *But that was so long ago! The world was different now*— Massey's voice sliced through brain tissue like a burning scalpel.

"Listen and listen good, Pat," he went on. "I'll bet my right arm to a stale doughnut that Ludendorff will be right in the thick of this."

"Ernst Ludendorff?"

"The one and the same. Our old buddy from the cloak and dagger days."

"He's German—"

"I know what the hell he is," Massey said with sudden impatience. "I also know he's been on the KGB lead team from square one. He's their best. And it's smart for them to use a German. *Any* edge is a good edge."

"All right." Elias spoke with sudden resignation, and Massey sensed he could feel an overwhelming tiredness in his old friend. Time to prime the old fire a bit.

"Senator," Massey spoke with a lift to his voice, "you consider me a pretty smart fellow?"

Elias offered a welcome laugh. "Come on, Caleb, what is this? Show and tell? You know what you are. You're a damned genius."

"Calling me names won't get you anywhere," Massey said lightly and then added a touch more seriousness to his voice. "Old man, you'll understand all this better when I tell you that compared to Vasco de Gama, who's like a reincarnation of Michelangelo, and he's their *primo* on their project, I'm just a kid in sixth grade."

"Is he your, ah, opposite number?"

"Uh-uh. Like most real geniuses he can't pour piss out of a boot without a roadmap. My man is Phil Mercedes."

"I know him. Razor sharp. Born leader."

"You got it. He's also an experienced military man *and* he's a realist. Most important is that he trusts me and I absolutely trust him." Massey glanced at his watch. "Senator, I'm running short on time."

"All right, Caleb, I'll back you all the way. Just a few moments more. What's the code name?"

"Dragonfly."

Elias laughed. "My secretary's phantom pet. Excellent. Who's the contact?"

"Luis Espinoza."

"The general? For Christ's sake, Caleb, he's been a thorn in our side for years!"

"Great actor, isn't he." Statement; not a question.

Elias chuckled. "Good night, Caleb."

"Night, Buster Brown."

Massey cut the connection, punched in a series of code numbers, waited briefly, then spoke. "Luis? Dragonfly here."

*   *   *

Massey returned to the alcove where Seavers and Scott waited for him. Kim held up his drink. "It's getting cold," she said, smiling.

He took a sip and held out the glass. "Your good wishes, and a successful trip."

Scott exchanged a questioning glance with Kim. "Uh, what about—"

"Check with the senator in your usual way," Massey said quickly.

"Where to, sir?" Kim asked, leaving no question that she knew Massey had taken care of their affairs with Senator Elias.

"You leave in the morning for Caracas. I suggest you find Stan Blake, fill him in, and you all make your flight on time. Your tickets will be waiting for you at the Eastern counter at Dulles. First class, I might add."

"Anything else, sir?" Scott asked.

"Yes. Why are you still here?"

Chapter VIII

"We are in great luck," the pilot said with a sense of excitement to the other three men in the pressurized cockpit of the powerful Yakovlev *Dark Falcon*. Colonel Karl Nikolaiev turned to look at his copilot. Colonel Leon Semyonov nodded his agreement and smiled. The heavy pressurized helmet atop his suit didn't move, but Nikolaiev saw his head bob in the glowing lights reflected from the instrument panel.

"Comrade Colonel, I have never seen such clear skies before in this area." A sense of quiet excitement came through in the words of Major Edward Naumov, radar specialist and electronics officer of the great-winged machine cruising eighty thousand feet over the darkened heartland of Venezuela. Displayed before them was an incredible sight. Caracas and the eastern coastline of the country lay far below as glowing and sparkling jewels. The Maracaibo oilfields had been a great area of pitch darkness punctuated with tiny flickering lights and then sudden gushes of flame as towers burned off the excess pressure of upthrusting gas and oil. Then they swept onward to swamp interior and turned their eyes from the earth to the majestic lift of the Andes far ahead. They were getting first light from a moon low on the horizon and the mountains seemed to float magically. But they were approaching swiftly their designated target area.

"Naumov," the pilot called through his helmet system, "is our course steady?"

Major Naumov shared the aft portion of the cockpit with Lt. Colonel Evgeny Evtushenko, their specialist in their elaborate camera and reconnaissance systems, and a mass of heavy equipment. They were two figures in pressure suits within a surrounding cocoon of elaborate instruments and equipment. "On course, sir." He studied the glowing scope target grid overlaid on a computer graphic of the land below. Everything was visible with a glance. "We will be in position to commence camera and recorders in exactly nine minutes, sir."

The pilot spoke again. "Evtushenko?"

"All is in readiness, Colonel. The equipment has been confirmed." He fell silent for a moment. "Colonel, there must be something very big going on down there. I am already getting indications of intense radiation in the infrared."

Nikolaiev pondered their situation and made a sudden decision. "Evgeny, start all recorders and cameras three minutes earlier than we planned. It would be stupid to miss any peripheral activity or installations because of a flight plan that idiot Platinov dreamed up."

Semyonov laughed. "Has that fat cow ever actually flown a mission?"

"Not in *my* machine," Nikolaiev said with a grim tone to his voice. "He farts. That man farts awake or asleep; it doesn't matter where he is. *Braaap, braaap!* I don't believe even a pressure suit would protect us. We would gag and it would take a month to fumigate the machine!"

The men laughed with him and Naumov's voice broke the laughter. "Two minutes to target run, Colonel."

They were suddenly all business, total professionals. "Very good. Everybody on their toes," Nikolaiev ordered.

"One minute," Naumov said.

"Ready," Evtushenko added.

"Colonel!" Semyonov said sharply. "I have a visual dead ahead!"

"Start everything rolling!" Nikolaiev commanded.

"Camera on, recorders on, radiation systems on," Evtushenko snapped.

"Can you see what it is?" Naumov asked.

"It is . . . a circle, a circle of lights," the copilot said slowly. "I don't understand . . . from this altitude, to see the circle itself so clearly . . . the thing must be enormous!"

Nikolaiev leaned forward. He saw the—whatever it was. A circle of light, the lights flashing around and around, a glowing disc of tremendous power output. "Damn you, Evgeny, is everything working?"

"Yes, sir, Comrade Colonel. Everything is working perfectly. We have full radar sweep, infrared photography . . . the scanners show the object clearly and— *it's disappeared.*"

"Over there!" Colonel Semyonov said in a half-shout. "I can't believe it! It's covered miles in just a few seconds!"

Nikolaiev saw it. "It's gone . . . no! There it is again. It must be very low, moving behind the tops of those mesas down there. Naumov, what distance to Angel Falls?"

"Sir, seven miles."

"There! It's going like crazy," Semyonov added. "I can see the colors now . . . they whip around and that machine, it is a huge disc . . ." His voice fell away as he realized what he was saying.

"A *disc*? Are you sure?" That from Naumov.

"I see it, the colonel sees it—Evgeny, do you confirm the shape on your instruments?"

"Yes, sir. A disc. It is moving, I mean, the instruments show it moves at better than three thousand miles an hour."

Nikolaiev laughed harshly. "In low atmosphere? Just above the ground? Impossible!"

Evtushenko spoke carefully. "Comrade Colonel, may I suggest you tell our instruments it is impossible?"

Nikolaiev did not answer for a moment. "I hope," he said finally to his reconnaissance officer, "that your instruments record accurately what our eyes tell us. Because if we return with only a verbal report of what we have seen we will all be in the psychiatric ward ten minutes after we land."

*   *   *

Captain Jesús Gomez stood in the back of an amphibious truck, a severely modified DUKW developed by the Americans for wallowing through ocean water, then rolling up onto beaches and lurching a path across swamps, grasslands or old roads. Jesús Gomez had been driving this particular DUKW for many years through the downcountry rivers and grasslands of Venezuela. At this moment, wearing army fatigues with a bright lightning-bolt insignia on his upper left arm, he also wore a huge grin. Ah, what a marvelous night, he thought. The stars were in their best form, splashing the sky from one horizon to the other, and the moon, a thick yellow orb crawling up over the mesa-silhouetted horizon, began slowly to add light to the shadowed earth. Gomez took a deep, invigorating breath. He loved the night, he loved the air, this marvelous country, he heard the roar of nearby rushing river and thundering falls as deep and rich music. But the grin was for a great winged machine, so high as to be hopelessly out of human sight, yet pinioned neatly on the gleaming surface of a radar scope. What a wonderful machine that could soar invisibly so many miles above the earth, faster than the bullet from a pistol, looking down on the earth from the heights of gods.

The grin remained as Gomez thought of the humans, not gods, in that machine his electronic systems tracked so faithfully. Humans of rigid thought whose technical competency could be reduced to startled imagination. A voice called out from the dim yellow night.

"Jesús! Have they taken the bait?"

Gomez looked out from the truck bed, barely able to see the silhouetted forms of Jungle Rudy and his daughter, Hilda. Beyond the two figures a huge helicopter hunched to the earth, enormous rotor blades hanging like the wet wings of a mantis. Its crew was within, sleeping.

Gomez waved. "They are good, these Russians," he called back to Jungle Rudy. "They will pass almost directly overhead and then direct to Angel Falls. I think it is time."

"Two minutes, I would say," Jungle Rudy judged from an ancient pocket watch.

"So it is," Gomez confirmed.

The seconds fled. Hilda nudged her father. "I wish I could see something."

"You will." Jungle Rudy pointed to the west. "Keep your eyes in that direction. A little more than a minute now."

Twelve miles west of Gomez, Jungle Rudy and the hulking chained mass of the helicopter, two men prepared to throw a switch. By their side a gasoline-driven generator thumped and *thu-wack*ed noisily in the night. Power at the ready as they counted down. One man called out the final seconds and then nodded. "Make magic," he said, smiling. His companion closed the switch.

Directly before them spread the results of their work earlier in the day. Sections of translucent piping filled with neon and other reactive gases. The piping covered a distance, measured in the greatest diameter, of nearly two hundred feet in roughly the form of a circle. When the switch closed, power flashed from the generator. A superpowerful neon circle exploded silently into existence, its glare lighting up the surrounding countryside. A deep fluttering sprayed back as startled birds dashed into the skies.

"Ah, is it not beautiful?"

"Wonderful! Truly it is magic!"

"Remember, exactly forty seconds and no more."

"Good, good. Only ten seconds to go."

"Power off *now*."

Power off. Retinal afterimages and ghostly swimming in the eyes. But not where the great ring had flashed so brilliantly. Only the barest of deep orange glows, fading swiftly.

"Look! Where Pedro and Maurice have been waiting!"

The two men looked to a low mesa eighteen miles distant across the rivers and the grasslands. Twenty-four seconds after their circular light blacked out another great ring of light burst into existence.

For thirteen seconds. Then darkness.

Nineteen seconds later another ring appeared, and then another, and another.

From eighty thousand feet the enormous fire-lipped disc seemed to race across the river and jungle country at incredible speed.

"Four o'clock, range nine miles, eight thousand feet below and closing fast. Radar confirmation, electronic countermeasures all systems are on. They are sweeping with ground radar and airborne radar." Major Edward Naumov was surprised and—for the instant he permitted this extraneous thought—pleased with his calm and crisp efficiency.

"How many?" Nikolaiev barked.

"In a moment, sir, I can—ah, four targets, Colonel, still closing fast, coming up level at four o'clock."

"Any sign of missiles?"

"No, sir. They have target radar locked on us."

"Decoys out!" Nikolaiev shouted.

Six small missiles spat with dark red flame from the belly of *Dark Falcon.* They whipped sidewards and down, each decoy missile emitting a shrill radar wave and flashing intense heat. If those fighters out there, and they could only be fighters, judged the Russians, the decoys should snare the missiles ranging in on the metal shape and powerful engines of the great reconnaissance machine in which they flew.

"Still closing, sir," Naumov announced.

"Sir, ready to fire homing missiles," Evtushenko said in a flat tone.

"Negative, negative," Nikolaiev said quickly. "We did not come here to fight." He paused a heartbeat as his right hand flicked away a safety cover to an emergency switch. "Prepare yourselves!" he sang out and snapped the switch to ON.

The night sky blossomed with dazzling yellow flame and violet shock waves as two liquid rocket engines exploded behind *Dark Falcon*. Instantly an invisible hand of enormous power pushed the machine through the speed of sound and far beyond, lifting *Dark Falcon* higher, toward the designated escape altitude of better than a hundred thousand feet.

"Missiles coming at us," Naumov announced, an icy hand gripping him as his radar tracked eight missiles accelerating from the still invisible fighters. His infrared scanners seemed to go mad with intense thermal signatures in the cold thin air of their altitude. Naumov felt thumping vibrations as Evtushenko responded to the warning of missiles and launched another brace of decoys.

"Colonel!" Naumov called out, a sweep of relief and laughter clear in his voice. "The decoys . . . the missiles have homed on them!"

Nikolaiev nodded. "We are safe. We will fly due south to Brazil and then to the east. Leon," he queried his copilot, "how long before we can rendezvous with the tanker?"

"Thirty-six minutes, sir."

Nikolaiev glanced at their fuel gauges readout. The glowing numbers pleased him. They had fuel enough to rendezvous with their tanker plus an hour's safety margin.

They would have an interesting tale to relate when they landed back home.

Jungle Rudy, Hilda and Jesús Gomez watched the flowering lights and starbursts expanding so high above them that no sound would reach the ground. Hilda pointed to the lights changing swiftly in colors. "What are they?" she exclaimed.

"Fireworks," Gomez laughed. "All kinds. The four lights you saw almost as a single light? Four of our jet fighters. They also launched missiles."

"You would shoot down an unarmed plane?" Hilda's voice showed concern and shock.

"They are not so unarmed," Jungle Rudy corrected her.

Gomez smiled at Hilda. "Do not worry, golden one,"

he said, using the name to mark her rich blond tresses. "The missiles carry no explosives. But the Russians," he grinned wider, "do not know such things. All those other lights. Decoys from the Russians to lure away our homing pigeons."

"But that sudden explosion—"

Gomez shook his head. He glanced at his radar set. The Russian machine was already beyond the range of his field equipment and he saw the four blips of the F-16's turning back to Venezuelan territory. "A rocket engine," he told Hilda. "A great burst of power to carry the dark machine higher and faster. A dash for safety."

Hilda was honestly confused. "You mean . . . they'll let the Russians get away? Just let them go?"

Gomez removed his headset and lit a cigarette. He leaned on his equipment. "But of course. How else," he asked expansively, "could those people return to Moscow with their pictures?"

"Pictures?"

Rudy gestured. "You saw the lights. The great rings of artificial flame, whirling around and around. From very high, Hilda, the lights are huge discs. The lights of one go out, another flashes to life. Again and again. You know what the Russians saw? A huge flying saucer, racing over the earth."

"And from now on," Gomez added, "the Russians will believe our scientists remain hard at work on a secret project in these hills and grasslands."

Hilda pouted. "They are no fools! I don't believe you can make them believe—"

"No matter what they believe," Gomez broke in. "They'll be confused, they must continue chasing after every ghost, and—"

"Jesús! Enough school!" Jungle Rudy called, waving his arm. "Come with me to the veranda. Hilda, go ahead, please and prepare the table. Jesús, I have wonderful Venezuelan rum and Swiss chocolate and marvelous Jamaican friends my gringo friend sends to me!"

* * *

"You know something?" Nelson Sanchez crouched beneath thick bushes in the heavy growth of the hillside along the mountain road and nudged Tony Pappas by his side.

"What?" Pappas hissed.

"I feel like an idiot doing this."

"All right. Be an idiot, then, but why do you ask *now?*" Pappas didn't turn to Sanchez as they spoke. He had his eyes set toward a military airport, aglow and flashing with the lights usually filling the darkness at such a time.

"Because we're whispering," Sanchez said. "Whispering, like idiots in a grade B movie or something."

Pappas turned finally, a strained look on his face. "Damn me if you're not right," he said with a voice raising from the whisper to normal volume. Pappas laughed. "Here we are, trying not to be heard from that airport, and they have jet engines howling and trucks running up and down the place—" He straightened from his crouch in the underbrush of the hillside. Between the two men stood a heavy tripod with a powerful long lens, and attached to the eyepiece section was a camera through which they studied airport activity with tremendous magnification. He turned to his left. Parked well off the road in the only level spot for hundreds of feet was their news van with MONITOR NACIONAL TELEVISION emblazoned on its sides. *How could we be so stupid as not to at least cover over that sign?* Pappas grumbled in self-criticism. *We might as well advertise . . .*

Against the night glow and starfield, and a low moon, he made out the figure of Angela standing atop the van, powerful binoculars to her eyes. *Even in the darkness she is beautiful,* Pappas mused. *That body—*

Her voice cut short his pleasant thoughts. "Quickly!" she said in a hoarse whisper. "They're coming in!"

Pappas nearly burst into laughter. All this skulking about on a hillside overlooking the Caracas environs. Nels was right. A cheap movie scene. But Sanchez listened instead of wondered.

"We're ready," he said, patting the camera. "Give me a position, Angie."

"There," she said, pointing. "To your left. I see four of them."

Sanchez adjusted his sights. He waved with one hand. "All right. I have them. I'm shooting now."

Far off across the countryside, landing lights wavering like great yellow eyes in the night, four jet fighters flared gently to the long runway and began their roll on the concrete. They taxied toward the end hangar on the flight line, where perhaps a dozen cars and trucks awaited them.

Angela Tirado climbed down the van ladder to join Pappas and Sanchez. "You have the pictures?"

Sanchez nodded. "A full roll. I've already changed film. But why are we taking pictures of airplanes landing in the night? What can we possibly do with them? They're so far away—"

Tirado half-turned to Pappas. "Four of those fighters, Tony. The best we have," she spoke quickly. She flashed a look of having bagged a difficult quarry. "Where *were* they? What were they *doing?* It's the middle of the night. There's no reason for them to—"

Pappas sighed. The world between military and civilian is huge, he thought quickly. "Angie, they could be doing *anything*." He shrugged. "Hell, I'm not carrying a crystal ball, woman. They could be on night maneuvers. Night formation training. An intercept of a bogey, something unidentified. *Anything*."

"Oh, come on, Tony!" she half shouted, one arm gesturing wildly in the direction of the military field. "You're a captain in our air force, remember? You don't need to *guess!* You of all people would *know*."

"Dammit, Angie, I don't know from crap!" he said with sudden impatience. "I'll tell you what I *do* know. Right now I'm freezing my ass off on a mountainside *with you*, taking stupid pictures of airplanes miles away from us, airplanes that fly at night all the damn time, *and I don't know why*."

"He's right, Angie," Sanchez joined in. "I'm turning

blue up here. So why don't you tell us what's going on?"

Tirado studied both men, but she kept her gaze leveled on Pappas. She spoke with deliberate patience. "You heard the reports of large Russian aircraft off our coast, earlier today?"

"Yes." He kept his expression blank.

"And now we have jet fighters all over the place, right?"

"We have fighters airborne," he admitted.

"And you don't connect the two?" Her eyes widened. "Tony, you swore you'd always level with me—"

"I *am*," he broke in quickly. "First, we've had large Russian aircraft off our coast for years. Their Bear turboprops; hell, they run up and down the east coast of South *and* North America. Those damn things can fly twelve thousand miles nonstop. And the Backfires from Cuba; what I'm trying to tell you, Angie, is that there's nothing unusual in Russian planes along the coastline."

"Nothing unusual in our fighters being up at the same time?"

"What's so unusual?" He shrugged. "Half the time we intercept them. The Americans intercept them, the Brazilians intercept them. We take pictures of them and they take pictures of us. Damn, woman, you're taking a lot for granted—"

"The hell I am," she snapped. "All right, Tony, you play your little game of see-nothing, know-nothing."

"Angie, please—"

"Load up, you two!" she said angrily. "Get the gear in the van. Move, move!"

Sanchez shouldered the heavy tripod while Pappas grabbed their battery packs and they started for the van. "Where are we going in such a hurry?" Sanchez called after the woman. "You said yourself it's the middle of the night!"

She stopped, offering a withering look over her shoulder. "We're going to the airport."

"*Which* airport?" Sanchez pressed, baffled.

"The commercial field, of course."

"But *why?*" Pappas added to Sanchez's queries.

"There's a commercial flight coming in from Europe in just about," she paused, glancing at her watch, "two hours from now. That plane is carrying Russian technicians and special agents. As tourists, of course," she added acidly. "And I want pictures of them. Good, clear pictures *and* video."

Pappas turned in resignation to Sanchez. "Doesn't this crazy woman *ever* know when to quit chasing ghosts?"

Sanchez shrugged. "Maybe *she's* got a crystal ball. Who knows? Let's go. *Anywhere* where it's warm."

General Luis Espinoza sat in the right seat of the jeep, nightpower binoculars to his eyes. He saw the two men and the woman and their van in a clear green light. "They're going back to their van," the general said to Major Raymond Velasquez at his side. He lowered the glasses and afforded himself the luxury of a thin smile.

"Raymond, that woman takes to the bait like a shark after a swimmer in the ocean," the general said. "I admire her. She has great spirit." He laughed suddenly. "And she has no sense. We kept her under arrest and threatened her and it all amounts to nothing. She smells a story and like the true professional, for her," he shrugged, "the hunt is on."

"Sir, you mean—"

"Yes, of course we set this up." Espinoza watched as the van lights came on and the sound of the engine starting carried thinly across the night. "We made certain she heard that unusual events were going on. The Russian planes. The Americans who act so mysteriously. And those so-called Russian tourists. Everything is *real*. It is not always precisely what it seems to be, but it is real. She is a true hunter, that Tirado. She does exactly what we wish her to do. Pursue the quarry. No wonder she is so good a reporter."

Velasquez nodded slowly. He had the general's full

trust. "Sir, does she know," he asked slowly, "about the
. . . project?"

Espinoza shook his head. "Not yet, not yet. There is
more bait to be scattered. We must let her learn more,
draw her willingly into the web. She is brilliant and we
have needs for her special talents. Soon, soon."

Espinoza pointed. "There. Those lights. One of ours.
We could follow her, but why bother? She goes exactly
where we wish her to go."

Chapter IX

"The Walls of Jericho, *circa Anytime Today.*" Felipe Mercedes spoke as much to some inner meeting within his own mind as to his scientists and technicians gathered in the claustrophobic security-paranoid entrance cubicle to the secret facility beneath the mountains that rose high above distant Caracas. Mercedes lifted one hand in a casual gesture that evinced a strange sense of power about himself and his group. His timing brought nervous laughs from those about him as loudspeakers from all four walls came to life.

"CLEAR THE DOORS. CLEAR THE DOORS." Mechanical voices tinged with overtones of doom bounced off wincing ears. "STAND CLEAR. STAND CLEAR. THE DOORS ARE OPENING. THE DOORS ARE OPENING."

Stupid machine-voice, Mercedes thought, grimacing. *I've got to get rid of that idiot voice box, get a woman's soft voice in here.* His thoughts reflected good sense. Most military services throughout the world had learned to their astonishment that a warning of imminent danger in an aircraft, or in a reactor system such as that in which Mercedes now stood, announced in a woman's soft voice brought swifter response than all the bells and whistles ever invented.

Then he cut short his own thoughts. The surface beneath their feet rumbled and the air shimmered from deep vibrations as infrasound spilled and tossed dust into the air about them. The thick concrete under their shoes rumbled with faint memories of earthquakes past as the steel wall split down its middle and groaned ponderously to each side, a magical separation on recessed tracks beneath and huge concealed hook rollers above. The doors thudded to a stop, sending more vibrations of low-frequency sounds into and through their bodies. For the moment they ignored the discomfort and failed even to step forward through the freedom of the now-open security walls.

Before them spread an incredible scientific Disney World. But no fantasy here except for the horizons never before crossed. Immersed as they had been with their laser program, embroiled with problems and success and failure, hopeful as they might be for their dazzling new craft, they were struck dumb with the sight their eyes struggled to take in. Lights and colors and sounds assailed them in a heady blast of science awhirl and blinding.

They moved forward slowly, a cluster of awestruck children shuffling into the new light. Except for Betancourt and Rivero, already accustomed to this new fantasy of scientific facilities and opportunity, they gawked and stared open-mouthed, half stumbling over their own feet. Here now was the dream come true.

Great laser-beam generators in long rows. Thick cabling, instrument panels everywhere, computer consoles glowing and spattering bright flecks of light, everything shiny and new and gleaming. The work crews in cleansuit coveralls, the walls and equipment marked and numbered properly. Judith Morillo moved aside from the group, staring about and upward as a devoted child's first visit to a soaring cathedral. "I can . . . I can hardly believe this," she spoke to them all, her eyes still drinking in the wonder about her. "It is like a church. It *is* a church!" she added with a sudden cry of triumph for what they had been given. Her eyes fixed on glowing letters spread along a curving wall, a sign of pride created at Mercedes' insistence, a reminder not needed, but treasured.

BIOELECTROMAGNETIC MANNED MATERIALS TEST COMPLEX.

"BEMAC," she breathed aloud, the word hallowed to her.

Dr. Mercedes and Vasco de Gama brushed by her. "No time for being dumbstruck right now," Mercedes said, not unkindly. "We don't slow up our work in here even if angels appear in our midst." Morillo hurried to catch up with the others sweeping along behind the scientists and a booming voice fell amongst them. Loudspeakers about the great domed center; Morillo was startled. She had looked at so many specific *things* in her first exposure to BEMAC she had failed to realize that what soared overhead was the upper center of a great domed structure.

"THE DOORS ARE CLOSING. THE DOORS ARE CLOSING. PLEASE STAND CLEAR. PLEASE STAND CLEAR. FIVE SECONDS, FIVE, FOUR, THREE, TWO—" The warning bell clamored. "—ONE, CLOSING."

The massive *thud* announced the dome experimental area closed off from the outside world. "Your attention, please," the voice of loudspeakers came to them. "All new arrivals please report to the safety viewing room to the left and above the entrance. The flashing yellow lights along the floor will direct you to this area. Please move into the viewing room as quickly as possible. Your assignments will be discussed with you following this next test. Thank you for your cooperation."

The new voice galvanized them to action. They moved quickly along the line of flashing yellow lights imbedded within the floor. As soon as they were within the room a technician counted off their number, spoke into a lip mike from his plastic helmet, nodded, and sealed the entrance door through which they had just filed. They all found places before a thick, wide viewing glass. As much as they wanted to voice their reactions and emotions, the urge to see as much as possible took precedence, and a rare silence bound them tightly together.

An electronic chime sounded and another voice came through the loudspeakers. There could be no mistake; whoever spoke now was long accustomed to obedience at such moments as the final count to a test. They listened to the test announcer, who remained invisible to them.

"Attention, attention, please," the voice called out with a smoothness surprising in a mechanical device. "Clear the central area. Clear the central area immediately. We are now T minus four minutes for a laser beam mirror test. T minus four minutes for a laser beam mirror test. Goggles will not be required—"

Morillo turned to Mercedes. "That's a surprise," she said, ignoring the loudspeaker. She gestured beyond the glass enclosure. "All that power out there, Doctor," she went on. "I recognize the generators and power systems and they're far greater than anything we've used before. Now we don't need goggles?"

Mercedes took her arm and moved closer to the window, a gesture and feeling of closeness he rarely showed, and even more rarely displayed so openly. "Judy, everything here will be a surprise. Everything here is well advanced over the equipment we used downcountry. It is the same equipment, in a way," he smiled, "only much, much improved. We don't need the protective goggles because with the test coming up we'll be tweaking down the beam intensity and—"

She stared at Mercedes with an urge to openly, even brazenly, disbelieve him. What he had just told her violated all the rules she knew governing the VHP, or very-high-power, lasers. "You're going to *tweak* one of the main BEMAC lasers?" Try as she might she couldn't accept his words.

Instead of a specific reply he nodded and smiled. "That's correct, Judy. I told you everything would be a surprise." He gestured beyond the viewing window. "Enough for now. Watch."

What poised there captured Judith Morillo, as well as the others. Their facial expressions glowed with expectancy and apprehension. Even as they waited they devoured the sorcery about them; even standing still they could sense and judge the enormity and complexity of the BEMAC installation beneath the steeply sloping mountain. The sense of grandeur and enormous power filled them all. Directly beneath the central peaking dome of the geodesic structure was the transmission heart and soul of everything they had done. And in every direction there snaked thick power cables, huge transformers, measuring devices, computers, instruments and gauges, control and display panels, high-up glassed-in control stations. Here before them was their new world of great curving mirrors and flat mirrors, mirrors of glass and steel and alloys, curved and concave and convex, and of a wild array of hues. Before them loomed and spread the magician's brew of laser fantasy, and even as they tried to absorb the wonder they felt the first great surge of power deep beneath their feet and literally quivering in the dust motes of air about them.

"Look! The dome! Straight up . . . it's opening!" No one recognized the voice but all eyes lifted to watch the curved geodesic ceiling split down its middle with its two halves sliding back and down. Each slid away a distance of twenty feet from where they had joined. The darkness of night hung like a thick mantle above.

"Fifteen seconds." The chant of the laser guru.

Lights dimmed, power surged, deep and mighty sounds rose about them, rattled molecules and tortured metal and wood and glass. Teeth grated painfully. Judith Morillo, unthinking, snatched at the arm of Ali Bolivar. The last seconds fell away.

Everything happened at once. Everything began and came together and started to end at the same instant. Gasps and unbidden shrieks from the watching group met the stabbing appearance, the burst into existence, of a faint blue-green light that faster than the eye could follow appeared to bathe everything within sight. The ghostly blue luminescence appeared, flickered, vanished. It was but the opening cry of light. Instantly behind the fleeing blue, sound tore against the viewing window, an explosive and sudden *CRAAAACK!* that one might hear from a frighteningly close blast of lightning. Tearing against the window as if seeking out the stunned group within came a pulse, a single instant wash of deep red, the hue of fresh blood; like the ghostly blue it exploded silently into being and was gone, leaving behind glaring retinal afterimages the eyes chased futiley.

These were but the opening sights and sounds of the full orchestration of power. Did anyone ever hear the cry of a wounded dinosaur in full pain? It could have been much what struck the BEMAC assembly, a shriek of raw energy, naked and stabbing tearing at the ears and the eyes and the brain and sending trillions of molecules dancing and vibrating, and before it was possible fully to comprehend this infernal sound there *appeared*, one instant not there and the next in full howling life, a green-glowing laser beam, fully fifteen feet across its perfect cylindrical shape, easily as measurable as a great rod of steel of the same diameter. Still they stared wide-eyed, issuing gasps and little cries of astonishment as they sought the origin of the terrible-wonderful light, and found it far to their right in the form of a great cannon, jammed with studs and bolts to steel flooring, festooned with cables and controls. It was all too much to follow in sequence as it happened; they caught mass impact and bits and pieces, lights and garish impressions; they struggled between sound and glare, and not until later when they saw slow-motion video of the event would they see that the light flashed outward from the cannon, exploded eerily from the faces of mirrors assembled in chain-reaction reflections on the opposite side of the geodesic dome and, still retaining its shape of glowing green steel, the beam raced with the speed of light, instantaneous to the human eye and its interpreting brain, about the mirrors and then fled almost vertically through the aperture straight above them, to rush off into the unsuspecting night.

Another cry of energy: deeper, a bass thunder from a kettle drum a thousand feet across struck with a stick the size of a sequoia. The laser snapped into memory. *It is there; it is not there.* The fastest rendition of those words was incredibly turgid movement compared to the lifespan of the massive laser beam. Had anyone among them ever tried to describe the sound, a sonic cry they'd never heard before, they would have deferred to the pilot among them, Ali Bolivar. "I imagine," he said later, "the guy wire from a telephone pole, one of those thick and very strong wires to hold the pole upright. If you strike them they give off a marvelous sound, a *twang!* that sounds like a zap gun in a science fiction movie. Now imagine a giant hand reaches down and pulls that wire, like the string of a bow, and lets it free in a sudden movement. It was like a thousand such cables going *TWANG!* all at the same instant. My bones felt like jelly!"

Light remained as a retinal imprint and memory, sound remained as jarred tissues and painful memory. Mercedes turned to Judith Morillo, now literally clinging for support to Bolivar's arm. Her cheeks were damp with tears and her eyes still wide with awe; Bolivar himself appeared thunderstruck with the speed and fury of what they'd seen and heard. Mercedes held the eyes of Vasco de Gama, who looked back with pure joy on his face.

De Gama laughed suddenly. "A tunnel! He has been talking all this time to me of a tunnel!" He threw his arms wide. "There is no tunnel . . . instead," he reached out his hand to touch the shoulder of Mercedes, "I find myself in a palace of the future!"

They threw their arms about one another, pounding shoulders, as the men and women about them, swept up in the fierce intensity and emotions, cheered and applauded.

Finally Mercedes stepped back. "Thank you," he said to the group. "And now, my friends, it is time to learn your new equipment, your new stations, and then," he added with a sweeping flourish, "I will work you harder than you ever worked in your lives."

Bolivar laughed. "Doctor, you make me feel like one of the maintenance workers at Disney World."

Few Americans ever took Roger Delgado seriously. As a scientist, that is. He didn't look like a scientist. In the midst of his fellow scientists he looked like a half-witted athlete who'd lost his way on the running track behind the BEMAC administration building. The simile fit well, for Delgado *was* a powerful athlete with wavy hair, tanned skin and a shining smile. He looked more gigolo than intellectual.

"He's the perfect man to work with the Americans on their SDI program," Felipe Mercedes long before had explained to General Luis Espinoza. "It's an exchange program which is something that still has the Americans perplexed. After all, what has Venezuela to offer for so vast and stupendous a scientific program?" Mercedes laughed at his own rhetorical sarcasm. "Only brains. Brains, intellect, accomplishment; that is all. The Americans know that Roger has something they want, but they're not certain what it is. So they will humor him and entertain him and try to woo him like a horny farmer chasing his sheep when no one is looking. Wonderful! Roger will be invited to play tennis and he is a championship competitor. They will offer him swimming pools when they have forgotten he has won Olympic swimming medals for us in the past. When he runs riot over their physical challenges they will turn to philosophy and chess, and Roger Delgado, I remind you, Luis, has met the Russians head-on across the chess boards and baffled *them*. Then they will try to charm his wife who is already a charmer of stunning beauty; she is our Venezuelan equal of Grace Kelly, and *she* will charm the wives of the Americans. Finally, after all this nonsense, what the Americans call so much folderol, they will get down to serious business."

And so it went. As Dr. Delgado moved into the stratospheric elements of the American SDI program he was permitted to share the problems still beyond the solutions the Americans sought so desperately. This was no magic carpet trip. "I lack what you seek, at least in specific terms," he told the Americans. "But we have come much further than you know in laser development. Do you know the name of Vasco de Gama? Ah, but you should, and I promise that *you will*. I see by your faces you are all from your state of Missouri. Very well, we will show you."

First there was the crystal, grown in laboratory con-

ditions under enormous pressure to more than a foot in
diameter. Crystal like none other, faceted intricately,
imbued with the quality of splitting coherent light beams
with absolute precision. "That is but a beginning and
only a part of the system," Delgado added, and displayed a complete test device. "When we add free-
electron laser pulsing to the crystal, beaming through
the crystal and emerging with many laser streams embedded within what *appears* a single laser beam, and
we *then* scatter the beams through reflection back to a
single point, then, gentlemen, we make the quantum
jump—"

Why the electron—no; the free-electron laser? "Vasco
de Gama years ago worked with microwave tubes,"
Delgado explained. "They produce incredible streams
of electrons that behave as coherently as the light does
in the laser. When de Gama further developed his
equipment he was able to create microwave tube streams
in variable energy levels. Then he went beyond anything we had ever heard of. His microwave tubes produced a *laser-styled visible light*. We all thought he was
crazy. Produce a powerful electron beam that works at
microwave *and* laser frequencies? Impossible!"

It seemed so. The average run-of-the-mill advanced
laboratory laser works like a pump. You take electrons
in a lasing medium—a high-energy particle soup, so to
speak—and kick hell out of them. What you're really
doing is accelerating electrons as they orbit their atomic
nucleus. Kick them hard enough and they begin to spin
in wider and wider orbits about that nucleus. When
you stop kicking, the electron drops back to its original
orbit. But it has more energy than it had before and to
become stable again in its orbit it has to release that
energy.

In the laser world, decay is a wonderful word, for as
the electron decays back to its original orbit *it hurls off
light*. It's possible to work with that light as particles, as
photons. And every photon that's whipped away from
the atomic nucleus has the marvelous ability to whip
out yet another photon. The net result is that the

energy level and the stream of photons goes up astronomically.

Next comes the equipment and the system to take all those photons and make something bigger, better, brighter, stronger and more of a tool than plain old light. The system that permits a freed photon to create yet another photon as it scoots from its old neighborhood of the atomic nucleus produces a veritable storm of particles of light. They're controlled, squeezed, pumped by electrical current to a reflecting mirror. Presto; the mirror bounces back the stream of light, all those photons marching in perfect harmony *at the speed of light*. And it bounces it back to another mirror, and back and forth and back and forth, all the time boosting its energy level. If one of those mirrors is only partially silvered then the beam finally smashes through and goes on to do whatever else is set up for its workload.

That's about as basic as you can get. The next basic building block calls for the use of a synthetic ruby, usually in the shape of a bar. The power source pumps away with swiftly increasing energy by boosting the electrons of the atoms in this ruby bar. To get maximum energy from the basic system, high-intensity green light is sent into the ruby bar. Atoms seem to welcome green light more than they reject that frequency and thus they're amenable to a mass frenzy of electrons whipping out photons, and photons creating still more photons, and when the capacity of that partially silvered mirror is exceeded, BAM! you've got a working laser beam.

Tickle the system by modifying the equipment and you can slice away a tumor on the surface of the human eye or you can slice a heavy combat tank in half, melting its steel as if it were soft butter.

None of the above satisfied Vasco de Gama and his research team. The promise of vastly greater energies and flexibility was their Holy Grail, and the path to heavenly reward for de Gama was nothing less than the free-electron laser. He hurled his beam of electrons into what seemed best described as a *wrangler*, built of powerful magnets of varying polarity. So the beam of electrons behaved differently from other systems. The electrons zigged and zagged with the speed of light, and what de Gama had latched onto was the incredible secret that all you need to do to get an electron to create a photon is simply to change its direction. A tweak will do. Tweak the path of the electron and it rewards you with a free photon. Do this on an increasingly larger scale and you get a controlled tornado of photons. The fancy name for it was synchrotron radiation. De Gama, a skilled horseman on the plains of Venezuela, preferred the term *wrangler*.

There were problems, to be sure. De Gama developed a laser beam fifteen feet in diameter to absorb the tremendous energies. His single greatest accomplishment came forth in mathematical theory. By placing an object in the path of the laser beam from its moment of weakness—the beginning of creating the beam itself—that object could be broken down beyond its molecular level to the level of the electromagnetic world—deep within the atoms themselves. At first they didn't know how or why; nothing they understood about free-electron lasers explained the phenomena. But that crystal . . . ah, it performed as a catalyst in the deepest chambers of the subatomic world. It froze the vibrations of the electromagnetic spectrum just so long as the object within the beam remained within this specific stream of particles—the photons—moving with the speed of light.

And since the photons were light, *and it is impossible for light to move at any speed slower than light itself*—a hundred and eighty six thousand miles a second—Vasco de Gama succeeded in erasing the electromagnetic structure of an object. By using his laser controls much the same as a throttle, although with incredibly greater precision, when he shut off the laser power the object reappeared in a different location along the path of the beam exactly as it existed before being subjected to the beam.

He had dematerialized matter.

And then reconstituted that same matter in a special position other than where it was dematerialized.

And nobody believed him. Nobody, that is, outside of a very small group of Venezuelan scientists.

And a handful of Americans.

Enter the Americans. Senator Patrick Xavier Elias; Caleb Massey. Each of these two men, given the full details of the Venezuelan program, placed a complete record of that program in a secret, coded secure depository. Elias didn't know the name of the man—or woman—selected by Massey to open that material in the event of their deaths, and Massey on his part had no idea of who the senator had selected for the same task, if the same fatal moment had been reached.

In return for what they received, Elias and Massey promised the Venezuelan team under Dr. Felipe Mercedes whatever they needed for their program, so long as Venezuela would continue to keep them updated on progress. Cooperation went to the point of stunned realization on the parts of Elias and Massey as to what the Venezuelans had actually done in their BEMAC program. Objects transported by the BEMAC laser beams progressed to animal tissue, chemicals, cultures; a bewildering variety of materials.

And finally to insects. Bacteria; viruses; basic cells; small animals. The rate of death and destruction was appalling, but the rewards of success were so incredible as to transcend any emotional or other objections.

They beamed larger animals and killed them, often horribly. Then their success rate improved. They went to human volunteers. At first jubilation swept their ranks. They were hysterical with joy, drunk with the wonder of their new powers. Their equipment grew. Massive facilities were made available to Mercedes and his team.

Then they tore Benito Armadas to bloody pulp and made of his beautiful young wife a weeping widow.

Claude McDavid met with Caleb Massey. "I need your help," he told the American.

"Name it," Massey said.

"We need more power to work with. Our reactor lacks the really enormous energy for full-scale *and safe* beaming. I have already had the facilities, the structural elements, prepared at BEMAC." McDavid took a deep breath. "I need a Mark Twenty-Nine reactor. Not the whole installation. Just the heart and the guts."

"That's just about impossible," Massey said.

"I'd like to have the impossible on its way in seventy-two hours."

"Hell, man, no way! It can't be done!"

McDavid smiled. "You may hold the entire solar system in your hands and you tell me no way?"

"Forty-eight hours," Massey said. He wasn't smiling. He just might have to kill with his bare hands to get BEMAC what McDavid said it needed. Immediately, if not sooner.

He got it.

Rogelio "Roger" Delgado emerged from his control room, wearing a combination of old army boots, a dirt-smeared face and streaked glasses, a lab smock wearing grease, dirt, carbon and parts of his meals of the last week, all topped off with a huge smile of greetings for Mercedes and his still slightly shocked BEMAC team.

"That was quite a greeting you arranged," Mercedes said after they shook hands warmly.

"Aha!" Delgado's smile broadened. "You knew it was me, you old goat?"

De Gama grasped the other man's shoulder. "Roger, my friend," he said, shaking Delgado gently, "who else lights up all the world simply to say hello?"

Delgado nodded. "Then I made the, shall we say, proper impression? Well, Vasco, we've followed your instructions to the letter. Claude McDavid pulled off a miracle—"

"You mean the—" De Gama seemed startled, disbelieving.

"The Mark Twenty-Nine. *Installed and operational.* I don't know how McDavid did it or what he promised the Americans, but it has all happened. We've tested out the systems. Power beyond anything we ever dreamed of having and you may begin your experiments whenever you're ready."

Vasco de Gama clasped his hands in triumph. "Tomorrow!" he cried.

Mercedes edged closer, speaking to anyone in the group who might have the answer to his questions. "What's the status of the satellite?"

Dr. Josefa Betancourt, white hair gleaming in the overhead lights, his farmer's eyes bright blue behind his glasses, nodded to Mercedes. It was difficult to think of this man as the true head of IVIC, but this sprawling installation had been created to help feed and modernize a largely agrarian society. BEMAC, despite its incredible promise for the future, was still a tenant of IVIC and its more immediate needs.

"There are some minor problems," he responded to Mercedes' query. "In your absence I took the liberty of talking with that American—"

"Massey?"

"That is the one, Felipe," Betancourt said with a nod. "Caleb Massey. The man of darkness who seems to know nothing but does everything. A man of great power. Well, we didn't go into the technical details, but he assured me that matters would be, to use his own words, well taken in hand."

Vasco de Gama showed doubts; a gnawing look and furrowed brow were signs they all recognized. "Are we to proceed strictly on the promise of this one man? A word by telephone? Felipe, we have such an enormous investment here—"

"You also have," Betancourt said with a touch of impatience, "the most powerful nuclear reactor this country has ever seen," he pointed to his left, "operating and awaiting your pleasure. Is that not good enough for you?"

Mercedes stepped in to heal any sudden breach. Scientists can be like finely attuned attack dogs, ready with the slightest provocation to turn on one another.

"My friend," Mercedes said to de Gama, "when we have been promised by Caleb Massey, count on his word as if it were my own."

Then there is the woman's touch. Dr. Rosa Rivero had calmed many a stormy moment. Elegant, gracious, a brilliant nuclear physicist and electrical systems scientist, she took de Gama's arm.

"Doctor, let us show you the power of the sun itself," she told de Gama. "Shall we let your own eyes tell you what you wish to see of the new reactor?"

Vasco de Gama looked chagrined, then brightened. He gestured to take in the entire group. "My apologies for seeming sharp. I am tired, edgy, impatient. Forgive any trespass on feelings; I meant no harm." He patted Rivero's hand on his arm. "Yes, of course. Let us go."

The others followed. De Gama spoke to Rosa Rivero just loud enough for the others to hear. "Perhaps history was wrong, my dear, to make Prometheus a man. It may well be the woman such as yourself who carries the fire for us."

Rosa Rivero's laugh was crystal. "You have been drinking of river water, I fear. Nevertheless, you are charming and I am flattered." They climbed up a winding slope. "Soon, my friend, you shall see this new reactor. We have been greatly impressed. We call it Vulcan's Hammer."

They stood before a wide viewing glass sheet. What they looked through was overwhelmingly deceptive. There were actually two sheets of glass and between them was heavy water, deuterium, sandwiched under pressure between the glass. And beyond that a system of mirrors so that what *seemed* to be directly before them was at least fifty yards distant, beyond multiple barriers of radiation and thermal shielding. A fluorescing blue-violet light poured from the reactor, bathing them in a glow of free atoms. A hush fell over them.

"All the power you will ever need," Rivero said quietly.

"How deep is the deuterium tank?" de Gama asked.

"Forty feet, sir. We have diffused the visible light by a factor of better than ninety-eight percent. The light we see? This blue-violet." She glanced at the others. "Unshielded, it would blind us all in a single glance."

Ali Bolivar pressed forward, nose against the glass. "It is difficult to conceive," he said, his voice muffled. He turned to Rivero. "You're at full power now?"

Rivero was delighted with his boyish expression. "No, no, Captain," she said, laughing softly. "We are at idle, what you would call a gentle cruise for your aircraft?" She pondered her words for a moment. "No, that will not do. The reactor is at rest. It runs at barely five percent of its power output at this moment, but that is more than the old reactor at *full* power."

Bolivar seemed uneasy. "And there is no danger? I mean, our being so close to this thing?"

"No danger?" She shook her head. "We have a beast under control here, Ali. But no matter how much control we never forget that behind all this shielding is an Atomic Genie, and it is always desperate to break free."

Bolivar grimaced. "Wonderful," he said.

The huge Lockheed 1011 slid earthward along an invisible electronic beam on its final approach to Caracas International Airport. Eastern Air Lines Flight 903 kicked out smoke puffs with a perfect landing, took the high-speed rolloff and slowed for the taxi movement to its gate.

Inside the terminal, on a balcony from which the entire terminal area, and especially arriving passengers could be seen freely, Angela Tirado, Nelson Sanchez and Tony Pappas stood by their video cameras with powerful zoom lenses. Angela held binoculars to her eyes as she scanned passenger unloading and then the immigration and passport lanes through which all passengers had to move single file.

"Look again at those photographs of the Russians," she told the two men. "We can't afford to make a mistake and—" Her finger stabbed forward. "There! In the immigration line! *Start rolling the cameras!*"

Through the binoculars she watched the three Russians and a fourth man she could not identify moving to and then past the immigration booth. The group of four men collected their bags and clumped together to pass through customs.

"You getting them?" Tirado shot at her crew.

"Perfectly. Just like home movies," Sanchez told her.

"All right, that's enough," she said. "Quickly, now, before they all go through customs, we'll set up the cameras outside, and—"

"*Hold it,*" Pappas broke in, taking her arm. He took the binoculars from her. "Wait . . . wait a moment," he added, studying the distant scene. He returned the binoculars to Tirado.

"Look at those three. Two men, one woman. One of the men is a giant," Pappas said quickly. "There's something strange about them. Quickly, get a good look."

Angela Tirado studied Kim Seavers, Morgan Scott and Stan Blake walking casually through the terminal lines. "What's so unusual about . . ." Her voice trailed away and she seemed puzzled. "Tony, you're right. But I don't know what it is."

"Watch how they walk, Angie," Pappas said with urgency. "The men, especially. They walk like big cats. Like a jaguar on the prowl. Angie, I know men like those two. Very special. Like the green berets, or special forces."

Tirado kept her eyes glued to the binoculars. "Americans?" she asked.

"No question."

"Then," she said firmly, "we need their identification, who they are, what they're doing here."

"Hey, what about the Russians!" Sanchez broke in.

Tirado glared at him. "Screw the Russians. We know who and what *they* are. But those three . . ." She let her words hang in the air. The two men looked at one another and both agreed on the same thoughts. *She smells a story. Anything can happen now.*

Far across the great sprawling terminal and lobby, in an alcove behind one-way mirrors, General Luis Espinoza and Major Omar Garcia of the Caracas police force studied a small television monitor of the three newsmen who had shifted their attention from the Russians to the Americans.

"Sir, it is almost time," Garcia told Espinoza. "The Russians will be outside any moment."

Espinoza smiled. "Three Russians and one very dangerous agent from East Germany," he corrected the major. "Your men are ready?"

Garcia radiated confidence. "Yes, sir. My best teams are on this assignment."

"Well, it's too bad," Espinoza said.

Major Garcia was startled. "Sir, is something wrong? Did I forget—"

"Forgive me, Omar, I didn't mean you or your men," Espinoza said, gesturing with a glove. "No, no, I meant those three. Our beautiful young lady, Angela, and the men with her. They watch the Americans so carefully they'll miss the *real* story. It is sad. That young woman will be furious. And I admire her. Well, as our American friends say, that's show biz. All right, Major, let's go."

Outside the terminal doors they found the usual scene of hectic and furious pedestrian and vehicle traffic. Cars, cabs, limos, vans, porters, passengers, officials, police, all in the wild swirl that attends every major airport. A long black limousine with Russian flags jutting from its front fenders waited to the side. A uniformed driver stood by the open trunk. The three Russians and the German came into view, porters carrying their bags. A cab burned rubber in a slam of brakes and almost hit the group. A porter shouted "Look out!" The group of four men jumped back, cursing.

Across the street, through a high-windowed observation room, Espinoza nodded to Major Garcia. "Just as planned," he noted. He wasn't looking at the Russians but at two additional porters who'd stumbled back with them and in the flurry of confusion switched one bag of the Russians for another that was a perfect duplicate. The authentic bag vanished with the porter in the swirling crowd.

The driver began loading the bags. The replacement bag came up just above the trunk lip and suddenly the bag sprang open, seeming to wrench itself free of the driver's hands.

Across the street Espinoza smiled. "Good springs," he told Garcia.

Two Russian automatic guns, stacks of bound money, and plastic bags with white powder tumbled to the ground. Everyone in sight of the scene froze. The Russians and their German friend stared in disbelief. Their driver dove for the guns and money and bags to cover what lay on the ground. He went flat as a policeman's boot ground heavily into his neck. The Russians looked up into the drawn guns of two police officers. One blew a whistle. Other police came running, drawing their weapons as they approached.

"Ah, a most notable scenario," noted Luis Espinoza. "Well done, my friend," he told Major Garcia.

"Thank you, sir. Later I will inform my men of your pleasure." He gestured to the scene outside the terminal. "Tell me, General, what you wish done with those men."

Espinoza began removing the wrapper from a thin cigar. "The regular routine, Major. Arrest, charges, wait for their consul to protest bitterly, call the newspapers and news television to get very good pictures, and then boot those people out of here on the next plane to Cuba. *Not* to Russia. Straight to Havana. We may as well add to their discomfort."

Major Garcia was openly delighted. "Yes, sir!"

Chapter X

"Now *this* is what I call some real digs!" Morgan Scott tossed his heavy bags casually to the floor by a deeply cushioned couch. He held out both arms and swung in a wide circle through a lavishly furnished apartment suite. He crossed the room to stand before wide picture windows. "Hot damn," he called out, "this is real creamy buttermilk, people."

Kim Seavers joined him by the window. She was almost speechless. Before them spread a dazzling panorama of Caracas with beautiful modern buildings, gleaming with the reflected late afternoon sun. Sunlight flashed and sparkled from the windows of thousands of cars pouring along the wide highways. Topping off the visual gourmet feast were high hills to their left and mountains to their right. Necklaces and pins of clouds hugging the sides and flanks of the mountains, pink and hazy violet in the afternoon haze and sun, completed the picture-postcard view.

"You're right," Kim sighed. "It's too good to be true. I feel like a little girl who just found out she's going to live in the castle at Disney's Magic Kingdom." Kim turned to find Blake far behind them across the huge living room.

"Stan, you think this will do—" She almost laughed aloud but settled instead for an elbow jab at Scott. He turned to find Blake. At the doorway to another room, Blake stood twice as big as life, almost dwarfing a beautiful dark-haired, slender woman. Maria Barrios had met them at the airport with a van, and from their first moment of meeting they knew they were with someone very special. It wasn't the obvious that brought them all up short as she introduced herself. Kim Seavers picked up every detail of perfect grooming and delicate touches blended with exquisite clothing; she looked for and found the details seemingly endless in every move and gesture. What Kim Seavers saw was close to perfection in the feminine ideal. Her speech, voice, bearing, manner, and an almost-physical aura of self-confidence all added to the picture.

Morgan Scott saw a friendly, doll-figure, lovely woman who was everything he didn't expect on his arrival in Caracas. To Scott it was simply automatic that they'd be met by an equivalent to their own selves; a strong, rugged, athletic—whatever, but someone who was in *their* field, not this childlike stunner of a woman.

And they were both taken aback with the tremendous impact Maria Barrios had on Stan Blake. It was like a water buffalo meeting a delicate nymph. Before six feet three inches and muscular bulk of nearly two hundred forty pounds, and with a body posture that seemed always on the verge of assault, Maria Barrios *did* appear to shrink to diminutive size.

Stark opposites they might be physically, but that's where the imbalance fled. Not even Blake's dominating bulk and dangerous psyche could diminish the awesome aura of this Venezuelan woman. Rather than her being overwhelmed by Blake it was the opposite way around. Stan Blake had been outgunned from the start.

Morgan Scott leaned closer to Seavers. "If I didn't know better," he whispered, "I'd say we're witness to the ultimate case of puppy love."

"Teenaged mush," she agreed, smiling.

"Do you think he knows we know?" Scott asked.

"He couldn't care less," Kim observed. "But if we don't break it up she's liable to drown the way he's drooling over her."

"Don't let him hear us," Scott said. "He'll have us with his steak and eggs for breakfast."

"Don't forget the vodka and potatoes and toast and cigar."

"Please," Scott said with a pained look. "I try to forget by noon of every day."

"Let's go," Kim urged, and they crossed the room to join the others.

Maria Barrios turned to greet them. There was no way Kim could miss the sparkle, the silent laughter, in her eyes. *But she's pleased; she's enjoying all this*, Kim judged to herself. *That's a good sign*.

"You are pleased?" Barrios asked them as they came forward. "We were hoping you would find these accommodations comfortable."

"Pleased?" Scott shook his head. "Miss Barrios, I—"

"If it will not offend you, especially since we will be working so closely together," she broke in, "I would prefer we know one another on a first-name basis."

Kim thought Stan Blake would tap-dance with pleasure.

"Of course," Kim said to the other woman. "I know what Morgan was going to say." Kim gestured to take in the apartment. "This is, well, it's fantabulous."

Maria Barrios blinked. "She means fantastic, fabulous, wonderful," Scott added quickly.

"Let me show you your rooms." Barrios led them through an enormous kitchen, a dripping-with-luxury jacuzzi room, through a door she unlocked with a coded pushbutton combination to reveal elaborate electronic and communications equipment within. "And here are the four bedrooms," she wound up the walking display. "Yours, Kim, over here. Morgan, here, and Stan, to the right. The fourth bedroom is set up as a guest room but with full working facilities."

"Who's that for?" Blake queried.

Maria Barrios offered a subtle shrug. "There will be someone at different times from the United States." She hesitated a moment. "Every now and then."

Scott turned to Blake. "The old man, maybe?"

"Which one? We got two star players, remember?"

"The senator?" Kim offered.

"Not *here*," Blake said immediately. "The old boy's strictly room service all the way. He likes a dozen restaurants within fifty feet of the elevator. He's straight hotel time, man." Blake shrugged. "Now, Massey might show up as a visitor. This place is just his speed."

Maria Barrios caught them by surprise. "I know the senator and Mr. Massey," she told the three newcomers. "Neither of them will join you here."

"Why not?" Scott asked.

"This is your residence *of record*. You won't *live* here."

"There goes the good life," Blake said sarcastically.

"It sounds like show and tell," Kim said.

"Or cat and mouse. A nickel gets you a buck that's the game," Scott added.

"Cat and mouse?" Barrios asked.

"Sure. It's an old American expression, ma'am," Blake said to her. "Game-playing. Now you see it and now you don't."

"Call it a facade," Kim explained.

Maria Barrios nodded. "I see what you mean. You're right, of course. This *will* be cat and mouse. Certain people will believe you live here. We want them to believe that. You will, of course, be busy elsewhere."

"Ma'am, you've told us where we won't be," Blake interjected. "Where *will* we hunker down?"

They couldn't miss the sudden shift in Barrios' mood; her lithe figure seemed to take on the tightness of spring-wound steel. "Forgive me. I should have said this sooner. Would you join me on the balcony, please?" She led the way to a balcony outside the living room and closed the door behind them, sealing them away from any means of detecting their conversation from inside.

"*Never* discuss where you will live or work or what you'll be doing in Venezuela, especially where you might be overheard," she told them.

"You mean this den of luxury is *bugged?*" Scott asked.

"Not yet, *I believe*. But most certainly it will be in the near future," Barrios replied. "And what you do here interests certain people we wish to keep guessing."

The three Americans burst out laughing. Barrios' eyes narrowed; she seemed both confused and angry. "I didn't realize I was so humorous," she said coldly.

Blake turned to her, his massive hands touching her

shoulders gently. It was like touching a child. "Ma'am—
Maria—no offense meant. We're not laughing *at you*.
Still," he shrugged, "it's funny. None of us have the
faintest idea of *why* we're here."

He dropped his hands, awkward at having touched
her in a society where such a move could be misinterpreted. Her eyes told him such concern wasn't needed,
then she turned to Scott.

"You'll pardon the expression, Maria, but what you
see before you are three mushrooms. Everybody back
home keeps us in the dark and feeds us horseshit."

She couldn't repress sudden laughter. "I see," she
said, smiling. "Then let us visit all these things about
which you know not the why, what or where."

"Lead on, lady," Blake told her with a grandiose
sweep of his arm.

They sat in a new Mercedes as Maria Barrios drove at
high speed away from the city, the road before them
ascending steadily. In the front seat Stan Blake shook
his head and smiled. "Maria, you change cars slicker
than anybody I ever knew. I swear this thing was
parked in the same space where you left the van."

"It was."

"That's all? No explanations?"

"If your records speak accurately," she said smoothly,
"you're quite capable of judging such matters on your
own."

"Neat response," Blake said with admiration for her
words. "Say nothing and intimate everything." He turned
to Scott and Seavers in the back seat. "Our driver is a
real pro."

He didn't get an immediate reply. The two passengers
in the back seat were staring at the roadside along which
Maria Barrios whipped their car with tire-squealing movement. "Stan, do me a favor," Kim told him. "Shut up.
Don't bother the lady. Have you even looked at this road?"

Scant inches separated their tires from a precipitous
drop of more than a thousand feet. "Jesus," Morgan
Scott murmured. "Talk about your Nightmare Alley."

Blake laughed. "What's wrong, boy? You look sorta white around the gills."

"You'd be white yourself, you musclebound mongrel," Scott growled, "if you were on *this* side of the car."

"Take a heap more than just a view to call me pale-face," Blake said, grinning.

"You know something?" Kim threw at them. "Nobody said a word to us about seat belts. That's all we hear back home. Buckle up, buckle up. Down here it's white knuckles up."

"Sure," Scott told her. "If this thing starts over the cliff you need a chance to open the door and jump."

"On *your* side of the car, maybe," Kim said, her voice tight as they rounded a hairpin turn.

Blake pointed ahead of them. "Hey, up there; see them? They look like astronomical domes. Right on that high ridge."

"You're right," Maria confirmed.

Blake studied her. His jaw tightened, a sign Seavers and Scott recognized. "The hell I'm right," Blake told Barrios.

Barrios smiled. "I have lied to you, then?"

Blake caught a side view from the winding road of the domes, reflecting sunlight. "Yep," he said after the pause. "You plumb lied to me."

Kim leaned forward, her hand on Blake's shoulder. "Stan, maybe we should wait until—"

"Wait, hell," he growled. "Nobody builds astronomical telescopes of that size this close to a city. The lights would make them useless." He jerked a thumb toward the domes. "They're a fake."

"Stan, you can't be that sure about—" Scott never finished as Blake cut him short.

"Let's not start *any* project," Blake snapped, including Maria Barrios along with his friends, "even if we don't know what it is, with bullshit. You know our rules, Morgan. *Everything* is straight arrow. None of this forked-tongue crap." Again he gestured to the domes. "Those are *not* telescope domes, dammit!"

The laughter from Maria Barrios came out almost impish in its bell-like quality. "Wonderful, wonderful!"

She turned for a moment to glance at Seavers and Scott. With her eyes off the road even for an instant, they flinched.

Barrios turned her glance forward, speaking as she drove. "You're right, of course," she said to Blake but including them all. "But they *are* real. They are astronomical observatories, but without the telescopes."

"That's a lot of trouble to fake someone out for nothing," Blake shot back.

"It is not for nothing, I assure you."

Kim leaned forward, her arms crossed against the back of the front seat. "What are they for, Maria?"

"I prefer to show you myself," Maria answered, a light touch of delight unmistakable in her voice. "Soon we will be—!"

As she spoke she was cutting a severe hairpin turn in the road. The dropoff to the edge of the car was higher than before and racing along so precipitous a roadway was producing an unmistakable sense of giddiness. And worse, as Maria made her turn, steering wheel full over and cutting the centerline as close as she dared, a huge construction truck came barreling around the turn, horn blasting, gears grinding, into what must be an inevitable sideswipe of their own car—

With skill born of long experience Maria snapped the wheel left, immediately right, rode brake and accelerator together, released the brake and with the left rear tire edging across the lip of the cliffside, brought the Mercedes slinging back onto pavement. Three Americans looked at one another with horrified looks. Blake pushed back in his seat to study Maria with undisguised admiration, then turned to look at Morgan Scott in the back seat.

"You know something?" Blake said quietly. "You're right. If I were on your side of the car I'd be as white as you look right now."

"Jesus," Scott swore softly.

"Amen," Kim said, finally breathing again.

"And this," Maria said without taking her eyes from before her, "is the *good* road."

* * *

They stood in dead center of the great BEMAC dome, diminutive figures in the bottom of the great geodesic inverted bowl, staring in all directions at banks of computers, control panels, generators, laser cannon, banks and great spheres of mirrors; the heart and soul of BEMAC. Glittering, humming, thundering sounds. Voices echoing, people all about them bent to their tasks. Maria Barrios had taken her three American charges through the BEMAC facility and now they stood by the transmitting platform, studying the sphere that would rise for a test or a mission; whatever it was, Maria had refused to go into detail, and the three Americans by now were determined not to ask questions but to let their hosts play out their own game. They turned as a group approached them and stopped, facing them.

Maria Barrios moved forward. "Ah, the moment for which we've been waiting." She looked from the newcomers back to the Americans. "I have with me Stanley Blake. He is our visiting giant. Here, his partner, Morgan Scott. And this lovely young woman completes their team; this is Kim Seavers."

One by one she pointed to the others. "This is Jorge Wagner. It is really Jorge Wagner, Junior but he dislikes the tag on his name, so we call him George. And this man with so much hair and the body of a gorilla is Alejandro Suarez. *This* lovely young woman completes their team; I give you Carmen Morales."

The Americans were surprised. Carmen Morales did *not* have the looks of a Latin; she was fair-skinned and had platinum hair so brilliant it reflected lights from about the dome.

Maria again took up their introductions. "These three young people are all graduates of the Venezuelan Technical Institute, as well as our military academy. But they are not all bookworms. One hopes for better things." Maria spoke with a warm smile, reflective of honest affection for the three. "They are all qualified paratroopers, they have competed with shining success in the PanAmerican Games as among our best athletes. They are qualified scuba and deep sea divers, all of them are accomplished mountaineers, they are paramedics, and between them they speak thirteen languages."

Maria Barrios glanced from one trio to the other. "You are all incredibly accomplished. It is a miracle that you all have so much in common."

They shook hands all around, with a great deal of silent "sizing up." Facial expressions and eyes tell much; the two trios found cautious high optimism for each other in that silent exchange. Alejandro Suarez, for all his massive bulk, moved with deceptive ease; this aroused the intense interest of Blake.

"Do we speak freely to one another?" Blake threw the question to the three Venezuelans. "No standing on ceremony, no thin skins, that sort of stuff?"

Carmen Morales laughed. "You have just said what we were hoping we'd hear from one of you. Wonderful! Obviously you have what might, without a warning, be considered a delicate question for us?"

"For him," Blake answered, nodding to Suarez. For answer the heavy man lifted an eyebrow, an unvoiced invitation for Blake to proceed.

"Ballet or fencing?" Blake asked without preamble. The others blinked with the abruptness of the question.

Suarez showed true surprise. His eyes widened and his head went back with laughter. "Marvelous! But we just met. How could you tell so quickly?"

Blake shrugged. "I guess it's all in the wrists," he offered as a lame joke.

"The wrists? Aha; you jest," Suarez said, not concealing his surprise and pleasure. "But you are right. Fencing *and* ballet."

Kim Seavers stared. "You? I don't mean to seem—"

"It is all right, Miss—"

"Kim."

"Good! It's all right, Kim. We will talk about it soon. And I will offer you the first dance."

"I accept," Kim said brightly.

The ice was broken and completely thawed within

those first few minutes. "You know," George Wagner said, "I'm sorry you did not meet Benito Armadas. He was our group leader and you would have liked him. What's that expression? All cut from the same stock?"

"It will do," Scott replied. "Where is this group leader? You sound like he's gone for good."

"No one comes back from the dead," Carmen Morales said quietly.

They studied the Americans for their reaction. Morgan Scott and Kim Seavers remained blank-faced; they had nothing on which to make any meaningful comments and a murmured, *Oh, I'm sorry*, would only have been insipid. Blake offered much the same reaction but with his own added fillip; he shrugged. A sudden silence began between them and Kim moved quickly to avoid a breach.

"We can't even comment on what you said. We have no idea what kind of work your friend was doing, how he died, or *why*. It's difficult to offer a response when you're in the dark about what's going on."

Carmen Morales flashed a smile of gratitude for her understanding; the relaxation among the group was almost visible. Wagner stared at the Americans. "You don't know?" He turned to Maria Barrios. "This is unforgivable. I thought they would be fully briefed before—"

Maria held up a hand to forestall any further questions to her. "We changed the procedures at the last moment, George. Since you six people will work together as a team, we decided it was best if you would brief your new partners yourselves. You may explain, well, everything." She glanced at her watch. "Forgive me. I am late and I must leave at once."

She turned to Blake. "You're in good hands."

He looked down at her from what seemed a great height. "Watch out for those trucks. Do I see you again?"

Their eye contact, brief but intense, shut out the rest of the world. "You will. Goodbye."

His eyes followed her every step of the way until she

was gone from sight. Blake spoke aloud, to no one in particular. "That's one hell of a woman," he told the world.

"That's one hell of a *lady*," Kim offered in mild rebuke.

Blake glanced at the Venezuelans. "Who is she?"

Suarez laughed, then let the laughter fade quickly. "You really don't know, do you?"

"Mister, we're set up to be a team," Blake said, neither warmly nor unkindly. "I'm not in the habit of asking questions for the exercise of flapping my mouth. No; I don't know who she is."

"Do you know the name Mercedes? Dr. Felipe Mercedes?"

"No."

"He's the director of BEMAC, which," Suarez gestured grandly, "is all this about us."

"What the hell is BEMAC?" Scott broke in.

"Bioelectromagnetic Manned Materials Test Complex," Morales added to the exchange. She laughed. "Very impressive, no?"

George Wagner bowed theatrically. "Welcome to the Devil's Brew. That's *our* name for this place."

"And the beautiful woman who interests you so much," Suarez explained, "is the secretary to Felipe Mercedes, who just happens to be the big Indian of this project."

Blake accepted the explanation in silence and Scott took the opportunity to touch upon what could be a sensitive subject. "This friend you mentioned; Armadas? What happened to him?"

Suarez's face seemed darker than its already cloudy hue, but it was a mood of memory rather than the present. "He was my partner," Suarez recollected slowly. "We did a full power beam transmission test at Devil's Plateau. When he materialized at the target point he came out spinning, moving at very high speed. He was also in a bias recovery when he should have been in the center of the receiver." Suarez took a deep breath. "He was, literally, torn to chunks and pieces."

A silence drifted among them. Scott fought it off with

effort; he knew he had to bring this out *now*. "Alejandro, please believe me when I tell you that we do not have the slightest idea of what you're talking about."

"But I'm starting to get the idea," Blake snorted. "Does it come under the heading of science fiction, or fantasy?"

"Shut up, Stan," Kim said abruptly, startling herself as much as the others. She was hanging on every word.

The stocky Venezuelan gestured to include the BEMAC dome facility about them. "Now is as good a time as any," he said with a shrug. He glanced at Morales and Wagner and they nodded assent. Suarez spoke carefully and slowly. "Have you ever heard of dematerializing an object, then transmitting the components as wave instead of quanta, by power beam, to a distant receiving facility?"

"No," Scott snapped. "Only in fiction."

"And," Suarez went on, "rematerializing that object in absolutely its original, absolutely unchanged form on arrival."

"Hey, you guys aren't talking about teleportation, are you?" Blake burst out. "Because if we're getting into a giant headshrink project here—"

"Nothing of the sort," Carmen Morales said. "We are talking physics and electromagnetics. Hard science, my friend."

"I'm damned glad to hear that." Blake had a look of distaste. "For a while it sounded like mental telepathy and little green men from Mars."

"What we do here is *not* fiction," Morales shot back.

The Americans looked hard at one another, then at the dazzling equipment surrounding them from every side. Stan Blake took a deep breath. "Look, I didn't mean to come down on what you were saying. I'm no scientist so I don't know enough to make a value judgement. But some things I do know, and what you're saying is way, way out. Mind if I cut some hard questions?"

George Wagner smiled. "Go ahead and cut."

"You're saying you really disintegrate matter. On the

molecular level *and* even deeper, down to atomic structure?" Blake was picking his words carefully, Scott and Seavers ready to add questions of their own.

Carmen Morales nodded. "Go deeper. Subatomic. Electron, photon. *Way* down deep."

"Okay. You disintegrate matter I can handle physically, you then zap it—"

"Think of it as a shock in the same vibration frequencies," Suarez offered, "of the material to be transmitted. If the shock is photon-administered we can match the frequencies. It's as if we disassociated the target material every particle from the other, but we freeze them exactly where they are in relationship of one to the other."

"Think of a computer," Morales added quickly. "You can disconnect all the internal terminals by a millionth of an inch. Everything is essentially unchanged but now you don't have a working computer. You have an assembly of parts. For that time everything is disconnected you have parts. You can transport them that way. Reconnect the works and, how shall I say it? Bingo! You've got your working computer but now it's in a different place."

"*And* a different time, of course," Suarez chimed in.

"Slower, slower," Blake protested. "Okay, now, you break down, or disintegrate under control a block of matter so that it becomes an electronically bonded soup—"

"Very good," Wagner slipped in.

"—and then you beam this glop with some kind of super flashlight, and when you zap it to where it's supposed to go, you're able to *re*integrate the glop into its original form, right?"

"Right," Wagner confirmed.

"*And*," Blake said carefully, "it comes out like it was before it went in?"

"You use different terms than we do," Suarez said, "but that is essentially the case."

"What a bunch of shit," Blake told them all.

"You really believe that?" Wagner smiled as he spoke.

"Jesus, you think I'm talking for the practice?" Blake snorted.

"Well, then," Suarez came in quickly, gesturing, "look around you. What do you think all this is for?"

"Hope, faith, charity, prayers, dreams, fantasy, belief, a roll of the dice," Blake said without hesitation.

"Hey, *we* didn't call this the Devil's Brew," Morgan Scott added to Blake's remarks. "But what you've told us goes against every grain of scientific foundation. At least," he appended, "what *we* know, anyway."

Kim Seavers stepped between the two groups, holding up both hands. "Hey, *everybody!* Wait a moment. We're getting off on the wrong foot. This is ridiculous." She turned to Suarez. "I apologize. We came here to work *with* you and it seems all we're doing is arguing." She took a deep breath. "We don't *mean* to. But everything you've said so far is so way out— "

Alejandro Suarez laughed. "There is no offense taken, my friends," he said easily. "Let me remind you of your *own* history. For two years *after* your Wright Brothers flew many of your scientists still insisted it could not be that man could fly a heavy machine under control through the air. And when you were building your atomic bomb in the second world war, one of your top scientists, an admiral, if I recall, told everybody he knew the whole project was the most damn fool thing ever thought up and it would *never* work. And who could possibly believe that men would ever go to the moon?" Suarez was enjoying himself. "There is no air out there," he held up a finger and pointed straight up. "So what is there for the rocket to push against? *Your* top scientists said that when they ridiculed your Robert Goddard. And your incredible science of bionics; when *that* came out it was ridiculed and sneered at, most especially by *your* doctors. You will forgive me, but the television series, the 'Six Million Dollar Man,' is especially popular in this country. Here children grow up in a world where everything that was once impossible is as ordinary as an automobile or a television set or a bicycle."

Suarez made a sweeping bow. "Welcome to the future. It is *always* impossible."

Carmen Morales laughed. "You all sound *exactly* like we did when we first came to this project!"

Before anyone could answer, a blast of sound, a savage *CRAAACK!* as if the very air had been split in two, burst among them. Over their heads a dazzling teal-colored beam of light snapped into existence and as quickly and brilliantly as it appeared it vanished with another ripping sound. The Americans flinched; their only comment was a reflex cry from Scott. "Holy shit!" he yelled. "What the hell was *that?*"

Carmen Morales pointed up and to their left. They saw a man waving from a glassed-in booth. "That's Doctor Delgado up there. He's our lead laser scientist. My friends, that is *his* way of welcoming you to BEMAC."

A chagrined Stan Blake looked up at the booth and waved back. "Whoever he is, he reminds me of King Kong. When *he* talks, *everybody* listens."

"Come with us," Morales said, leading them across the floor of the dome. They went through an airlock door, emerged onto a long corridor, wide and well illuminated, talking as they went.

"You've kept this incredibly quiet," Kim Seavers said to Morales. "I mean, we've never heard the first word about this place."

"You're not supposed to," Wagner replied.

"We've had a laser biology program here for years. Most of the animal tests have been done here. They still are," Suarez explained. "Dr. Edith Hernandez runs the program."

"You said it's been here for years," Scott said. "Is that a part of this transmission project?"

Carmen Morales nodded. "Yes, but for short-range work only."

They stopped before another airlock, went through the required stops for the air chamber to be sealed, waited for the warning and clearance lights, and watched heavy doors slide apart for them.

"We're now in computer master central," Morales explained, leading them on.

"That's why the compression? Full climatic control?" Scott asked.

"Correct," Morales told him. "From here we're going to the biology labs."

Kim Seavers hurried to walk alongside Morales. "I'm anxious to see *that*," she said.

They moved through another airlock chamber, emerging in a circular waiting area. Before them was a thick wireglass door with the sign BIOLOGY LABORATORY.

"We have another name for this area," Wagner said. "We call it the Time Lock."

"You'll explain what that means, I guess," Stan Blake said drily.

"Soon, soon," Wagner laughed.

They stood before the door, TV scanners covering them. Laser scanners, barely discernible, passed over the badges worn by the Venezuelans. Morales looked up, obviously to a concealed microphone.

"Dr. Hernandez, we have the visitors—the new team members—you've been expecting."

A green entry light glowed as a woman's voice came through a speaker. "Yes, yes. Hello, Carmen. Please; come in."

The door hissed open. Once inside the biolab they heard it close behind them with a solid thud. Morales led them into a smaller domed chamber. Along one side stretched long rows of clear transparent cylinders, each cylinder end embedded within what appeared to be generating equipment. As they came closer they saw that the opposite ends of the cylinders contained dazzling curved mirrors. Power cables snaked underfoot as they walked, computer banks on each side glowed and seemed to spatter lights of every color. Finally they stopped before a huge curving wall of cages filled with rabbits, dogs, cats, guinea pigs, monkeys and other animals. A woman emerged from behind the cages and Dr. Edith Hernandez stood before them, totally unlike anything the Americans expected. A radiant smile overwhelmed all else as they studied a woman about fifty years, plump, with reddish brown hair, a huge bosom and a well-worn lab coat. Hernandez was at once a grandmotherly-warm woman and a very hard and competent no-nonsense scientist.

She was also very gracious. "My new friends, welcome," she said with both arms extended. "Welcome to my humble madhouse."

"Thank you," Kim Seavers spoke for her group, taking Hernandez's hand.

The elder woman's eyes gleamed. "Ah, you are one of those, I see."

"I don't understand," Kim said, taken aback.

"You like animals. You *love* animals. You are what I call an animal person." Hernandez smiled warmly. "I can always tell."

Morgan Scott turned from his study of the computer banks. "Wagner told us they called this place the Time Lock," he said.

"A good description," Dr. Hernandez confirmed. "Here we can lock Time in place, freeze it, so to speak." She studied Scott's expression, her eyes shining. "Of course you don't believe me. How could you?" She took him by the arm. "But come with me and I shall explain."

They followed Hernandez and Scott down a long room with more of the transparent cylinders lining the walls. Within many of them could be seen more animals. Finally they stopped before a thick door. Hernandez motioned to a lab worker and he moved long handles to unlock the door. "This is the cold room," Hernandez said, leading Scott and the others inside.

For a moment Kim Seavers stumbled. A look of shock appeared on her face as she brought a hand instinctively to her mouth, on the thin edge of vomiting.

Before them stretched long racks of livers, kidneys, hearts, entire heads, intestines, eyeballs, sexual organs, limbs, sheets of tissue and red meat and other parts of animals.

"Oh, my God," Kim said finally, her face white.

Chapter XI

"If you wish to know the effects of moving out of time, then, my dear," Dr. Edith Hernandez said with understanding of Kim's near-violent reaction to the sight before them, "you use what God gives us for testing."

Stan Blake had already moved up to Kim to support her by an arm. Gently, he helped her forward. "Hang in there, kid," he whispered to her. She looked at Blake with a rush of gratitude. "After dark," he went on in his confidential whisper, "we'll come back here and I'll show you my new creation. Chicken livers and gumbo soup and black olives for eyes, and—"

Kim jerked away violently and slammed a fist against Blake's shoulder. A mosquito might have flown by him for all the physical reaction he showed. He grinned at her. "Better now?" She smiled wanly but nodded as color returned to her cheeks.

Edith Hernandez took her hand. "There is more, my dear. Some not so bad, some worse. But it is all necessary."

Carmen Morales came to Kim's side. "This, here, *is* the worst. We call it the meat locker for good reason. Don't let this old Indian grandmother fool you. One side of her heart is iron and the other is hopelessly soft. She works very hard to keep the iron side before us."

Kim squeezed Carmen's hand. "I'm fine now. Let's go."

They went through another airlock chamber but minus the heavy security trappings, warnings and lights. As the second door slid wide before them they almost stumbled with surprise. Once again they found themselves unprepared.

"It's like . . . damn, this is the sort of laboratory my father dreamed about all his life," Morgan Scott called to his friends. "Look at this place!" Gleaming plastic, steel, glass and banks of test equipment, monitoring panels, computers and equipment strange to them filled the dome-shaped room into which they moved in a loose group. Hernandez led them directly to a large cylinder; through a transparent material they watched a coruscating band of teal color. A steady power hum vibrated the air about them.

"That color," Blake observed, "it seems to follow a shifting magnetic source."

"You are absolutely right," George Wagner said as he joined Blake. "That sound you're hearing? A minor problem of energy interference. We feed from two separate sources so that if there's the slightest interruption in the primary, the alternate line has equipment to sense even the beginning of a deviation and cuts in automatically."

"You use the nuclear reactor?" Scott asked. He and the others had clustered about the cylinder.

Wagner nodded. "That's our first primary."

Carmen Morales and Kim Seavers were sticking close to each other. "You couldn't have come at a better time," Morales told her, the others listening. "We're about to see the end of a test program that's been under way for nearly six months." She laughed, a bit nervously. "And I wish I felt more confident about the results than I really do."

Hernandez gave Morales a sharp, disapproving look, but before she could voice a reprimand a loud bark behind them drew their attention. They turned as a lab worker approached with a large beautiful dog on a leash. Kim's face brightened at the sight of the thick-haired black, white and rust animal. "He's beautiful!" she exclaimed. The dog went directly to her. "I've never seen an animal like this. What is he? What's his name?"

Dr. Hernandez's dark mood was gone. "His name is Magnum," she said, sharing Kim's obvious pleasure as the dog licked her face. "He's a Bernese Mountain Dog, from the Bern Mountains in Switzerland. They have the Alps and we have the Andes. He loves Venezuela."

"We celebrated their arrival with champagne," Morales added. "They were eight weeks old then."

"How old is he now?" Kim asked.

"Eight months."

"You said something about more than one dog?" Kim asked. "Where's the other one?"

No answer came. The silence seemed deafening. Finally, as faces turned to her, Dr. Hernandez moved closer to the cylinder. She pointed to a nameplate at its base. Kim leaned down to read the plate. "Cassy," she said aloud, looking up. "That's the dog's name?" Hernandez nodded.

Kim's eyebrows raised. "I'm getting the idea that Cassy is," she gestured to the cylinder, "in *there?*"

"Yes," Hernandez said. "Magnum's sister." Hernandez took a long, shuddering breath. Her own unease began to show. "Magnum is eight months old. Cassy is eight weeks old." A grimace appeared on her face. "We believe. *We hope.*"

Stan Blake peered into the cylinder. "I guess you mean by circling around this subject that Cassy's been in here for a while?"

Hernandez's face now showed no emotion. "Six months."

Blake's voice was flat-toned, very tight. "You said she's only eight weeks old."

"Yes."

"Wait a moment!" Scott broke in. "That doesn't make sense. This dog, Magnum, is eight months old. Great; nice doggie. Then you point to this thingamajig here and you tell us you've had the dog's sister in there for six months, *and she's still only eight weeks old?*"

"That is the case exactly," Hernandez told him.

Kim left the dog before her to study the cylinder,

from one end of its thirty-foot length to the other. She stared at the light gleaming, shifting its focus in maddening slow motion. Kim looked up to Hernandez. "Doctor, all I see in here is this light. I *don't* see any dog."

"Part of those lights are Cassy."

Kim started to speak, held her tongue, then took the plunge. "You are telling me you have a dog reduced to free subatomic particles in this electromagnetic matrix, or soup, or whatever it is, *in here?*"

"Yes. And," Hernandez said with sudden warming to her voice, "you're closer to reality than you believed. You used the term electromagnetic matrix. That is excellent. Every living creature has an EM signature—"

"Excuse me," Scott broke in, "I'd like to be sure we're always using the same terms. EM is electromagnetic?"

"Precisely," Hernandez replied as if she were talking to a classroom. "An EM code is as individual as a fingerprint or a retinal pattern, or a voiceprint, or a subtheta brainwave. We break down that code and program it into the biosciences computers. That gives us the frequencies, down to an individual atom and lower, to immerse the living creature instantly within its own special frequency. At the same time, and I speak of *precisely* the same instant, we fire the laser."

Carmen Morales could hardly contain herself as she saw the three newcomers drawn into their reality of fantasy. "That laser beam," she rushed to follow Hernandez's words, "strikes the animal at the exact instant we've programmed the laser with the animal's EM frequency. In other words, there's a perfect match of the codes." She held up two fingers. "Two things happen. First, we've disassociated the atomic structure of the animal. *Before any time passes*, that structure is fully absorbed in its own code within the laser beam. We bounce the beam back and forth between," she pointed, "those mirrors, so that what we're transmitting, or carrying along within the beam, is really an electromagnetic pattern."

Hernandez nodded her approval. "When we complete the transmission we switch off the beam. That step rematerializes the animal to exactly what it was, in terms of subatomic and electromagnetic structure, when we fired the laser."

Blake, Scott and Seavers were openly dumbfounded. Suarez turned to Blake. "What would you say if I told you I can walk on water?" Before Blake could answer he pointed to Morales. "And *she* can walk *through* water just as you walk about this room; and, finally, this one," he pointed to Wagner, "breathes water without gills?"

"I'd say you were a sneaky son of a bitch and you're talking about water," Blake snorted. "Liquid, ice and vapor."

"Aha!" Suarez said. "And what if you knew nothing of these different states of matter of water? It would be magic or it would be impossible, *but it would be real*. And not only that, with this same water I can expand objects, crack mountains or slice steel with absolute precision. Everything you've heard so far is on another plane, but it's just as real."

Kim Seavers turned to Hernandez. "Doctor, can I go over this once again?"

"Of course, my dear." Hernandez folded her hands and waited.

"You put an eight-week-old puppy in there—"

Hernandez scratched Magnum's ear. "His sister."

"—and broke down her entire structure into God knows how many trillions and trillions of atoms and subatomic particles, right?"

"Yes."

"And realigned; no, *froze* her electromagnetic pattern, and every thought in her brain, every synapse, every cellular action, every twitch of her genes, and you mixed it into this laser soup, and you've kept her here for six months—" She stopped for a deep breath.

Hernandez smiled. "Yes, yes."

"—without food, water, air, temperature control or *anything* she needs for sustaining life, and now, I have to presume this is what you're after, you're going to put the whole mess together again like some super sub-atomic Humpty Dumpty?"

"You said that beautifully," Hernandez replied. "You left out only one thing. The key to everything."

Kim blinked. "What?"

"On the electromagnetic pattern scale there are no such things as air or food or water," Hernandez said. She pointed to the cylinder. "There is one more thing missing from there."

"For God's sake, tell me!" Kim almost shouted.

"Time."

"What?"

"No time."

"I—I don't understand."

Carmen Morales came to her side. "In that cylinder, so long as that laser beam is active, there is no time. *Time doesn't exist in there, Kim.*"

Scott couldn't hold his silence. "How the hell do you stop time?"

"I'll be goddamned." They turned to look at Blake. "I'll tell you how they do that," he said to Scott. "The same way Good Old Al said it could be done."

"Good Old Al?"

"Yeah. Einstein. Time dilation. Holy shit. Out of the equation into the laser fire. I'll be damned."

"Mr. Blake, you surprise and enormously please me," Dr. Hernandez said with obvious pleasure.

"What the hell are you two talking about?" Scott demanded.

"Relativity," Blake said. "Einstein's brain game. When a physical object is accelerated to the speed of light, all subjective time ends. Stops dead. Quits. Ceases to exist."

"Einstein also said," Kim added carefully, "that you can't accelerate a solid mass to the velocity of light, because it would then have infinite mass, and you cannot accelerate an infinite mass."

Scott was hanging on to his disbelief with all his strength. "But that's classroom *theory!*" he shouted.

"No it's not," Blake said, his intrigue growing with every moment. "Hell, Morgan, it's like flying. Until an airplane flew it was *all* theory; then overnight it was art and science. It's the same thing here. At least," he grinned, "until *their* theory takes off and flies." He patted the cylinder. "The key is in here. If that damn dog has been dematerialized into its EM glop, then it's moving with the speed of that laser beam bouncing back and forth. And since a laser beam *is* light and therefore moves with the speed of light, then there's no time—subjectively—inside that cylinder."

Blake studied the Venezuelan group; they deliberately held their silence and let him run with the ball. Blake didn't miss a bit of it. He laughed abruptly, looked at Seavers and Scott and pointed to the Venezuelan group. "You know what they're doing? They *could* tell us the answers we're dragging out with a lot of hit-and-miss work on our own. They won't." Blake set his jaw. "Okay, so we'll play it the way Dr. Hernandez obviously would like this to go. Blind man's buff, right?"

Edith Hernandez offered him a fleeting smile, but that was all. "Now comes the neat trick," Blake went on, shrugging off the silence. "It's just like you said, Kim. They've got to get Humpty Dumpty back on that wall with his eggshell in one round chunk like before the big fall. All the pieces back the way they started out."

He patted the cylinder again; he laughed suddenly and harshly. "There's only one way to find out. They turn off the power and we see what's inside here. Maybe, fricaseed dog and scrambled hair and feet."

"Dammit, must you say *that*?" Kim asked, making a sour face.

"Hey, don't kick on me, little sister," Blake protested. "*I* didn't put that dog in there. You don't like the menu, you talk to the madam over there," he said, nodding to Hernandez.

The elderly scientist took no umbrage with the sarcasms and clear disbelief. Edith Hernandez had been this same route with too many of her own peers to show thin skin. "If our theory is right," she said slowly to the newcomers, "and until this moment we *have* been right, then there is *not* a dog in that cylinder."

"Do we assume," Scott said acidly, "that you're the female Merlin and you've got a giant frog in there?"

Hernandez laughed. "*That's* a fresh approach! No, young man," she went on, back to being serious. "What we put in that laser beam six months ago is an eight-week-old puppy. What is in there *right now* is a puppy that is *still* only eight weeks old. Time, for that animal, has not existed for these past six months."

Blake offered a crooked smile but a tone of compassion. "If your calculations prove correct."

"Yes," Hernandez said.

"Please!" Heads turned to Kim Seavers. "*Do it now,*" she pleaded.

Hernandez studied her own group; one by one they nodded. "Notify Dr. Delgado," Hernandez spoke suddenly to Morales, and they heard the voice of a determined, serious scientist. "He'll operate the laser master controls. And bring Doctor de Gama here at once. Is Felipe Mercedes here?"

"I'll get him," Wagner told her and left.

Hernandez turned back to the Americans. "You're welcome, in fact, I wish very much for you to be here when we actually open the tube."

"I wouldn't miss it for the world!" Kim exclaimed.

"You realize we may fail," Hernandez warned. "The sight may not be—"

"Ma'am, just turn off that super flashlight," Scott broke in. "We won't bug you and we'll just turn up Kim's stomach controls."

Hernandez nodded, dismissing any problems from the three before her. "I must get certain medical equipment ready. Alejandro, you stay by the instrument console, understand?" She held out the leash to Scott. "Hold Magnum for me, please?" She turned to walk away.

They waited in silence until the Venezuelans began to regroup. People they'd not seen until now entered the chamber; Hernandez returned with several medical aides. Doctor Delgado took control of the laser systems. They saw Felipe and others standing on raised observation platforms, observing visually and on closeup television monitors.

Delgado's voice came clearly across the chamber. "Your attention, please. We will have power off in sixty seconds at the top of the minute. Start the count."

A wall speaker replied immediately. "Yes, sir. The count starts in twelve seconds for a sixty-second count."

Time crawled. The glowing red numbers on the large digital counter on the wall seemed to change slower and slower. Scott pulled the big dog closer to him. The Venezuelan scientists edged closer to the cylinder as the seconds dripped away.

"Ten seconds."

Is that goddamn clock stuck?

"Three, two, one, *POWER OFF!*"

The floor trembled. Teal-colored light within the cylinder flashed and then pulsated swiftly. Delgado operated controls on the cylinder; instantly, all light within the cylinder vanished. Delgado turned to glance up at Mercedes; the director, tight-lipped, nodded. Delgado slid back a section of the cylinder. For a moment he stood frozen, Hernandez by his side, also a statue. Slowly she bent forward and extended her arms into the cylinder.

No one breathed.

No one spoke. They couldn't.

Edith Hernandez straightened slowly, her head lifting and turning, lips trembling, tears streaking her face, her arms cradled across her bosom. She moved one arm.

A beautiful Bernese Mountain Dog—

—puppy—

licked her face.

Magnum barked madly. Hernandez held out the eight-week-old Cassy to Kim Seavers, almost beside herself with her own tears. She clasped the animal, hugging Cassy to her.

Blake and Scott stood to the side, trying to separate themselves from the emotions and near-pandemonium now racing through the group. Alejandro Suarez joined them. Even the burly Venezuelan seemed overcome.

"That's one hell of a job your people did," Blake said.

"Thank you." Suarez looked at the group near-hysterical with joy, then looked back to Blake. "But this has been the *easy* part."

"Hey, man, this is your turf," Blake told him. "You tell us what comes next."

"People," Suarez said.

"In that firetrap?" Blake said, pointing to the cylinder.

Suarez grinned and clapped Blake on the shoulder. "I've ridden that firetrap, as you call it. For a few minutes only, I admit, but—" He ended his words with a shrug.

Blake's eyes widened and Scott stared. "You look like you're still all in one piece," Blake observed.

"Well, this Time Lock, everything you saw," Suarez demurred, "this is really easy. I mean, you get in, you're naked, and they throw the switch—"

"My God, what does it feel like?" Scott burst out.

"That's the strange part," Suarez told them. "You don't feel *anything*. Not going or coming back." He shook his head. "No, no; that's wrong. That's for people *outside* the cylinder. Inside it's lights out and lights on *and that's all*."

"I'd say you were a fruitcake if it wasn't for that damn dog," Blake said quietly. "Obviously, it works. But there's got to be more than this. I can recognize volunteer time when the clock strikes. And it's banging away loud and clear."

"Very perceptive," Suarez complimented him.

"The big dome," Scott broke in. "That's the real merry-go-round, isn't it?"

"Your expressions are certainly different," Suarez said, not unkindly. "Yes, my friend," he told Scott, "the big dome is it." He studied them carefully. "Let me not make wrong conclusions I will regret. You are volunteers?"

Blake nodded to Kim Seavers, just yielding the puppy

to Carmen Morales. "Us and her," he said. "The Three Musketeers. No sense at all. We're volunteers. Now that we've joined up, what's next on the agenda?"

"Distance transmission in the main laser beam. From here to another place. Far away."

"How far is far?"

"*Miles.*"

"Whoo-*whee*," Scott said.

Blake spoke slowly, yet with disarming casualness. "Lights out, lights on?"

"Oh, sure," Suarez confirmed. "*If* everything works. I mean, if everything works exactly the way it's supposed to."

"And if it doesn't?"

"Then you will join Benito Armadas."

"Terrific," Scott said.

"There is no mincing words," Suarez said firmly. "You come out of that beam wrong, and it's like all the devils in hell are waiting to rip you into bloody pieces." He offered a thin, almost sad smile. "Are you willing to risk that, my friends?"

Stan Blake locked eyes with Suarez. "Not yet."

"Oh?"

"Not until I have at least one date with Maria Barrios," Blake said. "Then you can bring on *all* your devils from hell."

Suarez stared, then burst into laughter. "You are a man truly after my own heart, gringo!"

Chapter XII

Stan Blake swirled the cognac gently in the snifter diminished by the huge hand cradling the delicate glass. He stared for a long moment at the candle flame glowing through glass and brandy. He moved the snifter slightly. Distant lights flashed like falling stardust, bringing him to raise the glass a bit higher. Glass and lights became a swaying curtain of sight beyond which he beheld the face that had so overwhelmingly captured him. Blake brought down the glass slowly to see Maria Barrios clear before his eyes. She sat comfortably in the wicker throne chair. She seemed able to reach to any possibility and drape herself with easy perfection. A simple black knit dress, almost but not quite body hugging, and a single strand of pearls about that lovely throat. For this moment the city lights, glowing and twinkling like magic gems scattered freely across the distant hills and slopes, meant nothing to Blake. Nothing beyond yet another magic feathering touch of this incredible scene. They sat across a low table on the veranda of Maria's home.

"All this," Blake said in a quiet, husky voice, "can't be real. Too fast, too wonderful." He gestured easily with his brandy glass. "It's a tough deal to wake up from a dream and still be in that dream."

Her smile seemed to brighten the candle flames. "It is real," Maria said. He heard a gentle sigh escape her. "I confess to you I had hoped for us to be together, but," she hesitated, "not for weeks to come." She sought and found his eyes and held them. "That is our way."

"I know, I know." He leaned forward, elbows on his

183

knees, as thoughtful about events and this moment as was the woman. "I'm, ah, grateful you understood why I called so much sooner, than, ah—"

"There is no need for concern." She cupped the snifter in both hands and observed him above the rim. "You do not have time to court me. I wanted, want, that to happen. But I also do not have the time. *We* do not have the time."

"I'm sorry about that, Maria. I mean, the whole idea of doing things the way you people do—well, it has tremendous appeal to me." He paused and she saw his jaw set. *The defense move*, she had already learned of Blake. *He is uncomfortable, awkward. I must be gentle with my giant.* "I've never been easy in moments like this—" He interrupted himself with a sudden and self-conscious laugh, and any touch of humor brightened him. "I was going to say I've never found a moment like this very easy, but that's crazy."

"Why?" *One word and it's a musical note . . .*

"Easy. I've never had a moment like this." He bit down on his lip, another sign of the struggle within. "I'm clumsy with women." He caught her eye, blinked. "I mean, there are women, there have been—"

"I don't need to probe your soul, Stan. I know what you mean to say," she spoke quickly, then eased her pace. "I am flattered."

"My God, I hope so. I'm a bull in a china shop—"

"You are too harsh with yourself."

"I can't help it." He shook his head. "This gets crazier with every moment. I want to blurt out a thousand things, but I can't, I shouldn't, and half the time tonight, Maria, I feel I've said the *wrong* things. I don't want to lose my chance with you, I, uh, shouldn't even say *that*, and," the change came instantly, "do I even have a chance with you?"

"Yes." He could barely hear her voice for the crashing of his heart in his chest. This tiny woman was destroying him.

He offered a rueful grin. "I, uh, well, I mean, Maria, among other things, you really caught me by surprise tonight."

"Did you mind?"

"Oh, hell, no! I mean, no, of course not. *Really*, I—"

"Should I have told you of my children first?"

"No, no, absolutely not."

"That," she smiled again, "might have sent you quickly in another direction."

"Goddammit, Maria, this ain't no one-night stand!"

Musical sounds of laughter. "Now, my gentle giant, you sound like the man I heard so much about today. The man with the bellow of the water buffalo and the claws of the jaguar, the man who speaks with the swiftness of the thrown spear. I confess to you, Stanley Blake, I wondered what had happened to that harsh and abrasive person I met earlier."

He appeared dumbfounded. "Me?"

"Ah, is that a wound in your chest your hand covers?"

Self-conscious, he jerked his hand away from over his heart, a motion of protest about the reputation she espoused. "I can't get over this. You absolutely overwhelm me."

"A wraith of a girl does this to a giant?"

"Yes," he said, with harsher emphasis than he intended. He wasn't sure if he detected a muffled giggle. It didn't matter. He was so devastated with this woman he doubted she could do or say anything to displease him. He looked beyond her to the city. "You know something, Maria? One part of me inside is boiling and twisting and sort of crazy. But the other part," he showed his own amazement at his feelings, "well, I haven't been this relaxed since . . . since, hell, I can't remember when I was *ever* this relaxed."

"It pleases me to hear that."

The next question burst, almost explosively from Blake, he'd held it back so long. "What happened to your husband?"

"A pilot in our air force." Her tone was predictably flat, no catching strings of emotion. Great strength lay within that wraith. "He was an instructor. Ritchie and his student had trouble in the air one night. He ordered the student to jump. The young man froze with fear. Ritchie refused to abandon him, so he tried to save the machine and the young man." She turned to look into the night sky. "Since that night two years ago I have been a widow. I was very much in love with Ritchie. Like many women to whom this has happened, I never imagined he could fade into the past. But that is, of course, where he will always remain. Like any other memory of younger days and times."

Blake rose slowly and walked to the balcony, turning to look directly at Maria.

"I want very much to see you again," he said carefully.

"I hope you will."

"There's so little time!" he said with a reburst of his anger. "I can hardly get away from, well, *you know*—"

"Of course."

"Dammit, I just found you, woman. Losing you, the *chance* to know you, drives me mad."

She stood by him at the balcony, her voice warm and soothing to him. "You do not yet have me, gentle giant. Time; we must spend that currency together for a while. Do not rush what will be."

"I know, I know," he agonized.

"But for now," she said, and said no more as she slipped into his powerful arms for a kiss long and deep.

She lay on her back, beautiful and blonde and nude. It was ridiculous, this was science and medicine and it was all so impersonal but she wanted to yell *Give me back that goddamned sheet!* Carmen Morales leaned down within the cylinder, rechecking the medical sensors attached to Kim's supple body. Edith Hernandez and the scientific team stood back, a touch of decorum in their distance.

Kim motioned Carmen closer. "Do we always do this scene the tits and ass way?"

Carmen giggled. "No, no. But the first time it is most necessary. We can't afford any misreadings because of artificial materials about your body. Except for those fillings in your teeth, for which the computer has compensated, you are as you were when your mother released you from her womb. Of course, you are much more attractive to men now than you were to little boys then—"

Kim rolled her eyes. "Get on with it, Carmen. My goose bumps are getting bumps."

"We're almost ready." Carmen extended a pill to Kim. "This is the radioactive dye. When you hear the countdown reach one, immediately bite down hard, okay?"

Kim took the pill between her lips. "Shure. We who arr about to die—"

Carmen laughed. "I'm going to close the lid now. Hold that pill between your teeth. You'll have two minutes. You all set?"

Kim pushed the pill into position between her teeth, mumbled, and nodded. Hernandez came forward and the two men closed the lid, sealed the tube, and waited for a light to change from red to amber. The amber light signaled the next event in the count. A speaker sounded.

"Test one four six nine. Countdown begins in four seconds, four, three, two, one, we are at two minutes and counting. Two minutes and counting."

The remainder of the two teams stood to the side. Stan Blake gestured angrily. "Dammit, I should be in there, not Kim."

Suarez gave him a look of surprise. "Why? We're all equal in this program."

"Screw that equal shit. Anything could go wrong and I'm better equipped, or even you, Al, to—"

Suarez broke in quickly. "Easy, my friend. Physical strength means nothing when you're in that laser beam. Besides," he gestured to Morales and Wagner, "we've all been through this test. She'll be fine."

Blake was far from convinced. He stood tall and angry, arms folded, jaw set in granite. His knuckles showed white.

Thirty seconds and counting.

Wagner nudged Morgan Scott. "The count is on automatic computer now."

The seconds dragged. Blake and Scott held their breath.

"Three, two, one, zero!"

Again the multiple events came in the form of a roar of sound and the flash of dazzling light. The dazzling teal reflected off everything in the domed chamber and the sudden crash of energy echoed and bounced, rattling loose equipment and vibrating dental fillings. The sound faded, the flash was gone, and where Kim Seavers had rested prone and nude there was only the glowing cylinder, the light changing in response to the writhing electromagnetic patterns within.

Scott wiped heavy perspiration from his upper lip as he turned to George Wagner. "Why'd she take that pill?"

Wagner knew Scott had been briefed several times, but the query released some of his pent-up frustration at standing by uselessly while this woman, so long his partner and so close to him, was gone, vanished, ripped by light into trillions upon trillions of subatomic particles.

"It's a radioactive dye," Wagner replied quickly. "The test system takes an x-ray of her exactly one second after she bites into the pill to release the dye. We'll have another x-ray of her exactly one second after power cuts off. If everything goes as planned, and it did with our team when we rode the beam, then the radioactivity won't have had time to move from her mouth into her throat."

Morgan Scott stared at the man leading him through the maze. He was more emotional than objective. "If, maybe, perhaps, could be, possibly . . ." His words came across angry and touchy. "It could also scramble her mind, couldn't it?"

Wagner knew the folly in backing off an inch. Explaining was one thing; placating something entirely different. "Yes, it could," he said without inflection. "Does that surprise you? I can't believe you came into this program expecting guarantees and insurance policies! We're—"

The wall speakers boomed. *"Three, two, one, CUT-OFF!"*

Again the sudden flash; this time, however, the power

groaned down into a deep basso rumble as it faded into the structure and was then no more. Blake and Scott hovered anxiously as Morales and Hernandez opened the cylinder. Neither man could breathe; they were as taut as coiled springs and they stared with mixed relief and disbelief as Kim Seavers sat up, Carmen Morales slipping a shirt about her bare breasts.

Kim looked about her, puzzled. "Did something go wrong? What happened? When do we start the test?"

Blake exploded with a shout of joy. His massive hand crashed in jubilation against Scott's back, pounding the air from his friend and buckling him to one knee. Scott staggered to the cylinder. Carmen Morales moved aside for him as he knelt and threw his arms about Kim.

"It works!" he shouted. "Baby, my God in heaven, *it works!*"

Kim still didn't understand. "But . . . but nothing happened. I mean, I bit down on the capsule and," she made a sour face, "it tastes, *yech*, like raw fish, and that's all. One bite and then they were opening up this fancy tin can."

Scott held her face gently in both hands. "Kim, you were gone *for ten minutes.*"

"I was *what?*"

"You've been gone *somewhere in time*—and you're back!"

Kim stared about the dome at the smiling faces, upraised fists of victory. Applause from the technicians began to sound in the room, echoing again and again. Slowly she moved her hands about her body, feeling her skin, her limbs, her face. She looked up at Scott and Morales and Hernandez.

"I . . . I can't believe it. I was really a . . . a force field? And now I'm . . . it's amazing."

Blake came over, bent down to hug her.

"Stan, I, can you imagine—?"

"Get the hell out of there, lady," Blake told her gruffly. "I'm ready to take that ride and you're holding up the works."

She studied the angry, granite face before her. If she

didn't know better she would have sworn she saw the glisten of one small tear at the edge of his eye.

"She's beautiful," Senator Patrick Xavier Elias said of the photograph he studied of Kim Seavers. "You say she's already been through what you people so picturesquely call the Time Lock? Reminds me of that old Irwin Allen television series. 'Time Tunnel,' I believe they called it."

Caleb Massey smiled tolerantly of the senator's unexpected reminiscence. Before he answered he let his eyes again sweep the heavily paneled office, the massive structuring that gave the private room a cloistered feeling. Then Massey gestured idly at the picture Elias studied. "Yes, she's been through," he said finally. "In fact, Patrick, all three of our people have now made the journey."

"They all remain right where they are, were," Elias said, showing the confusion that always seemed to attend the technical aspects of the program, "and yet they've made a journey at the speed of light."

"Through time," Massey emphasized again as he had done many times before.

"You can't separate time from space," the senator said abruptly. Massey's attention quickened. "She was moving through time but her foundation, the dome, was moving through space as well. A change in spatial positioning, I suppose you call it?"

"Yes, yes," Massey said, showing his surprise. "Where did you suddenly learn all this?"

Elias smirked. "My grandson. He's a whiz at this sort of thing."

"What else did he tell you?"

"Oh, a bit of this and a dash of that. But he emphasized that you can't change—I mean, you simply cannot separate time and space. If Kim, this young beauty, went through time, she was also moving spatially. For example," said the elderly man, warming to the moment, "the installation in Caracas is moving at about a thousand miles an hour. The earth's rotational speed at the equator, I believe."

"Yes," Massey said. "Go on, man!"

"And the earth, which is tilted a good bit on its axis, also wobbles on its axis. Um, something like a spinning top leaning over at an angle. Right?"

"Right as rain, you old bat. Any more?"

"Well, the earth is in orbit around the sun. According to young Albert—his father named him after Einstein, you know—well, young Albert emphasized to me that the earth falls about the sun in its orbit at a real dandy clip. Something on the order of sixty-six thousand miles an hour."

"Eighteen point five miles per second; right. More?"

"Well, he began to lose me after that. He said lots of mumbo-jumbo about the sun being in orbit about a massive black hole that was the gravitational center of the galaxy and—well, he lost me there. But I did get that one point, Caleb. You can't move *only* in time *or* space, correct?"

"You've said it perfectly."

Elias's mood sobered. "You realize what this means, then?"

"Sure I do," Massey said, almost off-handedly. "In a way, it means the biblical truth. You can keep going into the future for super medical science. Incurable doesn't mean death; it means being put on ice, figuratively, frozen in time, really, until science catches up with whatever's trying to kill you, and cures you."

"People will go to war over this, Caleb."

"So what's new?" Massey shrugged. "They've gone to war over a broad, for Christ's sake. Helen of Troy for one, remember? But I know what you mean," he added quickly. "This is a hell of a lot more incentive than the best piece of ass that ever came along."

"You have a way with words," Elias said drily.

"But you're right. War is in the picture with this little doo-dad our Venezuelan friends cooked up."

"Never forget that there's two sides to every coin, Caleb."

"I'm way ahead of you, Senator."

"My God," Elias said, almost whispering. "We could

have kept Einstein alive, or a modern-day Moses, or Puccini—think of all the magnificence that died with Puccini."

Massey had a deadpan expression. "Hitler, Mussolini, Stalin— "

Elias shook his head. "The world's not ready for this."

"Dammit, don't give me piss-ant moralizing! I came here for a hard decision, Patrick!"

The senator waited a decent interval. "Tell me what you want," he said finally.

"They're going to run into trouble in Venezuela," Massey said ominously. "Real trouble. The kind that kills. It's the transmitting system itself. Not the concept or the operation, but a fault in the—well, just accept that beaming an advanced biological system isn't quite perfected yet."

Elias's eyes widened. "Advanced biological system?" He snorted with open disdain. "You've joined the enemy, Caleb. Is that how you now spell human being?"

"Man, woman, child," Massey whipped back. "That satisfy your moral minimums?"

"Don't get into a pissing contest with me."

"I don't mean to," Massey said by way of apology. "Let me stay on track here. Any long-range transmission of the mass and complexity of an adult human, or humans, spells trouble."

"*You* spell that out, dammit."

"One chance in six that every long-range beaming will result in serious injury or death."

Elias stared hard at his friend. The old senator blinked several times. "That's unacceptable."

"I agree. We don't want measurably acceptable suicide odds before we even begin."

Elias gestured uncomfortably. "Do they—I mean, Mercedes's people, know this yet?"

"They suspect it but they don't *know* it. This Delgado fellow is an absolute genius. He doesn't sleep much lately. Every night he's searching for a flaw he feels but can't pinpoint."

"Then how do *you* know so much! I know you're very, very good, Caleb, but—"

"You know Claude McDavid?"

Elias's eyes narrowed. "Yes. He—why, of course. We set him and, um, that other fellow, up with dual citizenship. What about McDavid?"

"*He* knows. He told me."

"That doesn't make sense. Why doesn't he tell Delgado or Mercedes?"

"Because he doesn't have any numbers. No hardware, no measurable data. It's something he feels in his bones, so to speak. Neither he nor I believe that Delgado or Mercedes is going to take on a major modification because of an ache in the back or the knee."

"*You* accept his hunch?"

"It's more than hunch. We've run it through the Greystone Mark Nineteen computers. They verify McDavid's hunch, as you call it. I ran the last Greystone runs myself. There's a problem, all right."

"You have the solution?"

"Yep."

"Is this problem what killed that young man of theirs?"

"Armadas?" Massey nodded, his voice a touch softer. "Yes, it is."

"Tell them *now*, then. Phil Mercedes will listen to you, or to me, or certainly to the both of us."

Massey shook his head. "Not yet, old man. This involves more than passing on the data. We'll have to get through or over or past Mancini somehow without spilling the beans. That won't be easy, even for you," he added quickly to forestall a sudden objection from Elias. "And if we slip up, well, I need some heavy bargaining chips. This can't be an all-Venezuelan or an all-American project. It's *got* to be a joint effort. When they run into their stone wall, they'll listen, and we'll cut our deal."

"You're getting cold-blooded in your old age," Elias said, a touch of sadness in his voice that was honestly felt. "You're putting up the loss of lives as a bargaining chip. Including *our* young people as well."

"Maybe you've forgotten something, Senator."

"Which is?"

"The names of all the streets at Edwards Air Force Base."

Elias raised himself a bit higher in his seat. A cheek muscle twitched. He hadn't forgotten a damned thing and Massey knew damned well he hadn't. Edwards Air Force Base. Named in honor of a test pilot who died there flying a giant all-wing machine many top scientists warned lacked stability, balance; all sorts of problems. The country needed a bomber that could fly ten thousand miles with a hydrogen bomb. Northrop's huge jet was a test program. It killed Joe Edwards and other good men. If there hadn't been the compelling need because of grim relations with the Soviet Union they would have gone slower with the great flying wing. But they didn't, and the test field out in the desert got a new name. There was something else. The "names of all the streets" at that airfield.

Every street was named for a test pilot who had died in a new flight program.

"I don't appreciate your remarks one bit, Caleb."

Massey saw he'd cut the older man to the quick. "I apologize, Patrick. I mean that. I also meant what I said about the need for a lever so we can cut a deal that brings us completely into their picture."

"All right," Elias sighed. "Lay it on me."

"I want to duplicate their BEMAC installation. Here; stateside."

Elias smiled. "That's *all?*"

"Hell, no." Massey smiled at his own audacity. "We'll need three satellites in geosynchronous orbit, our own master computers, Greystone series, a training and operational facility, my own team and—"

"Stop!" Elias coughed and took a moment to sip brandy. "Where? Your own setup, I mean."

"The old solar energy facility in Florida. It's actually on Cape Canaveral, north of the port inlet and just off to the boundaries of the Trident sub base. It's surrounded by a coast guard station and the air force launch spread on the Cape. There's also a bunch of DEA and Customs setups there. It's got outstanding security, and all the other activity, as well as the commercial and sports fishing fleets, will cover our bells and whistles nicely."

Elias pictured the area. He nodded. "You've chosen well. I can swing it with the committee," he concluded. "That takes care of the appropriations and the manpower. But I *can't* get it past the president with Craig Mancini guarding the gates. He won't go for it. He hates you, me, anyone associated with us."

"I've always wondered why," Massey mused aloud. "The *real* reasons, I mean."

"You know why! The bastard hates you even more than he hates Hispanics. Come to think of it," Elias said, scratching his chin, "he hates just about everyone who doesn't fit in the category of WASP."

"With a name like Mancini?" Massey made it clear he didn't agree.

Elias laughed. "With all you know you've much to learn. When it comes to things like this, deep emotional hates and the dark side of people like Mancini, you're still a tadpole kicking up shit in a small pond."

Massey laughed. "Thanks for the compliment." The laughter fell away and he looked seriously at the senator. "Tell me, old friend, what if I bring you Mancini's head on a silver platter?"

"What the hell does that mean?"

"The head will have a spike right through the lips so they don't flap too much."

"Careful, Caleb Massey. I won't cotton to dirty pool. We've had more than enough crap in our government with Watergate and Iran and—"

"*I won't fake a thing.*"

"You seem damned sure of yourself."

"I'll bring you something he'll want so badly he'll do *anything* to get it. He plays ball with you and me, he gets it. Otherwise—"

"That's got the smell of blackmail."

"You bet. The worst kind. Or," Massey appended, "the best. I give you my word it's clean."

"Blackmail, eh?"

"Clean."

Elias smiled. "Do it."

Nelson Sanchez adjusted the headphones connected to the electronic equipment strapped to the wall of the helicopter. He listened intently while he kept his eyes steady on several glowing gauges and screens before him. Seated nearby, Angela Tirado divided her attention between Sanchez and the earth's dark surface below, pierced by bright lights scattered below and the orange glow of Caracas in the distance through a thin cloud layer.

Through powerful binoculars she saw tiny spears of white light and the red afterglow of vehicles on the winding roads. She had an excellent view of the big white astronomical dome atop a distant ridge; she moved the glasses slightly and studied two more domes on two other mountain spines; one closer and the other in the far distance. The one that held her attention the closest she knew to be part of the sprawling IVIC research facility that covered nearly an entire mountainside and upper ridges.

Her body tensed as she saw a crack appearing in the IVIC dome; no, not a crack. The dome was opening. Quickly she looked at the next nearest dome. It too was opening!

She nudged Sanchez. "Anything?" she shouted.

He lifted one earphone. "Some sort of countdown. It started about thirty seconds ago."

"Countdown? To what?" she pressed.

"Can't tell, Angie. Whatever their radio signals are, they're being scrambled. I'm getting a power pulse and a wave but I can't pick up any details."

"Keep trying. Let me know the instant you get anything definite." Sanchez nodded and concentrated again on his equipment.

Angela moved forward to join Tony Pappas up front. He motioned to the headset and microphone. She slipped on the equipment and nodded. "Tony, Nels is picking up a signal he can't read, but to me it sounds like a countdown. There's no earthly reason why that research station would be so active at this time."

"I think he's right," Tony replied, swinging the helicopter around in a gentle wide turn. "I'm getting a lot of hash on radio." He paused significantly and pointed to an electronics panel. "And the nav equipment's twitching like it's gone bananas."

She studied needles swinging without any seeming purpose. "Which means?" she asked.

"A lot of very powerful signals. They're interfering with everything."

"But why *now?*" she pressed.

"It's four o'clock in the morning, Angie. No commercial flights operating now so there's no interference with their navcom systems. The military work UHF. That's ultra high frequencies above the band I'm getting."

She pointed to the main IVIC dome. "One gets you ten it's tied in with that," she said quickly. "Two of the domes have been open for a—"

The night split in two. Rich teal light, as hard and sharp as a steel cable, flashed into being. The country-side flashed in response and the dazzling light was gone. The earth was familiar again.

"Good God—there it is again!" Angie shrieked.

Pappas blinked rapidly, still half-blinded by the after-effects. "The same light we saw at Angel Falls—"

"Did you see how it happened?" she said excitedly. "It wasn't there and then it *was* and then it was gone! How long do you guess—"

"Two seconds, Angie."

She looked pained and frustrated. "Tony, what in the hell *is* it?"

"I don't know, girl." She studied his face; he was as baffled as herself.

She pressed the intercom button again. "Nels, did you pick up anything when that light flashed?"

His eyes were wide and he had his headset in his hand. "I sure did," he said, in obvious discomfort. "An icepick in each ear. Every needle on this equipment snapped to full overload, then it snapped back to normal. I never ran into anything like it. It's an energy overload. That's all I can tell you."

"Anything now?"

"Yeah. Same as before. A lot of radio transmissions but it's all code-scrambled. I can't touch it."

She pointed suddenly with one hand and gripped Pappas's shoulder with the other. "Down there!" She was pointing at the IVIC dome. "It's closing, Tony! It's closing! Whatever's going on *has* to be tied in to that place. Tony—*land down there!*"

He stared down at the IVIC grounds, pointing to the towers with red flashing warning lights. The nuclear reactor building was bathed in white and yellow floodlights, amber glows marked the parking lots. Pappas shook his head. "Angie, that's a federal security area. Absolutely prohibited even for flying over it, let alone landing. We set down there and they'll—"

"Land this son of a bitch, Tony!" Her face was white with sudden fury and she jabbed her finger toward the ground. "Damn you, *land down there!* Kill the engine, deadstick it in—I don't care, *but land!*"

He didn't bother with a reply. The helicopter started down in a wide descending circle.

What Angela Tirado pursued with enthusiasm but blindly, had already happened. Several minutes before Pappas began his descent into what he knew was going to be one huge lump of trouble, all attention in the BEMAC dome had focused on an elaborate lexan and steel sphere twenty feet in diameter. The sphere held dead-center position of the dome. Electrical cables snaked everywhere to and from the transmission platform. Everyone on duty was working; everyone off duty was also there, watching.

High above them the great dome was open to the night. Cold air flowed downward, a blessing in disguise from the heat of the equipment in the dome. Felipe Mercedes and Rogelio Delgado for the tenth time in as many minutes had checked the exact alignment of the laser cannon. Digital timers everywhere ticked away the last minutes and seconds of the test under way.

Dead center in the great sphere, standing on a platform within the sphere, Stan Blake stood tall and relaxed, wearing a tailored flight suit streaked with strange glistening wires and slim cables sewn within the suit fabric. On his left chest was a large medallion patch of black, run through with a jagged bolt of green lightning. He watched the technicians about him nod finally and leave the sphere. Blake glanced at a wall timer. Three minutes for the team to complete their last-minute rechecks of the system. George Wagner and one technician remained. They closed the faceplate of a pilot's pressure helmet, turned oxygen flow to full on; the oxygen flowed from two solid metal canisters. Oxygen turned to metal under crushing pressures of a diamond anvil. A touch of electrical current and one small canister released in a controlled flow as much oxygen as a tank as large as Blake himself.

Wagner tapped his shoulder. "Everything feel okay?"

Blake nodded. "Right on the money, George. Full oxygen flow." His voice came muffled through a vibrational speaker.

"How's the chute?"

"I wouldn't know I was wearing it if I hadn't seen it." Strong webbing harness had been sewn into the flight suit, and an extremely thin and lightweight flatpack showed only as the slimmest bulge along Blake's back.

"Everything looks great. Two minutes, Stan."

"Got it." They shook hands warmly and then Blake stood alone on the platform.

"*One minute and counting.*"

The deep power hum built up from its basso groan, increasing in frequency and volume. Dust trembled in the air throughout the dome as the last seconds fled.

"*Thirty seconds and counting.*"

Blake rechecked his positioning. He slipped without thinking of the movement into a fighting crouch.

"*Five, four, three, two, one, FIRE!*"

Green hell stabbed into Blake's eyes. A dizzy sensation, icy cold and at the same time as piercingly hot as a burning needle, slashed through his body and brain. He felt a strange lurching sensation as if something was twisting *within* his body. For a moment he rocked off balance; his physical instincts kept him erect and sure-footed. He had just enough time to hear the blasting roar of the laser and then sound and light vanished.

Blake blinked his eyes. Before him spread the dome. *But that wasn't George Wagner looking at him from beyond the transmission sphere.* Carmen Morales showed a marvelous smile beneath a face streaked with tears. But that was crazy. Carmen was in Dome Two for this test and—

He'd done it! He had ridden the beam! He'd been beamed from one dome to the other!

He stood erect, his clenched fist stabbing up above him, a wave of triumph galvanizing his whole body to wild energy. *"Hot damn!"* he shouted to the anxious faces staring at him. *"It works! IT WORKS!"*

A roar of joy swept through the dome as dozens of people rushed toward the receiving platform, shouting congratulations. Carmen Morales threw her arms about him, kissed him on the cheek and held Blake at arm's length.

"How are you? *How are you?*" Excitement rattled her voice. *"How did it feel?"*

Blake hugged her, then moved apart slightly so they stood side by side, her arm about his waist, his over her shoulder. He spoke to the group collected beneath them as much as to Carmen.

"Baby, this is an E ticket ride!" he announced. He planted a loud kiss on her forehead and turned to face the team still overwhelmed with their success.

"I'm ready for the round trip!" he shouted.

Dome Two shook with the cheers and whistles that met his words.

Chapter XIII

"Freeze!"

Nelson Sanchez was caught with one foot still on the step to the helicopter cabin, the other foot in the air reaching for the ground, when the voice barked harshly at him. Booming from a police loudspeaker he felt it almost as a shock. Sanchez froze. He had just time enough to realize that the metallic clicking sounds he was hearing were automatic weapons being readied for immediate fire. He had just that amount of time and no more to do all these things because he was caught between a rock and a hard place—the helicopter step with one foot, empty air with the other, being blinded by police searchlights, and the momentum of his own body still seeking ground.

Gravity and momentum won out over choice and prudence as Sanchez's foot searched frantically for solid ground and found no solidity in empty air. In a desperate attempt to keep from falling face first onto the ground, fearing any sudden movement might precipitate twitchy fingers on triggers, Sanchez flailed wildly with one hand for the handrail on the side of the cabin entrance. He missed. His right foot skidded to the right and his left hand banged painfully against the handrail, tearing skin from the knuckles. There was no stopping now. The police and security officers behind their blinding flashlights stared in disbelief as Sanchez appeared to be propelled wildly from the helicopter cabin, one foot splayed right, the other twisting backward, his left arm bent and the hand drawn inward and his right arm stabbing the air madly for the support that wasn't there.

With an unplanned screech of pain and anger Sanchez did an awkward twisting half-gainer flop through the air, tumbling as he fell, doing a complete roll with his body, and landing face first in rocky dust. He impacted with an audible *thud*, his nose mashed sideways against his face and his body collapsed in slow motion behind him.

His worst danger now as he lay on the ground like a crumpled, broken Raggedy Andy doll was that one of the men with a gun would be laughing so hysterically he would squeeze the trigger without realizing what was happening, bringing an unprecedented and immediate end to the life of one young Nelson Sanchez.

Sanchez came slowly to his knees, pausing like a battered animal on all fours. Blood dripped from his nose, his cheek was gashed, dirt caked his face and he spat dust and pebbles, both elbows were torn through his jacket and one knee jutted from torn pants. He looked ahead of him and saw only the blinding lights of the cars and all those people with guns. The helicopter blades had slowed down to no more than a lazy *whop-whop-whop* above him. Mixed in with the whistling, slowing sound he heard a rasping choke, what seemed to be a strangling cat. He turned slowly. Now he could see as he looked behind him.

The strangling, whistling sounds came not from the helicopter but from Angela, leaning against the cabin door, holding her sides, nearly choking as she struggled not to scream with the laughter that kept forcing its way from her mouth. Sanchez blinked. Angela was on her feet, one hand still covering her mouth. Behind her, garish in the multiple lights, the helicopter shook strangely, a rocking motion unlike anything he'd ever seen. He caught a glimpse through the front cockpit window of Tony Pappas with his face against the window, shaking uncontrollably with what Nelson sourly judged must be more hysterical laughing.

Angela had him by his right arm and was pulling upward with all her strength to get him on his feet. He stumbled to one knee, cursed the stabbing pain and wiped his mouth. "Come on, Nels," Angela implored him. "You've *got* to get on your feet. Think of how undignified you look with your face in the dust." She started to speak again and all control left as she burst out laughing.

A voice, seemingly connected only to thin air, came again from behind the lights. "You are under arrest!" the voice boomed. "Stand apart from one another with your hands in the air! You in the helicopter! Come out immediately with your hands up!"

Angela looked toward the lights, still supporting Nelson Sanchez. "You idiots, he can't stand! He's hurt! Some of you heroes come down here and help him!"

"This is your last warning! Stand apart or we will shoot!"

Angela stood straight, glaring into the lights, and slowly brought up her free hand closed into a fist except for a rigidly extended middle finger.

"You have ten seconds to—" The loudspeaker voice went dead as they heard a sharp retort. This time a nonmechanical human voice emerged from the glaring lights. "Idiot! Shut up!" The voice grew calmer. "Madam, we understand. Your man is hurt. Please remain where you are."

Angela half-turned her body but made certain not to move her feet. "Tony! Get the camera rolling!"

Highlighted forms emerged from the lights. Angela and Sanchez stared at what must have been twenty automatic weapons pointed at them and the helicopter. A man in military uniform came forward, glanced at Sanchez, motioned for several men to assist him. The officer turned to Angela. He offered a slight bow. "Madam, I regret to inform you that you and your group are under arrest—"

"No shit, Charley Brown," she murmured to herself.

"What was that, madam?"

"Nothing, nothing," she said quickly.

"Is that your pilot still in the helicopter?"

"Yes."

"Ask him to come out at once or we will go in to drag

him out. That would be unnecessary violence. Please, Miss Tirado."

She didn't bother spending time on wondering how he knew her name; that would come later. She turned to face the helicopter and motioned to Pappas. "Come on out. It's party time and we—"

A terrible sword of green so bright it dimmed the lights still playing on them crashed instantly into being over their heads. It seemed to tear the sky in two and then, before she hardly started to flinch, it was gone. She stared upward; it had been so incredibly close. "I must be losing my mind," she murmured aloud again.

Tony Pappas joined her. The officer studied him, motioned two soldiers to check him for weapons. "You will cooperate?" he said to them.

"Of course," Angela told him.

"You had to land? An emergency, perhaps? A forced landing?" the officer asked, and Angela judged the queries to be for the record.

"No," she said. "No emergency. Call it the responsibility of their press to the people. We landed to find out more about that green light."

The officer looked her square in the eye. "What light?" he said.

Flanked by two technicians, George Wagner walked casually across the floor of the BEMAC dome and stopped before the ramp leading to the spherical transmission platform. All about him, as he stared upward at the great sphere, the world was glowing lights and gleaming reflections. Wagner turned slowly, immensely pleased with everything he saw. He knew every control, gauge, handle, instrument, lever and connection in the dome. That had been his specialty as a BEMAC team member: not merely to ride the beam when that moment was reached, but to have a "falling blanket" knowledge of the systems so that he could always envision the operation as a single action rather than many interconnected steps. The technicians checked again the wire terminals and FM transmitters built into the electromagnetic striping of his jumpsuit, talking quietly in mike-and-headset gear to the main control room. Suarez, Scott and Seavers stood by, waiting and watching. A technician came up to Wagner.

"Sir, we're almost ready. The director and his staff are on their way here now for your test."

"Good," Wagner told him. "Tell them I'm ready. Even anxious to get this show on the road."

They all turned their heads at the sound of jet engines and heavy rotor blades. Through windows they saw the flashing strobes of several helicopters. Kim turned with excitement to Suarez. "That's Stan and the others in the second group." She clasped her hands. "I still can't believe it. Stan's made the beam flight and it was only a few days ago he considered all this," she gestured, smiling, "to be so impossible!" She pointed, squealing as would an excited little girl. "There he is!" She dashed away to the entry platform where the helicopter had landed on its return flight from Dome Two that had received Blake. Kim raced past the scientists without a glance to throw herself into Blake's arms. She held his head in both hands and kissed him wildly.

"Hey, you'd think you were just a little worried," he said, gruff and warm at the same time.

"You big galoot," she said with mock anger. "You had me scared to death."

"Why? Think I'd get lost?"

She pushed him away, ready with a nasty comeback, but before she could say a word he smiled and winked. "Thanks, kid." They walked arm in arm down the stairway into the dome. Technicians and workers broke into applause as they recognized Blake.

"*Commence countdown in five minutes. Commence countdown in five minutes.*"

The wall speakers broke up the moment of genuine warmth. "Back to basics, kiddo," Blake told Kim. "The boss man briefed me on the way over. George ready for the big boom?"

"I hope so," she said, not able to match his banter. "Dammit, Stan, every test we make bangs on another door that no one's ever opened before. How can you be so flip about it?"

"When being serious gets you somewhere any faster than a ride on the irreverence train," Blake said, mocking her, "you come tell me about it. But for now," he whacked her hard but lovingly on her backside, "off you go."

Blake hurried to join the group with Felipe Mercedes. Hernandez and Delgado were walking away to reach their respective control and monitoring panels. Mercedes climbed to the dome center by the transmission sphere to talk with Wagner.

"You're ready, George?"

"Sir, I'm *eager*."

Mercedes smiled, a fatherly expression. "So I see." He put an arm about Wagner's shoulder. "Now listen to me, young man. I know you Wagners. Always so hellbent for leather. Your father and I were *both* like that, so don't try to fool me about anything."

"No, sir."

"You understand your mission? *Stay as still as you can*. That is very important, George. If you don't and you get to the edge of the circle, well," Mercedes squeezed Wagner's shoulder, "I should not like to be the one who has to tell your father you've been hurt."

"I promise, Doctor. As still as a statue."

"*Bon voyage*, my young explorer," Mercedes said as he left.

Wagner turned to greet Blake. "Well, Superman himself! The man who travels with the speed of light!"

They shook hands warmly. "Congratulations, Stan."

"Thanks. You ready?"

"In a minute. But tell me," Wagner pressed, "how'd you enjoy being zapped?"

Blake shook his head in a gesture of disbelief. "I still can't believe it happened. I mean, on either the personal or the objective level. Taking the second part first, it's still, well—overwhelming is a good word for it. It's tough to push aside everything you ever learned as being impossible."

Wagner smiled. "And the personal?"

"What's there to say, man? One moment I'm *here*, standing like I'm made of concrete, and the next instant, before I even have time to blink, I'm over *there*. I've been asking myself all this time since the test, *what happened*?"

Kim Seavers had joined them, listening quietly. Now she spoke in response to Blake's last words. "The big difference is that George won't have to walk back. Or fly in the chopper like you did," Kim told her teammate. "He gets zapped out to Dome Two, he kisses the mirror and he's back here almost before he left."

Mercedes's voice came through the loudspeakers. "Ten minutes, ten minutes. Everybody take your positions, please. We are now in the active count. I want every man and woman here to be a complete professional from this moment on."

Kim hugged George Wagner. She hated these final moments of waiting the most of all. Then she and Stan Blake left for their positions for this test with medical monitoring. Everything went smoothly down through the count, all systems operated, power buildup came in like honey and the minutes dragged along second by slow second. But then, like all countdowns, the last grain of sand falls to the lower half of the hourglass.

Kim couldn't disguise the cold in her heart or the fear showing on her face; the very expression she showed to the world unnerved Stan Blake, who placed great credence in the incredible accuracy of emotions preceding a man's push into his future. He heard her counting aloud in a whisper she had no idea anyone else could hear.

"Three, two one, fly bright and true, my friend, have a—"

The blast of energy, sound bullwhip-cracked and light screamed silently.

"—nice trip."

George Wagner would be immersed in a flood of energy to convert him to the stuff writhing within stars and he would whip outward and all his being in the massive laser beam would rebound from the mirror and snap him back to the platform in the center of the high sphere.

Kim heard her own voice tinged with terror, heard the sound before she even knew it was herself as she stood on her toes, straining, every muscle pulled, eyes bulging. *"He didn't come back!"*

George Wagner in that blink of an eye was gone. *In the same blink of an eye he should have been back.* All they would have seen was barely a blur of focus of Wagner, if even that much. The human eye doesn't really measure up in efficiency to the speed of light.

But you didn't need super vision to see that the transmitting platform in the sphere was horribly, fearfully *empty*.

In Dome Two, bounce-and-return foci for the laser beam transport of George Wagner, cold fear leaped into the heart of every person involved in the test. The northwestern wall of Dome Two, now garishly open where the observatory dome had split to leave free space for the laser beam, remained open to the cold night air. Normalcy disappeared in the dome center where there had been the receiver-and-bounceback installation. It was still there but piled in a heap of metal and glass with viciously sharp edges, either collapsed into a pile of gleaming junk or hanging and swaying from connections somehow still unbroken. At the instant the laser beam with the dematerialized George Wagner appeared, before pieces began to rain down, the facility was untouched except for a space, a circle, fifteen feet in diameter, punched right through the center of the dome.

And beyond, at the southeastern wall, where the observatory dome remained closed, cold air now flowed and the people within could see stars. The opening to the outside world was exactly fifteen feet in diameter. The hole was scalpel perfect. A laser beam fifteen feet in diameter with the soul and body and spirit of George Wagner had been here . . .

* * *

On the downside of the mountain ridge of Dome Two, rocks, trees, loose soil and the debris of the observatory dome wall, including electrical cables, bricks, neatly severed steel, plastic and other instantly-created debris still tumbled, slid and fell mindlessly toward lower levels.

Twenty-seven miles to the southeast of Dome Two, as a laser-borne crow might fly with unerring and unbending accuracy, stones, dirt, bushes, branches and dust threw up a minor spray of collapse, falling away downslope. Had someone been watching, and could see in the dark, they would have made out a raglike human form, moving with no more volition of its own than broken branches.

Kim Seavers' voice cut like a siren through BEMAC. "Where is he? *Where is he!* Goddammit, somebody say something! *Do something!*"

By her side Blake, imperturbable, granite-faced as usual in an emergency situation, held an earset to his head and spoke calmly into the lip mike. "Blake here. Tracking, do you have a fix?"

"Blake, we can't talk with you. Yes, we've got a fix, working on one. We're giving it to Mercedes right now. Come on up." The line went dead, Blake tossed it aside, turned to Kim Seavers and jabbed a finger before her nose. "Shut up and come on." He grasped her wrist and took off at a run with Kim dragged behind like a child.

They burst into the Tracking Control Room, drew themselves up short. One glance told them any conversation at this point would only interfere. Blake held Kim's hand so tightly it hurt the woman; Kim didn't mind. Pain suppressed her deep urge to scream from anger, hurt, frustration. They recognized Aura Moreno and Ramon Gonzales at their scope panels and readout displays. Gonzales spoke into his lip mike with the professional, smooth tone of a former air traffic controller.

"We have a tracking signal," he said with an almost sleepy calm. "Twenty four point three miles bearing outbound two one seven degrees. Signal strong. No movement."

Mercedes spoke quickly but very clearly into his mike, his voice carrying to every unit of BEMAC. "Start the helicopters! All pilots in your seats ready for immediate takeoff. Paramedics, take the lead helicopter. Night vision crews join the paramedics. Sequera, what's the status on that searchlight Caravan?"

Paulina Sequera's voice came back on the open line. "Standing by, crew ready, sir."

"Launch them immediately to the coordinates from tracking. All light systems ready to flood the area. Oh, yes; notify air traffic control to block off the areas involved."

"Yes, sir."

Mercedes didn't hear the reply. He was already running from his control station to reach his helicopter. Blake was caught by surprise as he watched the BEMAC crews slip into their assigned slots for just an emergency situation as was happening now. Those with outside needs were running like hell. The others remained glued to their stations to coordinate the work of those going outside. Neither Blake nor Kim Seavers had any assigned post under these conditions. But staying still and waiting wasn't Blake's style. He took off at a dead run, almost dragging Kim with him. They made it through a door held open, saw one helicopter with only two people in the cabin. Blake lifted Kim through the door and leaped in behind her. He stabbed a finger at the pilot. "Go, go. GO!" he yelled. They joined the other choppers in swinging full-power takeoffs and headed for the unknown.

Flashing red and white strobes reflected along the face of Angela Tirado in a strange pattern created by the distant bright lights shining through wire-braided armor glass. She rested her arms on the high window ledge and then her chin on her arms, staring at men and women running, vehicles dashing in all directions, and five helicopters performing wild jump takeoffs. The scene was one of fine orchestrated frenzy, emergency teams operating full-tilt but with an efficiency that comes only from skill and practice. *Well, this is something of an improvement over a cold jail cell with iron bars*, she told herself, but not very convincingly.

She turned from the scene she wanted desperately to get on videotape. Not too easy with all their equipment under lock and key and armed guard. She looked across the room at Sanchez and Pappas. Tony was sprawled on a couch, stocking feet propped up on pillows and sleeping like a baby. She hated him for his ability to do that; the moment he was free of any immediate responsibility he could fall into a deep sleep anywhere.

Sanchez wasn't so fortunate. He sat upright in a lounge chair, his knees tightly wrapped, his face raw and bandaged, and he appeared to ache everywhere. She sat nearby. At least he didn't have any broken bones from that incredible pratfall he'd performed from the helicopter under all those bright lights. A doctor had examined him; whoever these people were, they'd whisked him through x-rays and then padlocked the three of them in this room. With amenities, no less, Angela thought drily. A fridge with cold drinks and fruit, a large coffee urn, even several packs of cigarettes for those who wanted.

She wanted. She lit up and blew out a sudden cloud of smoke. The roar of a helicopter passing directly overhead brought her glance up to look at the ceiling.

These people were incredible. What was the official line? *Absolutely nothing out of the ordinary is going on at IVIC*, they told her. And right outside this building it looked as if the nation was mobilizing to repel an invasion!

They swept over Dome Two like the charge of the Light Brigade, helicopters slashing the night with whirling blades and jet engine exhausts, strobes flashing and landing lights on full to illuminate the ground ahead of them. Blake and Seavers looked down as Dome Two swept beneath them, bright floodlights on the ground shining on the perfectly formed hole that had been laser-blasted through the far wall. Then they were beyond the ridge, pounding at top speed, the choppers vibrating and shaking from the energy poured into the rotors. Blake kept his eyes moving to find the single aircraft that would be orbiting overhead the predicted impact point of the laser beam that had swept George Wagner from all visibility.

"I see it," Kim said, nudging Blake. No mistaking the aircraft. Four dazzling floodlights poured a great cone of white light on a ridge directly beneath the aircraft and the helicopters darted forward. In the five machines radio headsets came alive. "This is Lead One to all BEMAC aircraft. The director wants only two machines to land. Lead will land and the chopper with Blake will also land nearby. Everyone else is to work the area for any signs of unusual activity. Everybody stay alert; we're going to have a lot of aircraft movement in a small area."

The two choppers assigned to the landing descended more slowly, deliberately, their own landing lights turning the tumbled ridge into stark highlights and shadows. Bushes and trees whipped wildly in the downblast of the rotors, dust flew about and even small stones sailed through the air. A blizzard of insects seemed magnified by the floodlights as they scattered from the noise, wind and light.

"Hold it!" Blake shouted to the pilot, grasping his shoulder. "Drop it down and—can you swing that light a bit lower?"

"Can do," the pilot told him, swung the helicopter around in a tight circle, then eased into very slow forward flight, the light retracing its former path. "There he is!" Blake called out. "Hold this for a moment," he ordered the pilot, and thumbed his radio. "Five to Lead One. We have a human figure on the slope directly before us. It looks like Wagner. He's face down and not moving. I recommend we land upslope at least a hundred yards away so we don't cause any windstorms by him. We're going to land now. Lead, I recommend you hover off to the side and keep your lights on him."

"Blake, this is Mercedes. Go ahead, quickly."

They hit the ground fast and hard in a violent storm of their own making. Through blasting dust ahead of them their landing light flashed across the unmoving human form they knew was George Wagner. Blake grabbed a paramedic by the arm and hauled him physically from the helicopter, then waved at the pilot. "Get the hell out of here!" he yelled. They bent away from the blasting storm as the chopper lifted and banked away for a downslope run from the scene. Blake, Seavers and the paramedic—his nameplate read MARCO RUIZ— scrambled over the treacherous ground as fast as they could run, in a crazy crab-crouching angle that kept their balance on the slope.

They were by the body. "We'll have to turn him over," Ruiz snapped. "I hate to do this, we don't know if he's broken his back, but—"

Blake and Seavers took position, Seavers by the legs and Blake the shoulders to take most of the weight. Slowly and carefully they turned Wagner onto his back, Ruiz holding the light. Wagner's face looked like hamburger and his jumpsuit was in shreds. Blake motioned for Ruiz to get to him immediately. "Kim, stand with your legs against George so he doesn't move downslope." Blake bent down with Ruiz. The paramedic looked up.

"We've got a heartbeat. Weak but steady. Weak pulse. Looks like internal injuries, not much external bleeding. He may have a concussion. He's really out. I'm giving him a shot to pump up his heart."

"Do it," Blake snapped. He watched the paramedic work swiftly. Ruiz glanced up. "Get another chopper in here right away. We'll cover his face with a jacket, load him aboard so we can get him to a hospital."

"We can't land a chopper here," Blake snapped, "and we'd be crazy to move him." Blake glanced up, recognized the chopper Ali Bolivar was flying. Blake motioned to Wagner. "Cover him," he told Ruiz.

Blake stood straight. A bright light from Bolivar's helicopter played on him. Blake signalled with his hands for the chopper to come in, then cursed himself for a fool. Ruiz had a walkie-talkie and Blake grabbed it. "Ali, Blake here. Come in from behind us. Can you hold that thing with the upper skid on the slope so we can load George? He's alive but we've got to get him to a hospital fast."

"Can do," Bolivar answered immediately. "Stay low, Blake. I'll be coming in right over your head."

Two minutes later Bolivar was doing his balancing act with the helicopter. They lifted Wagner into the cabin, Blake slapped Ruiz on the back. "Go with him!" he shouted, then grabbed Seavers and ducked down as the chopper lifted straight up, banked sharply and broke away downslope.

Moments later other figures approached from the helicopters that had landed on the ridge. Mercedes and Suarez were in the lead of the group. Above them, the plane still circled with its bright lights and a helicopter hovered to the side, in radio touch, ready to direct bright floodlights at any area they pointed out.

"Doctor, it's obvious he hit about a hundred yards upslope," Blake said, pointing to an area that appeared scrubbed of its loose debris. "See over there? He hit, and he bounced, and I think he was unconscious when he came down the slope. Otherwise he could have grabbed anything to slow him down instead of falling this far. That brush over there? It's broken; it slowed and it stopped him. Maybe saved his life. Ruiz said he's worried about a concussion and some internals."

Mercedes looked up at the possible impact point, then turned to look below them. The slope went steeper downhill for another several hundred yards. "If he hadn't stopped here," Mercedes said slowly, "he'd have fallen the rest of the way."

"Those are rocks down there," Suarez added. "I know

this area. If he'd kept going, George would be dead right now."

Blake looked at Mercedes. "What the hell happened tonight?"

Mercedes met his gaze. "Let's go back and find out." He held onto Suarez's shoulder for support to climb back up the ridge. "Alejandro, you come with us. Kim, I'd appreciate it if you went to the hospital for—"

"Of course," Kim broke in. "I'll call you from there with any news."

They gathered about a graphic display console on the main floor of the BEMAC dome. Behind and above the group rose the transmitting sphere on its three slender but powerful support legs. It seemed a fitting background to their gathering. Tables and chairs had been brought to the console area, and the assembled group prepared to spend the night with coffee, tea, juices and sandwiches.

"We have some hard and fast decisions to make tonight," Mercedes told them. "Not guesswork, mind you. But we can't avoid risks, despite what's happened tonight and—" he had a fleeting memory of Benito Armadas, "what's happened before. Every time we endure a setback we learn something new, our capability goes up along with our comprehension of what's involved here. I want everybody to understand that. *We are going ahead with the program.* We're going to take risks. There's no way around that."

He sipped at hot tea. "I want to make something else very clear. I believe I have, and you people also have understood the enormous significance of what we're doing. We've also had top government support, but until a little while ago even I dared not hope for the strength behind us. When we returned tonight, I had a message to call our president." He paused for the effect his words would have. "I spoke with Luis Cesar de Verde. He knew everything that happened tonight. He asked questions with discernment I never knew he had. But most of all I've been asked, directed, whatever, to

move along with our program, no matter what the
odds. I fear President de Verde is willing to take even
greater risks than any of us. However, he left no doubt
but that we continue as an autonomous group. We set
our own schedules." He paused, sipped tea, let his
words sink in. "Any questions before we start?"

"Any more word on George Wagner, sir?" He recognized the girl with the question. Mernet Antonetti, one
of their computer specialists.

"Yes. George was critical for several hours. His internal injuries were greater than believed. But they've
stopped the bleeding. He's had several ribs broken and
what appears to be a cracked shoulder blade. Possibly a
broken pelvis. Anyway, his condition is upgraded from
critical to guarded. I believe George is in for a long
hospital vacation. I'll make sure he has pretty nurses."

His last words and his smile broke the tension that
had gripped them all. It was an unspoken signal they
could now get down to the work at hand.

"George will be all right," Mercedes went on, "but
we have a problem. Obviously, we had some kind of
power overage. I don't know if we can call it a surge
when George made his test, but whatever happened
the system went to overload." He looked about at his
group. "Right now we don't know *why*. And I'll repeat
what we all know; George is fortunate to be alive. Like
it or not that's the way it is."

Dr. Delgado brought a large computer screen to life
with animated graphics of the laser system and the
BEMAC facility. "Look here," he announced as he
referred to the screen. "When we fire for a test we set
the laser beam for a specific distance. Or we go for a
direct or even a double or triple mirror bounce back to
the transmitting point. In any event, we fine-tune the
power input to get the desired output results. We have
some slack, as you can see here, but our slack is measured in *inches* and now we're dealing in miles. So
we've got to be extremely precise in everything we do."

Lorena Fieger motioned for a question and Delgado
nodded. "Do you get the problem in transmission at its

origin, sir, or at the destination? I mean, can't we adjust the beam power *during* a test firing?"

Dr. Delgado smiled but there wasn't any humor in his expression. "The problem, miss, is that our laser beam *is* controlled. It's got a definite end to it. Think of the beam as a fluorescent light tube, and you can easily imagine the beginning and end, or simply the two ends. When we made the test with Wagner we preset the distance to the target mirror in Dome Two, but we also kept up a feed of continuous power so we could get the bounceback to this facility."

Delgado smiled wanly and took a deep breath; Mercedes nodded encouragement for him to continue. "Obviously our calculations need work. We overpowered the system for Wagner's test. We simply don't know why, but the beam with Wagner in dematerialization stage as an EM field hit that mirror in Dome Two with all the force of an artillery shell. Considering the mass involved we might as well have beamed a bulldozer against that mirror system."

For the first time Delgado offered himself the luxury of an intended smile. "There's hope, of course," he went on after the pause. "We believe we'll have the truly precise fine-tuning we need to beam living targets successfully. *And* return them safely," he added with a flourish. "Now, Dr. Mercedes has something special to tell you."

The two men waited until the screen showed changing graphics. "Dr. de Gama will join me," Mercedes said, "in describing what we considered a, well, a classic case of serendipity."

De Gama went directly into his report, referring as he spoke to the computer graphics display. "In refining our power flow we discovered we can beam to a great distance without having to reboost during the transmission. Put as simply as I can, think of an electrical power line, what we see crossing the countryside. There's always a loss of electrical energy when you move along these lines, and along the way we use booster stations to keep up the desired energy levels. That's what we've done with the BEMAC laser. When we beam from here to Station Two, to get the bounceback we've had to add energy to the system at the point of mirror reflection. Each time we moved to a different bounce point we needed to add energy."

De Gama took a deep breath. He seemed hesitant to make his next statement. "We've recently moved to power levels at the boost source far greater than anything we ever anticipated. Virgin territory, so to speak. And something incredible happened. The laser beam seemed to sustain itself with virtually no loss of energy and, we are daring to hope, without *any* loss of energy."

Morgan Scott glanced at Stan Blake, who raised his eyebrows in a silent groan. He might as well have stood up and wondered aloud, *What's happened to the laws of motion? Of conservation of energy? Of the rule that there ain't no free lunch anywhere in the universe?* Morgan Scott did it for him, albeit much more gently and politely.

Scott raised his hand. "Sir?" Vasco de Gama nodded to him. "I don't want to make this a classroom," Scott said, "but from what I remember about energy and the laws that affect it, even the light from stars traveling through open space gives up its energy."

"True," de Gama said.

"Then how is it possible to get a beam that is boosted only once and doesn't *lose* energy without a kick in the ass?"

To his surprise de Gama and the others laughed. "You have a way, the three of you, of saying complicated matters with a most elegant simplicity," de Gama said. "And your point is absolutely valid. The answer, my friend, lies in two areas. One, the beam *does* give up energy, but so little and so slowly we can't measure the loss yet. Or, two, and this may truly be the answer, there is an unknown factor that helps the laser beam boost itself."

"That's pretty tough to swallow," Scott answered immediately. "It's like saying you reach down and grab your bootstraps and lift yourself into the air."

"A perfect example," Mercedes said, "and with more accuracy than you would ever dream. I believe that we are dealing with an unrecognized but beneficial factor here. Let me take a moment to digress. Several of my American friends, many years ago, worked an experimental aircraft program in the United States. It was a truly remarkable project. You may remember it. North American, which is now Rockwell International, built a huge bombing airplane. Your air force called it the XB-70 Valkyrie. It was far bigger than the B-1 now flying. In fact, it was considerably bigger than even the Concorde supersonic airliner."

Mercedes smiled at his own recollections. "Here is the point of all this. This monster aircraft, more than thirty years ago, far bigger than the Concorde, began to fly faster than any of the designers or pilots ever expected it to fly. Do you understand? I don't mean by just a few miles an hour. They hoped this airplane would fly at twice the speed of sound, oh, fourteen hundred miles an hour. Instead, when it went to full power at high altitude and reached its designed maximum speed of fifteen hundred miles an hour, *it began to accelerate*. Do you understand what I say? It picked up speed and it accelerated by *five hundred miles an hour!* It had no more power, it did not dive but flew in level flight, and it was now cruising at two thousand miles an hour." Mercedes smiled. "By all the laws of physics and aerodynamics this was absolutely impossible."

Scott showed sudden fluster. "There's no trick answer to this, is there?"

"Oh, no! Never!" Mercedes exclaimed. "There *is* a bootstrap effect involved. No one had ever considered it before, had never encountered it before, so it came not only as a surprise but as a shock. How could an airplane suddenly fly faster by five hundred miles an hour than all computer and engineering predictions promised? How could this be possible? It could *not* be *im*possible, because it was happening."

Blake gestured idly. "Doctor, the suspense is killing us."

The group laughed easily. "The answer was the shock

wave in the supersonic regime created by this Valkyrie. All airplanes flying at supersonic speed create such a wave, of course. But the design of this machine was so unique that the airplane rode its own shock wave, which applied pressure from behind the bottom portion of the fuselage."

Blake stared. "You mean like a surfboard?"

Mercedes smiled. "Once again you prove the master at simplification. Exactly; like a surfboard. There must be the initial power kick, of course. The airplane has its engines, the surfer has the wave, we have the energy in electrical form derived from the nuclear reactor. Now, the best part of all this is that there is so little loss, and we have tried diligently to find it, that we are now convinced we are actually getting an energy *gain*. We don't know how or why, but it's there, and—" his tone grew serious, "we intend to use this gain in a way we never dreamed possible."

Mercedes turned to Vasco de Gama. "Doctor; please?"

"If we are correct and our tests continue to confirm our theory, it is now possible to use a carefully, a *most* carefully selected energy level, and beam from here to Dome Two, bounce from their mirrors to another station and keep right on doing a bounce with the beam until a preselected destination is reached."

Carmen Morales shook her head in both amazement and disbelief. "Sir, won't we need the receiver station at the final landing?"

"*No.*"

The word settled like a huge exclamation point. Every one of these people had worked with lasers of all sizes, colors, prisms, holograms and power levels. You *could* preset the distance you wished your laser beam to travel. It was like turning on a flashlight, setting the beam for twenty feet, and the beam would stop dead at twenty feet. But the flashlight had to be coherent wavelength: the laser, and not random or chaotic light as poured from household bulbs or tubes.

"I can see by your faces," de Gama said with pride, "that you have already gone beyond my words. And you're right. We can preset the beam with exact coordinates such as latitude and longitude. Knowing these coordinates, the distance involved, figuring *everything*, then, let us say, we can beam from here to a target fifty miles distant and drop the package—inert or alive—safely to that destination."

Stan Blake's mind had been whipping along with every word. Unaware, he'd risen to his feet. "That's *without* a bounce?"

Mercedes and de Gama answered in unplanned chorus. "Yes."

"You're *certain?*"

"Not *that* certain that I would make the next trip, Mr. Blake," de Gama said.

A roar of laughter met his candor. Blake grinned and gestured his own agreement.

"And that is why," Mercedes said, "the next beam riders will be dummies."

"Hey, I thought we already qualified for *that* job!" Blake called out.

Mercedes shook his head; this man was irrepressible. "You're very much alive, Mr. Blake. But you lack certain qualifications for the dummy runs. The beam riders will be heavily instrumented mannequins."

Kim Seavers waved her hand. "Sir?" Mercedes nodded for her to go ahead. "You can use either the bounce mirror *or* fly—ride, I mean—without the mirror?"

"That is correct."

"The laser is line-of-sight," Kim went on. "That means your transmission is limited to horizon lift. You can't transmit over the horizon in a bend."

Dr. de Gama nodded. "Also correct."

"But if you used an airborne mirror—a balloon, an aircraft, or even a satellite in orbit, especially geosynchronous orbit, and you have the self-sustaining power you've described, then you could beam *anywhere,* right?"

They didn't miss the sudden shift in mood. Mercedes and de Gama exchanged a hard look, and Delgado moved forward in a subtle gesture to bring the conver-

sation to an immediate halt. Mercedes became, from
one moment to the next, *too* casual.

"Well, theoretically, Kim, almost anything is *possible*.
Probability is another matter entirely." Mercedes made
a show of looking at his watch. "I don't mean to put you
off, Kim, but we're now running late on some important scheduled tests. We'll pick up on this conversation
at a later time. Everybody, this meeting is over. Thank
you for your time, we'll keep you posted on Wagner's
condition, which we all pray will improve. Everyone is
free to return to work."

Blake and Suarez moved idly to the side of a computer console away from the rest of the group. Blake
fixed a steady gaze on this Venezuelan he had come to
like so much. "You get the feeling the old man put off
Kim?"

Suarez snorted with disdain. "Put her off?" he said
sarcastically. "Man, he almost sent her smoke signals to
shut up." He shook his head. "The old man isn't like
that, Stan. I've worked under him, with him for years.
He's never cut someone short. Makes you feel that Kim
stepped across a line they never suspected she knew
existed."

"I got another feeling, Al," Blake said, a grin forming
on his craggy features.

"I get three guesses, right? I'll take only one."

"Yeah. We got some long trips scheduled for us."

Suarez laughed. "And no room for whiskey or a tooth-
brush, right, gringo?"

"So, let's get that drink while we can," Blake said,
slapping Suarez mightily on the shoulder.

Blackbeard stood haughtily in dead center of the
lexan transmitting platform in the dome high above the
floor of BEMAC. He wore a fierce teeth-gritting snarl,
pirate attire, a black patch over one eye, a grungy
beard, boots, and long braided hair. "You know something?" Alejandro Suarez said to Morgan Scott. "That is
the first man to ride the beam with a steel pipe up his
ass."

Scott laughed. Suarez was right. The instrumented mannequin stood angry and menacing only because of the steel rod jammed into what was an unfeeling mannequin posterier to form a triangular platform balance. "Well, he looks halfway human," Scott said with admiration.

"What? How can you say that?" Suarez held a beefy hand over his heart. "That beard, that hair, that moustache! It's human hair, my friend, so part of Blackbeard is a part of us. We collected from many people so that all of us will feel we are traveling with our blackhearted friend up there."

"Test Five One Eight, five minutes and counting . . ." sounded the speakers.

"Let's go," Scott said. "We're on tracking for this one." They moved quickly to the tracking booth, standing behind the operators. The minutes fled, the seconds fell away, they felt and heard the familiar sounds of power charging to mighty levels and there was almost the sense of ozone stippling the air about them a split-second before the laser cannon blasted; to their slow human eyes the great beam snapped into existence down its tube and flashed from the many mirrors to envelop the Blackbeard within the lexan sphere.

Before they heard the CRACK! of sound Blackbeard *seemed* to blur and shimmer.

"We have transfer! We have transfer! Holy Jesus, he's here and—" The speaker gulped air, gasped. "This is Dome Two! We have transfer." The light exploded silently through the dome aperture, flashed throughout the mirrors, the observers in Dome Two had a ghostly image of a fierce pirate on the bounce platform and then there remained only rolling thunder.

Ali Bolivar and Carmen Morales unknowingly held their breath, staring down through night sky. Dazzling green filled their world, reflected fiercely within the cabin and off the windows of the helicopter at six thousand feet. From their height, an absolutely straight and intense line of green fire appeared on the country beneath them, snapped into existence at a sharp angle from a distant dome, and snapped again into existence in another direction.

Morales slammed a fist into Bolivar's arm. "It works! It works!" she shrieked.

"St—uh st—uh—station Th—Three . . . Uh, I can't believe this, it was here, it's here, I mean, the light, I think I saw someone on the platform . . . I must be going crazy . . . a b-b-beard and a crazy hat . . . it was here and it's gone . . ."

The green flash still reflected throughout BEMAC Dome as the transmitting platform in the lexan sphere shimmered again, twisting the eyesight of observers, and Blackbeard was again in clear focus. It took several moments for the observers to confirm that this was a *second* laser flash; there had been only a split second, a fraction of a second, between the initial and the followup appearance of the beam. Blackbeard seemed to shimmer, but there he was, as if he had never flashed at the speed of light from BEMAC to Domes One, Two, Three and back to BEMAC. Not until the stammering, shocked, awed reports came in from the other Domes did they truly have confirmation. With rising excitement they checked and confirmed what they hoped to see on their instruments. Suarez swung Kim Seavers about wildly, and a suddenly irrepressible Stan Blake grabbed and fiercely kissed Dr. Edith Hernandez, who spluttered and turned beet red. All about them were the cheers and shouts of the duty crews.

Mercedes, de Gama and Delgado looked up from the master data display. "Perfect," Delgado said quietly, but with a look of cautious triumph. "No anomalies apparent," de Gama confirmed. They looked at Mercedes. He thought for several moments, then nodded to a technician.

The loudspeakers boomed. "Prepare for Test Five One Nine. Test Five One Nine will commence in thirty minutes. Repeat, we have a test in thirty minutes. Three test riders."

Technicians carried the three instrumented mannequins to the platform within the lexan sphere.

Test Five One Nine went perfectly.

Mercedes turned to Delgado. "Give everyone a break for food. One hour. I intend for us to work the night through."

"Yes, sir."

"Test Five Two Six in twenty minutes. Two instrumented riders and six animals in cages. There will be six living animals in cages. We are at T minus twenty minutes and counting . . ."

Chapter XIV

"Coffee?"

Felipe Mercedes opened his eyes slowly. He was slouched comfortably in the conference-room lounge chair in a high wing of BEMAC. His eyes blinked as he stared, for the moment unfocused, at General Luis Espinoza. "My goodness," Mercedes said quietly, "did I really fall asleep?"

"Your allotment, my friend, is thirty minutes," Espinoza said, smiling. "But no, you didn't fall asleep. You were struck unconscious by some very large and invisible rock, I would say. That describes how swiftly you left my company."

"You said something about coffee? Ah, there really is a God who takes pity on old and tired men. Yes, please, General. Black and hot and a touch of the sweet."

"I'm not sure if you're describing coffee or how you like your women, Phil."

"Hah! Speak for yourself, you steelbacked popinjay. The coffee, if you please."

Soldiers in the room exchanged uneasy glances. *Never* had they heard *anyone* speak to the general in such a tone! And with such insults! They eased their tension when they saw no sign of resentment on the part of Luis Espinoza. These two must be very old and good friends, indeed.

Mercedes sipped slowly at first, then drank deeply of the invigorating, nearly scalding dark liquid. "You know, Luis," he told Espinoza, "it would be convenient if I could simply take this stuff by intravenous injection."

Espinoza scowled. "If you scientists had your way you'd develop a pill to fulfill your sex for you."

"You go too far, my friend," Mercedes warned.

Espinoza laughed. "Never so far as to take a pill instead of a woman. Besides—" He ended his words in mid-sentence. Two armed guards stood by the open door, Angela Tirado between them. Immediately Mercedes and Espinoza rose to their feet to greet her with full courtesy. Angela Tirado walked forward slowly; she noticed the guards had not followed but had been dismissed by the general with an easy gesture. The move did not please Angela. She would have preferred to kick this martinet in the groin just as hard as she could.

"Miss Tirado, sit here, please," Mercedes told her, offering a slight bow and motioning to a chair to her right.

Her eyes seemed to flash and they saw her jaw muscles knot. "I'll stand," she said coldly.

Luis Espinoza sighed. "Ah, let us not go through *that* again!" He offered her the flicker of a smile. "Miss Tirado, let me say quickly that you have been mistreated. You have been arrested, although your arrest was for due and unquestioned cause. I will note for the record that you have also been kept in confinement, most obviously against your wishes. But perhaps most important of all, you have been deceived. That means you have not fulfilled what you call your oath to serve our people through an open and free press."

"I—"

"Please; a moment more. Now that I have verbalized at least most of your angry feelings, I offer you and I hope you will accept my apologies, and those of Dr. Mercedes as well, and now will you *please* sit down!"

Angela stared in disbelief. She moved to the chair and eased herself to the seat, her eyes glued to Espinoza, her expression mingled relief and bafflement. Mercedes poured coffee into a cup and slid it before her. "It is very good, Miss Tirado."

She shook her head. Mercedes persisted gently.

"Please, I assure you. If you don't need coffee now, you most certainly will very shortly."

She slid the cup closer to her, watching the two men as if they were mad. "What in the name of God," she asked slowly, "is going on here?"

Espinoza motioned to the aides in the room to leave. He held his silence until the room was cleared of all save himself, Mercedes and Tirado, then he nodded to Mercedes to proceed.

Mercedes glanced at his watch. A smile appeared on his face. "Well, Angela Tirado, better than any words, we will show you."

He pressed a button on the table. The room lights faded and full-wall drapes to his right slid open smoothly to reveal a wall of thick glass. Tirado was on her feet immediately and to the window, staring down at the stunning BEMAC dome complex. A loudspeaker on the wall behind her came alive.

"—three, two, one, *fire!*"

The huge rod of blazing green light speared across the dome and instantly, faster than any eye could follow, zigzagged into existence through the mirrored facets and blasted out of the dome aperture. Angela shrieked, recoiling by reflex, falling backward and tripping. Helpless, about to tumble to the floor, she felt the general's strong arms supporting her. She looked up wildly as a clap of thunder pounded through the walls. She winced, fought for her balance and dashed back to the window.

She spun about again, her eyes wide. "I swear I saw three people in that . . . that sphere . . . and they were blown to bits by that light!"

"Light?" Mercedes queried gently. "Surely you can do better than that, Miss Tirado," he chided. "A reporter of science and technology using so common an expression? You disappoint—"

"*Laser!*" she screamed in sudden fury.

"Better," Mercedes complimented her. "*Much* better."

"Those people!" Her hand swung behind her, pointing beyond the window. "I *saw* them! I *know* I saw them! Then that awful light . . . and they're *gone*!" She stared with widened eyes. "You're . . . you're no murderer," she said as she gathered her strength and sensibilities.

"Conclusion, Miss Tirado," Mercedes said, a bit sharper this time. He snapped his fingers as he spoke, digging at her. "Draw the conclusion. Come, come, woman, fulfill your reputation! You're right. I'm no murderer. Neither is General Espinoza, so—"

"Then . . . they weren't real?" Her eyes went back and forth between the two men. "Anthropomorphic dummies?" she asked hopefully.

"Dummies, mannequins; any description will do. And yes; they duplicate many human aspects and they are fully instrumented."

"They really *were* there, weren't they? I remember," she said suddenly. "The countdown, three, two, one and then that light and when I blinked, that sphere, whatever the hell it is, was empty." She blinked. "And that light! It's the light I saw down at Angel Falls, and, and . . ." She took a deep breath. "Have I really been seeing what I think I've been seeing?"

Mercedes offered a genuinely warm smile. "Yes."

"The mannequins . . . where did they go?"

"Sixty miles from here," Espinoza replied. "Dome Two. I know it's no secret to you, Miss Tirado. You flew over all three domes several times the other night."

She gestured with both hands. "Wait, wait . . . let me think. That light. It has been, *is*, the same light? Angel Falls? What the Russians reported? What they saw from space? The airline pilots . . . and . . ." Her voice trailed away as she waited for the answer.

"Yes," Mercedes said.

Tirado was as wary as a cornered jungle cat now. "No UFO's?"

"Two answers. The first is for this room only. No; no UFO's," Mercedes said. "That's unofficial. Off the record."

"And the other answer?"

Espinoza returned to his seat and poured coffee.

"Would you mind if I smoke, Miss Tirado? And for yourself, a cigarette?"

"God, yes." She took the offered cigarette, lit up and sucked smoke deep into her lungs.

"That second answer?" she repeated.

"It stands in two parts," Mercedes told her.

"What the hell does *that* mean?"

"It means that you and, we hope, just about all the press media, will keep right on reporting UFO sightings. And," Espinoza stressed, "so will the airline pilots, the cosmonauts, the Americans and the Russians making their secret flights—anybody and everybody who even thinks they saw a UFO. There won't be complete agreement, of course." Espinoza leaned back in his chair and flicked a cigar ash to the floor. "There will be detractors. People who insist the UFO's are nonsense, that people are seeing meteors, helicopters, airplanes, marsh gas, or that they're hallucinating. But," he shrugged, "you know that cross-section of humanity better than any of us here."

He leaned forward, suddenly intense, very serious. "We *want* the world to be on a UFO kick, or whatever it is they call a new rash of sightings. We want controversy about UFO's. We want everything except an accurate description of what you saw a short while ago."

She eased back to her seat. "Coffee, *please*," she told Mercedes. "Very black, strong—" She almost grabbed the cup from his hands and drank the still burning-hot liquid. She stubbed out her cigarette, saw Espinoza already offering another. She lit up, starting to select her words more carefully.

"We are," she said with exacting precision in her speech, "talking about a laser beam, correct?"

Both men nodded.

"I mean, it's one hell of a laser beam, the light that poured forth from the mount—" She shook her head. "Forgive the biblical approach, but—well, I never dreamed you could even *think* of a laser beam of such incredible size! The power . . . it must be fantastic! You would have to—" She stopped as realization came home

to her. "Of course," she said as conclusions appeared
one after the other. "The IVIC reactor?"

"Not the one you've seen before," Mercedes said.
"An incredible new facility. Flown in secretly from the
United States. Far more powerful than you might even
dream of."

"The *Americans*?"

"I would have sworn you said gringo," Espinoza said.
"But perhaps," he shrugged in an eloquent gesture, "it
was only your tone of voice."

She seemed thunderstruck. "The *Americans* . . . working with *us*, on a secret project?" She studied the two
men. "I've never known the Americans—your gringos,
General—not to claim credit for everything. Except, of
course," she added sourly, "if the Russians didn't claim
it first."

"Americans, no Russians, and despite your past poor
record with our northern friends, we have not only
their full cooperation, but tremendous support and,
most precious of all, *silence* on this matter."

She thought of past events at the international airport. Pieces that had never made sense began to fit
together. She also saw the smile on Espinoza's face,
knew he understood her own thoughts on the setups,
the facades, the absolute control Espinoza had used.
Well, those details can come later, she told herself.
What counts now is the big stuff—

"Why did you destroy the instrumented dummies?"
she asked suddenly of Mercedes. She felt all news-
woman again.

"We didn't."

"I saw that beam vaporize them!"

"Don't always trust your eyes," Espinoza offered.

"You wouldn't go to all that trouble to make them
invisible," Tirado said slowly as she thought furiously.
"And you wouldn't need the other—" She sat up straight.
"You fired the beam from this dome to another, and
then it fired again to another dome, so you're testing
power of the beam . . . but, then why the dummies
. . ." She snapped her fingers. "*My God, you even told*

*me before but it never registered. You said the dummies
went sixty miles from here!"*

Mercedes nodded. "Precisely."

"But . . . that would make . . . no, no," she shook
her head furiously. "That's too far out. Way, *way* out!"

They held their silence.

"A t— a tr—" She fought to say it aloud.

"It's the only one of its kind in existence, Miss Tirado,"
Mercedes said to help. "And you are correct despite
your struggle to accept what you were always taught
was impossible. It is a laser beam transporter."

"You used the beam to transport those dummies from
here to the other dome?"

"Yes."

"But that means—I mean, a laser is light, and light
cannot travel slower than its own speed, what makes it
light . . . you transported those things *at the speed of
light.*"

"Yes."

"That's impossible."

"You look strangely like a woman," Espinoza said,
not unkindly, "hanging desperately to disbelief so she
knows she is sane. To accept the impossible—?" he
shrugged.

"You're telling me to throw away all the physics I
spent years learning in school?"

"Close to that, yes," Mercedes said. "You see, my
dear, that is precisely what *we* had to do."

"May I come back to this subject later?"

"Of course."

Her hand pointed to her side. "That large man, he
has the build of an ox and the color of a man from
Samoa, or Hawaii, or whatever; I recognize him. He's
American."

"Of course you recognize him," Espinoza said. "We
made certain you got clear videotape of Mr. Blake and
the others."

"The other man and woman, they're here, too?"

Espinoza nodded. "Yes. They're part of this team."

"There will be more of them," Mercedes added.

"This is all so . . . so incredible," Angela said, sagging in her chair. "You *arranged* for us to get video of the Americans?"

"True."

"I suppose you conveniently got rid of the Russians, too."

"Precisely."

"It was all *orchestrated?*"

"Only *we* knew," Espinoza stressed.

"This gets wilder with every minute," Angela said. "Who else knows about this? I mean, outside of your obviously tight little bunch here. Any media people?"

"You and you alone," Espinoza said.

"*Only* me?"

"Only you," Espinoza reaffirmed. "To the rest of the world it's all UFO's, mass hysteria, hallucinations and perfectly normal objects in the sky." Espinoza paused and glanced at Mercedes before looking back to Angela. "We need your help in keeping it that way."

"You need me—" Her mouth seemed to hang open before she brought her lips together firmly. "I hope you don't mean for me to—"

"Yes," Espinoza broke in. "To lie for us."

"Now wait a moment. I—"

"To lie for your country," the general said flatly.

"For the future," Mercedes added quietly.

"Goddammit, General, I'm not—" Her eyes widened as another memory charged to the forefront of her thinking. "You said I was the only member of the news who's aware of what's really going on. But if I recall correctly, and I damned well do, Tony Pappas only *acts* as a member of my team. He's military; guard or reserve pilot in our air force."

"Long ago he was assigned to you," Espinoza said.

"*Assigned?*"

"That is correct."

"To spy on me? What in the—"

"Never to spy on you. To *protect* you."

"I don't understand."

Espinoza sighed, glanced aside to flick an ash, then

smiled, on the edge of open laughter. "In the outside world, Miss Tirado, you have the reputation of a lunatic. Do not be insulted, please; in this respect it infers you will stop at nothing to get your story, whatever and wherever it might be. That means you do a great deal of flying. When we planned, long ago, to use your services, to join you with us, we selected the brightest and the best of all our young pilots. That man is Icarus Pappas: a gift from the ancient legends, so to speak, to Venezuela. He was assigned to be your pilot specifically because of his superb piloting skills. The fact that he is also a journalism graduate is no accident. You will have to take my word for one thing: Tony Pappas *never* reported one single word about what you planned, or did." Espinoza stiffened his demeanor. "We do not break our own rules and we do not spy on our friends."

Angela smiled at Espinoza, throwing him off balance with her reaction to his speech. "You just maneuver your friends, is that it?"

"Don't you, Miss Tirado?"

Damn, this man was fast!

She nodded her head, wet her forefinger and held it up. "One for you, General. But this isn't over yet. If I read you right, from everything you've said and what's happened already, your program calls for me to front for you, and for Dr. Mercedes, here."

"In a way, yes."

"So let's call it like it is. You want me to *lie* for you."

"Call it as you see it; lie, deceive, front, propaganda, public relations—whatever. You of all people know the full truth is rarely what is offered to the people." Espinoza made a face. "They *hate* the truth," he said harshly, "especially when it is about themselves. Would you like to do a story on the intelligence, literacy, culture, technical acumen, operatic abilities, steelworking skills, and other characteristics of our most primitive citizens, on the basis of comparison with the best of other cultures? If you did that, and were so foolish as to venture downcountry, likely we would find your head impaled on a stick in the jungle."

"They would have eaten the rest of you first, of course," Mercedes added cheerily.

"The lie is not the issue. The purpose, the *intent*, of the lie is everything. We're not here to hurt our people, or those of any other country. That is the essential factor with which we're dealing," Espinoza said with disarming candor. "If, Miss Tirado, you wrote a whole series of lies and you, *you* and your lies, prevented a nuclear war, would you lie?"

"Well, I, that's a totally different—"

Mercedes half-rose from his chair, pointing to the interior of the BEMAC dome. "Down there, Miss Tirado," he said with utmost gravity to his voice, "is a weapon that can be mightier than all the hydrogen bombs ever built. Greater than all the missiles and warheads assembled by all nations. Yet it can be wielded in a way that changes the future course of mankind *and it needn't kill a single human being*. It imprisons no one, and leaves man the dictator of his own integrity. It is not our intention to interfere with human conduct in such a manner. But the international ship of state is in very rough seas and there are perilous rocks all about us. We want to help steer mankind's passage through those rocks to some point in the future where, hopefully, the madness of international arms contests can be put behind us."

Felipe Mercedes drew himself up straight and stern. "If you tell the true story of what we are doing here, Miss Tirado, you can wreck all those hopes."

Angela suffered a terrible sinking feeling. Her hand moved in feeble protest. "But I—"

Luis Espinoza looked at her in a way she'd never seen before, harder than steel and yet with a humanism she never suspected in him. And a pride that seemed to burn from his eyes. "For the first time in our history, Venezuela, a small country, not even remotely a military or industrial power of any consequence, can influence the future run of history."

"And I repeat," Mercedes added quickly, "quite possibly prevent a nuclear war from shattering this planet."

She fought down her own fluttering hand. "But—but, *why me?*"

"Because," Espinoza said in a no-nonsense voice, "you're the best-known, the most popular, *and the most believed* news reporter on television throughout all of South America. To say nothing of the islands off our coast, up through Puerto Rico and Cuba, through Central America and Mexico. And with the Latin population of the United States increasing so rapidly your newscasts are growing in popularity in North America as well."

"*And* you broadcast in both Spanish and in English," Mercedes threw in as an added fillip.

By now she held up both hands, waving her arms in an attempt to hold off the onslaught aimed at her. "Wait; wait, *please!* How could little Venezuela possibly accomplish what you say? What has eluded *all* the nations of the world?"

"We won't tell you more right now," Mercedes said. "There are good reasons for the manner in which we've exposed you to our project. When you leave this room, you're free to move through this facility, to talk to anyone, to draw your own conclusions."

Angela leaned back in her chair, her professionalism taking fast hold of the situation. "And if," she said slowly, "I choose not to play your game?"

"Then, Miss Tirado," Espinoza said in a voice that revealed nothing of his thoughts behind his words, "we have misjudged you badly. You, *and* your principles. Did you think all this was arranged so lightly?"

"It would be incredible, would it not," Mercedes said, his voice just above a whisper, "that if there were a chance to avoid that ghastly nuclear war we all fear so greatly, and *you* were the one to destroy that opportunity . . ."

"That's one hell of a squeeze play," she answered in a quiet but heated anger.

Mercedes smiled. "Yes, it certainly is." He gestured with a smooth, gentlemanly grace. "Shall we go?"

* * *

Two hours later, her head spinning from the avalanche of detail and equipment she had seen, studied, had explained and demonstrated, Angela Tirado was desperately ready to see her first laser beam transmission test from start to finish. Felipe Mercedes had excused himself from the extensive tour and explanations. "You watch the test, Miss Tirado," he told her warmly. "I will oversee the affair, and the good general shall be your companion." They walked slowly through the main floor of BEMAC dome, Tirado following closely whatever piqued her attention. And for the first time since she had been brought into this astonishing place she heard angry words exchanged. She looked up; on the work platform surrounding the lexan beamsphere she saw several people and two dogs. She recognized the American woman, Kim Seavers. Carmen Morales and Dr. Edith Hernandez were still strangers to her.

She studied the two animals, a young puppy and a dog she judged to be about one year old. Their markings puzzled her. "General, what are those?" she asked, gesturing.

"Swiss Mountain Dogs. The big one is Magnum, and the pup, Cassy."

Angela noted that both dogs were in heavy harness, the pup irritated with the weight and feel of the leather bracing, the older animal, however, unaffected by what he wore about his body. The American woman was staring down the elder scientist, Hernandez.

"Dammit, Edie," she said angrily, "there's no reason to send *these* dogs!"

Dr. Hernandez folded her hands before her, clasping her fingers together. "Kim, you know they're scheduled for—"

"Screw the schedule," the American retorted. "Send a rat, a monkey; send a whole goddamn bunch of rats! You've got enough of them back there!"

Hernandez turned to Morales. "Carmen, can you talk to her?" she said, nodding at Seavers. "I think Kim has gone slightly mad. Perhaps it's the altitude—"

"Very funny," Seavers said acidly. "Send a damn goat, Edie!"

Carmen Morales put her hand gently on Seavers' arm. "Kim, the dogs are in the schedule. It's more than that and you know it. Specific body mass, size, the EM pattern we have on them, the—"

"*I'll* go. Send me instead of them," Kim persisted.

"You will *not* go instead of them," Morales snapped. "What is this? National Dog Week? Save a canine for Jesus? The dogs take the same chances we do and you know it."

Hernandez lost her patience. Her voice took a sharp and critical tone. "They're in the countdown to transmit," she said harshly. "Both of you, stop bickering *now* and get down or I'll have you carried physically away from here."

Kim placed both hands over her heart; on her face was a look of pure astonishment. "Me? *Us?* Bickering?"

Hernandez pointed a steely finger. "Get down, *now.*"

She jostled the two women from the platform and turned back to the animals. She secured them both by a slim cable to the transmitting floor. Espinoza pointed to the cables. "They'll remain tethered until exactly one second before zero," he said of the dogs. "Then the cables are freed."

Angela didn't answer immediately as a wall speaker intoned the countdown. She walked slowly with Espinoza toward a reviewing booth. "It's funny, General."

"Share your humor with me, then."

"What you two said to me before. About how important all this is? The course of history, and so forth?"

"Yes?"

Angela tried not to be overly sarcastic. "Imagine. The future of the world rests in the heart of a woman who weeps for a dog."

Espinoza stopped and turned to her. "Tell me, Angela Tirado, would you have it any other way?"

"Damn you, General, you—" She smiled quickly. "No, I wouldn't."

They were safely within the reviewing area when the

count fled to zero, the energy groan built up, alarming
Tirado, and she felt the world was about to end when
the laser beam crashed into existence and the ripping
CRACK! assailed her senses.

She really didn't hear or feel anything for more than
a moment as she stared, gaping, as the two dogs vanished. *Seemed* to vanish. One instant they were as large
and solid as life; the next, they seemed ghostly. She
stole a swift glance at Seavers and Morales. Morales'
face was like stone. Seavers was biting her lip, near to
crying.

Tirado looked back at where the dogs had become
phantoms. She swore that's what happened, but the
next instant, almost as fast as the first sound and fury
pounded her, another green flash and a lesser crash of
sound, and a very solid, normal puppy yelped in fright.

Seavers dashed up the steps to the platform, snatched
up the puppy and cradled Cassy in her arms. The
mountain dog licked the tears on her cheeks.

"I'll be damned," Angela Tirado said.

Seavers looked up. "Murderers!" she cried.

The men and women in the dome laughed and
applauded.

Chapter XV

Blake, Morales, Suarez, Seavers and BEMAC crews gathered about the transmission sphere, placing three dummies in position for beaming. They were unusually quiet, showing an air almost of depression. Their problem was revealed in their facial expressions when they handled the mannequins, the three in full dress combat gear including knives, autorifles, grenades and other weapons. Mercedes watched from the side, then moved closer to talk to his team.

"You understand this test?" he said to the group. "We beam these three on a direct shot to Dome Two, then to Three, and a longer transmission back to here with our dome used as a final receiver."

They seemed to listen half-heartedly. Mercedes was puzzled until Carmen Morales spoke directly to him. "Doctor, why the weapons?"

Mercedes didn't appreciate the question, but he covered his displeasure. "This test is to research a deployment possibility. Consider, if you will, a type of dangerous situation. The presence of police or soldiers at even a short distance becomes critical. In a negative way, let me stress. Imagine the cabin of an airliner with three hundred passengers, including many women and children, and the hijackers ready to blow up the plane. They have every approach to the airliner covered with weapons, and at the first sign of attack they'll not only shoot back but they'll start killing the helpless passengers. But what if we could beam a combat team directly *into* the cabin of that airliner? Or a building? Or a missile silo installation?"

240

Morales and the other beam riders exchanged hard looks. "I understand what you mean, Doctor Mercedes, but I, uh, I mean, *we*, never thought of this program for that kind of purpose."

"Then think about it, Carmen. It is all about real life." Mercedes looked about them. "All right. Enough talk. If you want philosophy, come to me later. Now; everyone to your positions."

By now the countdowns were pat affairs, everyone from director to the technicians moving with practiced and confident ease. The now-familiar loudspeakers chanted. "Test Six One Four, sixty seconds and counting . . ."

The deep groaning energy roar, green fire blazing, thunder, and blurs where there had been three mannequins.

In Station Two, everyone stood by, anxious to *not* blink when the beam smashed in, mirror-bounced, and moving faster than any eye could follow, snap-whipped the mannequins on their lasered path to Dome Three. The countdown from BEMAC Dome sounded from Dome Two loudspeakers. "Three, two, one, fire!"

Instantly the transceiver station and apparatus in dome center of the station exploded. Multiple blasts of flame and searing explosions tore outward, hurling steel, plastic and lexan violently away, striking equipment as well as helpless technicians on duty stations. Arms, heads, legs and torso parts of mannequins, wires streaming, internal parts sparking and blazing, whirled through the air. Smoke boiled upward and bizarre clanking and metallic ringing sounds came from debris falling downward.

The master control technician stared, frozen in disbelief. On every panel OVERLOAD signs flashed repeatedly. Another man ran to the panel, reached past the master control technician still frozen and unmoving, and yanked the EMERGENCY POWER CUTOFF handle down to OFF.

No one needed to say the test transmission was a horrible failure.

* * *

Sunlight, bright and warming, streamed in through the open windows of the ANYTHING ROOM. Here in a hall-sized gathering place, men and women tinkered with oddball equipment, met for technical bull sessions, or gathered away from the mainstream of hectic BEMAC life. Wall charts, computer terminals, cables, tools; the room was a monument to tinkering on a grand scale. Along one wall filled with old and battered but comfortable couches and lounge chairs and bean bags, intermixed with tables loaded with different kinds of coffee, soft drinks and fresh fruit, the human heartbeat of BEMAC had gathered to bear the burden of last night's disaster.

There was an absentee in their midst. Almost always, some measure, no matter how small, attended these gatherings. For this moment levity was banished. Delgado disliked smoke-filled rooms; he put aside his usual objections to the heavy cigarette and cigar smoke in the room and accepted the clearing effect of air-conditioning outlets and open windows.

Felipe Mercedes rustled a stack of papers before him; technical readouts from the recent disaster. "We know what happened," he told the group. Heads turned and bodies shifted to transfer full attention to the BEMAC director. "It's all here," he said, tapping the papers. "Indeed, we were able to suspect what we theorized *before* the test. Miss Morales, especially, as the spokesman for our teams, will doubtless be relieved that we had considered an event that will please her, and I ask her to note," he looked at Carmen Morales with a mischievous glint to his eye, "that our failure is her success."

Morales looked at her friends about her, shook her head and shrugged.

"We have confirmed," Mercedes went on, "that we can't transmit anything through the beam that is molecularly unstable."

"Do you mean, more specifically," Blake threw out, "that you can't *successfully* transmit an unstable molecular substance?"

"Thank you," Mercedes came back graciously. "Your words are more accurate, of course. Yes, we can transmit, we can achieve dematerialization, but arrival and rematerializing is where it all comes apart. And violently."

"Sir, you're referring, essentially, to explosives?" asked Carmen Morales.

"Absolutely. Any kind, apparently," Mercedes confirmed. "Let's say that in all the tests so far nothing of an explosive nature ever arrived without tearing itself apart. We've made sure to use minimal quantities, otherwise we'd have destroyed the receiver stations."

Morgan Scott gestured for attention. "But *why?* We go through fine. Animals have gone through. And you've transmitted all kinds of nonbiological material before."

Mercedes nodded to Dr. Delgado to take the query. "Any biological mass," Delgado began immediately, "a living mass such as yourself, can be worked skillfully within the beam because of your EM pattern. We can match the two; the EM pulse of your being with an EM pulse we can program into the beam, and we have great leeway. We don't need exquisitely sensitive fine tuning, so to speak. But that's why every one of you are given such exacting EM pattern screening tests. Our American friends, for instance," and he acknowledged Seavers, Scott and Blake, "never knew until after they arrived in our midst that they'd been screened, checked and their patterns coded down to the *nth* degree back in the United States. Otherwise, if they hadn't fit within the extremes of the beam, they would not be here now. So if you're of the right pattern, you mix with and flow with and *become a part of* the beam. If you're too far from the broad swath of the brush, so to speak, you don't come out of the beam the same as you went in. We just can't put you back together again."

Kim Seavers made a rude noise. "Doctor, we call that the Humpty Dumpty syndrome."

"A child's fairy tale, but absolutely correct," Delgado said, smiling. "Now, we *can* send someone through the beam even if they're off the pattern. They can wear a special suit or outer covering that has the proper EM

pattern of another person, or a suit with a pattern
encoded within the beam and locked into the computer. In effect, the suit acts as their own skin and they
make the transmission successfully. And what we're
talking about here is on the electromagnetic level. You
must separate EM from molecular."

Mercedes put down a coffee mug. "First, understand
that TNT, or any other explosive," he picked up on
Delgado's descriptions, "is extremely unstable as a molecular entity. Now picture a block of TNT dematerialized
and then resubstantiated on arrival at its target point.
Laser beam or not, we're dealing here with acceleration. Call it deceleration, if you wish, at arrival. Sometimes you arrive with the kick of a mule."

Alejandro Suarez waved a beefy hand in the air. "A
very *big* mule, Doctor!" he called out.

"And who would know better than those of you who've
made the trip?" Mercedes agreed. "Now, sometimes
you stop with a jolt. We never know how hard a jolt,
but when that laser stream decelerates down from light
speed, it is, molecularly, a *tremendous* jolt."

Suarez was enjoying himself. "It's not so bad, sir.
You're going better than a hundred and eighty six thousand miles a second, and then, you come to a dead
stop," he snapped his fingers, "like *that*."

"And if you're carrying a gun with live ammunition,"
Mercedes offered, "or a hand grenade, or a rocket, or
primer cord, or even RDX, when you make that stop
that explosive goes off and whoever's carrying it is—"

Morgan Scott bounced up and held his hand and
fingers in the shape of a gun. "BANG! BANG! BANG!"
he shouted, then grinned. "You are one very dead
sucker, man."

Through their exchanges General Luis Espinoza had
maintained a stony silence. Now he looked directly at
Mercedes. "That is not the kind of news," he said drily,
"I relish taking to Fred Carrillo."

"I understand," Mercedes said, appearing subdued
with the name and the subject.

"Hey, who's Carrillo," Scott sang out, "and why's he

such hot snot?" A titter ran through the group at his words.

Even Espinoza, despite his grim demeanor, smiled. "Mr. Hot Snot, as you so inelegantly describe him," Espinoza said, "is the special advisor to Luis Cesar de Verde, who is the president of Venezuela. Mr. Carrillo *just* happens, as well, to be the man who approves the funding for this project. It is expensive to the point of agony. If Carrillo believes this agonizing to have a future benefit to our country, the project continues. If this value eludes us, if Venezuela cannot show a return for what is a staggering investment for a nation our size, then this project becomes second-rate research. Does that answer your question, Mr. Scott?"

"Sure, sure; sorry I seemed so snotty myself," Scott said quickly. "I didn't mean to come down like that, General, and I apologize."

"You're telling us," Blake entered the exchange, "that you've got to keep your man happy, is that it?"

Espinoza nodded. "Yes."

"And by *happy* you mean our being able to carry out certain jobs," Blake shot at Espinoza, "that call for the use of firepower, right?"

"That, my friend, is the idea," Espinoza said with the barest trace of a smile.

"Not me!" Carmen Morales called out. "Count me *out*."

"General!" Suarez was standing. "This is the first anybody has ever spoken to us about *our* using *guns*. Besides, if we're that good, *and we are*," he gestured to take in the teams, "all of us, then we do *not* need guns or explosives to do our work."

"Whatever the hell that is," Blake finished for him.

"Alejandro," Espinoza said to Suarez, "you would use a bow and arrow against terrorists?"

"It was my impression," Suarez said slowly and carefully, "that all this, everything BEMAC represents, was on a much higher scale, for a greater purpose, than to be simply another SWAT team."

"Hey, General," Blake said, standing beside Suarez,

"excuse me for busting in on what sounds like a family affair, but Al's right. Whatever you've got in the back of your noggin for us, there's more ways than guns to do—well, hell, I don't know *what* we're to do."

Mercedes rapped the table before him. "Gentlemen, please! We're meeting on technical matters, not bashing one another about guns good or bad. Please!"

Espinoza pointed a finger at Suarez and Blake. "Meet with me immediately after this meeting." Then to Mercedes, "My apologies, sir."

Still annoyed, Mercedes turned his attention back to his group. "On a point of *scientific* inquiry, are there any questions on the explosives issue?" No one spoke. "Good. Now, we will repeat the mannequin beam tests as before but with one critical exception. No explosives or sensitive material of any kind. When those tests are completed, I have scheduled twelve more tests with riders in the beam. When *those* are successful, and we will take every step forward one at a time, we will begin the experiments, first with the animals, to transmit from here to a mathematical point rather than a dome receiver."

Gasps of surprise and murmuring swept the group. Kim Seavers rose slowly. "You mean . . . transmit by beam from here to a . . . to a *theoretical* arrival point? We beam to where a big computer marks a big X in its electronic brain?"

Mercedes hesitated before replying. When he spoke his answer caught everyone by surprise. "Does that bother you?"

"*Bother* me? Taking a shot into an unknown any of us can hardly understand? *You* don't understand, Doctor. *I'm volunteering right now for the first ride!*"

Blake nudged Suarez and spoke in a loud stage whisper. "It's just like I told you, Al. Body by God, brains by Mattel."

Kim turned and held up her right hand in a fist, middle finger extended. The team members applauded and whistled their approval.

* * *

"T minus four minutes and counting."

The loudspeakers by now were background hum to the beam riders. They had committed to so many tests their own sense of timing allowed them to move with clockwork precision. Suarez and Blake stood in the platform of the lexan sphere high above the dome floor. In addition to their special jumpsuits, they wore crash helmets, grappling hooks and lines, flashlights and a variety of other equipment catalogued and set up for the tests.

"This time, baby, it's hang on tight," Blake told Suarez.

"One hand or two?"

"Arms linked. My left, your right," Blake said. "We give it the big try, man. We go out linked and maybe we'll be able to pull our arms apart when we pop from the beam." He grinned. "Otherwise we're liable to arrive at Dome Two with my hand going in your ribs and coming out your ass."

"You should be so lucky," Suarez tossed back at him.

"Three, two, one, fire!"

Energy howling, light ripping outward, the doom boom, as they'd come to call the thunder roll following the flash, and Blake and Suarez were gone. Twenty minutes later they were back, grinning like idiots. They'd emerged from the beam in Dome Two, shucked their gear, slipped on new equipment, and had been boosted back to "Home Plate" by the Dome Two transmitter.

Scott and Morales made the next "flight."

Kim Seavers and a new team member, Danza Cuyagua, a huge Indian whose parents still lived in huts down the Amazon, boomed out on the next test. It went beautifully.

Angela Tirado stood with General Luis Espinoza in a viewing booth overlooking the BEMAC dome; to her right twenty TV monitors permitted the onlooker to zero in with a zoom lens on any activity within the dome. The theory behind this installation was that whoever was in that viewroom would never have gotten there without very good reason, so there wasn't anything to hide, and zoom closeups eliminated many questions about who was who and who was doing what. That's the way it was *intended* to function, but the human psyche being what it is, with old habits deeply ingrained into everyday human function, it was never surprising to those who devised the system that their best efforts would almost always be ignored by reflex action. Which is why Angela Tirado, watching two beam riders, trailed by technicians, walk across the dome floor to the stairs leading to the lexan transmission sphere, stiffened suddenly and, unaware of the act, sank her nails painfully into Espinoza's arm.

"I don't believe—no; it *can't* be!" she exclaimed as the general manfully did his best not to remove his arm or at the least clap Angela on the side of the head to free himself.

For an instant before he replied, Espinoza glanced at the television monitors, the camera controls, and all the facilities made available to zoom in tight on any face or object in the huge facility—all of which were being ignored by a woman who'd cut her baby teeth on electronic and television equipment and employed that equipment to become one of the world's best-known newscasters. Instead of tweaking a dial, she held her death clamp on Espinoza's arm and with her free hand pointed to the two jumpsuited beam riders.

"*Tony!* Isn't that Tony? *What's he doing down there?*"

"Pappas and Suarez are about to make another test." The general glanced at a glowing situation board. "There it is," he told her. "Pappas and Suarez and, um, about four hundred pounds of assorted materials and equipment."

"Since *when?*" She released her grip, to the silent but everlasting relief of Espinoza, continuing to point with one hand and brush her hair from her eyes with the other. "I knew he was *busy,*" she went on, "but this, *this,*" she gestured wildly again, "is plain damned ridiculous!"

"You didn't know?"

"Know *what?*" she said, nearly shouting at Espinoza. "When did he become a glory boy? Hell, General, *he's my pilot*. Oh, I know, he's in the air force reserve, and you can always call him to active duty, but he's *my* pilot and he works for *our* news company."

Espinoza laughed. "Then it's easy to understand why he's so busy. He's like a man holding down three jobs and—"

"He's like a one-legged man in an ass-kicking contest," she stuck into his sentence.

"Yes, yes, and most likely on thin ice, too," Espinoza added, still laughing. "Tony Pappas is rather remarkable. He does all these things and he does them well."

"How long has he—"

"Since the beginning of the program."

"You mean he's always been a part of this BEMAC Disney World and he's been *spying* on me?"

"Providing you with *our best pilot* for *your* safety is hardly spying," Espinoza said, elevating himself to a higher level from the barbed remarks. "But if you wish to consider that it was vital to us to know what the press knew or believed or suspected, why, then by all means go ahead and judge Pappas to be a spy. The fact that he'd give his life for you shouldn't matter at all."

"If I were a man, General, I'd—"

"You? Making a distinction between man and woman? Is that personal or professional, Miss Tirado?"

"Why do you always call me Miss Tirado when you're on your high horse, and Angela when everything's hunky-dory?"

He blinked. "Hunky-dory?"

She waved away the moment. "Forget it."

"As you wish. Did you check the time? Aren't you scheduled to see a UFO tonight with your own lovely eyes? I understand it will be an exciting first-person report."

She stared coldly at Espinoza. "Oh, I'll see them, General. And right on schedule." She grimaced. "But I'll be damned if I *like* what I'm doing."

"Yes, yes." Espinoza's voice seemed far away. She turned to see where he was looking. The count intoned through the speakers, energy soared, light blazed and the thunder bullwhip slid beneath her skin. She shuddered.

Pappas and Suarez vanished.

Green light grew from ghostly white into multiple ringed teardrops, expanded into eye-stabbing globules, and then surrounded a huge gush of savage orange-yellow flame pouring straight down, flanked by two wasplike lances of white-yellow fire. Flame and smoke tore madly across the launching platform, bellowed with a Minotaur-like roar as the powerful Delta rocket booster slammed upward from the holddown arms of Pad 17B. Cape Canaveral Air Force Station fell away like a huge deflated rock beneath the accelerating booster, its cry of power changing to an enormous, hollow boom of an acetylene torch reaching desperately for the vacuum of space.

Caleb Massey leaned against the side of the door to the communications van on Cape Canaveral. Massey didn't look like the Massey most people knew, with a wig, skin dye, and the uniform of an air force sergeant. He preferred his name not to be included anywhere in the list of government and military personnel involved in the launch. He blinked in the glare of the rocket howling up and over, not bothering with the binoculars hanging by a strap from his neck. He wasn't here for sightseeing. He spoke into a thin pencil microphone before his lips.

"We got a beauty, old man," he said with a quiet and deep pleasure. "This is the last one."

Only Massey heard the voice of Senator Xavier Elias in his headphones. "Did we confirm orbit on the other two?" Elias asked.

Jubilation came through in Massey's usually controlled tones. "Yes, *sir*. The shuttle crew threaded the needle perfectly. We've got two birds in synchronous orbit, *confirmed*. And the way this one is going: listen—"

He turned up the launch control speaker in the van and the voice of Delta Control came through loud and clear. ". . . and coming up on two minutes into the flight. On my mark, plus two minutes and counting, *mark*, and we're well into a perfect flight . . ." Massey cranked down the volume.

"By tomorrow night we should be in business, old man."

"It can't be any too soon. Look, Caleb, as soon as you wrap up your details down there, I'd like to see you one on one."

"How's the club for coffee? Eight sharp tonight?"

"Do it. See you then."

Kim Seavers climbed the stairway to the platform of the lexan sphere. Groups of people paused in their work to watch as she reached the transmission level. "You know something?" Suarez said to Blake and Scott, standing with him in a separate group. "That woman looks better in a jumpsuit with all her gear than most beautiful women do in a bathing suit. I don't know how she does it."

"Well, it's a hell of a lot more than just shape," Scott said, his voice snappish.

Suarez nodded slowly. "Easy, my friend. I have come to know and love her as much as both of you."

"Sorry," Scott said. "I know. I guess we're all on the thin edge right now."

Kim looked as if she'd stepped out of a futuristic science fiction film featuring beautiful women in dazzling attire. It wasn't too often you saw a woman's body well defined in a pressure suit which, in Kim's case, was emergency-situation-only outerwear. The BEMAC patch with its lightning-bolt insignia reflected glittering light, and the markings of her suit only served to emphasize the beautiful body within. Carmen Morales stood behind Kim, holding her lock-and-seal helmet. Another technician went down a checklist inspecting oxygen, radio, barometric pressure solenoids, harness and parachute, survival kit and other gear.

"Hey, I meant to ask you guys," Scott said suddenly. "The general, remember? Said he wanted to have a private chit-chat with you two heroes? What's the poop?"

"One guess," Blake said brusquely.

"No second chance, huh?" Scott grinned. "Tell you what, sweetheart. One buck gets you ten you two are not cooperating, you're stubborn, unfamiliar with the real world, that there are times when guns are absolutely necessary, and for the good of all mankind you've got to be prepared to use whatever weapons they give you, and don't give the general any snot."

"*Very* good," Suarez said. "I am impressed. I will tell Blake not to take your bet."

"And if you don't join the team, wear the school colors, and agree to kill, maim and slaughter when it's to make people free and happy, you're off the team," Scott added.

"What'd you do? Get a transcript of the meeting?" Blake asked.

"Nah. Just a wild, crazy and I'll bet astonishingly accurate guess."

"Guess, my ass," Suarez chimed in. "One last question. What was the outcome?"

"You politely told the general to get stuffed."

"Bingo," Blake confirmed.

"And since you're still here," Scott concluded, "it's either abeyance time or he was simply putting you two to the test."

"I think," Suarez said to Blake, "he is some kind of goddamned psychic, the way he got all that. Not only—"

"Hold it," Blake broke in, gesturing. "Here comes the old man."

Felipe Mercedes joined the group on the transmitting platform. He checked Kim's equipment, spoke quietly to the people readying her for her laser transmission test. The three men moved in closer beneath the platform to hear the exchange above them.

Mercedes faced Kim squarely, one hand on her shoulder. "I want to be absolutely certain you understand the risks you're taking. All our tests so far have been with the mannequins or the animals and this is the first time we're going so far with—"

She placed a gloved hand on his, smiling at the concern mirrored in his face. "Doctor, thank you, but I *know* the game plan. I'm the first walking, talking doll to take this trip. I drew the short straw fair and square.

It's *my* turn to go, it's *my* decision." She glanced at a wall timer, her impatience showing. "Please, let's get on with it."

Mercedes nodded. He turned to the assistants. "All right. Seal the suit, check all pressures and communications and we go five minutes after you give me the ready sign."

With those words the technicians and engineers returned to their control and monitoring stations. Several of the support team members gathered at the large computer graphics display of Moreno and Gonzales. This was obviously no simple repeat test; the air was electric with nerves on edge everywhere.

Blake and Morales stood together before the computer graphics display; the screen showed BEMAC on a map, marked by a single green light, and connected by a glowing line straight out of the atmosphere to a satellite in geosynchronous orbit at 22,300 miles above the planet. A flashing line reflected straight down from the satellite to an airfield near Jungle Rudy's camp near Angel Falls.

Blake's jaw muscles pulled into knots with the anger boiling within him. He glared at Mercedes. "Goddammit, he shouldn't send a *woman first*. I should go, or Alejandro, or Tony, or—"

Morales's look didn't hide her scorn. "Oh? Do you all have special talents as men that Kim lacks as a woman?"

"You're damned right!" he snarled at her. "It takes a man to—"

"You tell me three advantages *you* have as a beam rider," she lashed back, "that Kim and I *don't* have. And you can exclude your balls, *Mister* Blake, because all they do on a job like this is get in the way."

He stared at her in disbelief, then shook off her retort. "For starters," he said, "she could easily end up in deep jungle country."

"Well, then," Carmen said acidly, "supposing you or I did just that. Ended up in deep jungle country. Who would be the superior? You or me?"

"*I* would, of course. Special forces training, combat in Central America—"

"Big deal." She couldn't help her own sarcasm. "You *trained*. How long?"

"Four months, lady."

"Hey, that's really terrific, Blake. Four whole months. *I grew up in jungle country.*" She laughed. "*You* grew up in Detroit." She held his gaze without flinching. "Do you speak any of the native languages in down-country?"

"Well, I, uh—"

"Do you know what plants are poisonous and those that are safe to eat? Don't even bother to answer. *You* don't. *I do.* And not only that, but—"

Pappas nudged Carmen. "Stop beating up on the kid, Carmen. Nobody can hear themselves think around you two."

Blake and Morales looked sheepishly at one another; they nodded their assent to save their exchange for later.

Mercedes's voice carried to them through the loud-speakers. "I want everybody to understand just what it is we are trying to achieve with today's test."

Those few words were enough to bring everything to a halt. Several fast glances at the wall countdown digital timers confirmed their thoughts; the count was on hold. Kim Seavers stood alone in the beamsphere, strangely enough the only person in the great complex not in someone else's company.

"In just a few minutes, if everything works as planned," Mercedes went on in a voice they heard only rarely, with his tones of concern, "we're going to transmit a human subject from this station on direct line-of-sight to a satellite now orbiting above the equator. That satellite is in the familiar geosynchronous orbit at just over twenty-two thousand miles. It's what we call a holding orbit. It matches exactly the speed of the earth beneath the satellite so that this particular satellite seemed to remain fixed in space. In fact, the satellite is due south of us right now, directly over the equator."

Mercedes paused only briefly. "The laser stream ejected from this site will reach the satellite mirrors and reflect back to earth. Not back here, however. Its arrival point is a theoretical fix in time and space. A mathematical determination. It is exceedingly complex and every possible factor known to science is accommodated, such as latitude and longitude. Also, the mean elevation of the target area is fed into the new Greystone computers so we have a very good chance for the human rider to reach the desired target with absolute precision."

Suarez leaned over to Scott. "What's that computer? A Greystone?"

Scott shook his head. "Damned if I know, man. When I heard it I thought he was talking about a Tarzan movie." Scott motioned to the speakers. "Hold it, Al."

"I'm aware you're all concerned, *we're* concerned," Mercedes continued, "about the inevitable problem on which we've all spent sleepless nights. What if the beam rider—what if Kim—arrives at a point in space and time that's already occupied, such as a tree or a rock or, one never knows, inside the stomach of a cow. We've provided for such a contingency. If there exists a major molecular mass at the point of appearance the beam goes automatically into a reject-and-return mode. In short, it doesn't cut off, but snaps back to its origin, and the person in the laser stream rematerializes right here."

Silence met the conclusion of his statement. There was little or nothing to say. Everything they'd heard had been hashed over a thousand times without benefit of this particular stage and audience. More than a few of the BEMAC crews took umbrage with Mercedes for selecting so sensitive a time to pontificate; to them there must be more a political than a scientific or a human need for his speech. Yet the usual catcalls and cracks from the group remained absent. Kim Seavers was still there alone on that platform, and *that* was all that mattered. It appeared as if the truth of *that* reality finally reached Mercedes as well.

"Kim, any questions?" Mercedes asked over the speakers.

She thumbed her forefinger-and-thumb transmission button that brought her voice into the loudspeaker system. "Yes, sir. I've been up here so long I need to go to the bathroom, but—"

She paused and seemed to grope helplessly at her suit. "All these zippers!" She paused again just a beat. "Can I go now, Daddy?"

A staccato, echoing burst of laughter swept about the dome, slicing away the tension that had built through the seemingly endless verbiage.

"Three minutes and counting, Kim," came Mercedes's voice.

The ice was broken, people talked easily, tended to their countdown lists, the control panels steadily pushed away the red and amber and glowed more brightly with green, and the final calls went out through the headsets and the speakers—

"Nuclear."

"*Go.*"

"Power systems and flow."

"*Go.*"

"Navigation."

"In the green. *Go.*"

"Tracking."

"Ready. *Go.*"

"Seavers."

"Light the fuze. *GO!*"

"Twenty seconds and on automatic terminal count."

A voice, unknown as to source, came into every headset and through the speakers.

"*Vaya con dios, little sister.*"

Blinding light.

CRAAACK!

Kim vanished.

Chapter XVI

Teal light glowed and the blood-curdling scream sounded at the same instant high above the Venezuelan grasslands and river country. The scream issued from an almost mindless fear, the cry of desperation of a human mind drowning in complete vertigo, the ultimate helplessness.

Kim Seavers gasped painfully for breath, falling without hope or redemption, falling into a pit without beginning or end, falling, falling—

Stop it! Stop it!

Her own voice came tremulously to life within her head. *Wha—I can't believe this, can't stop falling . . .*

The jungled horizon with upthrusting blocks whirled madly. *You've got a horizon, you little idiot. You're not falling down a pit. The horizon! The horizon! Think, THINK! ACT!*

Her eyes bulged and she gasped air like a fish thrown onto a beach. She closed her eyes for a moment, forced sense into her own mind and head and body, spoke aloud, a tremendous relief accompanying the sound of her own words, gasping and labored though they were.

"Easy . . . easy . . . relax . . . falling but it's . . . nothing wrong . . . falling . . . I'm tumbling, the danger is this tumble . . . can't open chute . . . got to stabilize . . . must stop spinning . . . must stop tumbling . . . DO IT NOW!"

She pulled both arms in to her chest, drew up her legs and snapped out all her limbs as if hurling them away from her body. At once the tumble eased, the spin slowed. Instinctively now, responding to past experience, her arms and legs moved like a woman swimming through air, *which is exactly what she was doing.*

She spoke again to herself, calmer now, listening to herself within her own mind. "Falling . . . but no sensation of falling . . . stabilized! I'm stabilized!" She fell with her arms out, palms down, legs bent properly at the knees, facing down, perfectly stabilized, no longer accelerating, the pressure of the air from her falling matching her weight.

"I . . . got it! I got it!" In her jubilation she knew she was missing something. *Check your altimeter, you asshole . . .* She grinned at her own mind's voice. "Yes, ma'am!"

The BEMAC teams shared the same sense of helplessness and fear. Most of the display screens and control consoles in BEMAC flashed a bloody red warning. Red glowed everywhere, reflecting from faces and polished equipment. Dr. Edith Hernandez seemed to wrap her arms around herself. *"My God . . . my God . . . she came out at eight thousand feet . . ."*

Morgan Scott had yanked a microphone from the hands of the communications console operator. "Come in, Kim!" he yelled. "Come in! Answer me, goddammit!"

Only the hiss of empty radio waves met his entreaties.

Jungle Rudy and his daughter, a small army of BEMAC technicians, and a backdrop of natives stared into the sky.

"I've got her! Holy shit, she's way up there! Right over the river!"

Heads turned to follow the falling speck.

Jungle Rudy's fists closed painfully, unknown to him, as if his squeezing could help the girl now barely a mile up and falling at better than a hundred and twenty miles an hour straight down.

Of all the people involved in the test, at this moment the calmest of them was now Kim Seavers. She was through her ordeal of total loss of balance. With vertigo behind her, her past experience as a skilled skydiver took over. There had been a terrible wrenching sensation that felt as if she were being turned inside out and that ripped a wave of nausea through her stomach. Then the vertigo, the helplessness of total spatial disorientation, and finally her own senses and her inner voice bringing her from her lethal funk. For now between her and death was nothing but empty air. The usual automatic barometric release that would have opened her chute at twelve hundred feet had been eliminated. "I'll never know where I come out," she had decided in their planning for the mission, "and I don't want no little dumb black box making any decisions for me."

But that too was behind her. She fell in stable position, all sensation of falling gone, watching the earth widening, objects expanding, as she plummeted, now comfortable, relaxed, *safe* in her falling. Downward gravity and resisting air pressure removed all acceleration. She took only a moment to realize she was back in an old and familiar element and that she was also wallowing in the sudden sense of security. *The earth is coming up too fast*, warned her inner self, and she *was* making out too many details. Both arms came in to her chest, her right hand grasped the D-ring, both arms snapped out, the D-ring in her right hand pulling free the cable. The pilot chute whipped away on springs and blossomed, filled with air and hauled out the rest of her main canopy.

Moments later she sailed gently earthward beneath the square rig above her head, descending much like a glider. But she was too low, she realized, as the river came swiftly toward her. Not enough wind to fly away from the wide waters, but she gave it her best, working the wind and her gliding ability to reach the nearest riverbank. She just had time to hear the cheers of the crowd about Jungle Rudy, a split second to decide to leave her helmet closed. There could be enough air in her suit and the helmet to provide some buoyancy, help her get to the safety of the ground along the river's edge.

Cold stabbed through her as her feet made their first contact with water; as she splashed down, frantically banging the heel of her hand against the emergency harness release she saw the first crocodiles hurling themselves into the water from the far shore.

On the riverbank at Jungle Rudy's camp, the voice of Felipe Mercedes burst through the speakers in the communications truck. "Base camp! Base camp! This is BEMAC. What the hell is happening down there? Come in, come in!"

No one paid attention. They were piling into motorized dugout canoes, pushing from shore under full power in a desperate attempt to reach Kim before the crocodiles got to her. High overhead, diving toward the river, was the first of three helicopters. Manuel Gamus in the lead chopper set Kim in his gunsight to lock her into visual position. To his left his copilot answered Mercedes's call.

"Chopper One here to BEMAC. She's in the river, made a successful splashdown, but we've got trouble. Crocodiles moving in toward her. We're going down as fast as we can. Over and out."

Kim looked at death, huge, knobby, angry red eyes and two enormous rows of teeth. She had her survival knife in her hand, waiting for the croc to go under to grab at her legs so it could twist violently and drag her under. If she timed it just right she might get one good lunge with the knife in the soft underbelly—

Another bellow of rage, louder, exploding about her from behind. The thought raced into her mind. *Say your last words while you can.* She felt peace descend on her. *Mary, Mother of God*—

The water exploded from the fury of the attacking monster. Blood and chunks of flesh tore into the air—

But she wasn't hurt! She couldn't identify the roar . . . her helmet! She still had the helmet closed! *Now* she saw what was happening. A long burst of machine-gun fire ripping through the crocodile closest to her— *that was the roar!* Another croc coming in fast, another burst of fire. More of the attacking monsters and she saw a second helicopter, swaying from side to side, its front a sparkling blaze of flame from several machine guns firing steadily at the crocodiles. Chunks of flesh tumbled through the air, bloody froth drifted before the wind.

The wind beat fiercely about her. A shadow closed over her. She turned in the water. All about her were the crocodiles and torn flesh and bloody foam as machine guns kept hammering. Then the shadow came closer, and a helicopter dropped directly beside her, one skid into the water, a gunner hanging on to the skid with one hand, extending his other arm to her. "Grab hold!" he shouted. "And hang on, lady!"

She snatched frantically at the bent arm, closed her fingers as tightly as she could, felt powerful muscles lock onto her arm and the next moment the river fell away in a giddy swirl of rocking motion, a wild ascent, machine gun fire and torn crocodiles all about her.

The chopper made straight for the riverbank. Jungle Rudy and his entourage stood in their long dugout canoes, cheering madly.

High above the hysterical scene, unnoticed by anyone on the ground or in the canoes, a bright flash appeared and with the sound of arcing electricity, vanished.

Caleb Massey poured strong, dark coffee into two big mugs on the table between himself and Senator Patrick Xavier Elias. He unscrewed the cap from a gold flask, held it poised over the senator's mug. "Want a whack, old man?"

Elias sniffed the air. "What the hell is it?"

"Pimiento liqueur. Straight out of an old black woman's shop in Kingston. Not available for sale anywhere."

"How'd you get it?"

"Mind your business. Yes or no?"

"Hell, yes. I'm running out of time at my age to try new things."

Massey poured for both of them, capped the flask,

opened his briefcase and brought out a box of assorted doughnuts. Elias made a rude noise. "We have some of the best chefs in the world and you come in here with Dunkin' Doughnuts, and you eat that trash with some of the most expensive liqueur in the world. You amaze me, Caleb."

"Smrff, itsbest, wantsome?"

"You shoved that whole thing in your mouth!"

"Gsnraff, uumph, uh huh, wantsome ornot?"

"Hell, no!"

Massey swallowed, studied a buttermilk doughnut, decided to be just a bit more couth, broke it in half, gestured to Elias with a cheery, "Here's how!" and crammed the half into his face along with finger-licking, lip-smacking sounds.

"Jesus Christ," Elias muttered.

"Uh huh." Massey gestured for him to get down to business.

"You've got us in hot water, Caleb."

Massey swallowed a big chunk of doughnut and belched. He took a long swallow from his mug. "So what's new? Besides, Patrick, there's no other way. You know the stakes that are involved here. When something is bigger than you ever dreamed of, you've *got* to take the big gamble."

Elias motioned impatiently. "Put those goddamned things back in your case, will you?" He rolled his eyes and waited until the doughnut remains disappeared into Massey's attache case. "Now listen to me, Caleb. Let me make all this very clear. The president's coming back next week from China. The moment he sits down in the White House, Craig Mancini will be sprawled across his desk screaming for blood. Mine and yours."

"Like I said, what's new?" Massey changed his tack. "All right, Pat. Does Mancini know about the satellites?"

"Hell, *yes,* he knows!" Elias exclaimed. "He knows down to the last nut, bolt and solar cell. Our only saving grace is that he's convinced it's an energy program. You know, solar power. The same stuff we've been trying to sell the country for years."

"Well, I told him we'd developed teleportation."

Elias stared in mixed disbelief and amazement. Massey took the long pause to cram the other half of the buttermilk doughnut in his mouth. Finally Elias found his voice. "You *what?* I mean, you didn't, oh, not really, now, you can't be that crazy—"

"Would you believe me, *smraff*, excuse me, Pat, would you believe me if I told you we had a teleportation development program under way? You know, you're here, and we go boola-boola, mumbo-jumbo, throw a little goose grease in the fire, and zang! you're a thousand miles away. Would you believe me?"

"Jesus Christ, *no*."

"Well, neither did Mancini. He frothed at the mouth, accused me of being loose with the taxpayers' coin, told me I was covering up an illegal program, so naturally," Massey swallowed the soggy remains of his doughnut and gulped coffee and liqueur, "I let it slip about the solar program. Told him, or rather, let it slip that we'd developed a new type of solar cell that made silicon look like asbestos where churning out electricity was concerned. *That's* why he knows so much about the, ah, solar program. Only he thinks it's in Arizona where we *do* have a solar energy program. A few extra numbers here, a bit more names there, a couple of top-secret reports twixt here and there and Mancini is off chasing the great god Apollo. Senator, let me tell you that we worked hard to head him in just that direction."

"That's *not* the issue, damn you. You challenged his position and his authority. You went over his head—"

"Around him is more like it."

"Dammit, don't you get picky with me! Don't you understand that all the funds for your pet project are *not* authorized? That when Mancini speaks to the president we're both going to be on the carpet? You think this budget deficit reduction program isn't the search for the Holy Grail? No more sacred cows in the federal barn, Caleb!"

Massey grew quiet and serious. "We can't tell it like it is?"

"*Absolutely not.*" Elias stole a furtive glance about him despite none being needed. "*No,*" he repeated. "For God's sake, man, you'll panic—*drop it, Caleb.* Stay with the program."

"Yes, sir. I get your message." Massey sighed. "All of them."

Elias studied his old friend. "You said you could bring me Mancini's head on a platter. Can you?"

"Yes, but—"

"But me no buts."

"Okay, okay. I can."

"Not can. *Will.*"

"I will."

Elias shifted the issue neatly. "Now, about the changes you were going to make in this project of yours. Have you implemented them yet?"

"We've got it more than started. The equipment is built. Mercedes still has his problems. McDavid and I have the answers."

"When do you drop on him?"

"Tomorrow. When I leave here it's straight to Caracas."

"What about your duplicate installation here?"

Massey smiled and leaned back in his chair, obviously enormously pleased with himself. "Now, Patrick, that's the *best* part of all this. We've duplicated BEMAC ONE down to the last nut and bolt. With the exception, of course, of the changes we know have to be made. In other words, I've already had built what Phil Mercedes is so desperate to get, even if he doesn't know about it yet."

"And you're waiting for?"

"It would be very stupid of me to get ahead of Mercedes in this program, especially since it's his own man who taught me what I needed to know to be so smart."

"I never thought of you as the diplomat."

"Surprise, surprise."

"Be serious for a few moments, Caleb."

"You sound ominous."

"I have some questions for you. Some technical points first which I want to record."

Massey's eyes widened. He looked about the private club. "In *here*. You can't use acoustic here, Pat. You'll need direct skin pickup from the throat and—" He stopped speaking as Elias handed him a slim leather packet. "Oh. Okay. Hold one."

He slipped the packet into an inside pocket, withdrew a flesh-colored tab that he pressed against the side of his neck, beneath his shirt collar. It disappeared. Also invisible was the ultrathin wire leading down to the recorder now within his jacket.

"Okay, shoot," he told the senator.

"Our people gave me this question. You're firing a laser beam. Fact. Also a fact is that when you fire a blast of light, *any* kind of light, you can't avoid a law of nature. Even the light from a star, from a supernova, gives up energy as it moves through space. You agree so far?"

"You go to the head of the class, Senator."

"When they beam from point A to B and back to A, do they boost the beam during that time when it's being bounced back from B for the return to A?"

"You mean like adding a power kick for a telephone line? Or a power line with transformer stations along the route?"

"That says it nicely. Yes, like that. Isn't that necessary? If you fire your beam and you want to get a bounce, what keeps the beam from losing power?" Elias frowned. "You can add a power boost with a ground facility, but you don't have that much energy in a geosat at twenty-two thousand miles."

"You sure have a hell of a conversation with yourself, I must say," Massey told him. "By the by, you're absolutely correct on all counts. Your reasoning matches what we had exactly."

"*Had?* Do I detect a past tense in there?"

"Yes, sir, you do."

"You've found something that negates all the stumbling blocks I just threw at you?"

"Yes, sir, we have."

"You frighten me when you become polite, Caleb. All right, if you've come up with the kind of miracle our top technical people say is impossible, well, that's why you've got that recorder going. Have at it."

"I've got to speechify."

"Speechify away, Caleb."

"Well, first off, we're not talking about your ordinary, run-of-the-mill laser beam." Massey paused to glance within his jacket. A glowing red dot told him he was being recorded. "Okay, now, neither am I talking about beam diameter or the power charge that kicks it off."

Massey finished off his coffee, poured a mug without the liqueur. "Most laser beams—almost all of them, save for the variations on a theme for specific purposes such as holograms or communications—are pure and simple coherent light. In terms of mass, as they pass through atmosphere or space, those mediums on the human scale might just as well not exist. But that term, *might just as well*, is damned dangerous, because *everything* that exists on the molecular level—that's you and me, old man—has measurable and functioning mass, even if you want to consider it infinitesimal. Out there in the real universe, the electromagnetic and subatomic universe, where God gets real serious about this stuff, you've even got things like neutrinos which have so little mass, and such vast penetrating power, that theoretically they'll zip right through fifty light years of solid lead without even thinking of slowing down. Because to a neutrino, lead isn't even a bad dream. So it's critical to understand how vast are the distinctions between what we call *our* reality and what really makes up the cosmos."

Massey sipped coffee. "Still with me?" Elias waved him on impatiently.

"Okay. Now think of light in a way you don't often think of that wonderful stuff that makes day out of night. Think of the proposals we still study for the great sailing ships of space that will cruise from planetary orbit to planetary orbit. Remember them? Enormous sails, miles wide and miles high, intended to sail the curving gravity lanes between worlds, eh? We could still build such a sailing vessel, Patrick, a spacecraft attached by cables to that huge, huge sail that would capture the pressure of the solar wind; much like a small gondola, a tiny affair, is attached to a great balloon. Now, this solar wind is enough to sail our ship. The solar wind used to blow the old Echo balloon hundreds of miles above and below its early orbit. So we have real pressure in solar wind, which essentially is a gale of electrons streaming out from the sun. An electron has such a low mass, maybe it's one two-thousandths of a neutron or a proton, but in that solar flood that howls away from the sun the wind of free electrons functions *exactly* like the wind that fills the sails of a ship on our oceans."

Massey took a long breath, finished off his coffee, reached for a doughnut, thought better of it, wet his lips with his tongue, and returned to the senator's request. "All right, now back to the laser beam. Specifically, the BEMAC beam. It consists of a hell of a lot more than simply light, coherent or otherwise. First, the beam gets a kick from hundreds of millions of volts, or billions; we can boost all the way up with that new reactor. Second, and now we're getting down to the nitty-gritty, in this beam we have dematerialized mass. That's the people or the objects we send within the beam. The mass functions as much as quanta as it does as wave and that, my friend, gives a damned appreciable gravitational function.

"That mass attracts other mass. I don't care if you use Newtonian mutual attraction of bodies or the Einsteinian warpage of time and space, but it attracts mass. It pulls in dust particles, meteoric debris, atmospheric particles, even heavy cosmic rays, which in this sense are really the nuclei of heavy atoms. This stuff—think of it as being sucked in toward wherever the beam appears and creates its gravitational whirlpool—this stuff pours in from all sides toward the beam. It impinges on the beam, it tries to fall into the beam, toward its center of mass, so that it exerts an enormous squeezing effect *that adds energy to the beam.*

"Think of a light beam again, if you will. Light itself travels at a finite speed, and this external mass is always trying to catch up with, or fall to the center of the beam, just as any other gravitational system functions. You remember the Valkyrie?"

Elias scowled. "I was one of the senators who was voted down on further appropriations for that thing. You're damned right I remember it. What has it to do with what we're talking about?"

"Phil Mercedes knows the beam should need a boost. BEMAC fires the beam, it bounces off one or two or three relay stations that do *not* add a kick in the slats, and yet the beam has as much energy as when it left the laser cannon, or sometimes even more. Mercedes calls it the bootstrap effect, just like we got when we found the Valkyrie flying a couple of hundred miles faster than we ever computed, because—"

"I remember," Elias broke in, pleased to add to this extraordinary descriptive scene. "The shock wave. It rode on its own shock wave. I used to watch dolphins riding the bow wave of a destroyer. No effort on their part except balance, and they'd surfboard for hours on the bow wave. All right. I get that picture. Go on, please."

"Well, since the beam travels with the speed of light, before any of the stuff it attracts can even get to it, it's moving out of the way, always staying ahead of the incoming material. There's so much energy here, and so much attraction of mass because the laser beam is moving dematerialized matter at the speed of light, that the incoming squeeze is one hell of a boost." He smiled. "*Still* with me?"

To his surprise the senator shook his head. "No, I am *not* still with you. Dammit, what you just said is impossible. All the laws of physics tell us that what you just described cannot possibly exist as a reality. Your whole theory might stand up, *except* for one absolutely unassailable fact."

"Ah, the great man is about to demolish in theory what we do in practice. Welcome to the club, Patrick."

"Get stuffed with *that* refrain, my friend. It's simple enough," Elias countered. "*You cannot travel faster than the speed of light.* That is an unshakable pillar of reality. You referred before to Einsteinian space. Well, why you would use Einstein as a proof of your theory, and in the next breath reject that same man's conclusions, is more than surprising to me. You said yourself that you can't accelerate a physical mass faster than the speed of light. Because *at* the speed of light, mass becomes infinite and you'd need infinite energy for further acceleration. So the whole thing bogs down. You get to light speed and time stops. Okay, we've got enough proof of that. But *not* this business of something moving faster than light."

Massey waited several moments before his reply. "You're wrong," he said simply.

"Wrong? *How?*"

"You're familiar with the term black hole? Or black star? Of course; I knew you were. Keeping things clean and simple, we accept that a black hole is the aftereffect of collapse of a super stellar mass after supernova explosion. There's the great outward blowout and then what remains collapses in upon itself in, well, the best guess is less than a trillionth of a second. When this mass collapses completely, what happens? Why can't we see it?"

"That's already high-school physics, Caleb. Because the gravitational field is so enormous that not even light can escape."

"Tell yourself that again."

"What?"

"Repeat your own words to yourself."

"I said not even light can escape the gravitational mass of the black hole. So?"

"So the inward gravitational acceleration is so great that it exceeds the ability of a photon moving at better than one hundred eighty six thousand miles a second to fly away from the black hole. Inward acceleration, Patrick, exceeds light velocity by numbers and scales we can't even estimate, *but we know it happens*. It's real. It exists. There *is* movement faster than light. Of course, Mother Nature doesn't like anything to screw with her best-laid plans of mass and energy, so if a black hole *is* created, it's invisible to us. Well, nature says, hey, out there, no dice. I won't stand for something going faster than light. *And the damned thing, for all intents and purposes, winks out of existence in our universe.*"

Elias stared. "Where the hell do you people dream up this stuff?"

Massey laughed. "My dear old friend, in our crowd we have a saying. *A stitch in time would have baffled Einstein.*"

"Me, too," Elias said. "You've given me a beaut of a headache." He gestured to the recorder. "Turn that damned thing off."

Massey returned the slim leather packet to the senator. "Now, briefly, Caleb, *briefly,* some questions to which I need hard answers."

"Go."

"Can you beam an entire team into Russia from Canaveral?"

"*What?*" Massey swallowed. "Not yet. Very soon."

"How soon?"

"Ten days. Three weeks. On that order."

"Have you ever heard of Dr. Peter Unsworth?"

"Yes. Why?"

"I want you to get a team into Russia, grab Peter Unsworth, and bring him back safely to us."

"You're incredible, Senator."

"That is not the issue under discussion."

"Where is he in Russia?"

"Three stories underground."

Massey felt his voice had gone hollow. "A mere detail, of course. Three stories underground. Interesting. Where in Russia, might I ask?"

"Of course. Three stories *beneath the Kremlin.*"

Elias stood and faced his lifelong friend. "But first, keep your promise. I want Mancini's head on that silver platter."

*   *   *

"Quiet in the studio!" The girl with two pencils stuck in her hair, a clipboard in one hand, wearing a headset and pencil mike, blouse halfway out from her skirt, and looking as harried as newsroom girls throughout the world, groaned at the confusion in the newsroom of *Monitor Nacional Television*. "We go live in three minutes," she said into her mike, knowing her words carried throughout the studio.

"Hey, we going Spanish or English on this one?" She recognized the voice but couldn't connect it with a name. No matter. Estrella Marquez had been Tirado's number-one assistant for three years now and she didn't bother with the little details.

"English," she said patiently. The whole newsroom was controlled pandemonium, but it was *always* this way before a livecast. Marquez had worked at major network TV news in the states, and that was crazy enough. Caracas newsrooms were insane. Angela Tirado came along and boosted that insanity to international popularity.

"One minute, one minute," sang out the voice in timing. A last-second thought hit Estrella Marquez. "Anybody listening in at control?"

"Hey, sugarlips, this is Eduardo. Go ahead."

"You got the stock footage ready?" She could have kicked herself as fast as she spoke. "I mean, the new news footage," she appended swiftly.

"Uh, yeah, that's what I thought you meant," came the voice from control. "By the way, this stuff is—"

"Knock it off, Eddie," Marquez said harshly. "We're coming up on live time." She'd have to watch herself. The tape they were running had been prepared with exquisite care and here they'd gone to all their trouble to have everyone believe it was as fresh as breakfast, and she was calling it *stock* footage.

"Fifteen seconds, fifteen seconds. Everybody knock off the crapola, okay? No replies, please."

Another voice called out. "Ten seconds, ten seconds, and we go live with Miss Tirado."

The seconds fell away, lights switched to colors announcing live studio and live mikes and cameras, and a serious Angela Tirado appeared on banks of monitors in the studio.

"Damn, but she is one beautiful woman," thought Estrella Marquez. "So how come she's also smarter than anybody I know?"

The beautiful face and shapely body seemed out of place with the sexy-husky but commanding voice that covered continents. ". . . and we have learned the source of all those strange lights in the sky that have amazed and baffled and even frightened people. Green shafts of light and explosive booms in the skies have been seen and heard across all of Venezuela. But we're not alone in these amazing phenonema. The lights and explosions have appeared in the heavens across Brazil, and Colombia and even as far north as Panama. Earlier today this reporter led a news team to the government research center for a revolutionary new—"

The large television screen on the far wall of the government conference room held the attention of Espinoza, Garcia, and a small crowd of Venezuelan military and security officials.

"—communications system. It's what scientists call laser fiber optics. It uses materials and systems the government considers to be highly secret. This reporter finds that attitude almost insufferable. Venezuelan taxpayers made this new system possible and they should know all there is about it. But I can tell you that in a single beam of laser light, pumped by the new fiber optics system, we can send as many as a thousand telephone calls and more than one hundred television frequencies.

"What is this worth? What does it mean? The answer is in that first question: What is this worth? Well, to whom? And *that* answer should rivet the attention of every man and woman in our fair country of Venezuela. This new system means a total revolution in world communications. It means that Venezuela can earn between six and ten billion dollars every year from patents and royalties."

Espinoza nudged Major Garcia. "That woman is a genius. What is of more interest to people than UFO's? Money! Especially to Venezuelans, if it means making money for Venezuelans. To say nothing of the national pride." They watched dramatic pictures of a laser beam firing with the appropriate sound effects and dazzling lights. Tirado quickly paraded vast sums of money in columns of numbers across the screen behind her and then returned to the main thrust Espinoza had worked out with her.

"We are bringing you other news as a world exclusive. The United States is already deep into this fantastic new project with Venezuela. Full cooperation is under way with experimental laser broadcast systems between the IVIC Center of Caracas and Cape Canaveral in Florida. So the strange lights that have brightened our night skies, that this reporter and so many other people believed to be UFO's, turn out to be a future of tremendous wealth for our country. One communications satellite system, using the new laser system we have developed, can carry more messages, phone calls, television frequencies, medical data and other messages, than all the satellites and microwave systems of the world, *combined*."

Angela pushed away the notes on her desk and swung her chair about, making it clear to her audience she wasn't bothering to read from notes or a teleprompter, but that she was speaking from the heart. "I will predict the future for you, my fellow citizens of Venezuela. I predict that the world communications satellite system as it exists now will be wiped out overnight. The satellites now in orbit will be thrown away as so much ancient garbage. The new team of Venezuela and the United States, thanks to our scientists, will emerge in one brilliant stroke as the undisputed world leaders of—"

Espinoza clicked the TV remote control at his chair and the set went dark. He turned to Garcia and there could be no question but that the general was *very* serious.

"Listen carefully, Major Garcia. The Russians have taken the bait. The rest of the world may believe what you just heard, but the Russians are, if anything, suspicious. They are more than capable with laser systems and they will have many questions. Which, of course, we will refuse to answer. Now, Caleb Massey is arriving tonight to meet with our people at IVIC. He will be coming in aboard a C-5, one of those giant machines. It will have very valuable equipment aboard that must be moved *immediately* to BEMAC within IVIC. I don't care what you do or how you do it, but nothing must interfere with that transfer from the military airfield to BEMAC. Take as many troops as you need. All the helicopters you want. Maximum security *must* be maintained from beginning to end."

Espinoza permitted himself the luxury of a brief smile. "The Russians know that Massey is to arrive tonight. They do *not* know what is aboard that airplane. They know about Massey, and they also know who are some of the people involved in our project. I have every assurance they will go after those people tonight."

Major Garcia didn't hide the misgivings he felt. "You take a great risk, my general."

"Of course, of course," Espinoza responded. His eyes seemed to flash. "That only makes the game all the sweeter, right?"

Chapter XVII

The subway train eased to a stop deep beneath Caracas. Doors hissed open and the cars disgorged hundreds of passengers, followed by a surge of other passengers waiting to be swallowed up within the cars. In the midst of the crowd leaving the train six men moved as a single group. Felipe Mercedes and Caleb Massey led the way. Four large and powerful men fell in with them, two behind and one on each side to flank the American and the Venezuelan scientist. Behind them the train pulled away and the station became relatively quiet. Mercedes pointed and they moved quickly in the direction of a long and steep escalator. One guard slipped before them to take lead position on the escalator, the other three men eased behind, sandwiching Mercedes and Massey between them. It all went smoothly and without direction spoken.

Mercedes leaned closer to Massey. "I don't know how they found out, but the Russians know you're here. *And* they are looking for you."

"It's nice to be popular," Massey grinned.

Mercedes didn't share his sense of humor. "Be serious, Caleb. They have orders to kidnap you."

Massey nodded. "I know." He gestured to take in the subway escalator. "All this was a beautiful idea. The Russians are predictable. If you're a big shot, then you've *got* to be in a limousine. That's where I'm supposed to be. Not here."

"General Espinoza planned all this," Mercedes explained. "Including the double who looks more like you than you do."

"I didn't know that. In the limo?"

"Yes. Much fanfare, too. Motorcycle police escort, flashing lights, sirens. Very exciting."

Massey frowned. "Well, you can fool them for a while but we're not working with any rank amateurs. This meeting you've scheduled, Phil. The Russians know where your office is located. Both at IVIC *and* here in the city. They'll plan on the both of us going to IVIC, and that's a dangerous road. Expect any problems?"

Mercedes smiled. "Problems? Meeting? What meeting? You're not here on business, remember? This is a cultural visit. You're here to be entertained. In fact, watch your step, here," they moved briskly from the escalator, Mercedes talking as they walked. "I was saying, we're on our way right now to the Caracas Cultural Center."

"Really? Where is it?"

Mercedes pointed a finger straight up. "Right above us."

"You're kidding," Massey said with an appreciative grin. "What's the program tonight?"

"Why, *Swan Lake.* Tchaichovsky, of course. What could be more fitting?"

"What about my team people?"

"The general assures me he's arranged a social affair for them," Mercedes said. "We'll meet them later tonight."

They turned left at a fork in the tunnel; the right way led to the street, signs on the left pointed to the entrance to the Caracas Cultural Center. The tunnel walkway widened, wall murals appeared before them, and they moved into a magnificent underground center that led to subways, parking garages, restaurants, parks and the Cultural Center itself.

Mercedes took a sharp right turn, holding Massey's arm, and the six men moved into a beautiful atrium. Massey heard a door hiss closed behind them. He turned and offered a mental nod in appreciation of the technique being used. The glass that had exposed the atrium to people walking by had polarized to an opaque sheet. Mercedes stopped before a large tree and the tree slid sideways to expose a curving tunnel. The six men walked into the tunnel, the tree slid back into place behind them.

Massey mumbled aloud to himself. "And I came down here to teach these people some new tricks . . ."

Mercedes smiled as he heard Massey's words. He didn't answer but stopped by a huge mural. The mural slid aside, they entered a large anteroom, the mural closed behind them. Mercedes stood before a shelf emerging from the nearest wall. It lit up and a glowing plate appeared before him. He placed his right hand flat against the plate. It was clear to Massey that an optical computer system was examining not only four fingerprints and the thumbprint but the palmprint as well. The light faded and flashed a soft green; Mercedes stepped aside and motioned Massey forward. Massey and the four guards went through the security clearance process, and entered a large conference room where scientists and technicians awaited them.

Massey went up to Claude McDavid. They clasped hands fiercely, two old friends meeting after an absence each found much too long. "It's good to see you, Caleb," McDavid told him.

"And you," Massey said.

"Everything you brought is already at BEMAC," McDavid told him. "I'm amazed the installation is that simple."

Mercedes coughed politely to break into their conversation. "Gentlemen, if you please? We'd like you to tell the rest of us."

McDavid laughed. "Forgive me, Director." He and Massey took seats at the table across from Mercedes. "Shall we get right to it?" McDavid asked.

"Please," Mercedes said, clasping his fingers together on the table before him, waiting.

"Simply put," McDavid began, "the problems we've experienced in the beaming have nothing to do with the *amount* of power we're using. I've checked that a hundred times. We have more than enough power to handle any assignment I can foresee."

"But it *is* tied in with the power?" Mercedes queried.

"Absolutely. Let me rid ourselves of one other problem area we considered. The computers. The Greystone is truly a fabulous development. Since I last met with you, sir, we've triple-checked the performance of the Greystone with a dozen other systems. So we've been going through a process of elimination."

Mercedes remained calm only with great self-control. "And?" he said quietly.

"It's the power flow," McDavid said. "Or, more specifically, the smoothness of the power flow. The best cables that exist cannot eliminate all fluctuations. The metal, the alloys, the connections; they can't be perfect and they're not. And the slightest anomaly in that kind of circuitry and power flow, with the enormous energies we're using, is magnified a thousandfold."

"There's no way to predict or to locate any such problem? Can't we tell when we're not coherent with the flow?" Mercedes pushed.

"No, sir," Massey answered for McDavid. "We ran into the same problem with SDI. I never thought I'd see Star Wars pay off, but it has. If you get so much as a twitch or a tweak in the power, you get a tremendous, well, call it *dis*harmony. Everything seems to be a contradiction in terms. But right now, our new equipment, as Claude has verified, is being set up at IVIC. We've already built the same facility at Canaveral and checked it out."

Mercedes nodded. "Briefly, for the rest of the people here, please?"

"We've had to eliminate power fluctuations in our most powerful laser and energy beams for the Star Wars program. We've had a devil of a time with it," Massey explained in the simplest terms. "We solved the problems by going to the new cryogenics systems, the superconductors that operate at the temperature of liquid nitrogen. That's a truly fantastic advantage for us. Working with liquid helium presented staggering problems, especially of consistent reliability. When you're getting down to absolute zero, you may get the temperatures but your equipment goes to hell on you. *Not* with liquid nitrogen. Your equipment remains stable. Using the new superconducting ceramics, we were able to develop and fine-tune our free electron lasers. We not only obtained enormous power but we also achieved something known as random coherency. By the way, we didn't have the right clues. This man," he motioned to McDavid, "did. He's the one who gets the credit for the brain work. We're just the plumbers and the mechanics."

"This random coherency," a woman asked. "I'm almost afraid to ask. Does this guarantee a smooth power flow?"

"Absolutely," McDavid said. "There's so much energy available in confinement it always maintains maximum output. By using the superconducting ceramics we've eliminated electrical resistance in the system. The result is what we call absolute flow. No matter where you look you get coherent flow. It doesn't matter *where*. That's why we call it random coherency."

Massey leaned forward. "In sum, ladies and gentlemen, when the superconducting equipment is set up, which should be by tomorrow night or the day after, everything you've ever dreamed of doing with BEMAC should be completely within your grasp."

The room went silent. No one spoke. In the sudden calm they could hear the faint strains of *Swan Lake* from the concert hall above them.

They moved like royalty through the crowded lobby of the Caracas Hilton. There exists an aura about certain people, a sense of the extraordinary that requires no words, that either "is" or never can be. Eyes followed Stan Blake as he towered above the throngs of people in the luxurious Hilton lobby. He wore a wine-colored turtleneck, a suede jacket, and he moved—he *glided*—like a human tank on skates. The first sight of Blake drew attention; a second look to show Maria Barrios on his arm brought gasps and whispered comments as to the identity of these striking people who had that indefinable air about them. A dusky Chinese red gown, slit along the legs, form-fitted Maria, who set off her jet black hair with sparkle diamonds.

Behind them moved another couple; the word now might have been "overpowering." Alejandro Suarez, barrel-chested, thickhewn through his arms, and the striking dusky beauty of Carmen Morales in gold and brown. Theirs, too, was that air of airs, that ultimate touch of silky confidence. Eyes followed the four of them through the lobby, along the thickly carpeted corridor among the restaurants of the hotel, past the elevators. Ahead of them stretched the luxury shops of the Hilton. To their left, great flowering plants and a wide descending spiral stairway to the ground floor and parking valet service.

They walked in pairs separated sufficiently to seem casual, yet close enough to speak with each other in subdued tones. Blake led the way with Maria. He fell back slightly in his position, still looking straight ahead as he spoke to the others, but especially to Suarez. "You see them, Al?"

Suarez looked at Carmen Morales and smiled broadly. But he wasn't seeing her; his eyes darted about the lobby and the corridor. Still looking at Carmen he answered Blake quickly. "Four is what I get. One by the elevator, three down the hall."

"Same as me." Blake smiled at Maria. "Let them make the first move?" he said to Suarez.

"Of course. It's not polite to do anything first."

"They won't make their move here," Blake cautioned. "It's too busy. People could get hurt and that means publicity and even some photographers wandering around."

"I'm so sorry, Maria, but he is less than blinded by your beauty," Suarez told Maria Barrios. "Amigo, you are right," he directed to Blake. "We came to dance and the time is close. See those stairs ahead? Turn left there. I will follow."

They went down the wide, winding staircase amidst glittering fountains and heavy foliage. Ahead of them, across a small lobby and beyond the landing, were the rest rooms. Closer to them were elevators with people moving in and out in a steady stream.

Blake stopped at the foot of the stairs. "Ladies, would you care to, ah, use the powder room?"

Maria patted his hand. "Of course. Thank you."

"We won't be long," Carmen added. "We'll meet you here."

"Be damned careful," Suarez warned them. "We have those four spotted but there could be more."

"Ah, I like men who worry about their little women," Maria said, smiling. "All right, Carmen, let them have their fun."

Morales kissed Suarez on the cheek. "Be careful, you ape," she hissed in his ear.

"Worry wart," he smiled back.

The two men waited until the women were within the ladies' room, then went into the men's room. They paused a moment at the door as Blake lifted his left hand to look at his watch. The mirror showed several men rushing down the stairs. Blake continued into the men's room.

"At least four. Big hurry," he said to Suarez.

"Get to the far wall. You set?"

"Hey, got a reception committee in a pocket."

They stood by the far wall, looking into a mirror to see behind them. The urinals were to their right. They stayed before the mirror until the four men who'd followed them down the stairs were in the men's room. Now they knew with what they had to deal.

The first man of the group held their eyes. "No trouble, understand? You come with us quietly. We wish only to talk. Otherwise," he smiled with half a mouth of stainless steel teeth and brought a long-barreled automatic from a shoulder holster, "we must use these."

Blake leaned against the mirror, thumbs in his belt. Suarez kept his hands folded, out of direct sight. They were cool as ice, jazzing with one another, seemingly oblivious to any danger.

"Hey, Al, he wants us to go with him."

"For once you're right, gringo. He wants to go bang-bang."

"Nah," Blake sneered. "See those silencers? No bang-bang. Maybe phht-phht."

"No way, ace. They'll never use them."

"I think you're a smart spic. Think they *really* want to talk to us?"

"Hey, sure, man, but not here," Suarez said.

"They might shoot us in the legs—"

"No way, old buddy," Suarez broke in. "We're too big and ugly to carry."

"And it would make a scene," Blake said, nodding. "Hey, lay it on me, man, which ones do you want?"

The four men with guns stared in confusion. "I like the one with the crewcut. Him and his buddy," Suarez said.

"Hey, good. I'll take old chrome mouth."

Chrome mouth made a threatening gesture with the gun. "You fools! I warn you we'll—"

Blake and Suarez moved with blinding speed and perfect coordination. In a single move Blake simply dropped to the floor, rolling to one side as he went. Suarez did the same and both men, still prone, each brought up an arm and wrist-snapped a small ball at the armed men. They *stayed* down, covering their eyes with their arms.

Two blinder grenades went off with sharp popping sounds and light that screamed into a man's eyes. The four men froze as statues, instantly blinded. Two fired shots wildly, one smashing a mirror and the other cracking open a porcelain urinal. In almost the same moment Suarez's arm went back and snapped forward. A small bola whistled away and whipped about the neck of the first man with the gun, jerking him wildly off balance. His gun went flying as he choked and grabbed at his throat.

"You shitbird!" Blake yelled. "He was mine!"

Suarez was diving for the floor again as a second man, screaming with pain from his eyes, emptied his gun blindly. Blake went in beneath the gun and came up with a stiffened hand into the gunman's armpit. His hand struck with the force of a wild-swinging axe. The man screamed, the gun tumbled away, and the man careened against a wall, half-paralyzed and in agony. Suarez was up and running; his target was just regaining sight and bringing up a gun. Suarez came off the floor and landed a flying dropkick against the gunman with a blow that cracked his skull and hurled him unconscious against a wall.

"Here—catch!" he heard Blake yell. He turned, saw that Blake had the last man in a stiffened reverse armbend and was swinging him around as hard as he could. Blake let him fly as if cracking the whip, Suarez laughed and held out a massive fist in a short, straight blow that pole-axed their last assailant.

Blake dusted off his hands, Suarez rubbed his palms in glee, then cried, "Oh, my God—*the women!*"

They plunged through the exit door.

They were too late.

It began shortly after Maria and Carmen took seats at the makeup counter. By angling their bodies the mirrors gave them the same sort of covering view the men had provided themselves in the men's room. Maria first saw the two heavy men with drawn guns burst into the ladies' room. Women backed against the walls or crouched in chairs, terrified by the sight of the guns, overcome by the sheer audacity of the two men whose every move spelled terrible trouble. The men had Maria and Carmen picked out and rushed them from behind.

At the last moment before hands reached them, Maria and Carmen spun about, each holding up a perfume aerosol spray, the triggers held down. A searing, burning liquid gas hit the two men with all the effect of a two-by-four. Their eyes seemed afire, their lungs turned to blazing coals as they sucked in the spray. Their guns went flying as they clutched at their throats, their hearts, beating fists against their eyes, screaming with pain.

Carmen came up first, a small, wicked curved knife in her right hand. With her left she grabbed a man's belt, the knife flashed in and up. The belt was sliced in two and the trousers ripped open. Maria came in from the side. Swiftly she snapped a plastic tie-wrap about the man's ankles, binding them together. Carmen had his hands pulled behind his back, another swift move with another tie-wrap and he was helpless. Down came his trousers and his shorts until he stood, eyes watering, lungs searing, heart pounding, and naked from navel to ankles, buttocks stark white. It took only seconds to repeat their performance with the second man, and one last move—Maria used the tie-wrap to bind them together, back to back, utterly helpless and totally ridiculous.

They walked primly from the powder room. Blake and Suarez came pounding around the corner, stumbling against one another as the women came through the door. The men heard shrieks and howls of laughter from within the ladies' room. Maria and Carmen took the arms of their escorts and Maria smiled in pure innocence at Blake.

"Shall we go?"

Blake half-turned. "Wha—what the hell happened in there!"

"What's all that yelling and laughing?" Suarez asked.

The women tugged at their arms. "Oh, you know. Some women get so excited at naked men in their ladies' room."

Blake and Suarez stared at one another, baffled.

Crowding in the BEMAC control room was a small army of technicians with Dr. Roger Delgado, chief laser scientist for the program. Delgado was not happy with the test under way. Felipe Mercedes was gone for some unexplained conference in the city, Dr. Vasco de Gama was off on a research trip; many of the top people were absent from BEMAC dome and Delgado had misgivings about being the man who had top responsibility for the test even if it was scheduled. But he had been assured and reassured by the teams. Dr. Edith Hernandez swung his doubts away. She had been at IVIC longer than anyone else and her sense of judgement was legendary.

"We're designed to operate on schedules with three different teams, Roger," she told him privately. "Everything *is* in order. You've got some of our best people on duty: Pappas, Seavers, Gonzales, de Lauro, Logan, and the rider, well, it's Morgan Scott and he's right up there with the best of them. If you cancel this test without good reason with which *they* agree, you'll lose their confidence. I'm telling you now, Roger, you'll be finished here except for your own research. But these people won't follow you any more."

They proceeded with the test countdown. Unknown to Delgado he wasn't the only one seriously upset with this particular test. If he had overheard Seavers and Scott, then Delgado would have dismissed Hernandez's warnings about future leadership and simply shut down until Mercedes or de Gama returned.

Morgan Scott stood at the base of the stairs leading to the lexan transmission sphere. He wore the same equipment Kim Seavers had worn in her mission of near-disaster. Except for his helmet he was "packaged and ready to go."

Kim fiercely contested the mission. "Morgan, you're *crazy* to fly this test now. After what happened to me," she gestured wildly, "how can you even think of doing a satellite bounce *at night!*" She drew in a sharp breath, held his arm. "Morgan, *please,* wait until we get the final results on my flight."

Scott had no qualms. To the others in the lexan area he was a picture of complete assurance. "Look, Kim, we *know* what happened on your bounce. You and I did six complete computer simulation runs, remember? Besides all the test runs everybody else has come up with. Everything checks out. The answers are all the same. Someone misinterpreted a reading for your test and punched in a few wrong numbers. *I* won't be crocodile bait."

"You're so goddamned certain of that!" she rebuked him.

"Of course," he grinned. "Didn't you know?"

"Know what, you asshole?"

"Crocs don't eat at night. No candles. Too dark to see, see?"

Tony Pappas was getting rattled with Kim Seavers's resistance. "Morgan, what's the difference in a few hours? We could wait for daylight. Mercedes will be here then—"

"What in the hell is the matter with you people?" Scott asked, and his question was sincere. "What's got you so spooked?"

"For one thing," Pappas replied immediately, "if something goes wrong in the coordinates, you've got more safety with daylight."

"Will Mercedes being here change the numbers in the computer?" Scott demanded.

"No, but—" Kim and Pappas chorused together.

"Then drop it," Scott snapped at them. "If you can't cut me some slack in worry time, back off and let someone else take your positions for this test. I mean it, people. Dammit, the numbers don't change if Felipe is here or not. We're way behind schedule. All that damn modification work has screwed up everything. If this test works out now we've done a lot of catching up. Besides, there isn't a bigger worry wart in the world than Delgado, and he *and* Edie have given this thing the green light." Scott pointed to the wall timer. "Three minutes. Shut up and stop arguing. Kim, seal the helmet. Tony, give me a final on the suit and the electronics."

He went silent. They looked at one another and shrugged and went through the final checklist, stood Scott on the platform, climbed down as the speakers chanted through the count.

"Sixty seconds and counting . . ."

Kim grabbed Pappas's arm. "I hate myself."

There wasn't anything for him to say.

"Terminal count. Twenty seconds . . ."

"Fire—"

Kim stared at the platform, now empty. "He's gone," she said mournfully.

Pappas fought to shake off the doom-and-gloom attitude. "You expect him to still be there?"

She glared at him. "I damned well wish he *was*."

The circle spanned a diameter of five hundred feet, dead-center of the military airfield. Lights ran the diameter of the circle to illuminate the entire area involved. Everything on the airfield that could move was shut down. No vehicles moved. All aircraft were secured. Even the external radar antenna that revolved day and night had been powered down. No one was taking any chances. Along the flight line, men and women of the Venezeulan Air Force stood ready by rescue vehicles and crash trucks to accommodate—they didn't know *what*, but stood by on orders. Helicopter crews sat in their machines, power cables plugged in, ready at no more than a signal to fire up their machines.

The minutes dragged. Men leaned back against vehicles to steady their binocular scans of the sky from horizon to horizon.

"What do we look for?" one soldier asked his companion.

"For something special."

"What kind of something special?"

"I'll be damned if I know. Just keep looking. If it's there you'll know it."

A group of officers clustered about a jeep with radio gear. A captain listened intently on his headset. He lowered them slowly. "Any moment now . . ."

The beam of teal light appeared instantaneously; one second only darkness broken by the artificial lighting, the next second a cylindrical green sun burst gloriously before them. *The beam's edge, cut off as though it had disappeared into another dimension, stopped on the boundary of the flight ramp.*

A blur appeared for an instant, ghostly in the intense light where the beam stopped just above the concrete. But the beam was along the edge of the circle five hundred feet wide, not in or close to its center.

The faces of men watching ran wildly through awe, surprise, shock and horror. Instinctive cries arose, men gestured helplessly, terrible slow-motion movement compared to what was taking place before their eyes.

Vision cleared as the light vanished and the men watching had a terrifying picture of a man in a pressurized jumpsuit and helmet hurtling sideways through the air, just above the ground, limbs flailing. With terrific speed Morgan Scott whipped between two stunned soldiers. A hundred feet away, along the line of parked jet fighters, his body crashed against the long pitot tube extending forward from a fighter plane.

The pitot tube went through his body as if he'd been run through by a knife under full gallop.

A medical team reached him almost immediately. The paramedics slowed as they approached. A sense of unreality grew ever stronger. Morgan Scott's lifeless body, blood dripping down his suit to the concrete, was above their own eyes. They saw Scott against a bright light of the flight line, backlighted in an astonishing effect, his head tilted, his legs together, arms flung outward, eyes open and lifeless.

No one could have created a more perfect moment and scene of crucifixion.

A colonel walked through the group, men on their knees, crossing themselves, murmuring prayers. He looked into the face of Morgan Scott and motioned to the paramedics. "Take him down. Gently, gently. Use a stretcher and place him," he pointed to the area well in front of the fighter, "over there. No one is to touch the body. Keep everybody well back until I give you further instructions."

A jeep stopped fifty feet away. A sergeant in the jeep held up a radiophone and pointed to the colonel. He went to the jeep and spoke into the radio.

"Colonel Escobar here. Go ahead."

"Colonel, this is BEMAC Control. What happened, uh, did Morgan Scott arrive? How is he? Have you talked to him? Can you tell us—"

Escobar knew immediately from the manner of the words pouring forth that BEMAC—whoever was on the other end of the radio—already suspected the worst.

There could be nothing gained walking gently on those distant sounds of hurt.

"Your man is dead, BEMAC."

"My . . . oh, my God." Escobar waited for the shuddering breath, the sharp intake of air of a man gaining control of himself. "What happened, Colonel?"

"Scott—first the beam appeared. All this happened almost instantly. There was only split-second variation in events, BEMAC. The beam appeared like a solid bar of metal, tremendously bright, like a long green sun. It ended, I do not know your miracles, but the beam ended just above the ground. Above the concrete, really. Just inside the circle we prepared. Scott emerged from the beam like . . . magic is the best word. He is not there; then he is there. But he was not centered in the circle. He appeared near its edge. When he appeared he moved with great speed. A horizontal speed, just above the ground, and he was just a blur his body moved so quickly. When the beam vanished Scott was still moving at his great speed horizontally. His body struck the pitot boom of a fighter plane. He was impaled."

Escobar took a deep breath. "All I may tell you that may ease your pain, BEMAC, is that Morgan Scott died instantly. We have placed his body on a stretcher and returned it to exactly that point where he appeared so suddenly. It is a great shame." Escobar looked at the still form on the stretcher. "We await your next orders, BEMAC. We are ready to—"

His voice shut off as if a switch were thrown in his throat. Escobar's jaw dropped as he saw a green haze twist into existence before his eyes; it shimmered and pulsed. *Mary, Mother of Jesus, this cannot be—*

"Colonel Escobar! What's wrong? What's going on down there?" shouted BEMAC Control.

Escobar shouted into the microphone. *"He's gone!"*

"What do you mean he's gone? Make sense, man! What's happened with—"

Escobar heard the woman's shriek through his headset, louder than the man speaking into the microphone. Her sudden shrill scream stopped the radioman's voice and Escobar could hear the frightened repetitive wailing, *"My God, oh my God, my God, I can't believe this, oh my God—"*

"BEMAC!" Escobar shouted into the mike. "What is it? What's happening—"

"He's back! It's—it's incredible . . . can't believe this . . . his body is back here with us!"

Chapter XVIII

A green taxicab led the way. The driver and two passengers were armed with submachine guns and equipped with two-way radios. Behind them came the long GMC Vandura, looking like any other van from the outside but equipped with armored glass, bullet-proof fuel tank, and tires that couldn't blow out. It stayed in radio contact with the taxicab in front and the delivery truck following the van. The delivery truck was a disguised SWAT vehicle, a rolling armory, and it expertly covered the van that contained Suarez, Blake, Morales and Barrios, and the driver. "Call me Hugo," the driver told them after their pickup earlier from the Hilton and as he sped away in traffic, the other two vehicles sliding neatly into their lead-and-trail positions. They were on a winding road leading up a steep hill north of the city; now the van headed downhill.

Blake peered through the driver's window. "This is interesting," he said casually to the group.

Suarez leaned forward. "What's interesting? All I see is a lot of traffic and a big city."

"That's just the point, bucko. You're looking at the same part of the city we left fifteen minutes ago." He gestured at their driver. "Hugo, here, likes to drive in circles. Maybe we ought to have a little talk with Hugo."

Maria's hand was on his arm immediately. "No, Stan. He follows his orders, that's all."

"What orders?"

"We're going to a meeting. He took the long way around to make certain no one might be following us."

Suarez jerked a thumb behind him. "Well, lovely

lady, that truck is sure as hell following us. It has been ever since we left the hotel."

Maria smiled. "That truck, and the taxi before us. We are all together."

"Where to?" Blake pressed again.

"The Caracas Cultural Center."

"But that's right across the street from the Hilton!"

"Of course." Maria smiled sweetly.

Blake leaned back in his seat. He took a cigar from his jacket and handed one to Suarez. "Little woman," Blake said patiently, "you got to admit this is a hell of a time for a *meeting*."

"Hey, gringo!" Suarez laughed. "You speak wisdom. What the hell time is it anyway for this meeting?"

Morales looked at Maria Barrios and rolled her eyes. "Ten minutes to three, my hero."

"Three o'clock in the morning, my jungle flower, is a time for dancing, drinking," he leered at Morales, "and making love to a good woman!"

The others laughed at Carmen's sudden blush. Hugo half-turned from behind the wheel. "There's a late news bulletin. The television, please? Turn it on to Channel One."

The face of Angela Tirado in the television news studio came through clearly. ". . . caused a major disturbance tonight at the Caracas Hilton, where a formal banquet was being held for the trade delegation from China. Six members of a Russian group who flew in from Cuba—"

They stared at one another, grins breaking, turned back to the set. ". . . were arrested and are being held without bail. Earlier this evening, apparently drunk, several of the Russians started a fight in the men's room of the Hilton—"

Blake and Suarez whooped with laughter as the screen showed the Russians handcuffed, clothes torn, in disarray and bleeding, manhandled by city police and being pushed and dragged from the men's room into the landing at the stairway bottom of the hotel.

". . . and had to be physically restrained by local

police before being handcuffed and removed from the hotel—"

Blake and Suarez were pounding one another on the back and shoulders. The women restrained themselves, barely, with smiles.

". . . while several other Russians forced their way into the ladies' rest room of the hotel, where angry women turned the tables on the intruders—"

They watched two Russians stumbling clumsily, holding up their trousers with one hand, pawing at their eyes with their other hand, jostled by police from the ladies' room. By now Carmen and Maria were leaning against one another, tears on their cheeks from laughter, while Blake and Suarez knee-slapped and howled. Carmen turned up the volume to hear above the uproar.

". . . and the official charges include public drunkenness, brawling, assault, invading the ladies' room, indecent exposure, carrying concealed weapons, discharging firearms in public, and resisting arrest with violence. We have it on good word—"

Maria Barrios turned off the set. "I can't stand any more," she gasped finally. "My sides, they hurt." She looked at Carmen, face buried in her hands, choking with laughter, and Maria burst out again in her own glee.

"Just what in the sam hell did you two *do* to those people?"

The women couldn't answer for the moment. They clung to one another, bodies shaking as they struggled for control.

Hugo called back from the front. "Miss Barrios, we're here."

They regained control and looked through the windshield as the van turned onto the service entrance roadway for the Cultural Center. Suarez leaned forward to tap Hugo on the shoulder. "I can't get any answers back here, Hugo. What's going on here at three in the morning?"

"*Swan Lake.*"

"What?"

"The program tonight, sir. *Swan Lake*."

"I mean *now*, dammit."

Hugo ignored Suarez. "Ma'am, we're here," he said to Barrios as he eased to a stop in a concrete tunnelway. The cab had stopped before them and the truck eased to a halt directly behind them. Hugo unlocked the doors from his seat. Immediately a panel in the concrete wall slid aside and two armed soldiers, as crisp as starch, opened the van door. "This way, please," the first soldier said.

Blake and Suarez stared at Carmen Morales. She looked back and shrugged. They followed Maria from the van. They went down the hallway, through several more doors, and were caught completely by surprise as they stepped into the conference room with so many key members of BEMAC. They recognized Mercedes and several others of the local team, as well as McDavid. To Carmen Morales, Caleb Massey was a stranger.

Massey came forward, arms wide and stood before Maria.

"Colonel Barrios," he beamed, "it is my very great pleasure to see you again."

They clasped arms warmly. Stan Blake stared in disbelief at the two obviously old friends. Then he looked at Mercedes, whose face told him as much as he might find in a blank wall, then back to Maria Barrios as if he were seeing her for the first time.

Finally Blake found his voice. "*Colonel* Barrios?"

Maria went to him immediately, took his hand and squeezed it gently. "Later, Stan," she said in a half-whisper.

"But I—"

"Please?"

Blake melted. "Sure, of course, anything you say—" he broke into a half grin— "sir, I mean, ma'am."

She released his hand and returned to take a seat at the conference table next to Caleb Massey. Blake joined the other rider agents. There seemed an electric tension in the air which, Blake judged, was certainly to be expected, what with the cloak-and-dagger routines before assembling here and, for that matter, meeting in a secret sub-basement of the huge Cultural Center. Mercedes rapped twice, gently, on the table to bring the group to order. He wasted no time in dropping his load of bricks right smack in their individual chests.

"I have bad news," Mercedes began, his face almost grey. "The BEMAC team carried out a spot-landing transmission tonight." He paused a long pregnant moment to look at all the faces one by one. "Morgan Scott was killed."

No one spoke. They froze in their chairs. Finally Blake rose slowly to his feet.

"What happened?"

"The only saving grace I can offer you," Mercedes said as kindly as he could, "is that he died instantly."

"Goddammit, you've already *told* me he's dead. I want to know *how*. And *why?*"

Mercedes looked at Massey and the American nodded that he would pick up the answer. "The how is simple enough to relate, Mr. Blake," Massey said. "We set up a target circle of five hundred feet for emergence from the beam." Massey paused and held up a hand. "Forgive me. I tend to think in terms of *we* even when I had no direct connection with a specific test. A target circle five hundred feet in diameter was set up in the middle of a military airfield. All precautions for noninterference rematerialization were carried out. Observers saw the beam appear in cylindrical form; that conforms to a nominal transmission. Morgan Scott emerged from the beam several feet above ground level; that's as close as we can determine now. But he was moving horizontally at great speed during emergence. Apparently the speed was so great it amounted to violent acceleration. Eyewitnesses reported his limbs were thrown backward from the body as he appeared to be hurled sideways. Well beyond the acceptance circle his body struck, and he was impaled upon the pitot tube of an aircraft. It penetrated his body at that same high speed. Death was instantaneous."

Massey held the eyes of the devastated Blake. It's not always easy to lock eye contact with a man who's just lost his teammate and one of his closest friends, but there wasn't any other way. "I knew Morgan well; very well indeed," Massey said directly to Blake. "Have I answered, for now at least, what you wished to know?"

Blake sat down, made of stone. "Yes," he said. His lips barely moved.

Massey turned to take in the entire group. "All right, this meeting has taken on new dimensions. I'm going to repeat certain matters so that I'll *know* we haven't excluded anybody from what they should know."

He paused only for a deep breath and setting his mind on the new course. "BEMAC has flaws." He let that one settle in for another long pause. "You all know you've got problems. *We* have problems. You more than me because you, some of you, are riding that beam. George Wagner's alive because he was *lucky*. That's the truth of *that*. Kim Seavers survived only because you people took every precaution you could anticipate and then some, and *then* she lucked out. It could have gone either way for her and no one knows that better than Kim. The grim reality of all this is that Morgan Scott didn't have that luck."

Morales sat quietly, her face streaked with tears. "These problems? Were they our fault? Could we have done something, anything, to . . ." Her voice trailed away.

"No one here is at fault," Massey said with sudden heat. "Not here or anywhere else. Dammit, I don't want anyone to start wearing a crown of thorns about this! This is *not* an inquisition! We're pushing hell out of a new frontier and when it comes to frontiers I don't care if it's ancient sailing vessels or the space shuttle blowing up at launch, *someone*, sooner or later, has to pay the piper."

He stopped long enough to light up a cigar and yank his necktie loose. He sucked on tobacco, exhaled a swirling cloud, and stabbed the air with the cigar. "Now for the *big* news. We've found the flaws in the BEMAC operation."

"When?" Blake asked coldly.

"Too late to save Scott's life, obviously," Massey replied bluntly. "But early enough to prevent—I hope—a recurrence."

Alejandro Suarez stood until Massey nodded to him. "Sir, I'm a bit confused. You know so much about," he gestured with both hands, palms up, "this entire operation, and it sounds like you've been a part of this operation from the beginning, but I've never heard of you or how you fit into all this, and no one has told me to listen to you the way we listen to Dr. Mercedes."

Mercedes half-rose from his seat. "Alejandro, he speaks for me. His words, my tongue. Will that do?"

"Yes, sir." Suarez sat slowly.

"For good reasons, there's a lot about BEMAC you don't know," Massey said, looking at Suarez. "The risks you've taken have been enough of a burden. Even the Russians don't *know* about the United States being involved. And," Massey smiled, "didn't you have your own personal encounter on that level this evening?"

"Well, yes, sir, sort of. But there really isn't very much diplomacy in the men's john," Suarez answered, unsure of how much to say. "Miss Morales and Miss Barrios also held a meeting, I understand."

His words brought tremendous relief of tension through the group. Massey let the knotted feelings ease for a few moments. "They were out to get information from you," he said after a while. "They would have done just about anything to get it. Drugs, torture, anything. By the way, I've been informed you were backed by a SWAT team in case things got out of hand."

"What the hell did we need a SWAT team for?" Blake asked, openly belligerent.

"Obviously you *didn't* need any help," Massey offered.

"Do the Russians know what BEMAC is?" Suarez asked. "I know you indicated they don't, but they were sure all over us tonight."

"They were taking a wild chance." Heads turned to the soft feminine voice of Maria Barrios. "The answer, Alejandro, is that to the best of our knowledge they do not know. We wish to keep it that way. If any one of us had been kidnapped by the Russians, removed from our control, the SWAT team had orders to kill the Russians *and*, if necessary, anyone they had captive."

"*We?*" Blake called out. "I don't understand much of this anymore. And what's this colonel stuff?"

Mercedes took the questions. "Maria Barrios you know as my assistant, my secretary. That is her cover on our project."

"Cover?"

"Miss Barrios is a colonel in Venezuelan intelligence. She's responsible for the Russian sector."

"Please, *please!*" Massey waved both arms. "May we go on? We can attend to these kind of questions later." The room quieted immediately, and Massey opened his attaché case.

Blake couldn't resist the moment. "Is what you're carrying important, sir?" he asked.

Massey looked puzzled. "Yes, it is."

"That opened awfully easy, *sir*."

"Only to *my* palmprint, Blake. If you had opened it you'd be missing an arm right now and this case would be a fireball. Anything else?"

"Nope. Uh, no, sir."

Massey handed a slim stack of photographs to Suarez. "Pass these around," he told him. Massey waited for the pictures to pass about the table.

He addressed his next remark to the group. "Tell me what you see," he said in reference to the photos.

Morales held up a picture. "It's BEMAC, of course." Murmurs of agreement met her words. Except for Blake. He stared hard at his photograph, then looked up to Massey.

"Cute. It's real cute," he said, heads turning to him. "It is *not* BEMAC."

Suarez moved next to Blake. "Let me see." He studied Blake's picture and then his own and placed the two photos together. "They sure look the same to me," he concluded.

"The photos are the same but not the place," Blake

told him. His finger tapped the picture. "Look here. See it? The beamsphere is not on its support legs."

Suarez wasn't impressed. "So? It's down for maintenance or something."

"No, you dumb spic. There *aren't any* support legs. Even the floor mounts aren't here." Suarez grabbed the photo. "And see that grid on the floor? Like a circle where you'd expect to see the support tripod? I don't know what it is but sure as hell it's not in *our* dome."

Suarez looked with admiration at his partner. "You're a pretty smart cat for a gringo, you know that?" He punched Blake gently on the arm.

"Look here," Morales called out with growing excitement. "Look at the power grid in your pictures. It's also different from what we have."

"Very good, all of you," they heard Massey. "Now, put those pictures aside for a moment. Refresh your memory about the straight-line beam jump that Kim Seavers made. As you know, she came out of the beam about eight thousand feet up. We know the rest." He looked about the room, then settled on Blake. "*But do we really know the rest of what happened?* Does anyone here recall what was also so different about that mission?"

Blake showed a sudden and growing excitement. "Hey, hold one! There sure as hell was something different." He glanced at Morales and Suarez before turning back to Massey. "After Kim was down, after they'd fished her from the water, there was, well, the best I can describe it was that we had a laser energy pulse. Some kind of final energy burst from where the laser beam had appeared."

Massey stared at Blake, expectant, deliberately not saying much. "*Where?*" he asked, voice cracking like a whip.

"Well, it's in the films and," Blake hesitated, his eyes wider with his own recall, "it was eight thousand feet up. Right where the transmission ended."

Massey swept one arm wide to include everyone in the room. "Do you know, *now*, what we experienced?"

Morales was on her feet, gesturing wildly for attention. "A rebound!" she blurted out. "We had a rebound effect!"

"We're back with the ghost of Newton," Suarez said, more reflective than the others. "The old saw still hangs in there. Every action has an equal and opposite reaction . . ."

Felipe Mercedes finally rejoined the exchange. "How right you are, Alejandro. Newton's ghost is *always* alive with us. And Stan is correct, as is Carmen. You don't lose energy because it vanishes as magic. It must go somewhere. *It must be accounted for.*"

"And the energy released by the beam at its target point," Massey added, "is *so* great there *should be* a tremendous heating and expansion of the surrounding air. Well, *there isn't*. No heating, no expansion, no explosion."

"The most exciting conclusion we drew, and it's now reality rather than theory," said Mercedes, as he and Massey tossed their data back and forth, "is that unless we modify the impulse, exactly seventeen minutes after firing the beam, the energy snaps back to the source."

"You mean the *full* energy?" asked Blake.

"Yes," Mercedes confirmed.

"With the original mass?" Suarez followed.

"With the original mass, *and more*," Mercedes said. "There's excess energy involved."

"All of you, listen to me carefully," Massey broke in. "Morgan Scott died tonight. But his death, the manner of his death, confirmed what we've suspected ever since Kim's ride. If you're in the immediate vicinity of the delivery point, seventeen minutes after being beamed to your target point, *you'll be snatched back by the beam.* You'll be picked up exactly as if you were in the beamsphere and returned to your transmission source."

"Jesus Christ!" Blake swore quietly. "You mean," he hesitated almost as if he didn't want to say the words, they seemed so outlandish, *"it's a round-trip ride?"*

"Precisely," Massey said. Mercedes was nodding vigorously in confirmation.

"Hey, that's one hell of a theory," Blake cautioned, "but—"

Massey held up a hand and Blake went silent. "Seventeen minutes after Morgan Scott died tonight," he said slowly and with great deliberation, "there occurred a laser flash at the planned target point. The people on that airfield had placed Morgan's body on a stretcher and carried it back to exactly where he emerged from the beam. When the laser flashed at the airfield the second time, Morgan disappeared. *A split-second later his body rematerialized in the BEMAC sphere.*"

"My God, that cannot be," Morales said quietly, more to herself than anyone else.

"I cannot really impress upon you," Mercedes followed Massey's words, "how incredibly excited we are about this. Theoretically before—and now, it appears, actually—we can beam you anywhere in the world by using our laser geosat bounce. Then, seventeen minutes later, if you're in that circle where you arrived, you're snatched out of thin air, collected as it were, and bounced back to the starting point."

"This has gone far beyond a scientific test program," Massey said, his voice and tone demonstrating much thought behind his words. "We now have one of the most advanced weapons this world has ever known."

"Or even dreamed of," noted Maria Barrios, speaking for the first time in the back-and-forth discussion.

Morales held up her photo. "This *isn't* our BEMAC facility, is it?"

Massey smiled. "No, it's not. But with the exception of some modifications, minor but critical, it's a duplicate of where you've been working."

"Where is it?" Blake asked.

"What kind of modifications?" Suarez said quickly.

"First, those photos were taken at the BEMAC duplicate in a concealed facility at Cape Canaveral in Florida. Not on the missile launch site but immediately south of it, where the government ran an experimental solar energy program for some years before closing the place. It was abandoned for years. We took it over. For many reasons, including security, it was the perfect choice."

"Those modifications?" Suarez pressed.

"I'll defer to Claude McDavid for your answer," Massey said.

McDavid spread papers before him. "Let me state, first," he began carefully, "that we have been working on megapower systems a very long time. Jorge Wagner and I have been involved in the American SDI, the so-called Star Wars program, for some years. Our specialty has been power, but above all, massive amounts of power—and even more important, *smooth*, absolutely smooth, power flow." He glanced at some notes and slid some papers to the side.

"Let me touch on BEMAC before I go further. Our facility here began with what we believed was sufficient power from the IVIC nuclear reactor. Well, before that, we had the experiments down south, using hydroelectric power from Angel Falls. That was clearly inadequate in terms of power supply and especially in smooth power flow. We found it essential to come to IVIC for the nuclear reactor and then we learned, to our dismay, that our system simply didn't grind out the huge amounts of power the BEMAC laser sucks up. Caleb Massey here, and a few other people in the American government, who we will *not* name, arranged for a new power core for the IVIC reactor. That gave us the power we needed. We were, in modern terms, right in the middle of Fat City where power availability was concerned."

McDavid rubbed his hands absentmindedly. "But we still ran into problems. They tore up our mannequins and other equipment, they did horrible things to animals, and they killed some of our best people. We identified the problems after those losses. Put simply, the system for transferring power from the reactor and the generators, to the laser beam cannon, is flawed. There are imperfections in metals and alloys. There's interference from electromagnetic and other effects. We ran into some really troublesome electric glitches in our cables. All this killed people."

McDavid looked to Massey and Mercedes. "Damn, I didn't mean to make this a lecture," he apologized, "but—"

"Hell, man, don't stop now!" Blake called out, with the others murmuring agreement.

McDavid nodded. "It won't take much longer. While you people were working on this laser system, BEMAC, Jorge and I were deeply involved with the Star Wars energy systems. Our specialty wasn't far out—no pun intended. In other words, we didn't work on the satellites or weapons in space. We concentrated on powering the ground-based lasers for SDI."

He glanced at his notes. "Our job was to explore the idea of storing huge amounts of power in a ground facility, and always have it available for immediate and full-scale use in the laser-firing systems. We called it SMES, or Superconducting Magnetic Energy Storage. There were two simultaneous programs. The Bechtel company in the United States, and a separate research firm that's a joint venture of Venezuela and the United States. That's us."

McDavid rubbed the side of his nose, a sure sign to those who knew him that he was getting down to the gristle of the issue. "Our approach to keep the genie of superpower under lock and key," he said slowly and carefully, "hinged on the success of superconducting materials. Using the supercold of cryogenic systems. Simply put, when you get the temperature down low enough in a metal, it loses all electrical resistance. If the temperature is close to absolute zero, you can kick off an electrical current and without ever adding more energy, it will keep right on circulating for, well, forever. So what we did initially was to produce a massive superconducting coil out of the purest materials we could manage. Then we placed that coil within liquid helium that was contained in a special tank, itself buried well beneath the ground. It was about as close to absolute zero as you can get. We gave it a real good shot of electrical energy and a year later we still had the same amount of energy in that coil as when we started.

For those of you who want a specific statement, the energy was stored as a magnetic field, and that field was supported by the current that kept flowing without resistance in the coil.

"Okay. The next step after being able to build huge amounts of energy and keep them locked up was how to open this Pandora's Box of raw energy and use it as a tool rather than as an explosive release. For about a year we restricted ourselves to burst transmissions. Finally we were getting four hundred to a thousand megawatts for better than ninety seconds *and*," he stabbed a finger for emphasis at his papers, "we got perfectly smooth flow to the lasers. We got so good at it that with our test equipment—and admittedly it's a massive, expensive, complex facility for test purposes—that, well, we could fire a beam to the moon and turn rock into molten slag. Now, I'll also admit that the moon is a nice fat target that's moving along slowly, but proof of concept was our goal."

He paused to sip water. "I'll do the wrap on this now. Jorge, here, and I did some experiments on our own, because we always had BEMAC in mind, although, you can appreciate, we never discussed BEMAC with anyone up north, with the exception of our grizzly bear, Mr. Massey. To get to the nut of all this, we felt BEMAC deserved something better than working with liquid helium. I mean, you're down to absolute zero. *Any* change in temperature and you're dealing with immediate imperfection. With the new superconducting magnets that work at higher temperatures, and I understand you've already had some briefings on this, we developed the same power-storage system with liquid nitrogen that we could do before only with liquid helium. To wrap this up, that system is being installed *tomorrow* in BEMAC."

He sipped water again, glancing at Massey, who nodded. McDavid took his seat and Massey stood, gathering his papers. "By now you may have figured why you're meeting in this palace of culture instead of within your own facility. Anybody care to venture a guess?"

Blake gestured. "You have all the signs, Mr. Massey, of someone who's laid a lot of groundwork. Something's coming down and it promises to be heavy. We going somewhere?"

"Bravo, bravo, m'boy! You," Massey pointed a finger at Blake, "are *so* right. You're *all* leaving for Cape Canaveral."

Suarez came straight up in his seat. "To Florida? When?"

"*Now.*"

"Now? What about our equipment? Clothes?"

"We leave from here," Massey told him and the others. "We leave from here in the midst of all those people and all those cars that leave here when the ballet ends. Ladies and gentlemen, this may be the first time *Swan Lake* was ever used as a cover, but now you can see why we're here instead of at BEMAC. A general exodus from the IVIC area would be like shooting off flares. When you leave here in small groups you'll be mixing in with the culture crowd. You'll be invisible. Felipe?"

Mercedes stood. "Whatever you need in the way of personal articles, and your equipment, of course, has been prepared for you in Florida. You may ignore the need for passports and other such items normally required. We will all go to a military field within forty miles of here. An Eastern Air Lines jetliner awaits us there. We'll look like any other commercial flight, you'll have the chance to sleep on the airplane, and we will land at a military airfield in Florida. Time is running out. Any last questions?"

"What about Kim Seavers?" Blake asked.

"And Pappas?" Morales added. "And the others?"

Mercedes smiled. "They're already on their way."

"One last question?" Blake said.

"Of course," Massey told him.

"It's almost *four o'clock in the morning*. How do you keep an audience in your theater that long, to say nothing of your performers?"

"*Very* good," Mercedes answered. "This is a charity

affair. For every hour beyond midnight that our performers continue to play music and to dance, *and* the audience remains seated, Monitor Nacional Television has offered to double the proceeds of the box office."

"Thank your lucky stars you've got a lot of music lovers in this town," Blake offered.

"To say nothing of the performers," Mercedes finished with a laugh. "The Moscow Ballet was *most* eager to perform for us."

Chapter XIX

"Not very big, is it?" Caleb Massey pointed through the window of the air force bus driving slowly past the missiles and rocket museum on Cape Canaveral Air Force Station. A balmy and moist breeze blew in from the beaches just to the left; compared to the cool heights of IVIC this was steamy jungle. But for the moment they ignored the weather. They had a new perspective of Caleb Massey; *he had been here for the development and launching of most of these missiles and space boosters.* He was walking history.

"We launched Al Shepard and Gus Grissom on that bird. A modified Redstone missile that grew right out of the V-2 from the second world war. In those days it was a giant. Now the damn thing looks like a pencil." Massey pointed out the rounded flanks and sharp fins of the machines that broke the iron bubble of gravity and gave man his first crude slingshots to hit earth orbit. "It all started with these pieces of hardware," he said, pointing out one rare vehicle after another. "There's the Vanguard. It's even skinnier than the Redstone and it was six times as dumb a thing as was ever built. An absolute piece of technical crap on which we should never have spent a dime. Over there? See that one with the black and white markings? That's the ancestor of *everything*. The V-2. Made to carry hellfire and destruction, and it did, and from that ancient mariner, everything else evolved."

The bus driver hung on every word. He took a lot of people on this road going south through Canaveral, but it was all too rare to have someone like Caleb Massey on board the bus. *He* had been here in the *old days*. He was a relic like the others, but he still walked and talked, while these were immobile monuments.

"That's the bird there, that piggyback job, that started all the modern propulsion systems," Massey was relating. "See the main rocket? They built those in two-engine and three-engine versions. And those same engines went on to power everything else. We called her the Navaho. Had a ramjet cruise missile on top. Took it up to speed and altitude and then kicked the ramjet loose."

Carmen Morales shook her head. "But isn't that how the space shuttle works? I thought the shuttle was a revolutionary concept?"

"Just shows you you can't believe NASA propaganda," Massey grinned. "There were a lot more piggyback vertical-boost programs before shuttle, like Dyna-Soar. Well, over there, that's the Atlas that carried our first astronauts into orbit. And there's the Titan that boosted the two-man Geminis. I'd forgotten what we had here. Look at them . . ." He was drifting off, wandering in his own memory as much as talking to this new generation. "There's Thor, and Jupiter, and Juno. Aha, didn't know we had the Shrike here. There's the Loon, and the Aerobee. Uh-huh; Scout, Nike, Ajax, Little Joe, Delta, Centaur, Matador and Snark, there's the Lark and Mace . . ."

Finally he fell silent. Carmen Morales leaned forward to his seat. "Where are you now, Mr. Massey?"

"Thinking, young lady." He smiled at her. "Thinking that when these rockets were flying, even like that Atlas-Aegena over there, and we had names like Orbiter and Ranger and Surveyor, well, it's hard to believe. Most of you in this bus, the rest of the young men and women who make up our project, *weren't even born yet*." He patted her hand. "That's what I was thinking, how wonderfully young and alive you all are."

Carmen couldn't help it. She hugged him fiercely. There were a lot of smiles at the sight, but no one laughed.

* * *

They rolled through heavy security gates. Twice the bus had to stop between heavy gates, blocking them in. Security guards boarded the bus to check their names and identification. Blake studied them, seemingly casual, but his practiced eyes missed nothing. As they rolled from one security block to another he turned to Massey. "First time I've ever seen security people like these who don't carry weapons," he said to Massey. Everyone turned to listen.

"You mean no guns?" Massey replied with a question.

"You got it, boss man."

"Those dogs with them are timber-shepherds. One third timber wolf and two-thirds German shepherd, and they've got a bite as strong as that of a pit bull, except they're far more intelligent, they each weigh about a hundred and forty pounds, and they are the best trained security dogs you'll ever see in your life. Much better than guns that could hurt or kill innocents."

"Makes sense," Blake acknowledged. "What else?"

Massey smiled. "You tell me, Stan."

Blake looked around as Suarez followed his eyes. "I'm starting to see what you mean. The fences. Electrified, of course."

"Of course."

"Those transformers. Automatic cutbacks in event of short circuiting? Someone knocks 'em out they come right back on?"

"Very good. Go on."

"This isn't concrete or macadam beneath us."

"Nope."

"Steel mesh and plate on multiple pistons is my bet."

"Correct. We can drop this whole bus into a big tank of water directly beneath us. No fast way out. Vertical slick walls. The drop traps but doesn't kill."

"Neat," Blake said. "That means you'd want to immobilize if you do that. So you've got gas systems down there."

"Uh huh."

"I can spot the rest. Let's see if amigo here has sharp eyes also," Blake said, deferring to Suarez.

Suarez grinned. "There," he pointed. "Sonic disruptors." They looked at innocent-appearing air-conditioning ventilator tubes. "And those big vent fans; ah, that is a nice touch," Suarez said. "Blinder lights when they drop out of place. You look into one of those and you don't see so good for a couple of hours."

"Hey, they got some neat-looking strobes," Blake noted. "If they're full steam like I think they are, they're vertigo inducers."

"They are," Massey confirmed. "Three seconds of exposure to them and you're on your belly falling into a forever pit. You can *not* walk or stand up."

"That's enough," Blake said. "Now I'll let the sandman in my room tonight."

They rolled through the final security systems into a sprawling solar-energy research facility. They stood in the hot Florida sun amidst racks of solar cells, mirrors, parabolic reflectors, steam plants, liquid-mercury condensers, strange searchlights, thick cables snaking about underfoot. "This place is a junkyard," Morales observed. The buildings about them were unpainted and scabrous. The whole place looked shabby.

Massey stood by a wide doorway. "Come on in, and welcome to Fantasyland where everything inside isn't what it looks like *outside*."

The door slid noiselessly closed behind them. Instantly cool fresh air enveloped them, bringing sighs of relief. They went through a second door. Before them the corridors were gleaming and spotless. Everything was brilliant, new, ultramodern; there was a sense of great power and serious purpose underlying the long corridors stretching away.

Several people in jumpsuits of different pastels and identifying numbers waited for them. Massey turned to his group. "You'll be shown to your quarters. Fresh clothing, personal and toilet articles, everything you need is here. You have exactly two hours to shower, clean up, change, and report to Briefing Room Six.

These people," he motioned to the waiting group, "will answer any questions you have and guide you around."

Blake turned from a sightseeing expression back to Massey. "What's the rush, boss-man?"

"You do your first full mission," Massey smiled, "*tonight.*"

They emerged from the nuclear reactor room, following the shielded tube into the power transfer dome, a nightmare of plumbing, pipes, cabling, computer banks, and a wall of gauges, vertical instruments and emergency control systems. The immediate world was a Babylonian bedlam of deep groaning sounds, high shrill screams from supercold banks and piping and on the floor, with eerie effects from banks of multicolored lighting, cold vapors swirled about their feet.

"This is a technological Dante," Maria Barrios observed.

"Nightmare in color," said Kim Seavers.

Suarez leaned closer to Massey and McDavid. "How do you control the power flow?"

"Think of a rheostat that locks in place whenever you stop moving it. It's set in thousandths. We can use that kind of control to set the rebound from only seconds to the maximum time of seventeen minutes," Massey explained.

"One thing I don't understand," Tony Pappas said aloud, craning his neck and turning to try to absorb the incredible machinery about them.

"Shoot," Massey said.

"In Venezuela, we're pretty well isolated," Pappas offered. "You know, it's wild country for the most part. Jungles, flood plains, desert, raw mountains. But here," he turned with both arms out, "the whole world is watching you. How can you possibly keep this place secret?"

"They're not watching us," Massey told him. "They see the space shuttle up at Kennedy. The Delta and Centaur and Titan launch pads. That's what they see."

"No, no, he's right," Carmen Morales broke in. "I saw the astronomical domes when we came here. It's obvious to the whole world that with all these lights around here, the space center and all these towns, to say nothing of that constant salt spray from the ocean, that you're *not* doing optical astronomy."

Massey laughed. He motioned for them to start back to what they already called Cape Dome and answered Morales as they walked. "Everything you've said, and that Alejandro said, is true. But sometimes the best way to hide something is to put it right under everybody's nose. What do we have here? Noise, bright lights, people coming and going at all hours—here, that's absolutely *normal*. Extra security? Hey, just try to get into the Trident complex. Right in our back yard we've got the giant base for the super subs that carry those Trident missiles. We've got a full coast guard station. Then there's the Cape with all the launches we do from there. *And* the launch center for the shuttle. We're surrounded by security. There's Patrick Air Force Base, and that's got a mob of combat aircraft. We've got those Fat Alberts, the blimps, up at thirteen thousand feet with their radar systems looking for drug runners. Plus the towns. This whole place is crazy with lights and noise. It's a perfect cover for us."

"And the astronomical domes?" Morales pushed. "*They* don't stand out?"

"Not at all! That's the beauty of it. This whole coastline is dotted with these domes. They contain huge radar systems as well as cameras and telescopes— theodolites—for missile and spacecraft tracking. They've been here nearly *forty years*. Ours is just one more dome. In fact, we've got six, all different sizes. Five are dummies. In fact, one of them is a bar just for you people. Like it?"

"One more question?" Suarez asked. Massey nodded. "Even with everything you say, the green laser is like nothing else here. How do we explain *that*?"

Mercedes laughed. "I'll answer that, Alejandro. You, of course, know of Angela Tirado."

"Ah, the peach of Venezuela."

"Peach?"

"Like a Georgia peach," Seavers broke in. "Young, beautiful girl."

"Well, that is a new name for me. She is a part of our operation. Have you heard her world-exclusive reports, as the Americans call it, a world scoop, of the new satellite communications system developed by Venezuela and being tested here? It uses a very bright laser beam. Miss Tirado calls it laser fibre optics. A lovely description."

"And no one," Maria Barrios added, "questions Angie. She is a firebrand. All fury and brimstone. She has been the best cover we could ask. People here *expect* to see the green laser. To them it is lovely fireworks."

"Fibre optics to make love by," Blake suggested.

"What?" Maria asked.

"Anything, for him," Kim Seavers smirked, "is to make love by."

Massey stopped by a large door and pushed it open. They looked upon a superbly equipped gym, swimming pool, and equipment testing facility.

"This building, from the outside," Pappas said, "it looks like a junkyard."

"That's the name of the game," Massey told him. "Okay, Blake and Seavers, you come with me. Everybody else, it's training time. You've been on your butts much too long."

Seavers and Blake exchanged glances; Kim shrugged. They turned to follow Massey. Several minutes later, after passing three security checks, they stared about them at an enormous mission planning room.

"No windows," Blake observed aloud. The walls were invisible behind charts, maps, technical sheets, photographs, long racks of communications electronics, computer consoles, TV monitors, and mysterious equipment they couldn't identify. Massey led the way to a round table and pointed to chairs. "Sit down, please." An aide appeared out of nowhere with coffee and fresh juice, and left.

Massey poured coffee. "I need a mission by two of my best agents. Specifically, Beamriders."

"We seem to fit that description," Blake said.

"You're also experienced on the beam. That's damned important. There won't be time for sightseeing. Besides, you're the best for this particular job. *And* it's vital training for an even bigger one to follow."

"What's the job?" Kim asked quietly.

"I can't say before I know you'll accept," Massey said carefully, "and I won't ask you to say yes before I tell you that we—no; *you* two—are taking a high risk."

Blake shifted uncomfortably. "No disrespect, sir, but why the hell don't you just get on with it?" Kim nodded her agreement.

Massey looked from one to the other. "That's it? No questions?"

"We don't kill," Blake said.

"Agreed," Massey told him.

"Name your poison, then," Kim added. "Sir, I guess."

Massey nodded. "All right, then. I want you to beam onto the thirtieth floor of an apartment complex in Washington, D.C. Not just onto, *into*, that floor. Specifically, to a certain room at a certain time, with unerring accuracy. It's got to be absolute. The Greystones have worked it out from a dozen different angles and all coordinates are down absolutely." His eyes were cold and unblinking; this was a man back in a harness he hadn't worn for a long time. "If we make one mistake, forget to cross one T or dot a single I, we could kill you."

"Go on," Blake said, impatient with the dire warnings.

"You beam in, do your work in sixty seconds flat, we beam you out."

"And you said no guns?" Kim queried. "Sorry, I forget. Guns are out for other reasons. No weapons, then."

"Costumes and a camera."

"*What?*" they chorused.

Massey didn't answer.

"He's grinning like the Cheshire Cat," Kim noted.

"Canary feathers and all," Blake added.

*　　*　　*

First they sealed off the entire facility with maximum security. Nobody in; nobody out. Then they doubled the security within Cape Dome. Only those necessary for the mission had entry. All observation booths and TV cameras were closed down.

It could have been BEMAC dome except for two major differences. Clouds of liquid-nitrogen vapor seeped through the cryogenic power storage area, rolling and swirling down stairways and creating startling effects from the many multicolored lights of the huge dome, a sight never seen in the Venezuelan facility.

And there was the beamsphere, exactly the same in size and shape and content, but unsupported by the tripod legs of BEMAC dome. The circular power grid along the floor and around the circumference of the sphere sent a tremendous lifting energy to the super-conducting ceramic material forming the framework of the sphere. The sphere levitated above the floor, or seemed to do so. "It eliminates interference from the supporting legs," Massey had explained, "and one more possibility of something going wrong is eliminated."

Caleb Massey and Felipe Mercedes had stood together in Control Central, feeling the power thrumming beneath their feet and watching the beamsphere rise slowly to its lock-and-hold position. "Caleb, if I didn't see this with my own eyes," Mercedes told him, "I don't think I would believe even you." He shook his head with wonder. "You're actually *levitating* a three-ton sphere!"

Massey refused any special credit. "Hell, Phil, it's either magic or it's superconducting ceramics. You know what's funny about all this?" He went on without waiting for a response. "The stuff we use for our power flow is made by the same laboratory that makes hydrogen bombs."

Mercedes frowned. "I know, I *know*. It's still so hard to accept!" He studied Massey. "The same formula you told me about before?"

"Yep. Same stuff. Yttrium, barium and copper in a platinum oxide, ceramics for binding, and—"

Loudspeakers throughout the Dome boomed their message. "Three minutes and counting. Seal all doors. Seal all doors. All personnel remain at your stations. All personnel remain at your stations."

Massey and Mercedes donned headsets and mikes. Massey's microphone now stayed alive. "At two minutes," Massey announced, "I want final confirmation all systems."

"Coming up on two minutes," Master Control intoned. "On my mark—*mark*! Two minutes and counting."

Voices carried from throughout the Dome.

"Reactor."

"Go!"

"Power energizer and flow."

"Go!"

"Beamsphere lock."

"Locked. Go."

"Dome open and locked."

"Open, locked. Go."

"Range safety."

"All green. Go."

"Beamriders."

Blake's voice couldn't be mistaken. "Zip-a-dee-doo-dah!"

"Let's do it," Kim sang out. "Beamriders, GO!"

"Terminal count coming up."

"Let's do it, baby," Blake called out.

"Terminal count."

"Hot damn," Kim said.

"Hold my hand, kid."

"Three

"Two

"One

"*Fire!*"

Green flash, ozone in the air, a cracking blast.

Teal hellfire stabbed away from the earth, guided unerringly to a satellite more than twenty-two thousand miles above the equator, whipped through angled mirrors, flashed earthward.

Kim Seavers and Stan Blake were in, were part of, *were the fire*.

Senator Patrick Xavier Elias stood waiting at the security door to his private apartment for Caleb Massey. His personal guard closed the door and, following the senator's orders, sealed the two men inside.

"Sit down, man," Elias said. "We're clean here. I've got all screens up."

Massey slouched in a deep armchair and took out a long Jamaican cigar and lit up with a smile of satisfaction.

"Goddammit, don't look so smug, Caleb! *Don't you realize you've failed us?*" Mancini sees the president tomorrow afternoon and he's got enough ammunition to bury us forever!"

He dropped heavily into his own chair, scattering an ashtray and cursing beneath his breath. He glared at Massey. "So we can kiss our precious teal ruby lasers goodbye and—"

"He's seeing the president tomorrow *afternoon?*"

"That's what I said, blast you."

"Plenty of time, then, Patrick, plenty of time. Do you want me to die of thirst, man? Where's the whiskey?"

"You've lost your marbles, Caleb. You haven't heard a thing I've said!"

"Me?" Massey sat up straight with a pained look on his face. "I heard it all. It's *you* who's lost his hearing. Whiskey, man!"

Elias sat back, slumping. "Hell, you know where it is. Get it yourself."

Massey returned with a bottle and two glasses. He poured with a flourish, held a glass out to the senator. "Drink up, man."

"Are we celebrating our own funerals?"

Massey downed his drink in a long gratifying swallow. He kept silent while he refilled his glass, then sat back. With his free hand he patted his jacket pocket. "Right here, my friend, I've got Mancini." He withdrew a videotape cartridge and held it up for Elias to see. "Not on the silver platter, but it's the same thing."

"A videotape?"

"Right."

"Who?"

"Why, Mancini, of course. And a few others."

"How long does it run?"

"Forty seconds or so."

"You *have* lost your mind, haven't you? What in the name of the seven blue gods of the Potomac are we going to do with—"

Massey held up a hand to end the sudden tirade. "Old man, you've always trusted me. Don't go bad now." A cold smile appeared on his face. "Get Mancini here. Tonight."

"Tonight?" Elias echoed.

"*Now.*"

"It's almost two in the morning, Caleb."

"My mommy gave me a watch. I know. Get him here."

"I can't—"

"Yes, you can. Invoke your position as head of the senate committee, you old goat."

Elias sighed. "It can't get any worse. Why not?"

"Hell, Patrick, he'll think you want him here to listen to you beg."

"I'm out of *my* mind. I ought to—" Elias cut himself off in midsentence, opened a panel on his chair armrest, tapped in a coded number. The phone was answered before the third ring.

"Mancini? Pat Elias here. Yes, yes, I know what damn time it is! Shut up and listen. As chairman of our senate panel, I'm invoking Article Four." He listened for several moments. "*Yes,*" he said firmly. "It's a fullblown emergency. I want you and no one else in my apartment in thirty minutes, or we go ahead without you, and you're locked out of *all* future sessions. Good."

He cut the connection and studied Massey. "Satisfied, you crusty old bastard?"

"Notice how willing he was to show up?"

Elias's face went through changing emotions. "Yes," he said slowly. "By God, you're right! I expected a lot more spit and piss from him. You know why, don't you?"

Massey held up the tape. "Silver platter time, old friend, silver platter time."

Twenty-two minutes later, by the clock, a chime sounded. "Go ahead," Elias said to the room.

A concealed speaker came alive. "Sir, a Mr. Craig Mancini is here to see you."

"Security check?" Elias asked.

"Confirmed, sir."

"Bring him in, please."

"Yes, sir."

Craig Mancini stood by the door, waited until it closed and locked behind him. He glared at the two men.

"Ichabod Crane, I do believe," Massey said with a cheery wave.

"You didn't tell me *he'd* be here," Mancini said icily.

"You didn't ask, either," Elias replied.

"I'll be brief," Mancini began.

"That's a change for the good," Massey chortled.

Mancini ignored him. "I'm here because the law calls for me, under Article Four, to respond day or night to your call. But tomorrow, Senator, I'm going to fry you coal-black!"

Massey put aside his nearly-empty glass. When he rose to his feet the jaunty air was gone. He faced Mancini directly.

"Mancini, you live on the thirtieth floor of the Masters Apartments. Is that correct?"

The unexpected question put Mancini off his speed. "Why, uh, what's that got to do with—"

"Dammit, just answer the question," Elias barked at him.

"Yes, I live there." Mancini came back quickly. "Where I live, however, is none of your damned business," he spat at Massey.

"Uh huh," Massey said, his attitude just a hair *too* congenial. "Now, the security at Masters is tighter than the Pentagon. You couldn't pound a needle up an elephant's ass trying to get into that place. Entry is permitted only with fingerprint and retinal identification by computer. Still correct?"

"Uh, yes, that's right, but—"

"All windows are sealed. All exits are from the building interior. You're nailed shut once you go into your own apartment. Am I still on target?"

"Cut the crap, mister, and—"

"No one gets into your apartment unless you let them in yourself, right?"

"I'm not going to stand for this shit any longer," Mancini snarled to Elias. The senator smiled but said nothing.

Massey's voice had become velvet. "*Mr.* Mancini, I've checked the security docket at your apartment complex. So I want you to have every chance to answer truthfully." He smiled again at the angry government official. "Now, did *you* let anyone into your apartment tonight?"

Mancini started to answer, faltered, his face turning red. He caught himself and set his face in a hateful look. "*No*, damn you," he shouted at Massey, and then, turning back to Elias. "You tell me what the hell all this is about or I'm out of here and I'll skin you two bastards alive tomorrow!"

"Stow it, shit bird."

Mancini gaped with Massey's remark. "*What?*"

"You heard me," Massey said quietly. He slipped the tape into the VCR on the bookcase, checked the television for ON, hit the PLAY button, and stepped back. "You'll just *love* this, Mancini."

Green light flashed from the screen, then flickered and washed out. The scene before them was obviously from a handheld camcorder, and just as obviously an amateur grip on the camera. The camera zoomed in to an eyeblink shot of Stan Blake as he lowered a plastic Darth Vader helmet over his face. The camera scene followed Blake-Vader as he strode down a hall, turned left around a corner, and caught Vader striding purposefully toward the open door of a bedroom. As the camera shot closed in the bedroom appeared in pink, effeminate detail. The view moved jerkily to the right to show Craig Mancini with a stunned look on his face, mouth gaping open.

"Holy shit," Elias said.

Craig Mancini wore women's panties with an open crotch, a stuffed bra and a bright red garter belt. Lipstick had been smeared garishly across his mouth. Reflected in the full-wall mirror was a naked man, also staring, his hand frozen in the act of masturbation. Immediately Vader was by Mancini's side, a gloved hand over Mancini's shoulder and cupping one full bra. "God, I love you!" Vader cried, as his other hand reached down to Mancini's open crotch and squeezed.

Mancini jerked back, eyes bulging, starting to scream. Vader waved gaily. "Ta ta! Love you, doll. Bye, now!"

The screen showed blurred movement as Vader moved toward the camera, then the camera whirled about to show Vader running down the hallway. Light flickered, the picture gave way to a flood of green light and the tape went blank. The sound track hissed steadily as snow scrambled the set.

Still without a word, Massey hit the EJECT button, removed the tape and handed it to the senator. Elias weighed it in his hand.

"I suggest," he said to Mancini, "you make some changes in your scheduled subjects to discuss tomorrow with the president."

Mancini shook from rage. His face livid, he could barely get his words out coherently. "You son of a bitch, not even this rotten blackmail will—"

Elias raised his brows in a calm surprise. "Blackmail? *Me?* Mancini, to hell with your bra and your crotchless goodies. You're not thinking clearly, man."

"Wha—what do you mean?" Fear had begun to replace rage.

"How did those maniacs ever get into your apartment if you didn't let them in yourself for a homosexual orgy?" Elias chuckled. "Hell, man, there's got to be a lot more tape where *this* scum came from! God, what a story! I can see it now—" Elias held up both hands in the imaginary camera frame, smiling. "America will *love* it! Craig Mancini and Darth Vader, and whoever else was that human puke you had in the bed, going at it full-tilt and . . ."

He let his voice change to ice as his words faded. He tossed the tape to Mancini. "You fuck up *just once* and I promise you every member of the congress and the senate will have their own copy of this video vomit. *And* the White House as well. You have my word on it."

Elias rang for his security guard. He stood to face Mancini and there was no mistaking the fire in the old warhorse. "Get out. Forget anything and everything you knew or heard or even remotely suspected about *any* project on which I or Massey might be working."

The door opened and the security guard bowed slightly to Mancini. "This way, sir."

Chapter XX

"Let me get this absolutely straight, old man. Despite everything you've told me, which makes this cockamamie concept triply impossible, you want me to put together a team and snatch Peter Unsworth out of Russia, right?"

Elias held out two shot glasses. When he and Massey each held one he raised his glass to his friend, they touched glass with an ominous *clank* instead of the familiar glass ring, and Elias nodded. "God help me," he said, taking a long swallow, "yes." He watched Massey dump his drink unceremoniously down his throat before continuing. "But," Elias said, shrugging, "after seeing that little home movie of yours—you know, you had everything except Shirley Temple and naked sheep in that little di-do—I'm inclined to believe you can do *anything*." He held up his glass in a final prefinishing salute. "Here's to our backward peasant friends in Venezuela."

"And a child in a *sombrero* shall lead them," Massey acknowledged. "You know they present us a problem."

"Who? Mercedes's people or the Russians?"

"Both," Massey said, fishing in his jacket pocket for a cigar. "The Russians for obvious reasons. They will take most unkindly to anyone kicking in doors three stories underground to snatch a foreign brain from under their potato bins in the Kremlin."

"And the boys in Caracas?"

Massey lit his cigar, tossed a match uncaringly onto the carpet, and puffed great clouds of smoke. "They got a rule with this BEMAC project. Their boys dreamed it up and *our* boys and girls have gone along with it."

"Which is?"

"They won't kill for *any* mission."

"Bullshit."

"You misread the signals, you old bastard. I'm not saying there won't be situations where they'll kill out of reflex or instinct or something like that, but they won't kill as an act necessary to carry out an assignment."

Elias raised a grayed eyebrow. "No guns? They won't take guns?"

"No guns. No explosives unless they work as tools. But refusing to take guns isn't a problem."

Elias sighed. "You and your fucking word games. Why not?"

"You can't send explosives of *any* kind through the beam. They got a bad habit of blowing up on arrival."

"If you can't carry guns then what's the beef? Didn't these people ever hear of other means of dispatch?" Elias belched. "Come to think of it, the Venezuelans have a history of slicing up and putting holes in people with spears, lances, bows and arrows, crossbows, poisoned arrows, blowguns, knives, machetes, clubs," Elias said brightly, "to say nothing of boiling oil, cannon, *and* all kinds of guns. In that way," Elias said smugly, "you might say they're almost like *us*."

"Almost, but not quite," Massey added. "They're really not nearly as bad. Don't forget *our* history."

"Screw history. *Why* won't they kill for a mission?"

"It's against their principles. It's immoral. It's downright sinful to them. They—and *they* includes our guys and gals—insist that there are better ways then deliberate homicide. They say it's time we started coming back from the brink to which we pushed ourselves with hydrogen bombs, et cetera, et cetera."

"God bless them. Makes sense to me. About damned time someone started thinking like that, too. Hip hip hooray for them."

"You still want us to get Unsworth?"

"Yes."

"He's *that* important?"

"*Yes.*"

Massey made a steeple of his fingers and peered through them at Elias. He burned a finger with a hot cigar ash and yelped. He flicked away the ash. "Any other immediate vital statistics?"

"He might, he *just* might, represent the single greatest advance in brain genetics in the human race."

Massey grimaced with distaste. "You're giving me a headache. What's so special about the old coot?"

"He reads minds."

"So do I," Massey answered immediately.

"What?" The question leaped from Elias.

"So do I," Massey repeated. "For starters, my own. I knew someone else who could read minds. My wife. She read mine like a damned comic book."

"She could *read* your mind by looking at the bulge in your pants." Elias put down his glass and leaned forward, cracking his gnarled knuckles one by one. "Time to get serious, boy."

Massey's eyes narrowed. Elias knew the signs. His old crony would be with it from now on. "Okay, lay it out," Massey said.

"He reads the minds of other people." Elias eased back slowly in his chair and frowned. "From what we've learned, that isn't *that* important by itself."

"Wait a moment," Massey broke in. "You're not talking about a super psychologist, are you? I've known people who could read other people, but sure as hell they weren't tapping into mental wavelengths. They're so good they could tapdance their way right around Freud or Jung or anyone you'd care to mention."

"No psychology here. I am telling you that Peter Unsworth can tell you, even if you're in a face mask so he can't *see* your steely eyes or quivering lip, what you are thinking. He can probe, also. But what's even more critical is that Unsworth knows how to amplify his ability so other selected people can learn the technique."

"You know you sound like you've lost a couple of

neck screws. Your head is waggling from side to side, old man."

"Oh, sure," Elias said diffidently. "I'm talking about a man, I'm talking *to* a man, who dematerializes human beings in a laser soup, locks them within a dimensional warp where time comes screaming to a stop, then flashes them about the world by bouncing them like so much ping pong stuff off satellites hanging over the same point on the earth, like some cosmic lanterns, and then he rematerializes them on the basis of what a computer spits out in little numbers as to where and when, *and I've got loose screws?*"

"My deal is science," Massey said sourly.

"And mine is?"

"Voodoo or some shit like that. You know how I feel about this psychic crap, you old bastard. Mumbo-jumbo, incense, calling up spirits, rapping on tables—"

"You idiot, I ought to rap you right in the head!" Elias said with sudden, unexpected enthusiasm. "You, of all people! Head in the sand! It can't be! Never happen! Impossible! Man can't fly, right? And Caleb Massey has a brick in his skull!"

Massey took a long time to study Patrick Xavier Elias. "In all the years I've known you, old man," Massey said quietly, "I've never heard you say those things to me, *or* get so bloody het up like you just did."

The senator fixed unblinking eyes on his friend of many years. "Caleb, there's no fun and games here. I've been on this Unsworth thing for a long time. It's for real. Whatever's taken place in his brain, his mind, the son of a bitch can—what the hell do you call it? hear, sense, discern, listen; *what?*—what someone else is thinking!"

"Does he pick it up in visualizations? Like pictures?"

"I don't know."

"Words? Breakdown of languages? Is there a crossover of languages so words translate image-wise to overcome language differences?"

"I don't know."

"How do you know what you *do* know?"

"CIA. M-Two. Scotland Yard. KGB."

"KGB?"

"It cost us perfect altered identities for an entire family, the cooperation of three governments, and several million dollars to confirm he's where I've told you he is. Sublevel Three, East Wing, Kremlin." Elias waved off any interruptions. "We don't know his range, how far away he can pick up something from another person's mind. Or, if his range is limited, how long it will be before it increases. Or if the Russians can find some way to electronically amplify what he can do. Needless to say, I don't need to draw you a map of what danger he represents if everything we've found out is real. *There's nothing this government does or plans to do he won't know.* You might as well consider the entire United States a shooting gallery. You might—" Elias sighed, his sudden flurry of energy abating swiftly as he sank back into his welcoming chair.

"Get him, Caleb. At all costs."

"Questions, old man."

"Ask."

"Single most important fact about Unsworth, aside from what you've told me. Think first, Patrick, please."

"He's a prisoner."

"Shit, I should have known."

"And he's blind," Elias added.

"*What?*"

"Totally blind."

"Do you want him dead?" Massey hated himself for asking the question. He'd become so enamored by his young men and women of the beamriding program he'd begun to accept their moral values.

"*No.*" Elias's eyes opened wide. "I think," he said in a hoarse whisper, "of what his mind is, might be, *could be.* I am left completely overwhelmed. Good God, he might just be the homo superior the geneticists have suspected might already be among us. That means he's the future of the human race. Dead? *Never!* You do anything, everything, sacrifice anything and anyone to get him out *alive.* Hell, if it would bring him to us I'd slash my own wrists and die happy, knowing I'd done one great decent thing for the future of man. Whatever," he muttered, "that might be."

"You have the intelligence data on *specifically* where and how they're keeping him?"

"Mostly. You get everything we've got. I don't think you'll be all that happy," Elias said moodily. "They're tight about this man."

"You said he was a prisoner. Did they take him? Snatch him?"

Elias shook his head. "Hell, the Russians never knew, or anyway never *believed* anything they might have heard about Unsworth. They had no reason ever to kidnap him. They couldn't have cared less about him. One more looney who escaped from Stonehenge, as far as they were concerned."

"He defect?"

Elias sat up. "Christ, I need a drink. This is the toughest part of all."

"Sit back. I'll do the honors. I think I need a blast myself." Massey poured, they drank, Elias spoke.

"Peter Unsworth is neither defector nor traiter. He is, in fact, a very decent human being and a dedicated scientist."

"You realize," Massey broke in gently, "you're speaking of him almost as a friend?"

"I don't know him," Elias deferred. "Not personally. But I recognize scientific spirit and dedication. For many years he worked with a research team at Oxford. He kept pursuing what he considered the holy grail of expanding human consciousness. Noetics, or whatever the devil they call it."

"The term noetics was coined by Ed Mitchell. Remember him? He walked on the moon with Al Shepard. Apollo Fourteen."

"All the better, then," Elias acknowledged. "But Oxford figured he was a complete nut and after some nasty confrontations they threw him out on his ass. He told Thatcher and Oxford where they could bloody well stuff their bloody science programs—you get the idea—and he trundled off to the United States. Well, he was laughed out of IBM, Rand, Sperry, Apple, Stanford, East Michigan, Princeton and God knows where else. Apparently what I've heard about psionics programs in our country is so much misleading tripe. Anyway, Unsworth, still trying to do his best for *us*, got in to talk to the people at National Security Agency. They humored him and figured he belonged on a banana farm. Frankly, they were *very* insulting."

Elias sighed. "We've fallen from grace where open minds are concerned," he said wearily. "But to wrap it up, *someone* should have known better. Because we found out too late that the Russians were real hot to trot with Unsworth. *They believed him.* If not what he could already do, at least his potential. When he was at his lowest, when just about everyone over here had insulted him, Moscow offered him the sun and the moon and—"

"Who handled it?" Massey asked.

"Mikhail Karkogin."

Massey's lips tightened. "Damn, he's the best. I know. I've had a couple of nasties with Mickey in the old days." Massey looked up. "How did Unsworth go blind?"

"That, my friend, almost shames me to answer," Elias said. "Because I'm as guilty as anyone else. Unsworth is Nobel Prize material. The man is dazzling. No one ever seemed to put two and two together. That this man of absolute genius *has been blind all his life.*"

"Jesus, you're not serious—"

"The Good Lord save me, I am. That simple fact, that he was blind and got around perfectly well without a cane or a seeing eye dog or a companion, or help from *anyone*, should have been great screaming flares in the sky to alert us. But we were even blinder than him—"

"None so blind as those who refuse to see?"

"Don't rub it in. I'm as guilty as the rest. Dammit, I'm an old man and I'm tired. Will you get Peter Unsworth for us?"

"How the hell do I know? *We'll try.* Question."

"Ask."

"What makes you believe he wants to come out? Or that he'd be willing to come with us?"

"We don't *know*. But a number of our people who had contact with Unsworth have become inexplicably convinced, absolutely positive, that's what he wants. Right now, that's more than enough for any of us."

"All right. The first thing we'll do is to—"

Elias's hand shot up. *"Don't tell me.* Don't tell me *anything*. Understood? You do the job and I'll pay the piper back here."

"It could cost," Massey warned.

"The stakes are higher than you could ever imagine," the senator said mysteriously.

Massey decided not to pursue any more of it. He rose and started for the door, stopped and turned. "One favor, Senator."

"Name it."

"Don't die on me, you old bastard. We need you."

The security guard opened the door. Massey had one last glance at an old man almost buried in his chair, looking terribly lonely.

The long, wide training gymnasium of CANAVERAL dome rang and echoed with vibrant activity, a giddy mixture of powerful machinery, of the voices of men and women harsh and taunting, shouting and yelling. Human forms bounced and slammed, fell and rose on the training mats in mock deadly hand-to-hand combat. Men and women climbed swiftly up hanging vertical ropes, crashed their bodies through a tight obstacle course, hung by parachute harness from other training devices.

Caleb Massey, Kim Seavers at his side, stopped to watch two agents charging an angry, large muscled figure. "Take him high!" one yelled, "I'll get his feet!" and the powerful defendant stood untouched and laughing as his attackers fell mysteriously not through him but an incredibly realistic hologram of the man.

"That is neat," Massey said in admiration.

"Watch Maria," Kim told him.

That surprised him. Maria Barrios belonged with Phil
Mercedes, not here. Then he thought of where he'd be
sending his team, and memory of Maria's fluency in
Russian and several dialects as well pushed aside his
questions. He watched Maria, crouched behind a desk
in the training field, three men rushing her from different angles.

In a blur she whipped a stubby pipe from her sleeve,
pressed a button and the pipe snapped out to nearly
four feet in length. In that same continuing blur she
had the fatter end of the pipe against her lips, and he
heard the barely perceptible hiss of air from the pipe.
He caught a glimpse of a slim projectile take the first
man in the neck. Maria half-rolled and a dart took her
second attacker in the arm. The third man was trying to
dodge when a final dart nailed him in the leg. Each
man went wildly rigid as the dart poison rushed through
their systems. They twitched for several moments and
lay still.

"It's only a training dose," Kim explained. "They'll
be out for two or three minutes, have a slight headache
when it's over. But it shows you what we're coming up
with."

"What the hell kind of narcotic is that?" Massey
asked.

Kim shrugged. "Don't know, sir. Maria brought it
with her. It's from downcountry Venezuela. The Indians who live near Angel Falls use it on their arrows and
blowguns. A full dose will knock a jaguar unconscious in
about four seconds. Same with a man. Instant nerve
paralysis and unconsciousness in four seconds."

"I'm impressed."

"You should be. We all get knocked out with it at
least once in training so we'll *know* its effect on a man
when we're on a mission," Kim explained.

Massey nodded. "Okay, kid, it's time. Get them
together."

Kim Seavers faced the room, blew on a piercing
whistle. Everything stopped; they turned to her. "Gather
round, people!" she called. "Big Daddy's home."

Massey winced but didn't comment on the name. He brought his wristwatch to his lips. "Code Dragonfly Prime. Execute full security. Nobody in, nobody out until release."

"Yes, sir," his watch told him.

Massey turned to the BEMAC crews and motioned for them to relax on the floor. He wasted no time on salutations.

"This is straight arrow, people," he began bluntly. "No innuendos. No fun and games. Straight talk. I have a mission. We're asked to execute as quickly as possible. Which means as fast as we select a team and get it ready to beam. *But*—" He paused deliberately, let the *but* hang in the air between them, let wariness and caution stab to the forefront of their thinking.

"—the nature of this mission means that whoever goes accepts tremendous risks. I can't minimize that. I'd planned on a solid six months of training and tests before anything with this kind of weight on it. I don't have the time. *You* don't have the time. I'm not assigning anyone. This is a case strictly for volunteers. If you volunteer for a mission about which I'll tell you nothing except that it's a critical assignment and the odds are against your returning, then I'll confirm that you're crazy. Hands up for go, down for brains and no."

He waited a decent interval. "I see. I'm disappointed. There isn't a sane person in this crowd. Twenty people, twenty-one hands. Blake, dammit, drop one hand."

One of the later teammates, Tad Crippen, waved his hand and Massey nodded. "How many go, sir?"

"Six. I'll tell you right now I've selected Blake, Seavers, Morales and Suarez. They have the most experience. I have a relative newcomer with us, who goes because he not only speaks perfect Russian, but he *is* Russian."

Maria Barrios turned pale. Blake gripped her hand tightly. Massey knew she figured the lead mission was a lock for her. If he didn't have this other rider—

Leonid Zhukov, squat, burly, curly-haired and powerful, rose to his feet. "I am ready, sir."

"He's not only crazy," Massey said with a hint of a

smile, "he's a crazy Russian. What *sane* Russian *wants* to go back to a country where there's a very big price on his head?"

That, he knew, answered many unasked questions in terms of the mission, even if it raised new ones among the group. The latter didn't matter.

Bill Coulter leaped to his feet. "I'll go."

"Hey, wait a minute!"

"Who the hell is he?"

"We all volunteered! What's the gig?"

Massey stonewalled the protests. "You all volunteered. You're right. So it's first come, first served. That's the team. Six go. *Be prepared for seven to come back.*" At the sudden rush of exclamations and murmurs he held up his hands. "No questions now on that point. Oh, yes, standard procedure. Three agents for backups and command and communications positions. Maria Barrios, Danza Cayuga, and Jim Sabbath."

He nodded to Kim. She gave the whistle a short blast. "All right, people. Primary team and backups in the planning room in thirty minutes sharp. The rest of you please return to your training schedules. That's it."

Mission Planning offered luxurious, warm, welcoming moods to its occupants, unlike any other room in the entire Canaveral BEMAC complex. Wood-paneled walls, thick carpeting on the floor, heavy drapes, a well-stocked bar and fridge, gleaming rosewood conference tables, and walls packed with electronic equipment beautifully ensconced within wood-framed racks. Dead center of the room was the main conference table, the space atop the table and above to the ceiling left open. The table center glowed softly. Caleb Massey, the six agents selected for the initial beamrider foray, and the three backup agents sat in a wide ring about the glow.

"In the event you people haven't noticed or been made aware of the fact," Massey informed the group, "Dr. Mercedes and his people are gone."

"I've noticed," Suarez told him. "But I don't know where they are."

"Caracas," Massey said, and as he expected his word brought signs of surprise. Massey pointed to Suarez and Morales. "You two are the only Venezuelan members of this team. Until and unless they become actively involved, Barrios and Cayuga fill the same position. They're Venezuelans and they're involved. Now, I don't say any of this lightly. Your mission is extremely sensitive on the highest political and national levels. We've made certain that Mercedes, and none of his staff, are aware of what we're going to do. That way they can't be blamed for anything if this whole affair comes apart on us."

Massey's gaze moved to meet the eyes of Suarez, Morales, Barrios and Cayuga. "Your loyalty from this point on must be to *me*. To me even more so than to BEMAC and everything you've worked for since you got into this program. That loyalty includes not saying anything about this mission, to Mercedes *or anybody else*, without my okay first. Can you four handle that? If you can't, please tell me now, leave this room and you'll never hear it mentioned again."

Carmen Morales. "To the mission, then."

"As far as I'm concerned," Suarez added, "*you're* the mission. No problem, man."

Maria Barrios and Danza Cayuga nodded assent.

Blake toyed with an unlit cigar. "The more you *don't* say, sir, the bigger this gets to sound."

"A keen observation, Mr. Blake. It's big. You're going to Russia." Massey paused. He knew the need for several moments of what he called "causation and settling" on the part of people dealt a difficult hand, no matter *how* eager they might be to test an unknown. For a moment he considered telling Blake to go ahead and light his cigar. He vetoed his own thought, and while his vocalization of *Russia* still resounded silently among his group, poured himself a mug of coffee, leaned back, and lit his own cigar.

Blake smiled at him. The smile grew broader when Massey blew out the match he'd used and tossed the box to Blake. The choice of wooden matches in an age of glitzy gold lighters said much between the two. For his part, Massey had always found the delay in interrupting talking, while he went through the "ancient" procedure of opening the match box, removing a single wooden match, scratching the match to fiery life and *then* lighting up, a remarkable wedge to separate emotions from sound thinking. He knew the method was taking its effect as several of the people at the table poured coffee or juice. *Watch the slump*, Massey told himself. *It's the angle of the body dangle in the chair that says so much.* His practiced eye showed him people ready to accept anything he might have to offer.

"You, ah, have a specific place in mind, sir?" Massey would have bet a hundred-dollar bill against a stale sandwich Zhukov couldn't have contained his curiosity.

"Kremlin," Massey said through a cloud of swirling blue smoke. *Goddamn good cigars, these Macanudos.*

Zhukov tilted his head back in a barely perceptible move and with his head still at an angle Massey knew was slightly unnatural, looked thoughtful and said, "Ahh." *I win again*, Massey told himself. *Every goddamn Russian I've ever known does that same damn routine when you tell them something they didn't know and they don't want to admit it out loud.*

"Ah, *what?*" Blake demanded of Zhukov.

The Russian smiled. "I like that word. Kremlin. It has a nice ring to it. Like rice *crispies*. You should spell it with a K instead of a C."

"Well, not really *to* the Kremlin," Massey added, and had their full attention once again.

Three of his agents immediately looked at Zhukov and said "Ahh," in unison. Laughter broke out among the group and fled quickly.

"Do we have to guess?" Bill Coulter asked. Massey took a moment to study Coulter before he answered. This was the only one of his agents he didn't know over a period of time or through a personal relationship. That always tugged at his CAUTION sign in his head, but Coulter had an incredible record. He was called *Machine* by his longtime associates. He had that magic sense, feel, touch and mastery of almost any kind of machinery. In today's world, unless you were running naked through the desert or the jungle, that could be one hell of an asset. He was also an ex-army assault force leader, a chopper pilot of no small renown and, Massey recalled, he delighted in risking his life in fragile winged things he built out of cardboard and aluminum tubing he flew off high buildings and mountains. Massey made a mental note to do some more digging on Coulter, but the man he saw was intelligent, sharp, athletic and—*Stay with the program, Caleb*.

"I don't want to keep you in suspense," Massey told Coulter. "No guesses. You're going *beneath* the Kremlin."

"*Beneath?*" echoed Seavers.

"Beneath," Massey repeated. "You're going to have to get through a triple ring of defenses, perhaps fight your way into a heavily guarded laboratory, kidnap a blind British scientist who can read other people's minds, stand off half the KGB and Kremlin military security, wrap the whole job in seventeen minutes, and come back safely." He puffed heavily as if he were trying to hide beneath the swirling bank of smoke. "Neat, huh?"

Carmen Morales let out a burst of laughter just a bit *too* shrill. Not fear, Massey judged; ridicule and disbelief. "We're supposed to do all this— Mr. Massey, you forgot one thing. You forget to mention that after we do most of what you just said, we've got to retrace our steps to return to the point of emergence so the beam can pick us up, right?" She stifled another outburst.

"Wrong," Massey said. "We'll be playing a variation on a theme."

That one drew blank looks. "I'll explain," Massey said, "and a little magic helps in that regard."

"Magic?" Suarez echoed.

"Sure," Massey said. He half turned and spoke to thin air. "Hey, Stoney, you awake and alive?"

A voice came at them from the exact center of the conference table. They stared at the glow in the air. "Yes, sir."

"Who in the hell is Stoney?" Jim Sabbath had sat with Cayuga and Barrios in a group, all three remaining silent as they absorbed instead of interfering with talk, but this last scene was one Sabbath couldn't let go by.

"Stoney's full name is Greystone. A very personable computer of very advanced capability and with some neat tricks up his electronic sleeves." Massey put aside his cigar. "All right, Stoney, let's get with it. Program One Six One Two Zebra Talon, activate."

"Yes, sir," said the voice without a body from thin air in their midst.

A gentle chime sounded. Within the open space, within the faint glow, a shimmering effect took place. Glowing lines appeared, bent and curved sinuously, colors emerging from nowhere, and out of nowhere, it seemed, there appeared a holographic projection of an aerial view of the Kremlin. "Hold it, Stoney," Massey said.

To his group. "Everybody know where they are? What they're seeing?"

Nods and murmured agreement came from about the table. "Okay, Stoney, let's go in."

The Kremlin seemed to expand as the observer's point of view fell gently from the sky. The building towers and walls rose up and filled the view of the "invisible eye" as the computer played its magic with the holographic data presentation. "Jesus!" someone cried out as they plunged *through* solid stone to emerge inside within a long, wide corridor.

Zhukov's voice, sarcastic and tinged with what could only be memories driven deep into the mind, came through the shifting lights and colors. "Home, sweet home," he said drily.

"Stoney, hold it here," Massey snapped. The holographic three dimensional view froze like a miniature dungeon before them. Massey turned to Zhukov. "You've been *inside*?"

"Well, of course. Yes, sir. I mean," Zhukov went on a bit more carefully, "I *worked* there when I was a Young Communist. Bright, eager, dedicated, committed. One of the finest. I was marked for great things in the future. Of course, at the time I was only a messenger."

Massey's face seemed to light up with the incredible news. "Only a messenger?" he echoed. "*Only* a messenger? What are you, Leonid, a gift from the gods? How in the hell did all this escape your records?"

"I suppose," Zhukov said, still with the sarcasm that carried his first interruption, "that your Stonewall computer—"

"Greystone."

"Whatever, sir—has flaws like the Lenin computers in there," he said, pointing to the Kremlin hologram. "Like all computers it is no more brilliant than the worst idiot who has a menial job somewhere at the bottom of the pile preparing personnel files for databanks. Maybe what I did when I was fourteen years old was not important to your people. But I *did* tell them, and it *is* in my records. The paper ones. You know, sir, the old-fashioned kind?"

Massey gestured with both hands to stop the conversation swiftly leading them from the issue at hand. He grabbed cigar and box of matches, withdrew a wooden match and promptly broke it in half without getting a light. He tossed it all to the floor. He stabbed a finger at the corridor before them floating in midair. "You know that area?" he demanded of Zhukov.

"To be sure, Mr. Massey," Zhukov said, much more easily now that he'd gotten rid of some buried memory bile. "I must have walked up and down those hallways at least a thousand times, and sir, that's no exaggeration. We were almost constantly on the go with messages. They were paranoid that the CIA had bugged just about *everything* in there. Hand-carried messages were safe."

"What about the sublevels?"

"When I was there, and please keep in mind it's been at least sixteen or seventeen years since then, they used the sublevels almost around the clock for communications. Cryptography and intelligence or even personal messages. Whatever they needed or wanted for security or privacy. All that's gone now. With communications satellites and the new computers they've moved the command communications centers about thirty miles outside Moscow."

"Forget that," Massey said, more harshly than he had intended. "Nothing personal, Leonid. Look, son, I know I'm repeating things but I've got to do that. Now, this particular level. You've walked through it?"

"Until my feet were sore," Zhukov laughed. "The hottest thing on the black market for our group were American sneakers."

"Who's there, on this exact level we're looking at, *now*?"

Zhukov squinted at the projection. He looked up at Massey. "This is up to date?"

"Stoney? You get that question?"

The dematerialized voice answered immediately. "Yes, sir. Yes, sir."

"What's he saying?" Kim asked, puzzled.

"Stoney answered both questions. The hologram data is up to date and he got the question."

"How accurate?" Zhukov asked.

"All available data is presented, sir," Stoney intoned.

"You'll excuse me, Mr. Massey, but that is the computer equivalent of a copout. It is saying maybe, perhaps, this is the best that the worst idiot you have has programmed me."

"I'll let you shoot the goddamned thing when you get back," Massey told Zhukov. "Now assume that it *is* up to date and that it's as accurate as possible. If you find any flaws or faults, just sing out."

"Sir, there are blanks. Personal things I remember. I wouldn't expect Stonewall to have that kind of data."

Massey didn't correct any computer names at the moment. "Here, use this laser spot," he said, handing a projection beam to Zhukov. He snapped it on and the tiny red beam broadened to an arrow wherever it was aimed. Massey glanced up instinctively even though he knew the pickup microphones were everywhere in the room. "Stoney, priority command. Whatever information you receive through the voice of Leonid Zhukov you will place in the data memory banks and adjust the holographic projection in immediate real-time. Confirm."

"Yes, sir."

"Leonid?"

The light searched the hologram along with Zhukov's memory. "Here, sir." Everyone leaned forward. "The defense system was built in four levels." The laser arrow moved with his words. "Correction, sir. Consider them as rings. A, B, C, and D. At first security in the system was made up exclusively of KGB guards; trusted members of the party, that sort of thing. They hated their work. They were like prisoners themselves. They just watched us coming and going. There really wasn't much else for them to do. They called it the Rings of Siberia. KGB headquarters put on a lot of pressure to change the system."

"Did they?"

"Yes. They went to computers—"

Massey slammed a fist into the palm of his other hand. "Hot damn!" He winced from his own blow. "Excellent, excellent!" He blew on his hand. "Go on, go on," he said with a sense of excitement.

"It's a very elaborate system. To get through the first two rings all visitors go through fingerprint, palmprint, retinal pattern checks; that sort of thing. When you pass A, here, you go through the process all over again to enter B." The laser arrow stopped at B. "No one goes past B Ring unless they have the highest security clearance. It's much easier to see Gorbachev than to get past this point."

Massey sat back, chewing on his lower lip. That didn't make sense. With the communications systems gone—

Blake spoke the question he intended to ask. "Leo, what's so hot inside, you know, beyond the B Ring?"

"I don't know." Zhukov shrugged. "It's been years since I was there."

Kim turned to Zhukov. "Any ideas?"

"Ideas? Yes. Of course," Zhukov said. "Mr. Massey,

tell your Stonewall that what I am saying now must be considered to be rumors. Crazy things. I never really paid much attention at the time. I was young, Moscow had more wild rumors than Washington, and I had just discovered that Russian girls were not built like Russian boys."

"I thought they were built like Ernest Borgine," Blake cracked.

"The boys or the girls?" Suarez asked.

"The girls," Blake told him.

"Shut up," Massey told them both. He turned back to Zhukov. "Can you tie in what you know about this system, these rings, and Peter Unsworth?"

"I've never tried to. I mean, I just heard about Unsworth right in this room for the first time."

"Knowing the system, where would *you* put Unsworth if you wanted him sealed off as much as possible?"

"Oh, no question." The laser arrow shifted. "Inside the D Ring. It's the very heart of the place, the innermost core."

"That," Massey announced solemnly, "is precisely what they *have* done. That much I've confirmed. Peter Unsworth is inside D." He took the laser pointer from Zhukov. He looked at his agents one by one, then began to point with the laser arrow as he spoke.

"By going to a computer defense system, I'm convinced the Russians have done us a tremendous favor. They don't know it, of course, because their systems, their planning, couldn't possibly have taken into account what we've got with our beaming system. Don't count the Russians short on brains for that, however. *Our* defense and security systems can't possibly have taken into account any beaming *by anyone*, let alone the Russians. But to stick to the issue. Our best help right now is the shortcomings of the computers. They can really be pretty dumb animals. I'll confirm Zhukov's thoughts on that matter, even if it means I owe an apology to Greystone. You read me, rocks-for-brains?"

"Affirmative, sir."

The laser arrow moved about. "If someone gets through

the first two rings, here and there," Massey continued,
"then the computer is programmed to accept them as
security-cleared."

"Sir, I don't understand." They looked at Carmen
Morales. "Why would the computer do a thing like
that?"

"Sir, may I?" Zhukov broke in and Massey nodded.
"He's right, Carmen. If you get through A and B, here,
here, then the computer's *been informed* that you're
acceptable. You *must* have full security clearance or
you'd never be on the edge in the C or D rings. That's
the critical point. If you go past A and B you're Mr.
Nice Guy, or else you're stopped dead in your tracks
before you go through B."

"Let me get that straight," Blake queried. "You cannot get into their inner rings, C or D, one or the other or
both, unless you're cleared?"

"Yes," Zhukov told him. "That's computer logical. No
clearance, no go."

"How serious are they about stopping people?"
Kim Seavers asked. "I mean, if they're not cleared and
they still try to get through."

"It sure as hell ain't Disneyland, kiddo," Blake said
nastily. He was getting more than a little upset with the
questions he heard, indicating all too clearly to him that
his fellow agents were less than understanding about
Russian trigger fingers.

"The standing orders in event of any *attempted* security breach have always been to shoot to kill," Zhukov
came back. "There are, at such a moment, no questions
to ask. Kill on sight. You see, since everyone in that
area *knows* those standing orders, no one is crazy enough,
even a top official, to try to throw around his weight.
There is no reward in being a *dead* commissar."

"Why are you so certain they'd shoot on sight even if
they recognized a top official?" Morales asked.

Zhukov smiled coldly. "Because if they don't, then
the guard or the soldier who failed to carry out his
orders is immediately brought to an inner courtyard,

the scene placed on closed television for all to watch, and *he* is shot down like a dog."

Bill Coulter raised his brows at Massey. "Boss-man, I sure hope you've got some super can-opener in mind."

"Son, that super-ape over there, Blake, said it best of all: that there *are* better ways than guns to do a job," Massey told Coulter. "Now, the *only* people who don't have security clearance and who can still get all the way inside those defenses, well," he said brightly, "they're all right in this room with me."

Blake's hand walloped Suarez across the back of his head. "Damn, we're dummies," he said with self-disdain.

Suarez turned with an astonished look. "Why *me*?" he demanded.

"Because Nasty Massey has been trying to get us to come to the conclusion that's so obvious it's been doing everything but dance a jig under our noses," Blake said with a grating tone. "Boss-man, gimme that pointer." Blake rose to his feet and the laser arrow stabbed into the holographic projection. "There's A and there's B. The two outside trouble rings, right? It's stupid for us to even think of busting our way in. It would be suicide."

The laser arrow moved. "But we can beam right in to," the arrow made a circular movement, "*here*. Right inside the third ring. We beam in here, we're past their defenses, and we've just shoved a load of logic right up the nose of their computer system." He tossed the laser pointer back to Massey.

"He's right," Massey chuckled. "He's right and he's right on. If you show up in Ring C you're safe. *You can't be in there unless the computer's security system passed you through as okay.* That's all the computer knows. If you're inside then the *only* logical conclusion is that the computer itself let you in. It's beautiful. It's Catch Twenty-Two in reverse."

"Sir, you were speaking before about a British scientist," Kim Seavers said directly to Massey. "You said he was blind—"

"And you said he reads minds," Zhukov added. "You are serious about all that?"

Massey leaned back, hunting for his cigar. He changed his mind and lit a fresh one, going through the slow routine of opening the matchbox and scratching up the light. "I am *very* serious. I don't want any of you to dismiss this as anything less than a life-or-death situation. You're going to risk your lives to bring Unsworth out of Russia and back to us here. Want any more serious *than that*?"

"That's Grade-A, pasteurized, homogenized serious, all right," Blake offered, refusing to let serious become grim.

"We have to kidnap him?" Suarez asked. "What if he doesn't like Blake's ugly face and he doesn't want to go?"

"CIA tells us he *wants* out," Massey said. "They also tell us the Russians will kill him before they ever let him go."

"Ah, a nice easy job," Blake laughed. "Everybody ready to kill this poor bastard."

"And us," Morales reminded him.

"This mind-reading," Zhukov joined in, "is it dangerous?"

"It could be. I don't know." Massey shrugged with his reply. "Assume he's for real. *You've got to do that.* CIA—which, by the way—is solidly supported by our other intelligence agencies *and* the British—"

"That makes it okay, then," Blake said tartly. "If Thatcher's Legions say it's okay—"

"Shut up, Blake," Massey said, but his tone wasn't angry. "We've been told," he said to the group, "that Unsworth is developing a means of amplifying his own ability. Like firing off a shotgun blast of mental energy so that he can affect certain people as much as he can tell what they're thinking. Does he have the ability to zero in on a single mind or is he jammed by mental crowd noise? Hell, I don't have those answers. But what if—the famous what-if scenario—in case of a war, he could detect through certain people what our weaknesses were? What if he could blind certain key people with brain-ripping headaches? It could leave them helpless."

"And what if he's just a nice guy?" Coulter asked.

"I don't know he *isn't* just a nice guy," Massey countered. "But the highest levels of our government, scientific as well as political, say to get him."

"Nothing to it," Blake said with a snap of his fingers.

"Sure," Suarez followed. "We go in and we bring him out."

"Very funny," Massey told him. "Let's get back to this fortress."

"That's nothing," Zhukov said. "You mean the fortress *within* the fortress."

Massey looked up. "Precisely. All right, people, button it up and pay attention." The laser arrow began to move again. "See those corridors? The whole place is crisscrossed with photocell beams and lasers. Two types: alarm and lethal. The laser alarms sound like wounded dinosaurs. And there's something else—" He lifted his head. "Stoney, some animation, please. Defense systems by the light."

They watched, fascinated as the hologram came alive. The corridors enlarged to reveal greater detail. Six figures moved along a corridor. Lights flashed, alarms screamed from the hologram, laser beams snapped wildly in random criss-crossing fire. The tiny human figures fell slowly, limbs tumbling away.

Suarez's jaw tightened. "Holy Mother," he said, his voice strained. "This is too fucking real . . ."

"That's us down there, isn't it?" Kim said to Massey.

"That's one scenario," Massey told her. "Wait, young woman. You haven't yet seen the tripwires. Stoney, let's have it."

The holographic projection jerked into motion. They watched a three-dimensional, living scene in fast reverse, dismembered bodies rushing together and everyone walking backwards until the motion stopped abruptly. The figures started moving again at normal speed. "This is the tripwire sequence," Massey said. "Stoney, let's have some greater detail."

The corridor enlarged again as did the figures. They watched, fascinated, almost hypnotized, by the computer three-dimensional animation *of themselves* moving ghostlike down the corridor. Alarms sounded from the scene before them, tiny silver lines flashed outward from wall slots and whipsawed like writhing tendrils. The wires cut the three figures to tumbling pieces.

"I think I'm going to be sick," Carmen said, hand over her mouth.

"Get sick *here* and you're off the mission," Massey told her.

"Holy shit, those wires could ruin your whole day," Blake said quickly.

"No telegrams, please," Coulter added. The joshing helped. Carmen swallowed hard, breathed deeply.

"Aside from your twisted humor," Zhukov told them, as he stared, fascinated, at the miniaturization of their own deaths, "those wires, if you're not prepared to avoid them, could cut even a horse into thin steaks."

"Leave it to a Russian. Chopped horsemeat. Yech," Blake said.

"Got any sheep? I'm in the mood for lamb chops," Coulter offered.

"Shut up, you idiots!" Maria Barrios shouted. She'd been slammed harder than she ever could have anticipated by the sight of a tiny figure with the doll-like face of Stan Blake being sliced to ribbons.

Carmen saved the moment. "How do the Russians get in and out?"

"You got that question, Stoney?" Massey said to the ghost ears in the room.

"Yes, sir. Tape rolling now, sir."

Tiny figures moved through the corridor, passed through doorways, rode up and down elevators.

"Ah, the old tunnel, it's still there," Zhukov exclaimed. "See? The arrow. To the left, please. Aha! See how the tunnel goes *beneath* the Kremlin meeting halls, to an elevator and then you go *up* into the complex?"

"This seem accurate to you?" Massey asked.

"I'm amazed," Zhukov told him. "How did you ever

manage to get such incredible detail of the sublevels of the *Kremlin?*"

"Would you believe," Massey said with a sudden grin, "that most of this information came from an obscure guide book to Russian history, and especially of the Kremlin?"

"But . . . *where?*"

"Moscow."

"You bought pictures of this in a Moscow store?"

"Pictures, descriptions *and* detailed drawings. Apparently neither GRU nor KGB thought it very important to check what had been published right under their noses. And very much in the open. But what you've added, plus our intelligence data, is what let Greystone put it all together in this nifty-dandy picture show."

Seavers peered intently into the holographic tunnels. "Sir, you have any bright ideas on how to live through those lasers *and* those wires?"

Massey at first seemed to ignore the question. "You have three days to train." He hesitated a moment. "Yes, Kim, we have ideas. Good ones. You'll have every chance to test them before you go. And any time you," Massey looked up, "or anyone else feels this is strictly a one-way trip, you may step down with no reflection on your membership in our elite organization."

"Bullshit, boss-man," Blake said scathingly. "We've heard about you before. You chuck out on a mission to which you're assigned, and they don't let you have asparagus or squash any more in the messhall. We know your type."

"My God, doesn't he *ever* quit?" Coulter asked.

"Oh, I forgot. If Coulter takes the dip in home waters instead of going fly-bye," Blake added, "no fried okra for him. We'll show his WASP ass a thing or two."

"Shut up," Massey said, almost by reflex. "Suarez, you were asking?"

"I don't like to ask this question," Suarez said slowly, his voice carrying a note of despair no one missed, gaining their instant full attention. "But someone has to, and even you won't talk about it so far."

"Have at it," Massey told him.

"What if we get in, what if everything works out the way we want, and the old man, for some reason, we can't get him out. It might be a problem we can't handle, or the old man could refuse. What do we do then?"

Massey laid down his second cigar. He leaned back slowly in his seat. "Kill him," he said finally.

The silence following those two terrible words was deafening.

"I don't believe," Kim Seavers said in a low voice, "I really heard you say that."

"I said it," Massey confirmed. "Those are orders from Washington. You can't get Unsworth out? He refuses to go? Kill him on the spot."

Kim's face worked through a paroxysm of anger. "*No— goddamn—way.*"

"Me, I'm with Kim," said Carmen Morales. "I would not kill him. Or anyone else. Or even you," she jabbed a finger at Massey, "for suggesting we do this."

Massey relit his cigar. His smile was pure snake. "Then we'll get a man to do the job."

"How about me?" Blake asked.

"Yes, how about you?" Massey repeated.

"Those are orders from Washington?" Blake said.

"They damn well are, mister."

"Well, then, considering everything you've said, and why we're here in the first place, why don't you pick up that phone over there and call them, and I'll get on the horn and I'll say, fuck Washington. How's that, boss-man?"

"You speaking for yourself or is this a caucus?"

Jim Sabbath jerked a thumb at Massey. "Who the hell is this guy? One minute I'm talking to a man I know and respect by name of Caleb Massey and now this shitbird appears in front of me."

"Cut some slack, Jim," Blake intruded. "I wasn't through. Didn't answer the man's question." He directed his words straight to Massey. "I talk for me. I'm *not* here to play butcher or assassin. Given very rare circumstances such as saving the life of a child, sure, I'd kill if that was all that was left to me. But it wouldn't be for any goddamn *mission*. Don't wave no CIA bullshit flag at me, Massey. Don't tell me all that crap again that 'Nam was for Mom and apple pie. *You* disappoint *me*, Massey."

"The last thing I figured you for," Massey said, almost sneering, "was a pattycake."

"Don't rile me, ex-boss-man. In this world it takes a lot more *not* to smear someone. Killing is almost too easy. I want to tell you about my old man. He got shot to shit in Vietnam. He was a real crazy brownskin. *He was so dumb he volunteered.* They shot his ass to pieces but he killed so many goddamned people on the other side, and saved so many on our side, they gave him the Medal of Honor. I watched his hospital plane land. The old bastard was more dead than alive. He'd lost so much blood he didn't look too brown, either. I know he hung on just long enough to come home to talk to me. 'I got to tell you something, son,' he said."

Stan Blake, the mean machine, the professional soldier, the ruthless killer, sat straight with tears running down his face. "My old man, he says, they give me this medal for killing over four hundred little brown people. Boy, he tells me, I didn't even know one of them. Never knew their names. I hardly saw any of them. That don't make no sense. I didn't even know what the hell I was killing them *for*. I found out. I had to die for *something*, he tells me, and his life is leaking out of him. I'm dying for you, son, he says, so I can prove to you that unless you got the most powerful reasons in all the world for killing, *don't*. I love you, boy, he tells me, and my old man, he dies right there on that goddamned airfield in my arms."

Blake wiped his cheek unashamedly as he stood straight and tall. "You know what was the worst of it? I didn't understand him then. I went to Grenada and I killed people there. I killed people in Honduras, and El Salvador and in Nicaragua, and it wasn't until we smeared a village in some Godforsaken hillside and I picked a

kid out of a burning hut and carried him in my arms
and he looked up at me and he said, *Why?* that I came
to understand my old man."

Blake pointed a finger at Massey. "Mister, I know
your record better than you think I do. I'd follow you to
hell and gone and back again. You're a brave man. A
good man. *But I won't kill for you because that's my
job.* You want a killer, go hire that crazy Rambo fuckhead
or somebody like him. Massey, I quit."

The others came slowly to their feet. Kim slipped her
hand through Blake's arm. She was crying. "Me, too."

"I guess I don't get no more asparagus," Suarez said.

Leonid Zhukov shook his head. "And I thought I'd
get some good borscht again. I'm out, sir."

"Count me out, man," Coulter said.

Massey stood to face them, his eyes going about the
room, meeting each man and woman directly. His face
muscles twitched and finally he spoke in an emotion-
choked voice.

"I am so goddamned proud of every one of you." He
swallowed hard. "You've all passed your biggest test.
Don't change." He fumbled for his cigar. "Get your
asses back in the training room!" he shouted, waving
his arms. "We've only got three days, you damn fools!"

Maria Barrios walked up to Massey and kissed him
lightly on the cheek. Her eyes were shining. She
squeezed his hand. She had said more than all the
words she knew.

A Russian KGB guard lunged with a bayonet at Kim
Seavers. She sidestepped in a sudden fluid motion,
slipped away from the lunging guard, tripped him,
spun him about into the path of Bill Coulter. A heavy
fighting staff, used for centuries by monks on lonely and
dangerous trails, whirled in Coulter's hands to crash
against the lower back of the Russian. His rifle flew
away wildly as he collapsed. Another Russian came
forward with a submachine gun blazing, this time at
Suarez. His body dropped almost magically to the floor,
his arm swinging around in an overhead toss, and the

small bola howled as it wrapped about the Russian's neck, a small steel ball cracking against his chin. He fell like a stunned ox. Suarez spun away, a blinder grenade in his hand, pin out and ready to detonate. More guards came running.

A whistle blew shrilly. The beamrider agents and the Russians stood upright, soaked in sweat, bruised, somewhat bloody, grinning at one another. In sweat-soaked gym clothes, Massey moved among them. "Not bad for amateurs," he said. He held his nose. "God, you stink. Everyone to the showers. Fresh clothing, please."

"We through for today, boss-man?" Morales asked.

"I said you stank. Fresh clothes and back here in twenty minutes. Then the *real* workout begins. Oh, Blake?"

"Yes, sir?"

"No asparagus *or* squash for you tonight."

Blake held up a thumb as he left for the showers.

Chapter XXI

Caleb Massey stood at the edge of the hand-to-hand combat mats, his recently fresh gym sweats soaked from collar to toe. He held a coiled whip in his right hand, and another looped about his left shoulder. For several moments he watched his team working out against their Russian opponents and then he blew a short whistle blast for their attention. Everyone stood at rest, grateful for the respite.

"That's it for the fun and games," Massey said easily. "Clean up, eat some iron rations, get into your Russian uniforms, assemble your equipment, and meet me in the game room exactly two hours from now." As Massey talked he worked the whip lightly, letting it float about easily through the air and lie on the mats as a loosely uncoiled snake.

Blake, Suarez and Coulter stood in a loose bunch, having just had a grand old time beating up on their "Russian opposition." They were too keyed up to come down easily. Every muscle shouted for more action. Suarez elbowed Blake.

"Hey, boss-man," Suarez called to Massey, "what for you got the whip?"

"Yeah," Coulter laughed. "You look like you're trying out for a part in *Raiders of the Lost Ark*."

"Nah," Blake joined in. "He's too fat. Too old. Too ugly. What the hell you gonna do with that dead snake, *sir*?"

"Exercise discipline," Massey said easily, passing the uncoiled bullwhip length through his hands. "Which, I note, is something you people have a great need for."

"Oh, my, this is too good to be true," Suarez said. He edged forward of the others. "Why don't you try it out on me?"

"Alejandro," Massey said wearily, "your assignment for now is to live, breathe, think and *look* Russian. Outside of learning to curse in Russian, I can't see much else you've done."

Massey smiled to himself. His people were so keyed up they were almost vibrating. No way was Suarez going to let *this* opportunity go by.

Suarez stood well before him, both hands beckoning. "Come on, boss-man, let's have your best shot with that piece of leather."

"Nope."

"How come, man?"

"Because I *like* you. Because I don't want you cut to pieces."

Suarez stood wide-legged, clenched fists solidly on his hips. Massey didn't miss him moving one foot slightly ahead of the other for a well-balanced fighting stance. Massey also knew that Suarez had spent years riding hard and tough on a Venezuelan ranch, that he was as much an expert with the whip as he was with those devilish mini-bolas he'd perfected on his own. Bola, whip, fighting staff, throwing knives, blowguns, bow and arrows, crossbows; name it and Alejandro Suarez was your man.

"Hey, amigo," Blake called softly from behind and to the side, "keep your eye on the old man. The fat bastard's got something up his sleeve."

"Sure," Coulter joshed, "and Al's walking right into it."

"Come, come, come, come," Suarez asked in a pleading tone.

"He's only a boy!" Maria Barrios called out. "A little native boy. Be easy with him, our leader!"

Grins all around. The "native boy" was more than two hundred forty pounds of knotted fighting muscle.

"I promise," Massey called back to Maria, but he didn't take his eyes from Suarez, who was beginning a side-to-side snake weave with his body. Massey lashed out with the whip. It sang through the air from its speed and the sound of a pistol shot rang out as the whip cracked. But Suarez was even faster; in a blur of motion he dodged the last, his arm came around and forward and down, he coiled the whip's end about his wrist and yanked with tremendous force.

Suarez leaned forward into the pull of Massey's body, prepared to come back with a tremendous yanking motion that would haul Massey stumbling from his feet. He stared in surprise as the whip handle came flying through the air. Massey stood straight, whip hand wide open, smiling.

"Hey, you forgot to hang on, boss-man!" Blake catcalled.

"Oh, my, he is being so nice to the little brown boy," Maria laughed.

"Watch him, Al," Coulter sang out in a second warning.

"He's right," Kim said, laughing. "Never trust a fat man who smiles."

"Yeah!" Sabbath called. "Especially when he's the guy who signs your paycheck."

"I know that look," Zhukov said of Massey. "He reminds me of an interrogator with the KGB."

Massey slowly uncoiled the second whip from his shoulder.

"Hey, I'm getting a second chance," Suarez answered the group.

"You really want a second shot at this?" Massey asked. "I'd rather let you off easy, amigo."

"You bet, fat m—"

In a blur Massey moved with startling speed, the whip slashing forward, but the tip moving almost leisurely through the air. Suarez laughed, his hand shot out to grasp the end of leather to wrap about his own hand. He began to yank hard.

Massey stood easily. They looked from Suarez to Massey and back to Suarez. A crackling bolt of blue lightning flashed about Suarez's hand, audible and deadly.

He yelled in pain, trying to draw his hand away from the writhing, flashing whip; the blue fire flashed up and down his arm and Suarez spun violently about to the mat, feet drumming against the padding.

Massey rotated a bezel on the whip handle. Blue fire ceased. "Help him up," Massey directed Blake.

Blake and Coulter dragged the shaken Suarez to his feet. He rubbed his hand and wrist, eyes still wide, body still aching.

"You'll be okay," Massey told him. "You got a low dose."

Blake came forward. "Man, what the hell *is* that thing?"

Massey handed him the whip. *"Be very careful,"* he warned. "Don't work it until you understand it." The others crowded around. "It's got a niribium powerpack in the handle that shoots a vibrating laser through fiber optics along its length. Low amps, ninety thousand volts. It reacts to biological electrical output. Low amps and a hell of a lot of volts. Anywhere from forty to four hundred thousand. Sixty thousand puts you down for sure. Double that and you're out cold for minutes to hours. Go up higher and you can turn the brain into steam. It would probably throw the heart into violent fibrillation as well. But," he added with a pause, "keep it down in the stun range and you can lay thine enemies low without killing them."

Blake stroked the weapon. "Beautiful . . . just beautiful. It's gorgeous!"

Suarez took the whip. "Boss-man, I got to hand it to you. You sure as hell had me fooled."

"Consider it a demonstration."

"How many of these we got?"

"Two."

"I want one."

"You've got it."

"I'll take the other," Blake said quickly.

"And the devil take you," Carmen Morales said, stepping in. *"I'll* take it."

"You?" Blake smiled.

Carmen took the whip. "Is it off?" she asked Massey.
"If the red light at the end isn't glowing, it's off."

She smiled sweetly at Blake, half-turned and in a motion faster than they followed the whip streaked out, cracking, and cut in half the towel Leonid Zhukov was holding. Again the whip cracked and Danza Cayuga danced as the tip barely stung his ankle. One more time, the whip snapping inches above Blake's head.

"Shit fire, girl," he told her, "*it's yours.*"

"Ladies, gentlemen." They turned to Massey, more from the tone of his voice than those words. The room went quiet. "It's time," Massey added. "Get ready. The show's on."

They assembled near the steps to the beamsphere. Four men and two women in Russian attire. Three men and one woman in military uniforms. One woman in a smart business suit. The last man in a scientist's lab smock. Zhukov was, appropriately, a full colonel. The levity attending such gatherings was subdued, almost absent and replaced with the knowledge on everyone's part that this was very much a "for keeps" operation before them. The three backups inspected gear and equipment in a final check, going through backpacks, battery belts and cables. Beneath their outer garments they wore bulletproof vests, as much festooned with equipment as to protect their bodies.

Zhukov hefted his gear. "It's heavy, but it is worth it. The guards don't carry rifles. They're all equipped with nine-millimeter automatics. These vests will stop anything from those weapons."

Blake raised an eyebrow. "You didn't mention no rifles before."

"The military cadre, the full soldier's group, they'll have the rifles and automatic weapons. But they won't be on post. They're strictly garrison."

"Let's hope they stay that way," Morales said soberly.

It was said, all that could be done was done. Power hummed in the dome, equipment glowed and flickered in standby, and from one balcony and stairway cold white vapors floated silently along walkway and stairs. Lights flashed like diamonds through the frosty living cotton.

Maria Barrios looked at the wall countdown timer, an unnecessary but instinctive reflex. Everyone knew what time it was; their clock was countdown, not that of the outside world. Massey came quickly to them. He gestured with a sheaf of notes.

"There's a last-minute change. Listen up, people." He held up a battery-powered hologram they could see from all sides. No one questioned what glowed softly before them; by now they knew the Kremlin sublevel area by heart.

"We're going to beam you directly to this anteroom," Massey said slowly, leaving nothing to question. "We've confirmed it's empty this time of night. We can't take a chance of beaming you any closer to Unsworth or into his laboratory, because we don't know where his equipment is, how crowded the place may be or who's moving around. If you beam to the lab and get a rebound, a rejection, we may never get this chance again. We did a very low power beam a short while ago from IVIC. It took a fast set of Polaroid pictures. The place, the anteroom, is empty. One light is on. The pictures didn't show any scanners, but—" he shrugged. "Anyway, that's it. To the anteroom, which leads, here, straight to the corridor and to that final elevator to Unsworth."

"And we've got a problem," Blake said quietly.

"Right," Massey confirmed. "A problem that may be a blessing in disguise. The problem is that we don't believe you've got a tinker's chance in hell of getting *back* to the anteroom in time for the beam pickup. And if you're caught in between you become the guests of the KGB right in their home turf."

Zhukov grimaced. "No, thank you. I would rather have a cyanide capsule in a tooth."

"This is your lucky day, Leonid. We're fresh out of cyanide," Massey said with the first brightening of their group exchange. "Pay attention, boys and girls. We're going to do a bias beam. When we drop you into the anteroom we'll also snap a beam in dead center of Unsworth's shop." The three-dimensional hologram glowed brighter in the area of the laboratory. "There's no problem with the bias beam because we're not sending in any solid objects so we won't get a rejection. At the same time, we're able to tell by reaction back here—or the Greystone computer can tell, that is—if the bias beam went into an open zone. If it did, that's where you get your trolley car to come home."

"Anyone ever try this before?" Kim Seavers asked.

"Nope," Massey said with sudden cheeriness. "But Old Stoney says it will work just fine." He gestured quickly. "We've tried it. Mercedes and his people have run about a dozen test trips this way and it's worked perfectly every time. That's how we know we can get a data feedback on the drop in the lab."

"*That* helps," Carmen Morales said.

"One last thing," Massey added, speaking quickly as time began to flee from them. "We believe there's a chance that if you show up in the anteroom, without the Russian security computer having you in its memory banks, then, if the autodefense systems are on, the lasers may just fire automatically."

"Terrific," Coulter said. "Send in a pig first. I like my bacon sizzling."

"But we already discussed that," Suarez said, puzzled.

"I know, I know," Massey told him. "So call me a worry wart. I want you on your toes *the instant* you know the beam fires. I want those protective sheets ready and in place *before you beam*. Got that?"

They nodded.

Massey took a deep breath. "Saddle up."

They went up the four steps into the lexan sphere. Everyone else stood well back or went to their assigned stations, freeing the transmitting area. Power built up about them; they felt it in the air, through the floor, a barely perceptible deep bass sound that was almost but not quite like the rumble of distant heavy thunder.

The wall speakers called the events. "Clear the sphere.

Clear the sphere. Power for lev coming on in thirty seconds. Stand by, please."

The sense of power became unmistakable. Vapors began to rise from the circular power grid about the outside base of the lexan sphere. Electricity raced through coils without resistance. The sphere began magically to lift as if it were levitating.

"Up, please!" Blake called out loudly in a singsong voice. "Tenth floor, ladies lingerie—"

The sphere stopped. The speakers kept control. "Sixty seconds and counting. Personnel in the sphere remain in position, please. Stand clear. Stand clear. We will go autocount at twenty seconds."

The great geodesic dome was surrealistically mad with the thrumming power, and the long-awaited surge of energy as enormous floods of electricity fed through the computer-controlled cables to the laser cannon. Final countdown lights flashed, vapor swirling madly from electrostatic forces, tiny tendrils of St. Elmo's fire spat and crackled about the room.

"Three, two, one, FIRE!"

Teal light flashed into space, carrying with it the bodies and souls of six men and women.

Chapter XXII

At the count of *"three"* the six beamriders crouched low, bodies pressed one against the other for support, all facing outward from a common center. Stan Blake had just enough time to call out, "Get r—!" when everything that was Stan Blake, body, mind and soul, became quanta frozen in timelessness. The beamriders themselves never saw the teal green slash of light; optic nerves don't work that swiftly. But there was no delay in six people working as a team operating as intended; they'd rehearsed the maneuver again and again in a race against themselves.

They never saw the huge anteroom within which a green cylindrical shape snapped into existence; as quickly as it appeared, vanishing. All about them, deep under the ground surface of the Kremlin, were metallic walls, sheets of plastic curling from disuse and stained with mildew, and all sorts of oddments of signs warning the occupants of old not to break this regulation or to behave in this particular fashion.

The beamriders saw nothing of the room because they weren't looking to see anything but a dull mirrored surface. At the countdown of three plunging to *Fire!*, on the other side of the world in a dome structure on the Atlantic coast of Florida, each agent with their left hand gripped a snaproll sheet of brilliant mirrored flexglas, and with their right hand yanked down on the roller, completely obscuring each person behind a sheet of maximum mirror reflection.

This was their shape and form and position as they materialized in the underground anteroom. They stumbled slightly from the beam drop of barely an inch above the stone floor of the anteroom, a materializing position worked out with exquisite detail by the Greystone computers and the initial beam firing with the Polaroid camera. But even one inch is enough to rustle limbs and rock a body.

"*Freeze!*" Blake barked at them all, and they hung tight, pressing harder one against the other.

By way of answer he received a sharp cracking sound and a red glow, and then another. "Jesus, those are lasers!" Coulter cried out.

"Stay still!" Kim shouted. "They're hitting us dead-on!"

Their reception exceeded anything they'd expected. Empty the anteroom might be; dormant it was *not*. The Russians apparently felt the need for security was still so great, all automatic computer detection and laser firing systems were fully active. Without proper clearance authority from their computer, the Russians left the laser defenses in the anteroom on full automatic. They could be turned off by only a few means. There would be a complete electrical failure of the whole Kremlin complex, or the security computer would register all clearances met as required and put the laser beam rifles on "HOLD." The third means of shutting down the system was to rip it apart, tear it up, *burn it out*—which is precisely what the beamriders were doing by huddling together in anteroom center.

Every time a laser beam fired with power to penetrate and burn its target, it struck one of the brilliant flexmirror reflective surfaces and bounced the beam back against the metallic walls of the anteroom. Finding the quarry was at first easy for the defense system. It used photocells and infrared trackers to pick up movement and/or body heat. If someone stood dead still in the anteroom the photocells, unless a beam was being cut by the unmoving target, had no work to do. But the infrared detectors worked thermally and anything over ninety-two degrees Fahrenheit brought heat homers to lock onto the source *and* to fire the lasers.

"This is a hell of a welcoming committee!" Suarez

grunted over the sound of lasers blasting, a metallic hissing and crackling sound. They knew that to stumble, fall or even to sway an inch too much could bring a pencil-thin laser beam tearing into and through one or more of their bodies.

"Hang in!" Blake said again. "It's working. Hear those sounds?"

It was the sound to make any target's heart leap with joy. The sounds of laser beams bouncing back from the flexmirrors and slashing through the walls and, finally, starting to burn through the very cables feeding power to the infrared detectors and the laser beams. The sounds were unmistakable: giant chunks of metallic chalk dragged across a high-friction board, a screech of metallic outrage as the power cables flashed and sputtered, short-circuiting violently.

"Smoke . . . I smell smoke!" Carmen Morales shouted. "Is it," she faltered with her own question, "us?"

"Hell no!" Blake roared. "The beams are cutting in and out. They're tearing the place apart." Debris spattered and banged against the flexmirrors as fiery explosions raced up and down and through the walls.

"They're dying out," Zhukov said, listening with the ears of a man who's heard defense lasers firing before. "We're almost safe—listen! The lasers have stopped!"

"Everyone stay still. I'm opening my shield just a hair," Blake said. He moved a convex mirror on a rotating swivel between the small space between his flexmirror and that of Kim Seavers. "My side is shut down," he said. "Al, give your side a look."

Suarez's mirror slid out, turned left and right and up and down. By way of answer he stood erect, letting his flexmirror snap back to a slim tube. "That's it. Everybody *move*," Suarez said with an unmistakable urgency to his voice. They let their mirrors roll up and jammed them into backstraps.

"Full arms, everyone, *now*," Blake snapped. He didn't need to. Everyone was yanking their weapons from their straps and velcro pockets. Suarez and Morales had their stunwhips ready to use at any second. The others prepared their wrist crossbow launchers, folding-tube concussion and blinder grenade launchers and assorted other devices of nonlethal mayhem.

Alarm horns clamored suddenly all about them. Reflex brought them spinning about, weapons ready for any attackers. The room remained smoky and spattered with burning debris, but unoccupied except for themselves. But they couldn't go anywhere until the alarms shut down.

"The monitors!" Zhukov urged the others. "Get to them *now* . . . they control the defenses." He turned to Coulter and ran to a wall. "The cables. They're exactly five feet off the floor."

Coulter joined him and the two men brought up pistol-like, thick-barreled laserguns and switched on their waist powerpaks. Intense beams of fiery red light blasted from the lasers, spattering molten globs of burning metal as they cut through the walls. Smoke boiled out and sparks continued to splash outward. "Just a bit higher!" Zhukov yelled. "I've got the first ones now!" Dull explosions from within the walls rocked them as heavy power cables and their feed systems short-circuited. The overhead lights flickered on and off. Without a word everyone turned on their miner's lamps in headbands.

"Blake!" Coulter called. "I think we got 'em! Check the scanners!"

Blake and Morales covered the anteroom. A dozen television scanners had moved back and forth. Now they jerked fitfully to stops and the small power lights beneath each camera dimmed like dying, tiny cyclops.

"We got them!" Kim shouted, jubilant.

"Get with it!" Blake bellowed. "We're running behind!"

"I thought this place wasn't guarded," Suarez threw at Zhukov.

"Just goes to show you, friend," Zhukov answered with a strained grin, "that you can't trust the Russians to do what you expect them to do."

"Can the chatter," Blake said angrily. "Let's get the floor cables." Seavers and Suarez, following assigned tasks, had their laser pistols close against the floor, slicing deep furrows in the stone metal. Zhukov hovered nearby, studying a schematic of powerlines. Coulter and Blake were at the main door leading to the waiting tunnel, looking for the easiest way through.

Carmen Morales ran to Zhukov. "Where's the cables for air conditioning?" she said urgently.

"We've got them already." Zhukov traced a line on the schematic and pointed to the exposed, laser-ripped flooring. "Right there. When you cut these cables you shut down the air conditioning systems ahead and behind us."

"Great," she said, reaching into her pack and withdrawing three heavy canisters with quick-release firing pins. She waited for further orders from Blake.

Blake turned from the heavy door leading to the tunnel. "Let's do it, troops. Fourteen minutes."

Zhukov joined them and the men slapped a shaped thermite charge against the door locks. A thin wire trailed behind them as they moved quickly to the opposite end of the anteroom. With everybody together, Suarez yanked a tubular device from a canister. Like a thing alive, the titonol metal jerked and expanded as if it were alive, forming a large wedge-shaped blast shield. Suarez pulled locking pins in place; he and Blake grasped handles within the shield.

"Hit it," Blake ordered Zhukov.

Zhukov twisted a handle on his waist powerpak. Intense flame ripped into the steel door and a heavy, dull explosion boomed about them, hurling out molten metal and chunks of debris. The shield shook and vibrated wildly from the impact of steel chunks, but held. Immediately Blake and Suarez released the grips and Suarez hurled the wedge to the side.

Morales glanced at a wrist gauge. "Everyone! Oxygen plugs! *Now!*"

They pulled small plugs from their packs and inserted them solidly in their nostrils. Oxygen flowed from the packs. Nose clamps assured they'd breathe nothing but pure oxygen if they needed to as they fought to break through the heavy defense door.

"Holy shit!" Coulter exclaimed, pointing behind them. A sickly yellow gas was seeping into the anteroom from beneath the door closest to them.

"Stan! It's mustard gas! We've got to get out of here!" Morales shouted.

"Get through that door!" Blake ordered. "And until we're away from this gas, no more talking! Use hand signals only. Clamp your lips tight. Let's go!"

They rushed for the door, still closed but *possibly* unlocked. If they needed more charges now they'd hurl mustard gas about them with great force and they'd need more than the nostril intakes to protect them. The door moved a fraction of an inch. Coulter made a wedge with his hands and pointed to the door. The signal was unmistakable. Unlocked, but jammed. Kim aimed her laser pistol at the line between door and frame, ran it down swiftly to clear any debris. Suarez grasped the heavy handle, Blake grabbed Suarez and with a tremendous heave the door dragged open slowly. They went through, turned and pulled it shut. No sign of gas showed.

"Kim, hit it with a weld," Blake told Seavers. Again the laser pistol went into action. She melted a chunk of door near the top, letting the molten metal run down, cooling swiftly. In moments, as it cooled, the door was effectively sealed shut. It would take another explosive blast to free it.

"Company," Morales sang out. They spun about from the door. Two men rushing toward them, grabbing for automatic pistols in leathered holsters. Morales yanked a pin from one of the canisters she'd been holding and hurled it ahead of her. A muffled explosion slammed hard air against them, but their eyes were clamped shut and they covered their faces as the blinder grenade went off, savage and piercing in the enclosed tunnelway. One man screamed; the other shouted, cursing, firing blindly with his automatic. They dropped to the tunnel floor.

"Put him away," Blake called to Suarez. The big Venezuelan held a blowtube in one hand, pressing a button. A compressed air charge whipped a narcotic dart into the throat of the blinded, wildly shooting Russian. He went backward as if hit by a truck, unconscious before he hit the floor. The narcotic dose would leave him that way for more than an hour.

They dashed down the tunnel. Unexpectedly a door opened to their left, in midcenter of the tunnel. A Russian guard stared in disbelief at them, gun in hand. He got off two shots before Blake came up under him, swinging his fighting staff. It caught the Russian on the side of the ear, pole-axing him. "Put him out," Blake ordered. He was taking no chances with unconscious Russians coming awake before the team's time ran out. Suarez fired a dart into the unconscious form. Blake and Morales were already tossing canisters into the guard recreation room. A blinder grenade went off with a dull booming roar and a smoke grenade followed immediately. "Jam it!" Blake yelled as he pulled the door shut. Kim hit the edges at once with the laser pistol. Metal ran molten; the door was jammed.

They ran steadily, crouching low. "How long does this goddamn tunnel go!" Coulter yelled. "Zhukov, you crazy bastard, what's happening here?"

"Keep running, keep running," Zhukov urged. "They've increased the tunnel length, that's all."

Blake turned, saw Zhukov running at a strange angle. Blood caked his left shoulder. Blake didn't need to ask whether he'd taken one of those early bullets. "Can you handle it?" Blake asked, running.

"It's a scratch," Zhukov said harshly. "Keep running. And watch out for another guard room. There *must* be another one that's not on our charts."

"Jesus Christ," Coulter said, alarm in his voice. "Look, they've widened the tunnel into a guard perimeter ahead of us!"

"Hit 'em!" Blake roared.

Blinder grenades flew down the tunnel into the widened space that formed the guard checkpoint. Smoke grenades followed, and Suarez went flat, snapping out narcotic darts as fast as he could. Sirens and klaxon horns screamed and blared, and they heard sudden gunfire, but they had the element of surprise. The scene was wild pandemonium as half-blinded, choking, gagging Russian guards either fired wildly with their pistols or struggled to see. Zhukov had been right. These men all had only their pistols. The regular garrison with heavy firepower and fully automatic weapons hadn't reached them yet.

Morales threw her canisters one after the other, as far ahead of them as she could toss the blinder and smoke grenades. Kim Seavers had dropped to one knee, firing steadily from a tube launcher. Vomiting gas shells mixed with the smoke; it would dissipate within thirty seconds, but that was enough for the Russians sucking the bitter gas into their lungs to stop as if hit by trucks, doubling over, retching violently.

"Amigo, the whips!" Blake sang out. Suarez and Morales rushed forward, whips cracking like pistol shots, the handles set to ninety thousand volts. Blue fire leaped and crackled wherever the whips touched human bodies. It went incredibly fast. More than a dozen Russian guards lay crumpled or twisting in terrible pain on the floor.

Several more guards rushed down the hallway toward them. Zhukov stood tall, pointing and shouting. "Behind you! Behind you, idiots!" he shouted in Russian. "Shoot, shoot!"

The men spun about, guns firing blindly down the tunnel at anything that might or might not be there. The beamriders came up fast behind them. The whips took out two, Kim nailed one with a wrist-crossbow dart, Coulter flattened the fourth with a blow to the back of the neck.

"More doors ahead. Keep going!" Blake bellowed.

A guard staggered to his feet behind them, holding his pistol in both hands. He emptied the magazine in their direction. Coulter spun wildly from three shots squarely to his back, bouncing off a wall, starting to go down. Blake caught him as Coulter hung on, gasping for air. "Just . . . just keep me . . . up," Coulter choked out. "The vest . . . stopped the . . . slugs. Out of . . . breath." Blake dragged him on down the tunnel, leaving the gunman to Suarez. A crackling display of blue fire and the Russian bounced several times on the floor, unconscious.

Several more men appeared, their guns still holstered. Blake dropped Coulter like a sack of meal and barreled into the group, the heavy staff swinging like a sword against heads, groins and stomachs. Four or five Russians were either unconscious or on their hands and knees, battered. "Put 'em out!" Blake shouted, going back for Coulter. Morales ran up, whip singing with blue fire. It was enough to get one good caress with the whip to put a man out of action for an hour or more.

They had no trouble getting through the next barrier. The door stood wide open. Zhukov ran ahead of the group, holding on to his bleeding arm. A dozen Russian soldiers appeared, chilling his blood. Zhukov gestured wildly with the pistol he'd grabbed from a felled Russian and shouted steadily to the confused soldiers. They turned and ran as he brandished the pistol. As they disappeared into yet another side door the rest of the team caught up with Zhukov.

"Leo, what the hell did you tell them?" Blake asked. "They just ran away."

Zhukov grinned hugely. "First impressions are everything. Here I am, a wounded Russian colonel, pistol in my hand, shouting orders. What else is there to do but to obey? I told them there was a large force of terrorists back in the first defense ring, trying to get upstairs to the meeting of the commissars on the second floor. I told them to take the emergency tunnel and get to the Kremlin chambers at once." He gestured ahead of them. "Keep moving, keep moving, Stan."

They ran on, Suarez helping Coulter, who'd had the equivalent of hammer blows to his back and lungs and was still struggling for air. "How'd you know about an emergency tunnel?" Blake asked Zhukov.

"I didn't," he said between his own struggle for air. "But if they'd made these many changes here, it made sense that they would have built a safety corridor. And," he grinned again, "I guess they did."

"Right ahead of us," Kim called to them. "The elevator shaft. I can see the doors." Moments later they were at the twin doors. "Al, Bill, Carmen," Blake said quickly, "check behind us. Lob a few smoke grenades as far as you can for safety. We've got to get this elevator to work."

He turned back with Zhukov at his side. Coulter had slid to the floor, back against the wall, taking deep shuddering breaths. He knew the bullets, prevented from entering his body by the flak vests, likely had broken a couple of ribs. There was too much pain and breathing was too difficult. But if he could just hang on a bit longer he'd make it. He looked up at Blake and Zhukov at the door. Zhukov banged on the buttons. Doors started to open, shook and quivered, jerked back and forth barely an inch or two, and jammed in place.

"When we cut the power," Zhukov said. "It's on emergency only now, but there isn't enough juice to operate normally."

"We'll have to blow it open," Blake said. "Give me a hand, Leo. Quickly."

They slapped thermite explosive charges against the lock of a thick service panel to the right of the elevator. "Do we need this much?" Leo asked, eyes wide.

"You got time to spare, buddy?" Blake shot back. "Everybody heads up!" he yelled, and twisted the igniter. They hugged the wall as the charge blew out the steel panel.

"Goddamn," Zhukov muttered. The wiring system was a mess. Zhukov studied it for a long moment, Blake's fists clenching and unclenching, then Zhukov grabbed two green wires and jammed them together. His body jerked convulsively as a charge of electricity tore into him. His head snapped back, his jaw twisting as he fought for breath. To his side the elevator doors crashed open. Before Blake could move Suarez was flying through the air in a brutal football tackle directly at Zhukov. His weight and the force of his sudden charge slammed Zhukov free of the wires. Eyes bulging, gasping for air, the others dragged him and Coulter into the elevator.

Seavers kept hitting the UP button. The others stared helplessly as Kim turned, despair in her eyes. Blake and Suarez wasted no time. They linked their hands and fingers into a step, Carmen Morales put a foot squarely in their interlocked fingers, and they heaved her up and held her aloft as she rammed her forearms against the access and service panels on the elevator roof. They came free with a clanging motion. She reached up and shoved them aside, looked up, a flashlight beam in her hand moving back and forth.

"Two ladders, side by side, straight up. One door three floors up. I can see it. Boost me higher."

They heaved and she went through the panel, turning to assist those below. Kneeling on one knee, she grasped Kim's wrist first, hauling up as she was boosted from below. "Don't wait," Carmen ordered. "Start up those stairs *now*. And have a blinder ready to toss the moment you're up there."

They sent up Coulter next so he could have as much time as possible to make it up what was a devastating climb for a man who apparently had broken ribs. Zhukov took the second ladder as Kim scampered up, followed by Coulter. Zhukov wanted to be first to the door at the upper level. He was the best prepared of them all with his colonel's uniform and language fluency to meet any "awkward" situations. Suarez lifted Blake to the opening and he lifted himself with levitation-like ease, the muscular Suarez following him the same way.

"Go ahead," Blake told Suarez. "I'll leave a gift behind." He placed a blinder grenade on one side of the hatchway and a smoke grenade on the other, ran a thin wire around some bent iron. It was virtually invisible from below. Anyone climbing after them would break the wire. The odds were also that anyone firing at them would cut the wires, and if everything went to hell in a basket, they could drop a concussion blinder and set the rest of the grenades off when it struck.

Above them, Zhukov and Kim were at the upper elevator doors. Zhukov climbed higher, reaching for the emergency handle to open the doors from the shaft. He pulled with all his strength. "Jammed!" he said in a hoarse whisper to Seavers. "Let me have a wedge charge. Quickly!"

He placed the charge at the base of the doors, passed the word down. Blake came up behind Zhukov. "When it blows, give it everything you've got," he told Leonid. "No matter what happens we've got to get as far inside as we can. Otherwise they'll pick us off like sitting ducks."

"Like Muscovy ducks, you mean," Leonid said with a humorless laugh. He leaned down. "Everybody, flatten yourself against the walls and hang on to those ladder rungs." He turned and held his hand out. "At the count of one," he added. "Three, two, one—" and jammed a live wire from his powerpak into the shaped charge.

The elevator doors blew completely away from the shaft opening, taking much of the blast effect with them. Over their heads, clinging as hard as they could to the ladders, the six beamriders rode out the booming concussion wave. "Hit it!" Blake yelled, and tossed a blinder grenade through the open doorway. Zhukov followed with a second, and they scrambled into what appeared to be a series of offices. A guard came around a near corner, grabbing for his pistol as he ran. Blake rolled over swiftly, slamming into his legs. The guard stumbled, falling forward. Zhukov grabbed his arm and yanked as hard as he could. The guard was carried forward by his own momentum; arms flailing, mouth open in the start of a scream, he flew out into the empty space of the elevator shaft. His scream echoed thinly about them as they moved as fast as they could out of the shaft.

Two more guards came about the corner, firing as they ran. Blake took a heavy blow to the ribs; only his kevlar vest saved him. His sudden gasp from the shot distracted the guards for a moment. Two whips cracked as one as Morales and Suarez lashed out, the whips slashing against the Russians' legs. Blue fire crackled, they spun about like rag dolls, unconscious before they crumpled.

Zhukov was already ahead of the others, Kim with him, stopping at corridor exchanges. Behind them a sudden roaring explosion as grenades set for ambush in the elevator roof went off with gouts of flame and a brilliant flash. Smoke boiled upward through the shaft. Screams and shouts came garbled through the uproar about the team. They ignored them, far more interested in the shouting and the pounding of feet coming toward them from the corridors that lay ahead.

Leonid Zhukov, his good arm held high with his automatic in his hand, ran straight *toward* the oncoming Russians. In his first glance he saw they were a mixture of soldiers with technicians, secretaries and scientists. Zhukov made certain to shout first and more loudly than anyone else. Cursing a blue streak against the idiots who would leave the Kremlin chambers open to the real assault rather than the fuss and bother of this decoy assault, he turned at least half the Russian troops in the other direction, running as fast as their booted feet would take them. But a group of mixed technicians and soldiers *fell in behind Zhukov* to protect and to follow him. No choice; Zhukov, still shouting and waving his weapon, went charging through a door into a room that promised to lead to another corridor.

Two Russian guards within, standing before an enormous computer console, opened fire immediately. Zhukov with first sight of the guards had thrown himself violently to the side, cursing as his injured shoulder slammed into a desk. Behind him several of the Russians who were following him screamed in a wild spray of a devastating bloodbath at pointblank range from their own men. Flesh, bones and blood spattered throughout the room, mixed with cries of pain and screams of rage.

In the confusion Zhukov stayed low and made it back

to the corridor. The beamriders came running up the hallway, unfortunately just as the enraged guards burst from the room where blood ran so freely. The Russians let fly a blast of heavy gunfire. Coulter took a blow to the stomach, stopped by his kevlar vest, but a second slug sliced open his upper arm in a painful but not crippling wound.

Carmen Morales was less fortunate. She seemed to be struck by a giant invisible blow and hurled against a wall. Suarez was right behind her, dodging, his arm snapping out the whip, catching the first Russian in the face. Blue fire ripped through his mouth and ears and from his nose; blood gushed forth and he was unconscious in midscream. The effect was enough to throw off the second guard. Kim nailed him with a wrist crossbow dart and he fell silently, face contorted.

Suarez was instantly by Carmen. Blood stained her left shoulder and her face was white with pain. A bullet had gone into her mouth at an angle, missing her teeth, and emerged from her cheek. It was a terrible and bloody wound but it wouldn't kill her, yet the pain was agonizing.

"G-go on!" she begged Suarez. "Get the h-hell out of here. The whip . . . give it to Kim. I'll stay . . . stay here . . . block them . . ."

Without a word Suarez jammed a handkerchief into her mouth against the cheek wound, hauled her up like a sack of dogfood and threw her over his shoulder. Coulter was on his feet, dazed but in control of himself, running with Blake. Zhukov caught up with Blake to help lead the way. Kim took up the rear of the procession, ready for anything with grenades and crossbow darts.

"It's the last corridor!" Zhukov shouted, pointing ahead of them. He ran madly ahead, the miner's light on his forehead moving so wildly it seemed like a flashing beacon.

He heard Seavers's scream from behind him. "Stop! Leo, it's a trap!"

He flattened against a wall, looked back to Seavers.

She pointed down the corridor to a TV scanner high on a far wall. "Leo, what the hell's that thing doing on? I thought we cut those cables! The transmit light is on!"

Gasping for breath, he spoke in short bursts of words. "Separate power line . . . must be. Can't get through . . . here. They're watching. This whole place . . . alive . . . with lasers. Got to knock out . . . scanner!" He turned to Seavers. "Kim, *don't go down that hallway.* It's a laser trap." He closed his eyes, murmuring in a sense of sudden, overwhelming defeat. "We came so . . . far . . . now . . . this . . ."

Behind him, the others came pounding up the corridor. Zhukov waved his arms. "Stop! Kim's down the corridor . . . she'll be killed . . . scanners working . . . the whole place is . . . alive with lasers!"

Blake stretched out an arm to signal the others to stop where they were. Without a word, Suarez eased Carmen to the floor, turned to cover them behind him. Blake called to Kim Seavers. "Hold it there! I'll help!"

"Stay back!" she screamed at him. He had no choice but to watch as she unsnapped the flexmirror she'd used before. She held it carefully top and bottom so that each side, her left and right, was covered by gleaming mirror. She took a deep breath and ran with all the speed she could manage down the corridor. She reached the farthest point she'd gone to before, and threw herself forward in a wild rolling somersault, going over and over in a blur of gleaming flexmirror and parts of her own body. Laser beams snapped steadily, angry blazing dragons biting lethally at her, reflecting from the flexmirror. The others stared, helpless yet awed, as Kim whirled down the corridor. A sudden cry of pain stabbed back to them as a laser sliced through an exposed area and burned through her jumpsuit leg and her own skin as well. Then she was by the far wall, directly beneath the scanner and she threw aside the mirror, climbed to her feet. She held the laser pistol in one hand, turned it on, reached high and jammed the pistol against the scanner. Ruby-red flame tore into metal and plastic; a shower of molten debris fell about her. She winced as particles hit her face, searing more flesh. Numb with pain, she waved a weary arm for them to come on.

"The light's out! She's done it!" Blake prodded the others. "Move, move!"

They came down the corridor, battered and besieged with wounds and pain. Suarez half-carried Carmen Morales, her face white, but regaining her strength. Zhukov held a hand to the shoulder where he'd been shot, but his eyes were bright and clear again. Coulter limped and swayed, a miracle in motion with broken ribs, hard blows and internal injuries from bullets slamming into his kevlar vest, his upper arm bleeding from a grazing bullet. Blake had taken several direct hits, but he was so powerfully muscled that the blows against his kevlar shield were like fly specks.

The corridor turned at a right angle by the scanner Kim had turned into slag. They pushed their way into a wide doorless anteroom, obviously a communications checkpoint where two huge Russian women came running at them from behind a counter. Blake didn't hesitate a moment. The beefy woman in the lead, a heavy stick in her hand, rushed him, swinging with all her might.

"Nice try," Blake smiled. His fighting staff caught her beneath the elbow and the sound of bone cracking was like a pistol shot. Blake didn't waste the sudden advantage. The pole whipped around, the opposite end came forward swiftly and she took the blunt end like a Mack truck directly in her chest. Her eyes bulged as she was slammed unconscious, tumbling sideways from her own momentum and the crushing blows.

The second woman was struggling with a holster by her side, the weapon coming into view as Suarez caught sight of the gun. His whip lashed forth, the tip curling in a blur around her wrist. Blue fire crackled, she screamed and the gun went flying as she jerked backwards violently, already unconscious.

"In God's name, how much longer does this go on?" Suarez shouted to Zhukov.

Zhukov pointed to a wooden door. "We're there. The women were guards to keep whoever's on the other side of that door inside."

Suarez turned to Seavers. "Kim, help Carmen." Kim nodded, put an arm about Carmen's waist.

"Hit it!" Blake yelled to Suarez. Both men stepped back, and ran full speed toward the wooden door. At the last moment they left the floor beneath them in flying kicks and their combined weight, with all their speed, brought their boots crashing with tremendous impact against the door. Wood splintered with a tearing crash, hinges ripped away and the door blew backwards. Zhukov ran past Blake and Suarez as they regained their feet; they followed Zhukov, the others coming behind as fast as they could hobble and limp.

They were in the research laboratory. Near room center, to their right, stood a man who could only be Dr. Peter Unsworth. He stood untroubled by the mayhem and explosions and crashing noises and flying dust and debris, staring at them with sightless eyes. He wore a lab smock. One hand rested on the table, another was in a pocket.

They felt wildly unreal, staring at the British scientist, whose eyes, unseeing, blind, seemed to bore right through them. Unsworth's hair was disheveled, and as he stood quietly his mouth opened slowly. The frozen tableau held for long, stark seconds.

"My God," Seavers said. *"He's mad."*

"Four minutes!" Blake shouted. "Al, cover us. Zhukov, look around, see if anything's going to be trouble. Bill, can you help with—no; you stay with Al. Kim, you help me with the old man, here. We've got to get him into a magsuit *now*."

Kim slipped her backpack from her shoulders to the floor, yanked open the velcro cover and pulled free a loose-hanging jumpsuit lined with magnetic metallic striping and threads and velcro bands throughout. At the top she shook loose a flexplastic see-through faceplate. The thought struck her as ridiculous. They'd made sure to bring a transparent faceplate *for a man who was blind*.

"Leo!" Blake called sharply. "Talk to him. In Russian. Tell him we're here to get him out of this place, to take him with us. He's got to get into this suit for safety."

Zhukov went up to Unsworth, touched his arm gently, spoke quickly but clearly in Russian. Unsworth looked right through him, then abruptly stepped backward along the edge of the table. His sightless face contorted with sudden anger; his blind eyes stabbed at Zhukov. He shouted angrily in Russian.

"What's he saying?" Kim asked.

"He's shouting at me, at us," Zhukov said, "to get away from him, to leave him alone."

Seavers moved to Unsworth, hoping a woman's voice would calm him. Unsworth scrambled away from them; in a sudden panic he stumbled by a chair, nearly falling. Kim rushed to help him, hold him up.

"Please, *please*, Dr. Unsworth . . . we're friends, *we're your friends*," she said, as calmly and yet as urgently as she could. "We want to help, take you away from here to safety."

In his blind panic none of them could fathom, Unsworth swung wildly at Kim. She blocked the blow. Blake held Unsworth as firmly and gently as he could. "Dammit, man," he railed in his frustration, "*we're friends—*"

Kim turned to Blake, despair stark on her face. "Stan, we're running out of time. I—I don't know what to do!"

"Whatever it is," he said harshly, "we'd better do it damn fast. We're going to have company soon and I have no doubt they'll be the heavies this time. The garrison here." He glanced from her to Unsworth. "We'll just have to take him whether he wants to go or not."

"*No!*" Her face seemed to twist with some inner agony. "No, I won't do it. I won't let you do it! Either he comes with us by his own decision or—"

Unsworth moved uncertainly but on his own closer to Kim. He seemed to be staring at her face, as though he had an unknown inner sight. The fear and anger he had shown faded as his hand reached out to touch Kim's shoulder, move up to the side of her face. A smile appeared; a smile and astonishment.

"You're . . . *you're thinking in English!*" he cried.

"I don't . . . what?" Kim stumbled in her answer, confused.

Unsworth's face was almost shining. "You're *thinking* in English! *You're not Russians!*"

Suarez's voice bellowed from the side. "Dammit, we've got less than two minutes! Do it, man, *do it!*"

Kim faced Unsworth directly. "What do you mean? How do you know we're not Russians?"

"He can hear us, Kim," Blake broke in. "If nothing else, the way we're talking—"

"*No!*" Unsworth shouted, laughing and crying at the same time. "You don't understand . . . *I'm deaf!* These people destroyed my eardrums. They're . . . I *can't hear* a thing you're saying . . . I can't see you . . . *but you're thinking in English!*"

Blake stared with wide, astonished eyes. "My God, he's doing it . . . reading our minds."

"Yes! Yes!" Unsworth shouted.

Seavers gripped the arms of the old man. She was going crazy trying to think her thoughts as hard as she could while she spoke aloud. "Doctor, if you understand what I'm saying, what I'm thinking as damn hard as I can, you've got to get into this jumpsuit. *Please* . . . we don't have any time left—"

Kim shut her eyes, facial muscles tense, her mouth set tightly, thinking with all her might.

A heavy explosion boomed from the corridor. They heard voices shouting in Russian. Blake spun about to see Suarez hurling gas canisters with all his strength down the corridor. Dull popping explosions and sudden bursts of light told him the gas canisters were blowing, mixed with the blinder grenades.

"One minute, goddammit!" Suarez shouted. "One minute and we go with or without him! Zhukov, help

Coulter and Morales over there. That's the pickup point
. . . move, dammit! *Move!*"

Kim's eyes snapped open. "The suit!" she shouted
to Blake. "Help him into the suit! He'll work with us!"

Blake held Unsworth's shoulders, Kim slipped the
scientist's legs into the suit trousers, wrapping velcro
fasteners into place as quickly as she could. They got
his arms into the gloved sleeves. Blake ran his hand up
the front of the suit, magnetic fasteners sealing wherever they touched. They pushed the helmet over his
head, Kim ran her hands around the neck rim.

"He's in," she told Blake.

"Hold him at pickup," he pointed. "Stay low, girl.
This is going to be a hell of a squeaker."

Coulter could barely move; Blake grabbed him by an
armpit and dragged him like dead beef into the pickup
area. The others huddled together. Only Suarez remained outside the circle. "All! Let's go!" Blake shouted.

"No! They're coming!" Suarez shouted. He paused to
hurl another grenade down the hall. A burst of machine-
gun fire ripped at them from the corridor. Suarez spun
about from the impact of bullets slamming into the
kevlar vest at stomach height. He hurled another blinder
grenade as he started to fall. A bullet clipped his knee
and he dropped heavily, cursing.

"Go on, dammit!" he called through his pain. "I'll
hold them—"

Blake dashed from the pickup circle. He heard Kim's
voice screaming from behind him. "Stan! Don't . . .
we've only got seconds to—"

He wasn't listening. He dragged Suarez to his feet,
turned his back to the pickup circle, and punched Suarez
in the mouth with all his strength. Blood flew. The
shocked Suarez, trying to stand on one leg, stared at
Blake, who bent forward, hit his friend in the stomach
with his shoulder in a running-start football tackle, hurling him backwards. He grabbed Suarez about the waist,
pushing with all his strength. Suarez fell, unable to
stand any more, one leg crippled, the other hopelessly
off balance, falling backwards, Blake gripping him with

all his might, *falling into the sudden dazzling green light* . . .

Russian soldiers in gas masks, deploying out to the sides from the corridor, burst into the laboratory, moving swiftly and expertly, machine guns hammering from one side to the other, their weapons shattering lab equipment. They stopped firing, staying low, moving cautiously to finish off the—

The long laboratory was empty.

Chapter XXIII

The young couple stood on the edge of their pent-house balcony twenty stories above the flat sands and moon-sparkling surf of Cocoa Beach. Theirs was a lover's night, a breeze wafting in from offshore, a moon sliding ever so slowly to the horizon. The surf came to them, musical in its splashing rhythm, a slow beat to their mood. No shortage here of magical gemstones to sigh gently on one's senses. To their left stretched the long curving flank of the Canaveral seashore, reaching all the way to the tip of the Cape, and in between minor galaxies of lights from homes and apartments along the beach. Bonfires winked in haze created by salt spray from the surf. Offshore the lights gleamed like diamonds scattered lazily in all directions. The shrimp boat fleet cruised in a slow formation for miles. A great palace sprayed light in a huge bowl; a cruise liner working its way slowly in toward Port Canaveral. All manner of boats and ships out to sea touched the darkness to the horizon. And still farther to the north, again to their left, were the lights and strobes of the submarine pens, the towers of Canaveral, and still beyond those upreaching beams, the lights marking the huge spaceport from where the shuttles flew. An intruder moved silently and ghostly at regular intervals; the Canaveral lighthouse sweeping its beam around and around as it had for years longer than these two young-sters had been alive.

No shortage of gleaming and sparkling gems in the sky. Helicopters drove back and forth, visible only by their lights, discernible from the powerful flapping monotone of great rotors and the harsh cry of jet exhausts. A launch was nearing, and of a sudden white lances spoked into the night as batteries of great searchlights surrounding a space booster clicked and boomed to life. The couple looked south and again the pearls that glowed and the gleaming lights marched on. Beyond Cocoa Beach rose a great golden spray of light from the flightline amber floods of Patrick Air Force Base. In the distance, over the ocean, they saw three huge and intense white lights start from tiny twinkles and become unbelievable brilliant globes: the landing lights of some great transport still concealed within the brightness of lights and otherwise shrouded in the dark.

"This is hard to believe," the young man said finally, making certain body pressed tightly against body as they looked and yielded to conversation of the moment.

"Remember that night at Disney World?" she asked. "I was so impressed with the boats on the water, and the hotel and the monorails—"

"And the palace in the Magic Kingdom?"

"Uh huh. But here . . ." She shook her head slowly, a romantic young thing, warm and rounded and lovely here at night, leaving behind her a daytime world where she commanded the skills of great computers and she thought in time measured in millionths of seconds. That was some other place, some other time. Yet—

"What's so hard to believe is that *all this is real*," she said finally. "That really gets to me. When I was a little girl I used to come down to the beach, up there," she pointed, "by the jetties, and we'd watch the rockets go up at night, and the whole sky looked like it was on fire, and it was *so* beautiful."

He lacked her words, the years of growing up in the midst of aimed fire and steel, but he was no less impressed. "Wow, I guess you're right," he said finally, wanting the words but suffering those riches.

The shaft of green fire saved the moment for him. One moment they held themselves willing prisoners of the night and the lights. In the next instant the wire-thin slash of green snapped into existence, a light that appeared instantaneously between earth and the shrouded heavens.

Then it was gone, remaining a bit longer as retinal after-reflection in their eyes.

"What was that?" she exclaimed.

He thanked his own private gods for knowing something, at least, about this sudden intrusion in their private heavens. "Oh, I've seen that a lot. Usually it's much later than now, though."

"What is . . . I mean, it was so *beautiful*, and it came and went like," she laughed, a wonderful tinkling sound to her young man, "well, like magic." She laughed again. "That's the kind of light Peter Pan or Tinkerbell would use to slide down from the sky."

"Well, in a way, maybe it's like that," he told her. "It's some kind of test, you know, a beam for sending television signals back and forth between satellites."

"Whatever it is, it was beautiful," she sighed.

"You know what I think?" He moved back slightly to face her. "I like to think about this stuff a lot. You know, daydreaming. Science fiction, like. Wouldn't it be something if we didn't need to use the rockets to fly into space? Like, maybe we could use something like that green light."

"Gee, I don't know," she said slowly, unrealizing that the world in which she spent her days was a miracle beyond dreaming to her own family only two or three generations removed. "How would something like that work?"

"Well, I don't *know*," he fought the words out, "but I was reading that it was impossible for sailors from a long time ago to imagine ever crossing the ocean, you know, without their *ever* once touching the water. The whole idea was real crazy to them. How could you cross the ocean without going in a boat? You *had* to go by boat. There wasn't any other way, and since you just *couldn't fly*, well, it was crazy."

He grinned. "So that's how I think about that light. Like, it's an energy beam. We send voices through invisible rays now, right? Voices and even pictures.

Television goes through microwaves, like those towers by the phone company building? Well, we could use things like that."

She laughed, and for a terrible moment he thought she was laughing at him. She wasn't. She was laughing at the idea, so unreal, so preposterous, of men going into space on a light beam.

"You know what?" she said to him. "Before I'd believe people could travel by light, I'd believe that one day we'll be able to talk to other people at a distance without radio, or television, or things like that."

"How would they do that?"

"Well, being able to send thoughts by thinking. You know, mental telepathy. Stuff like that."

He laughed. "Wow, you're really awesome, you know that?"

"Well," she retorted with her favorite girlish pout, "I'll bet," and she snuggled closer to him, her full breasts hard against his chest, "I can tell right now what you're thinking."

He grinned. "You bet," he said, and kissed her.

Chapter XXIV

The huge clamshell doors of Canaveral Dome came together with a deep, low-booming rumble and a final massive thud. No one heard or paid attention to the sound. All eyes in the great dome stared at the seven figures huddled together within the lexan transceiver sphere, now lowering steadily and smoothly. All other activity within the dome ground to a halt, everyone staring at the dome. Only a few among them expected, *hoped for*, the presence of a seventh person. The other technicians and scientists, and the remaining cadre of beamriders, had known nothing of the attempt to bring back anyone. They found the sight of seven, one wrapped in a loose magsuit and helmet, beyond their understanding.

Massey had expected the worst. The sight of his own people as well as Peter Unsworth was beyond his wildest expectations. It didn't take him more than a single glance to confirm his fears, as well. Several people in the group, hanging together as tightly as they were, prevented him from sorting out who had suffered what, but the pained expressions on faces and the blood spattered on their suits was message enough. He had a full medical team standing by, paramedics and two of the finest doctors from the navy, the latter chosen for their security as much as their medical skills.

"Timmins! Brudos! Get in there!" he called to the medical team. They moved forward, pushing aside other people who gawked at the sight before them as the sphere rested on the dome floor. The doctors and paramedics moved to the group. Stretchers were brought to the sphere as bodies began to separate. Right behind the doctors, mixing in with them were Maria Barrios, Jim Sabbath and Danza Cayuga.

They brought Bill Coulter from the group first, face white and drawn, grinning through set teeth to hold back the pain. Dr. Timmins hovered over him. Coulter looked up at Massey. "It was one hell of a ride, boss-man." He winced with the effort of raising up on one elbow and talking. Massey went to his side. Every glance brought his pride soaring.

"Shut up," he told Coulter, but the words carried deep affection with them. "How bad is it?"

Coulter turned his head to Dr. Timmins. "Shut up, and talk," he grunted through his pain. "Ornery old son of a grizzly bitch, I swear." Timmins moved his hands across Coulter, when the beamrider agent cursed with renewed pain. "Easy there, doc. *Very* easy, if you please." He swallowed hard. "I think I've got a couple of busted ribs. My stomach don't feel so good, also." He closed his eyes for a long moment. "Goddamn arm's sorta messed up."

Timmins turned to a medical team. "Get him to surgery immediately. Dr. Wells is waiting there. Okay, move him out. Gently, damn you; *gently.*"

"Hey, I got to . . ." Coulter was on the edge of fainting. His voice began to fade. "I got to . . . to report . . ."

Massey touched his shoulder gently. "Later, hoss."

They wheeled Coulter away. "He's bleeding internally. I think we're looking at a punctured lung also. Did you see that kevlar vest? It looks like they were shoving pistons at that man."

Massey nodded. "Get to the others," he said, moving closer to his group. Dr. Sam Brudos stood before Carmen Morales, whose face and neck were covered with blood. Her jumpsuit showed dark stains from heavy bleeding. The doctor carefully removed the handkerchief from her mouth. Someone behind him murmured, "Jesus . . ."

Massey gave him a look that would have frozen a polar bear. He turned back to see Carmen pushing away the doctor. She could barely talk and was obviously in great pain. "Alejandro," she forced out through her torn mouth. "Take care . . . Alejandro . . . hurt bad."

Suarez had been so quiet, staying so much in the background, they'd ignored his remaining seated, looking all the world like a heavy buddha. Massey went to the sphere, gently removed Suarez's hands where he'd held them so carefully over his knee. "Jesus goddamned Christ," Massey swore softly. Suarez's whole knee and leg were caked with blood. Massey stared at white bone through the torn leg of the jumpsuit. Massey turned; both doctors were tending to bad wounds. Massey gestured for two paramedics. "Don't waste a moment. Get this man to the medical ward at once. *Stay with him, understand?* Don't leave his damn side until a doctor gets to him." Massey turned back, knelt down before Suarez.

"Ever think about having a bionic knee?"

"You sound, uh, damn . . . sound like I'm a candidate."

"You are. You take any morphine from your kit?"

Suarez shook his head slowly. "No time. Had to keep my head . . . clear." Massey hadn't realized how badly he must hurt.

"Where else, Alejandro?" he asked as softly as he could.

"Got some stomach pains. External. Kevlar stopped a bunch of rounds."

"Your mouth . . . what happened?"

"What's it look like, boss-man?"

"Your lip is split wide open. Loose teeth. How—"

Suarez grimaced in a horrible grin. He lifted an arm painfully and pointed to Blake. Blake stood to the side, Maria Barrios clinging desperately to him, her face buried in his chest. Massey knew she was crying.

"Big dumb son of a bitch . . ." Suarez forced out painfully. "Punched me . . . like to . . . tore my head off."

Massey stared. "What?" he exclaimed. Softly then, "But how . . . why?"

"Bastard . . . saved my life. Kiss the . . . ugly gringo for . . . me."

Massey stood. "Get him the hell out of here. On a stretcher. He's not to put any weight on that leg." It took the two medics and Massey to get the big man onto the stretcher; they wheeled him away swiftly.

He saw Zhukov seated on a stretcher; medics were cutting away his shoulder clothing to get to the wound. "Leonid . . ." Massey started, but the Russian interrupted him immediately. "Flesh wound. I'll be fine. Take care of the others." Zhukov looked around. "Kim; where is she?"

My God . . . Massey thought frantically. *Kim, and Unsworth!* He saw them well to the side of the others, a group of people about them, staring, mystified, at the British scientist. Kim was removing the last of the magsuit and helmet they'd placed on him, and it wasn't until he was much closer that Massey saw that Kim herself had taken some nasty punishment. He looked from her to Peter Unsworth, his sightless eyes staring straight ahead of him, turning slowly back to Kim. None of the uproar appeared to have the slightest effect on him. Massey started to speak to Unsworth, then a lifetime of hard experience ruled his emotions. You take care of your people who are hurt, *first.* Everything else comes later.

He leaned down for a close look at her leg. "That's a nasty burn," he said, looking up at her.

She nodded. "Laser. Forget it. We'll deal with it later. The laser's antiseptic, remember?"

He stood. "Kim, for Christ's sake, you've got burns on your face."

Her eyes locked with his. "*Later*, sir." He knew an imperative when he heard and faced it. He nodded, turned to Unsworth, to that sightless figure, looking so frail in this huge place.

Massey extended his hand. "Dr. Unsworth, I'm—"

"He can't hear you," Kim broke in. Massey's face showed his puzzlement. "The Russians . . . for their tests. They destroyed his eardrums. He's deaf."

Massey couldn't help staring; even knowing the old scientist couldn't see him, he still felt uncomfortable with his own shortcoming of a rude stare. Peter Unsworth smiled.

"Hello, Caleb Massey," he said.

A physical blow couldn't have dazed Massey more than those few words, at that moment, only seconds after learning that the man before him was blind *and* deaf.

"How? Uh, hello, Dr. Unsworth . . . Kim, you said he couldn't hear me? But he knows my name . . . he knows who's standing here before him!"

"Yes, sir. That's right." Kim was smiling.

"But how could he . . ." Massey's voice trailed away. His own eyes widened and his mouth opened; he felt he was gaping stupidly and forced his mouth closed.

"Don't be embarrassed," Unsworth said, offering a kind smile with his words.

"He's really—" He let the question hang.

"Yes, sir," Kim said, and she was clearly and tremendously proud of this man who had linked his arm in hers.

"You're— No, don't *say* it," Unsworth told him. "Think your name. Spell it out letter by letter. Better yet, think of seeing your own name in full, dominant and bright, like an electric sign against a dark background."

Massey frowned and concentrated.

"You're really working much harder than you need to, Caleb Massey." Unsworth extended his hand and they clasped.

"My God, I am so pleased, so tremendously pleased, that you're safe and with us," Massey said. Immediately he turned to Kim. "I feel so *stupid*, speaking aloud, knowing he can't *hear* what I'm saying, and yet, I *want* him to know what I'm thinking, saying, what I want him to know!"

"It will take some time, Caleb Massey. May I call you Caleb?" Unsworth asked. "I am *so* tired of those stiffnecked, no-imagination, bullheaded, blockbrained Russians—"

"Yes, yes; of course!"

"Then, please; my name is Peter. I am weary of officialdom, Caleb."

"Sir, let me make it easier," Kim said. "Think *and* speak aloud when you communicate with Dr. Unsworth. If you try to separate the two it simply causes turmoil in your own mind, and it confuses him."

"Muddies up the water, it does," Unsworth said.

"Forgive me," Massey said hastily. "I haven't had the decency to ask if you're hurt, or tired, or—"

Unsworth held up a hand. "First things first."

"Of course."

"Where in the bloody hell *am* I?"

"Sir, Dr. Uns—Peter . . . the United States. Just on the south edge of Cape Canaveral. That's on the Atlantic coast of Florida."

"Your space center?"

Massey thought of the rows of giant towers, huge rockets blazing their way into the heavens.

"Now *that's* the way I like a man to think!" Unsworth exclaimed. "Three-dimensional, full-color thinking. Thank you. I know where I am now." He frowned. "How in the hell did I get here? This young lady started several times to explain, but it has been quite exciting and, I must say, most confusing."

Massey created a mental picture of himself, facing Unsworth, both hands raised with his palms facing the scientist.

"All right," Unsworth said affably. "I'll wait. But it was quite a ride, I'll tell you." He patted Kim's hand. "My dear, look at the gentleman, please. Stare at him. Concentrate on his face in total, then concentrate on his dominant features."

They stood this way for perhaps thirty seconds, until Unsworth nodded. "Well, now I know what you look like," Unsworth said. "A cross between a grizzly bear and a subway car, I'd say."

"But how—"

"I see through her eyes, Caleb."

"Oh. Is there—"

"You're damned right. I thought you'd *never* get around to it." Unsworth licked dry lips. "Good Lord above, how I need a drink—No, *no*. Not water. What a horrible thought. And *not* tea. Don't go provincial on me, old man. Relax. Scotch and soda. If you're still barbarians over here in the colonies, make it scotch neat."

A technician standing behind them gestured to Massey. "I'll take care of it immediately, sir. Scotch and soda."

"Make it a double," Unsworth said.

"Yes, sir." The aide took off as if propelled by a cannon shot.

"Let me not continue to be such a poor host," Massey said quickly. He thought up images of medicine, pills, RX symbols.

"No, no; I'm perfectly all right. Exhausted, and I shall likely perish before you get me that drink. There is something I'd like, Caleb."

"Name it, Peter."

"You old fool, get this girl some medical attention. I know she has a nasty burn."

"Kim, the doctors are waiting for you," Massey said. He saw the stubborn look on her face. "Don't argue, dammit! Join us in the lounge as soon as they get through with you. That's an *order*, Kim!"

She nodded slowly. "Thank you. It *does* hurt a bit."

She started off but Unsworth gripped her arm. "One moment. A small favor, please. Caleb, will you look at this young woman for me? As I asked her to do with you?"

It was strange, making an intense study of someone you'd known so well and so long, and seeing so many things you'd never seen before, thought Massey.

"Yes, it is that," Unsworth told him. "Thank you. She's a very lovely young woman. Kim, off with you," and he pushed her gently.

Massey moved to take Unsworth's arm. The scientist raised his hand. "*You* look where you're going, Caleb. I can see through *your* eyes."

Massey took his arm. "I don't know if you're getting this picture, Peter Unsworth," Massey said slowly, trying to create a visual image of *Massey* stumbling, "but I would feel a hell of a lot better if you let me add some physical input to your walking about." Massey was perspiring. "I don't think you have any idea of—" He created a mental picture of Unsworth with a stubborn look on his face, while Massey stumbled about him, his hands tearing out his own hair in gobs and flinging them about wildly. He replaced the scene with another of a calm, serene Massey and Unsworth walking together with Massey's hand guiding Unsworth by the arm. To finish off his three-dimensional image within his mind he thought of the night sky and scrawled a flaming *PLEASE!* across the heavens.

Unsworth chuckled and slipped *his* hand through Massey's arm. "All right, Caleb. It appears this is going to be more difficult for you than it is for me."

Massey nodded. Clouded in thought he nearly tripped over cables stretching across the floor. "Watch where you're going!" Unsworth warned.

Massey stopped, not believing what was happening. *I still can't believe this . . . he's blind, and he's deaf, and he's telling me how and where to walk because I'm bumbling about like an idiot.*

"True," Unsworth said.

The scientist stopped in midstride. "How bloody unthinking of me," he said quietly. He turned to face Massey. "I'm turning this way because I see myself through your eyes. If you can see my eyes directly I can see yours."

Massey made a small, "Oh."

"I have been terribly rude, Caleb. I can turn off my ability to read, or to think or feel or understand your thoughts, however this functions. I don't know. But I feel I'm intruding, and I am disturbing you greatly. If you wish complete isolation from me, if you wish your privacy absolutely not to be disturbed, you need only say so."

Massey ran the problem through his mind. He had

mental pictures of himself mopping a sweaty brow, of confusion. He threw up clouds of question marks, then emblazoned the word NECESSARY in his mind.

"All right. But I can make it easier. You're getting dizzy trying to communicate in a pattern you've never known. It's really much easier for the young people, you know."

WHY?

"Because you are a hardboiled old egg and the best changes in you, the vital young juices that take us into the future, have been boiled out of you. The others still slosh about in their minds and they are quite susceptible to change. It will take you longer. Now, let me make it easier on both of us. When you wish to get a clear message to me, Caleb, leave aside your mental images for a while. Take your time. Think in terms of words flashing by, as if on a screen. Or a line from a typewriter. Let the words move from right to left. I will literally be reading those words, and we will have greater clarity."

THANK YOU.

"And if you wish me out, my new and unbalanced friend, send me a mind picture of a very large wooden door with iron bars holding it shut. When I see that door I'll go no further until you give me permission."

THANK YOU.

"Stop thanking me and get me my damned drink!"

Chapter XXV

"How many people in Venezuela know about this?"

Caleb Massey asked the question of his friend seated before him. He felt uncomfortable trying to walk around the heart of the issue with the two young people seated nearby, but the senator had told him, "Let it out; they know."

Senator Patrick Xavier Elias, wearing the soiled clothes of a retired fisherman, right down to the rumpled hat and assorted lures and hooks, paused only briefly before replying. "Two. Felipe Mercedes and General Luis Espinoza."

Massey frowned. "Mercedes I understand. But the general? I don't get that one, Patrick."

"Luis Espinoza is one of the finest astrophysicists in the world," Elias said easily. "Very few people know that. His military reputation is impeccable. He's such an iron-assed old martinet that no one ever associates him with anything else except a spit-and-polish, by-the-book general of Latin extraction. Behind that front, and it is not a facade, is a brilliant scientist."

"I don't see how he could do it all. The man is—"

"Espinoza trained himself to sleep two hours a night. Every *other* night," Elias stressed. "He lives both lives with equal alacrity, intelligence, and results. *And* as a general, who also works with the Venezuelan national guard, which is the true police force of that country, he's in a perfect position to support BEMAC, and Mercedes, of course, and also to assure its isolation and security."

"He knows all of it?" Massey pressed.

"He knows everything we know," Elias replied.

Massey sat back in the old leather chair, stained and cracked like the others in the old Titan blockhouse on Cape Canaveral. There could hardly have been a better site of security than the long-abandoned launch complex. The main outside doors had been welded shut years before. The windows were all armored glass, structured to withstand the direct hit of a flaming, exploding Titan rocket powerful enough to hurl a four-ton Gemini spacecraft into orbit. The only way in or out of the blockhouse was through a tunnel deep underground. That led to a smaller security blockhouse, right now guarded both by electronics systems and a dedicated team from the FBI.

"How many people, all together, in this country?" Massey said, renewing his questions.

"Right now," Elias replied, "there is myself. You make the second. Do you know Frank Bemis? Well, he's in the senate with me. He flew on three shuttle flights as an astronaut. An absolute crackerjack who's always lived three or four years in the future. I needed an opposite number for obvious reasons. Frank Bemis is it and he's number three."

"Who else?" Massey pushed.

"Mitch Carruthers. I believe you know him."

"Yes, of course. Computer genius. Believes in force fields and EM matrix systems for computers."

"Carruthers designed your super Greystone as a side job, Caleb. Since this whole thing began he's spent all his time working on a computer system that we can integrate with the unique abilities of Peter Unsworth."

"That makes four of us, then. Elias, Massey, Bemis and Carruthers," Massey reviewed. "Unsworth, of course, makes it five. Plus Mercedes and Espinoza. That's seven."

"Make it eight."

"Who the hell else?" Massey said angrily.

"Kim Seavers."

"Kim? *Kim?* How could she possibly know about—"

"Unsworth told her."

"In the name of God, *why?*"

"Because she's established what he describes as the most incredible rapport with him. Same wavelength. Same frequencies. Harmonics. I don't know all the reasons," Elias added by way of mild protest, "but he's got them. He also told me that he insists on a young mind being involved. Too much petrification with too many old bastards. He also pointed out that without Kim there isn't a single woman in this project, and to him that's a terrible, terrible mistake."

Massey thought that over. "We couldn't stop that if we wanted to," he agreed. "But why is it so important· that there be a woman involved?"

"I asked him the same question."

"And?"

"He said to me, 'What if *they're* women?' He almost bowled me over with that question. He's right, of course. That could be what we'll find. And we needn't get into this in a chauvinistic limousine, he added. It might be the last mistake we ever make."

"Jesus Christ," Massey murmured.

"That, too, is a distinct possibility, according to Unsworth," Elias replied. "Are you quite through mumbling?"

Massey waved him on.

"You forgot to ask me what that young man is doing in here," Elias needled him gently. "*And* that young woman."

"My God, I'm getting old," Massey said, sinking back again in his seat.

"Quite true, Caleb, but then, consider the alternative," said the senator. "This, by the way, is Ted Wright. And the young lady is Liam Carruthers."

"The same?"

"Yes. She's Mitch's daughter."

Massey nodded to the two young people. "Forgive me if I refer to you in the third person," he told them. "It's not personal."

"Yes, sir," they chorused.

"Why are they brought in?" Massey asked.

"They'll work the ASCOT."

"What the hell is the ASCOT?"

"Carruthers's super computer. He calls it ASCOT. That's not an acronym, by the way. He picked ASCOT because he says the damned thing tied him up in knots since this project started. Ted and Liam will both handle all programming. Each will always back up the other."

"You haven't got anyone else under the rug somewhere, have you?"

"Word of honor. Eagle Scout, Fourth Class Beer Drinker and all that. No. No one else, Caleb. And we don't bring in anyone from now on without your say-so. You didn't have that privilege before because it didn't mean very much. Now that BEMAC is real *and* we have Unsworth—or, more properly, since Unsworth has joined us—the privilege is yours. And so is a great deal of power. We will go along blindly from this day forward to provide you with everything you need. Do you understand?"

"Yes. It's too bad it has to be that way—"

"Of course it *has* to be that way. You'll be bringing in more people. As soon as you start getting this thing under way you'll have to select members of your beamriders who'll make the trip. They'll have to know everything, of course. Strange to say, they'll be under your orders, but the only way you can be successful is to give them their heads. This cannot, this absolutely *can not* be a case of anyone following anyone else's wishes, desires, orders, commands, what-have-you. It must be from the heart and the soul as well as the mind, or we don't stand a prayer."

"The soul, you say," Massey replied with some acid. "I've never seen one of those."

"Look more closely in the mirror, my old friend. That is the one reason above all others, not ignoring your many and considerable talents, why you were selected for the position you're in."

"Are you staying here or going back to the Hill?"

"For the next few days, Caleb, you old bastard, you and I are going fishing."

"We're *what?*"

"We're going fishing. On a big damn lake some-where. I used to do that with Phil Wylie when I was a snotnose senator. We'd talk things over, let them sort themselves out. You've been driving too hard for too long. You don't relax any more. You by God *need* some space and time of your own. We're going to fish and we're going to exchange philosophies. Your people need at least ten days to learn, to get to know one another, to become a team, and they don't need you looking over their shoulders and meddling. You go back into harness when you're fresh and alive again."

Elias stood up with a groan. "Let's go. I heard of an absolute beaut of a black bass that has my name on it."

The old senator was right on target. Caleb Massey returned to CANAVERAL dome ten days after the private meeting in the old Titan blockhouse with his batteries recharged, the lethargy of the long earlier travail behind him. He itched to get back into harness, to bring together his team in a way that had not existed before. And everything he had ever known before, no matter how outlandish, crazy, impossible, fantastic or any other adjective that might fit, was utterly small peanuts compared to what he was now up against.

He would send his beam agents on a long voyage. The "long" was measured only in miles, the distance from A to B. The voyage itself in terms of time would be meaningless, since in the laser stream they would be somewhere beyond time. Yet it would be a trip beyond anything they could imagine, with a purpose none of them had ever dreamed of, beyond even dreams and fantasies.

And it would be possible *only* if he could bring together all the many parts. *Only* if he could create an element of true *gestalt* among those involved. The psychological barriers seemed insurmountable. Removing one's ego from the forefront of the brain and placing it far behind other priorities was a mental exercise that in history had received much bowing and scraping but damned little truth or reality.

The key to it all, the hard nub of what might happen, what *must* happen, and successfully, was Dr. Peter Unsworth.

Who ever expected the saviour would be blind and deaf!

They had become inseparable, Unsworth and Kim Seavers. Massey had never experienced anything like it. However they had come to communicate, however they had managed so total a mental integration, was astounding. It had happened before, of course, sometimes with identical twins, of whom folklore was filled with wondrous tales. But these two weren't twins and this wasn't folklore.

"What I need to do," Kim explained patiently to Massey, with Ted Wright and Liam Carruthers privy to every word, hopefully comprehending the emotions involved, "is to translate for Dr. Unsworth." Kim showed a sour expression. "Translate is such an *inadequate* word, Caleb. Transliterate is better but it's still a shortfall for what I'm trying to say."

"Keep at it," Massey urged. "I'm slow, girl, but I'll give it my best shot. And I really *need* to know."

She sat with Unsworth, the old man comfortable in a suede jumpsuit that kept his frail body warm and yet provided a feel of body luxury he hadn't experienced in many years. After the coarse clothing of the Russians almost anything would have been an improvement; this had a personal, warm, human feel to its touch. Kim's hand almost always rested in the hand or on the arm of the old scientist, as if their feel, their touch, was as important as what Unsworth tried to communicate to her, and she to the two young ASCOT programmers.

"All right," Kim said, settling her thoughts. "So far as we know, the only person who's ever received the message is Peter Unsworth." She paused a moment as his head turned to her, an instinctive response to whatever communication existed at that moment between them. "I want to make it absolutely clear that I used those words, 'so far as we know.' Dr. Unsworth has told me, and he's repeated it so many times it's clear he regards it as much more than the equivalent of a religious litany, or something on that level, that *he* doesn't *know* that he's the only one. He knows only that he received the message *in his mind*."

"Once?" Massey asked.

Kim nodded. "Yes. Just once. But—"

Unsworth squeezed her hand gently. "Excuse me, my dear." The sightless eyes turned to Massey, unsettling; blind but driving powerfully, it seemed, right through his own eyes to the back of his skull. "Let me not fault Kim. Caleb, it's almost impossible to express in words the impact of the message. I can do it to some extent with her. We've made the bridge between us. But I cannot expect her to bear that intensive or complex a torch. So; may I interrupt?"

"Of course, of course."

"Kim obviously has told you the message came to me but one time." A rapturous look appeared on Unsworth's face. "It was, at the same time, devastating in its impact, yet as subtle as a falling snowflake in its delivery. It grew within my mind, like a field of flowers in a four-dimensional garden. Does that sound crazy? I well imagine it might. I would react with some suspicion to such a statement. In your case, Caleb, you are fortunate enough to have our finest technology, mixed as it is with intensely human people who feel and grasp and emote with one another, and—"

Unsworth stopped, his face revealing only that he searched his own mind. *Or someone else's.* "You have the proper word, Caleb. Yes, *gestalt* is it. A fusion of minds so effective, so penetrating and embracing, that they are able to think and comprehend as one. I do not talk about the Tibetan prayer rooms or anything of any religion. This is entirely different." He frowned. "Forgive me; I ramble. I don't intend to, but awesome, devastating, shattering; they are all inadequate.

"The flowering of four-dimensional thinking, that will

have to do, Caleb. The intrusion, into my thoughts, into my mind, came so subtly, the single petal of a tiny flower that stayed with me, growing and nourishing. I believe the message was delivered in a pace determined by my own ability, or capacity, not simply to receive, but to absorb, and then, to understand."

Without a spoken request, Kim placed a mug of steaming broth in his hands. Unsworth blew against the mug, sipped slowly.

"Are you still with me, Caleb?"

"With some difficulty; yes." Massey painted the picture of the words, bright and clear, in his mind.

"Well, I don't blame you for feeling a bit muddled. It's beyond difficult. Well, I've said that enough," Unsworth nipped at himself. "All right. The message at first, in terms of specifics, was formless. Flowers, subtlety; that sort of thing. It was like a glow within my mind that refused to go away. Aha! I have it! Think of a hazy, even a diffuse, crystal ball within your mind. It's there for a reason. It contains a picture. It contains many pictures. Those are the harbingers of the understanding— the message—to come. I believe the flowers were a clever way to gain my attention, to bring me to concentrate on the crystal ball, which in mental image could be something I held in one hand, like some silly fortune teller, or as big as the sky itself. Obviously, I looked. I looked deeper and deeper, and as I did, the impressions, the message, *messages*, became clearer. God's truth, Caleb, I was both fascinated and utterly confused."

He drank more broth, thought for a long moment. "Then, in that crystal ball—in the crystallization of muddled thoughts—I first saw the castle."

"Castle?" Massey echoed.

"Oh, yes," Unsworth said with a deep smile. "A castle."

Massey's own mind ran away with him. Immediately in his mind's eye he conjured pictures of castles as he knew them. The marvelous structures of Bavaria, looking down on the forest hills of Germany. Castles of fairy tales, huge and foreboding. Massive walls, dark greys;

inside, dark with flickering smoky torches, horses crossing the bridge over the moat, courtyards of cobbled stone, winding staircases, evil spirits and knights—

"No, no, *no*," Unsworth broke into his wanderings. "This is no trip to the land of Oz! Nor is it a tour of castles haunted by ghosts and foul deeds. Forget the castles that rise on our world, Caleb. Ignore all that you have known or might know of such things."

His hands moved as if he were trying to grasp the mental images within his mind. "Crystal. Glass. Showers of light. The sun everywhere. Glowing from within. Brilliant. Wonderful. *Radiant.*" He sighed. "Do these words help, Caleb? They are woefully inadequate. Create a picture in your mind, Caleb Massey. Bring forth your childish dreams, your fantasies, wonder of wonders, magic, fairy tales, beauty . . ." His voice again faded as he dwelt in his own thoughts.

Kim turned to Massey. "What we've been doing is trying to capture everything Peter's told us," she said slowly and carefully, "and program it into the ASCOT."

"You're what?" Massey couldn't believe it. "How can you bring a mental picture, especially what *he's* describing, into an electronics system? He spoke of looking through a crystal ball that's as large as the sky, and you're going to put it into an electronic-mechanical device flat as a board—" He cut himself off in midsentence. *Of course; first the computer. The graphics displays.*

"You get the picture from him?" Caleb asked Kim.

Her face brightened. "*Yes*. He paints his pictures with words and descriptions. But little by little he's been able to place images in *my* mind. Then I work with computer graphics myself. I place the patterns on the screens. It doesn't matter if they're inadequate at first, because each image is one step better than what I might have had moments before. Once I get started, I can describe to Ted and Liam what I'm seeing in my own mind. By working together we expand the scene. If the light is wrong, here, we brighten or soften it. If this tower is too wide or too low, we change it."

"Building blocks of images," Massey murmured.

"In a way, yes. But our building blocks are soft and wonderful. You *must not* use the old standards, sir."

"I'd like to see what you've come up with so far, Kim."

"Please; wait just a bit longer?"

"Of course. You're running this show," Massey said. "I'm more than satisfied to be the student. *I* need to learn."

"Thank you. Now, as I build the scene, correcting all the time, Peter can read the picture in my mind. I look at the three-dimensional graphics. *He sees in his mind what I see with my eyes and bring to my mind.* Do you understand now? His mind guides my thoughts, my hand, my concepts and impressions. Ted and Liam constantly improve and make accurate what I learn from Peter, and he in turn immediately sees my faults or blemishes or shortcomings."

"And it works, I would imagine, from the way you're telling me about it."

Her face was radiant. She had come alive in a way Massey had never before seen in *any* woman. Something utterly, wonderfully beautiful shone within Kim Seavers. It was almost a physical force to him. At any moment he expected to see a golden aura begin to shine about her. Without his bidding, that scene appeared in his mind, servant to his racing thoughts and his imagination.

"I like that," Unsworth told Massey.

"What?" Massey asked, jerked back to reality.

"Forgive the intrusion, old man. She is doing extraordinarily well."

"How far have you come in all this?" Massey asked Kim.

"I'm not sure because I don't know how far we still have to go." She showed a touch of deep concern. "What I'm doing, what *we're* doing, with this transfer of what Dr. Unsworth sees, or has been sent, into the computer is only a part of this program. Oh, I know that sounds complicated, maybe even silly, and it doesn't make sense, *but it does*, truly, it does. We must take

this one step, one phase at a time. And Ted and Liam
must be capable of knowing as much as *I* know, so that
they can use the ASCOT to bring out as realistically as
possible what we've been doing." She took a deep
breath, grasping Unsworth's arm. "Does that make
sense?" she begged of Massey.

"Barely. It would help a great deal if *I* could see this
castle or whatever it is myself."

Kim turned to Liam Carruthers. "How far have we
gone beyond the graphics?"

The pretty, dark-haired girl, whose father had created this monument of electronic genius, looked for
Ted Wright to corroborate the words she would use.
"We're ready—but I want to confirm this from ASCOT—
for the full-effect holographics."

"I'll do that," Ted Wright said quickly and quietly.
He turned from her to address his keyboard. His fingers flew as he "talked" with ASCOT. *A whole new
generation, a whole new world, and new minds in a
universe I never knew at his age,* thought Massey as he
watched the young man. He turned to Unsworth who
was smiling. Massey conjured a clear mental picture of
himself and Unsworth seated at a scarred table in a
dungeon-like room, pushing little rounded sliders on an
abacus.

A chuckle escaped Unsworth. "Oh my, how true,
how true," he said to Massey. "You learn quickly, my
friend Caleb."

A mental picture of the words THANK YOU in fireworks brilliance flashed in Massey's mind.

"ASCOT's ready," Ted Wright said.

"Sir?" Liam Carruthers looked at Massey. "We can
proceed now."

Massey turned to Kim. "All right?"

"Yes," she said. Without any sign of contact, Unsworth
nodded his assent.

The lights in the computer bay began to dim. "No;
wait. Just a moment," Kim said quickly. "Sir, one last
note. What you will see is what Dr. Unsworth saw *after*

weeks of the message first being received. It's important you understand that. It didn't happen right away."

"I understand. One question. The message originated from what you're about to show me?"

"Yes." Kim nodded to Liam and the lights grew dimmer.

Massey felt his heart beating faster.

Darkness.

In the room center, a nebulous light. Swaying curtains of hazy glow. Formless shapes intertwining, bringing forth colors, shifting, challenging the eyes and senses to follow. Lines and forms emerged from the diaphanous scene as the computer rolled the data through its electronic ganglia and brought three-dimensional holographic reality from the birthing of the unknown.

Massey felt his long-held breath gushing from his lungs. He forced himself to breathe evenly, taking in long, steady gulps of air. His vision cleared. He had an incredible urge to float away, outward from his physical self, into the gleaming edifices rising holographically before him.

The castle . . . it's real. My God, it's real! A castle of unknown metals, of alloys never known until this picture, of colors that shimmered and glowed and whispered up and down and through ramparts that seemed always to be reaching higher and higher.

But a castle like none other, like none ever seen or known.

Then it hit him, a mental blow that struck every nerve of his physical being.

The castle rested on no surface.

A castle without turrets.

No drawbridge.

No defenses.

No surface? No! It hovered . . . it levitated? It was suspended in thin air . . .

That can't be.

He stared at the hologram, so starkly real and yet a phantom of reality, fully three-dimensional, absolutely real as if he observed the castle from afar, from a height.

It's not floating in thin air.

There's no blue to the sky. But it's day. No blue to the sky. No clouds. The sky is black, velvet black, impossibly devoid of all light. No; there's more. There! Lights in that sky.

His eyes hurt. Not lights. *Stars. Forever and ever, stars, glowing, gleaming, shining. They don't sparkle. No . . . no twinkling.*

Of course it's not floating in thin air. Or on thin air. There can't be air if it's daytime and the sky is black.

It can't be a castle.

He heard the voice of Peter Unsworth. "You're almost there, Caleb."

Massey spun about, staring into the sightless eyes, trying to open his own mind. He felt staggered, off-balance.

"Easy, easy," Unsworth said soothingly. "Yes, my friend, you're right."

Massey had judged what he saw. He'd judged it, figured it out, but had refused his own mind the reality of what hovered before him.

"It's the moon, isn't it?" Massey said aloud finally, his own voice mocking all his senses of what's real and what isn't.

"Yes," Unsworth said.

"*Our* moon?"

"Yes."

"That's why the sky is black. No atmosphere, no refraction of sunlight from floating dust or water vapor or air . . ."

"That is true, Caleb."

The truth continued to hammer Massey.

"That . . . is not a castle," he said finally.

"It seems a castle, but you are right. It is not so," Unsworth said.

Massey looked almost frantically back and forth from Unsworth to Kim. "Then what in the name of God *is it?*"

"Don't answer," Unsworth said to Kim. "He must say it himself. He knows the answer."

Massey sagged in his seat.

"I don't think I *want* to."

Unsworth smiled, knowledge and sadness mixing in his sightless expression.

"It is never easy, Caleb Massey, to advance through thousands of years of civilization," Unsworth said as if from a distance, "to march through time, from one age of enlightenment to another, through the golden eras, the blossoming of thought, the conquest of vast frontiers, all the things that we have done, and then to face the truth."

A tremendous sigh went like an invisible wind through Unsworth. "I have lived with this . . . I do not know how long, but I have lived with it alone. It seems easier," he faltered, pushed himself on, "yes, it *is* easier, not to be alone when you learn that you are an aborigine. How does it feel, Caleb, to know that you still walk with a spear in one hand and a dusty cloth about your loins, through the deserts?"

Massey looked at the castle suspended above the surface of the moon. "There's no earth in the sky."

"It may not be seen from the lunar farside," came the answer that Massey already knew.

"It's a ship," Massey said, yielding all his disbelief. *Accepting*.

"Yes. A vessel beyond anything we can even dream of," Unsworth said. "In my own feeble way, Caleb, I do not believe what we see is truly that vessel. I am convinced neither the eyes nor the mind of man may comprehend its true shape, or *lack* of shape, or its size, or even remotely what it looks like."

"Then . . . then why do we see it as a castle?"

"Would *you* take the aborigine into the heart of a nuclear reactor, Caleb? Into the savage heat, the blazing radiation, the controlled death? Would you plunge him unprepared into such a terrifying spectacle and experience?"

"So the castle is . . ." He struggled for the words. "It's the protective fantasy of our childhood dreams."

"To be sure," Unsworth said.

"Call it Camelot," Kim said to Massey. "It will do as well as any. And it is much safer for us."

Massey looked harder, trying to penetrate the veil of Camelot. "A star vessel," he said hollowly.

"Beyond *that*," Unsworth said.

Massey studied the old man. "You're reading my mind. So easily."

"Not so. You've *opened* your mind. It's one of the first steps."

"*The message!* The message . . . *this is it?*" Massey gasped.

"Nothing so easy, Caleb."

"Then—"

"All you have learned so far, you know. Does that make sense?"

"No, I— Wait; *yes.*"

"Of course," Unsworth said.

"But then . . . the message you've talked about. What is it?"

"A summons."

"Summons? To . . . up there?"

"Yes. Up there. To the far side of the moon."

"Who sent it? Did they . . . is that what you received?"

"*They* sent it. I have no idea or concept of who or what *they* are. But the summons is unmistakable. It calls for us to meet a schedule."

"Schedule? This is crazy," Massey objected. "We're being summoned to the far side of the moon by a—a, well, a people, a race, from within a ship that looks like a castle but in reality is beyond our concept to perceive in its *real* self?"

"Precisely."

"When? I mean, by whose time? What reference?"

The blind man motioned to the two programmers. Ted Wright's fingers flashed across the keys.

The castle dissolved in a shower of sparkling lights. In its place appeared a representation of the solar system. Nine planets. Many moons. The light of the sun, obviously, vastly dimmed for purposes of presentation in this three-dimensional world of electronic fantasy-reality. Massey felt strange looking at the blue-white marble third from the sun. He felt stranger looking at the earth's moon, knowing what hovered effortlessly on its hidden side.

"Seeing it like this," Massey said aloud, "it diminishes what we did with Apollo. It was so incredible. Getting off this world. A quarter million miles to that airless nothing. Landing one ship after the other there. Men walking there. Riding those crazy lunar dune buggies. *But we did it.* On this scale," he said sadly, "we haven't yet made it around the block."

"Look at the position of the planets, Caleb." Unsworth again gestured to Ted and Liam at the controls of ASCOT. "If you would be so kind," he said to Liam. "The dates as we recognize them."

Glowing numerals appeared magically within the orbs of the solar system.

"That's less than a month from right now!" Massey shouted.

"Yes."

"We're supposed to get there *in less than a month from today?"*

"Yes."

"But we don't have the ships any more!" Massey shouted, anger bursting through him. "Dammit, Unsworth, you know that! The Apollo fleet . . ."

"I know. Junk. Rusted metal. Museum pieces. Broken dreams. A magnificent journey outward smashed at the peak of its success." Unsworth offered Massey a sardonic, humorless laugh. "Columbus turning back when land was just over the horizon. The Wright Brothers trashing their splendid little machine because of one miserable failure after another, with *their* dream only a wisp of wind away from them. Shall I offer more?"

Sightless eyes lay behind the arms that stretched out. "They were watching us, Caleb. I don't know how, or why, but they were watching us. Out of the mud, burr and fang and claw into steel and blazing fire and we were on our way, and we went to the moon and then we turned our backs on ourselves. Forgive my words,

Caleb, but we pissed on our own feet when we quit. We didn't go far enough."

"And how far is *that?*" Massey asked with bile in his throat from the bitter pill dissolving within him.

"They left a marker for us. A message. A monolith; I don't know what it was. Is. I don't know. But they told me, in whatever incredible way they have of telling me anything. They left a message for us on Mars. That message was a key. Before us waited the Rosetta Stone to open to us the roads that cross the universe, *and we pissed on our own feet!*"

Unsworth trembled; an icy wind rattled his old bones as thoughts churned angrily within him. "My fellow men, my race. We turned our backs on ourselves. *We quit.*"

"*So what the hell are you trying to tell me, old man!*"

"Ah, your mind is a blazing, white fury, Caleb. Your juices flow glowing with life. That's good."

"Answer me, damn you! You're their telephone system! *Pick up the goddamned phone and tell me what they want!*"

"Oh, it's not what they *want.* It's what they're offering us."

"And that is . . ." He shook his head wildly. "No; *don't tell me.*"

He could feel Unsworth's mind within his own, expectant, waiting, hoping.

"They're offering us a second chance," Massey said, the fury gone like a sudden gust of mindwind.

"Yes, they are."

"But we don't have the ships! And we could never build them in time to—" He fell silent, staring, feeling Unsworth join with him.

"That is right, my friend," said Unsworth. "You have less than one month to send your people, Kim and the others, to that castle on the far side of the moon. Caleb, Caleb," he said softly, "don't even think of the technical. Don't bog down your thoughts with mechanical things. *Think of the castle and know we must be there, we must send our best to them, within the month.*"

Kim Seavers reached out to rest her hand on Massey's arm. "If we don't," she said in a voice of velvet, "they'll go away. They won't be back."

Massey took her hand. "And we will be left alone," he said.

"Forever," she told him, her voice trembling suddenly.

He reeled back in his seat. "The laser beam . . . our project. That's how we'll go, then."

"You have much to do and little time in which to do it," Unsworth told him.

"How incredible," Massey said to them both. "It's as if we developed the laser system . . . the beaming . . . barely in time."

"If? *IF?*" The voice of Peter Unsworth roared from him, energy impossible from the old man.

"Do you really believe that rod of green fire happened by accident?"

WILL *YOU* SURVIVE?

In addition to Dean Ing's powerful science fiction novels—*Systemic Shock, Wild Country, Blood of Eagles* and others—he has written cogently and inventively about the art of survival. **The Chernobyl Syndrome** is the result of his research into life after a possible nuclear exchange . . . because as our civilization gets bigger and better, we become more and more dependent on its products. What would *you* do if the machine stops—or blows up?

Some of the topics Dean Ing covers:
* How to *make* a getaway airplane
* Honing your "crisis skills"
* Fleeing the firestorm: escape tactics for city-dwellers
* How to build a homemade fallout meter
* Civil defense, American style
* "Microfarming"—survival in five acres
      And much, much more.

Also by Dean Ing, available through Baen Books:

ANASAZI
Why did the long-vanished Anasazi Indians retreat from their homes and gardens on the green mesa top to precarious cliffside cities? Were they afraid of someone—or some*thing*? "There's no evidence of warfare in the ruins of their earlier homes . . . but maybe the marauders they feared didn't wage war in the usual way," says Dean Ing. *Anasazi* postulates a race of alien beings who needed human bodies in order to survive on Earth—a race of aliens that *still* exists.

FIREFIGHT 2000
How do you integrate armies supplied with bayonets and ballistic missiles; citizens enjoying Volkswagens and Ferraris; cities drawing power from windmills and nuclear powerplants? Ing takes a look at these dichotomies, and more. This collection of fact and fiction serves as a metaphor for tomorrow: covering terror and hope, right guesses and wrong, high tech and thatched cottages.
